THORNAPPLE

BOOK THREE OF THE POISON GARDEN

JENNIFER ALLIS PROVOST

BELLATRIX PRESS

Contents

1. No Doctors — 1

2. He's Been Spelled — 7

3. Shopping and Secrets — 17

4. Amir — 29

5. Mermaid Cove — 35

6. Found Her — 46

7. Oranges and Truth Spells — 51

8. One Night at the Louvre — 56

9. Curses — 59

10. Foresight, Again — 64

11. Fate, Evil or Otherwise — 73

12. A Witch's Debt — 81

13. Boxing Lessons — 91

14. Ned Burroughs — 97

15. Family Ties — 103

16. Poor Pacheri — 118

17. Wizards Are Real? — 127

18. Awful With A Purpose — 134

19. None Of This Is Right — 138

20. That's The Spirit — 141

21. Secretive, Even For Witches — 157

22. Jemima — 164

23. Alex Was Never Cursed — 169

24. Sweet Rolls — 177

25. Cats and Crossbows — 188

26. Magic on the Roof — 194

27. Tunnels in Time — 201

28. It's a Map — 210

29. Let's Go Back To When It All Began — 214

30. Foxglove Tea — 223

31. In the Cottage — 228

32. Very Large Cougars — 234

33. Cider and Rabbit Stew — 242

34. Laundry Day — 247

35. Bones — 264

36. The Letter — 271

37. New Plan — 283

38. We Need a Bigger Gun — 289

39. Little Sand, Little Magic, and Boom — 301

40. Partners — 309

41. Happy Birthday! Wait, What? — 316

Wolfsbane — 324

About The Author — 328

Chapter 1

No Doctors

Dan shook his head. "I don't know about this."

"Do you have a better idea?" I countered.

He frowned. "No."

"Neither do I."

Our current questionable idea was to have me sit under the light of the full moon while Tessa magically examined me and tried to glean some information about my curse. Since this curse hadn't been present when I was born, and Gran hadn't detected it on me until I was eight, it could have come from anyone and anywhere—but I was dead certain this was my mother's handiwork. Let's just say she's never been in the running for parent of the year.

In order to accomplish this grand feat of curse detection, Tessa, Dan, and I were in Dan's backyard setting up a magic circle on his well-tended lawn. Luckily, he wasn't one of those fools who opted for the lawn care company that doused its clients' yards in chemicals to keep the grass green for longer than it was meant to be. Since this sort of ritual was best conducted with the subject—in this case, me—in direct contact with the earth, his freshly trimmed lawn was an ideal location.

Gran's yard would have also been a good place, mostly because the earth there knew me, and the familiar setting would offer an extra bit of protection. But my father was there, searching every spell book and grimoire he could find, and this spell required me to be completely naked. While I don't mind nudity, being a grown woman naked in front of my dad was something to be avoided at all costs. Besides, Dan had a nice tall stockade fence, which would keep out the neighbors' prying eyes.

"It's ready," Tessa said. She'd drawn a circle of salt on the lawn, and set five white pillar candles at the cardinal points. "I even brought you a pillow," she added, indicating the purple cushion in the middle of the circle.

"You're so good to me." I kicked off my sandals, then I pulled my shirt off and handed it to Dan.

"Do we all need to be naked for this?" he asked.

"Only if you'd like to be," Tessa purred.

"Tess," I admonished, "stop trying to embarrass him." I slipped off my shorts and handed them to my increasingly flustered partner. I had to admit, Dan was pretty cute when he blushed. He frowned at my bare body, then he leaned over and kissed my temple.

"Anything goes sideways, yell," he said. "I'll have you out of that circle in a hot second."

I gripped his hand, as much to reassure myself as him. "Tessa won't let anything happen to me."

With that, I stepped inside the circle and sat cross-legged in the center, my butt on the cold grass while the cushion supported my back. Once I was seated, Tess entered the circle and poured out the last measure of salt, thus closing the spell around us. She snapped her fingers, and the five candles lit as one.

"Whoa," Dan said.

Tessa glanced at Dan and grinned, then she focused on me. "You know how this goes," she began. "Clear your mind, but make note of any stray thoughts, especially persistent ones."

"Got it." I shook out my arms. "Are you starting with my head?"

"Your fingers, actually," Tessa replied, then she grasped my left hand and began probing the skin between my fingers.

"Are finger curses common?" Dan asked.

"I depends on the purpose of the curse." Having finished with my left hand, Tessa scrutinized my wrist, then my forearm. "If you want to impede someone's ability to write, or perhaps play an instrument, the fingers would be an ideal location."

Dan grunted. I flashed him a smile, and let my eyes close. The spell intensified, making my limbs feel like warm molasses. "This feels nice," I mumbled.

"Don't get too comfortable," Tessa warned. "I need you to stay awake."

I nodded, but I felt my consciousness drifting farther away. Tessa's fingers were hypnotic as they glided across my skin, the soft thrum of her magic soothing my soul. But even as I was soothed, something deep within me woke up.

Something that didn't want to be found.

I tried to tell Tessa, but my throat was thick, my tongue heavy. I didn't know if she'd relaxed me to a place beyond words, or if the curse was keeping me quiet. I suspected it was a bit of both.

Oblivious to my issues, Tessa completed her inspection of my arms, and moved on to my shoulders. She knelt behind me, and paused.

"Eli, what's this in your back?" she murmured, stroking her hand down the length of my spine. Her hand moved lower, toward the darkness within me. The grayish tendrils of the curse snapped a warning, then she paused. "Dan, help me lay her flat."

"Why isn't she responsive?"

"She's too deep in her trance." The cushion was moved aside, then I felt Tessa's hands under my armpits and Dan's under my thighs as they laid me flat on my back. "But she can hear us, and knows exactly what we're doing."

"I think I messed up the circle," Dan said.

Tessa didn't answer him. Instead, she pressed her hands over my heart, then my stomach. She followed the tendrils down to my lower abdomen, then she gasped.

"What is it?" Dan demanded. "Is she okay?"

"The curse is in her womb."

I was still out of it as Tessa blew out the candles, and Dan bundled me into a blanket and carried me inside. After he situated me on the couch, I heard him and Tessa talking in the kitchen.

"How long will she be asleep?" he asked.

"She's not sleeping, she's entranced," Tessa said. "As for how long she'll remain entranced, it's hard to say. Alex sometimes goes in so deep it takes him days to surface, and Eli does take after him."

"Speaking of taking after, did this curse offer any clues as to who put it on Eli in the first place?"

"No, but there is a decidedly feminine feel to it."

"Great. We only have half the population to work through." I heard the fridge door open and shut. "Think it was her mother?"

"I don't know. Honestly, I know very little about Christina, so I can't speak to her motivations, but she was Eli's mother. Why would a mother curse her child? And her womb, no less."

Dan grunted, which was his go-to response whenever he felt like he was in over his head. "Should we take her to a doctor?"

"I don't need a doctor," I mumbled.

"You mean a conventional mortal doctor?" Tessa asked. Evidently they hadn't heard me. "And tell the doctor what, that she's about to birth a curse?"

"Is that going to happen?" Dan asked. "Will it... come out of her?"

"No doctor," I said, a little louder. When they kept talking, I waved my arm to get their attention, and rolled right off the couch, blanket and all. I heard footsteps, then Dan's warm hands were under my shoulders.

"Hey, babe," Dan said as he lifted me off the floor. "You going somewhere?"

"No doctor," I mumbled. Dan sat on the couch with me on his lap. "Hate them."

"All right. No doctors."

Tessa smoothed back my hair. "Eli, honey, you'll be out of it for a while yet. Want me to wait and drive you home?"

I pried my eyelids open and stared at Dan. "Can I stay here?"

"Of course you can."

Tessa squeezed my shoulder. "Call me when you're up to it," she said, and she let herself out of Dan's house. Once she was gone, Dan tightened his arms around me.

"Tell me what you need," he murmured against my forehead.

"I'm fine," I said. "Tessa's right. It takes a bit to come back from a trance."

"I don't like seeing you like that. Scary."

"After everything that happened the other day—witches, car crashes, and the rest—me lying on the ground is scary?"

"Yeah, well."

Dan didn't say anything further, but as he tucked my head underneath his chin, I realized why he was so nervous. His wife had died right here in this house, and I bet he was the one who found her—and I'd just willing gone into an immobile, nonresponsive state. Sometimes, I was really dumb.

"I'm sorry," I said. "I should have prepared you for what it would look like."

"It's okay. I know for next time." He paused before asking, "Does it hurt? The curse, I mean."

"I didn't even know it was there." I swallowed. "What do you think it means?"

"Hell if I know, but we'll figure it out. We always do."

Chapter 2

He's Been Spelled

When I woke the next morning, it took me a few minutes to figure out where I was. Since my apartment had been blown to bits by Nathaniel and Amir's supernatural pissing contest, I'd been bouncing between my old room at Gran's and Dan's house, the former mostly for clothes. I'd tried sleeping at Gran's for exactly one night, but my father and Tess got into a fight—or, as Dad put it, an intense debate—and I drove myself to Dan's in the middle of the night. Dan hadn't minded, and truth be told, I preferred staying at his place. However, staying at his place for more than a few nights in a row was an awful lot like living together, and that was something I couldn't process just yet.

I had bigger items to process first. Much bigger.

Since lying in bed all day wouldn't help me process anything, I pulled on one of Dan's tee shirts and went in search of him. What I really wanted was to go for a run, but all of my running clothes had been destroyed when my apartment blew up. Add to that the loss of my laptop, client lists, and the rest of my belongings, and suddenly spending the day in bed seemed like a great idea.

I found Dan pacing in the kitchen with his work phone to his ear. He was nodding and frowning, neither of which were good signs. I went to the far side of the kitchen and started watering the potted herbs, and tried not to eavesdrop.

Dan ended the call, then he stood behind me and wrapped his arms around my waist. "You have no idea how much I need this."

I turned around and embraced him. "What happened?"

"That was the chief. Apparently, your place blowing up has been deemed suspicious, and he wants you to come in for a statement."

"That's understandable," I said, but Dan wasn't done.

"Thing is, he couldn't say why it's suspicious. Arson and Bomb scoured the wreckage eight ways to Tuesday and found no evidence of foul play. There is no reason to suspect you of anything, yet they do. Makes no sense."

"They think I blew up my own apartment? For what reason?" I didn't have renter's insurance—which was foolish, my now-homeless self realized—so the explosion hadn't left me in an enviable financial situation. If it hadn't been for my older belongings I'd been too lazy to move out of my grandmother's house, I would own almost nothing.

"Not only that, they aren't looking into anyone else. Not your neighbors, not the building owner, nothing." My jaw tightened when he mentioned my neighbors. All in all, twenty-three people had become homeless after Amir worked his time spell, which destroyed my apartment and ultimately rendered the rest of the building uninhabitable. I knew Amir's actions weren't my fault, but I still felt awful. "And there's the thing with Jada."

I leaned back and regarded him. "What about Jada?"

"That was my case, and ever since she disappeared from the hospital, it's pretty much gone to hell in a handbasket. I'm off the case, probably for good."

"But we still need to find her!"

"We will. We'll just have to do it unofficially."

"Everything I do is unofficial." Dan laughed, and I decided to change the subject. "After we hit the station, want to go shopping?

I really need clothes, and some other stuff." I'd raided my closet at Gran's, but those old shirts and jeans only took me so far.

"Sure. Maybe you can give me a makeover while you're at it." He got serious, and added, "And, we need to talk to Tessa about your curse."

"Yeah," I said, even though I never wanted to think about this stupid curse again. "We do."

Soon enough, we were in the rental car Dan had picked up after his own truck was totaled, and on our way to the police station. I noted the way Dan had set his jaw, his white knuckles where he gripped the steering wheel, and felt a new wave of guilt and shame.

"I'm so sorry," I blurted out. "I never meant to for you to put your job on the line in order to help me."

"Why are you sorry? You haven't done anything to me." Dan glanced at me, and saw me wringing my hands. "Listen, I may have done some questionable stuff, but my reasons are my own. You've never made me do anything."

"But, what if you get fired?"

"Then I get fired. Life'll go on." He pulled into the station's parking lot and found a space. "Can I tell you a secret?"

"I guess."

"I never wanted to be a cop, and if all of this ends I really won't miss it." He shut off the car, then he unfastened his seat belt and faced me. "I like helping people, but I don't need a gun or a badge to do that."

"I thought you liked being a police officer."

"I do, but I like other things, too." He got out of the car, and I followed suit. "Come on. Let's see how much trouble I'm in."

Dan opened the station door for me, then we walked inside with his hand on the small of my back. I smiled up at him, but he was staring straight ahead, grimacing. I followed his gaze and saw the police chief, Louis Renault, scowling at us.

"About time you got here, Lyons," Chief Renault barked. "My office. Now!"

"Wait here," Dan murmured, then he followed the chief into his office. I sat in the waiting area, straining my ears for any sounds that escaped the closed door.

"The chief's out for blood this time," Jill Sanders, the department's forensics specialist, said as she entered the waiting area. "He's been complaining about Dan's cases all morning."

"Does he always single Dan out?" I asked.

"No," she replied. "Chief's usually pretty even-tempered. Whatever's gotten him all worked up must be big."

"Must be." I looked toward Renault's office, my imagination running wild with images of Dan getting screamed at by his irate boss. "Is Dan in a lot of trouble?"

"I really don't know." Jill watched me for a moment, then asked, "The girl that went missing from the hospital, she was your friend?"

"Yeah, we knew each other back in the third grade," I replied. "I didn't see her for twenty years, then poof! She was back in my life, causing a ruckus."

Jill pursed her lips, then she looked toward the chief's office window, obscured by blinds. "A ruckus is one way to put it."

The office door banged open, and Dan exited the room. Behind him, a red-faced Chief Renault followed. The chief fixed me in his gaze, then he pointed toward the interrogation room.

"Moore, in the room. Now!"

Jill and I shared a glance, and I asked, "Is it even legal for him to question me?"

Dan shrugged. "Under these circumstances, not really. Up to you if you want to do it, babe."

"What's the worst that could happen?" I got up and entered the interrogation room, if for no other reason than to get this over with. Renault shut and locked the door behind us.

"Dan can't be in here with us?" I asked.

"No." Renault paced in front of the two way mirror. I wondered if Dan was watching us, or if a camera was recording the room. I hoped so, just in case. "Your apartment blowing up has made things very difficult for me."

"Me, too." When he paused in his pacing to glare at me, I added, "I am homeless, now."

"You're not playing house with Lyons?"

"I'm a grown woman. I don't play house." I almost added that it was none of Renault's business where or who I lived with, but something was off about him. "Is there something about the explosion I can help with?"

"You can tell me how it happened."

"I don't really know," I said, which was the truth. I had no idea how Amir destroyed my apartment. It could have been the spell I detected, or an entirely different spell I'd never noticed. For all I knew he'd used an old fashioned pipe bomb. I only knew that Dan and I had barely escaped with our lives. "We were in my apartment, noticed a few things out of the ordinary, and in an abundance of caution we left. We'd only just gotten outside when it blew up."

"By we, you mean you and Lyons?"

"Yes."

"Why was he with you?"

"We were both at the college, and he'd offered to drive me home."

Renault's scowl deepened, and I wondered if my truthful answers were mucking up whatever enchantment had been laid on him—and that was the moment I realized he'd been spelled. But the question remained, who had spelled him?

"Does Lyons drive you around often?"

I shrugged. "He had the nicer car. Why are you so interested in Dan?" I leaned across the table, and said, "He's single, you know. Want me to talk to him for you?"

"What? No, no, that's not what I'm supposed to ask you about." Renault closed his eyes and blew out a breath. "What are you and Lyons plotting?"

"Um, nothing. And even if we were up to something, you don't have any say in what I do, and who I do it with." I winced at my wording, but Renault didn't seem capable of responding to my half-assed puns in his current state. Despite his partial incapacity, I reminded myself that he still had an entire building full of armed officers at his command. If I pushed him too far, I'd probably regret it.

"I need you to stay away from Lyons," Renault said.

"Okay. Can he still drive me home?"

Renault blinked. "You said you were homeless. Where are you staying?"

The skin prickled on the back of my neck. That sensation heralded my foresight, which was my least helpful gift. I waited for it to subside, then my foresight told me to say, "A motel on Route Ten."

Renault paused. "Route Ten, you say?"

"Um, yes. Route Ten." I gripped the edge of the table, trying to get my breathing under control while the blood rushed in my ears. My foresight had just given me a hint, and I needed to follow it through.

If this was the sort of spell I thought it was, Renault would relay that information to whomever was holding his leash. "It's okay if Dan drives me to where I'm staying?"

"Yes, he can bring you there."

"Great. Are we done here?"

Renault nodded, then he unlocked and opened the door. I got out of there before he could change his mind, and almost bumped into Dan as he walked out of the observation room.

"Were you watching?" I asked.

"Yeah." Louder, he added, "Let me bring you to that motel."

"Okay," I said, just as loudly. Acting gigs were definitely not in our future. "Let's go."

As soon as we'd turned the corner, and were out of sight—and hopefully, earshot—of the chief, I whispered, "Who here can you trust?"

"Besides you?" Dan rubbed the back of his neck. "That's a short list."

"Think fast," I said, then I saw a length of straw blonde hair. "What about Jill?"

Dan must have agreed, because he yelled, "Sanders! My office!"

"You don't have an office," Jill yelled back.

"Yours, then." When Jill looked like she was going to haul off and punch him, he added, "Please?"

Jill looked at me. I spread my palms and smiled, then Jill stalked toward her office door, gesturing for us to follow her. Once we were all inside, she slammed the door shut and rounded on us.

"What's this about?" she demanded.

"I'm pretty sure Chief Renault is possessed," I replied; nothing like leading with the most important facts.

"Really?" Dan asked; crap, I should have warned him.

"Yeah, he's totally acting weird," I said. "Or maybe he's just enchanted instead of a full blown possession, but either way we need someone to keep an eye on him."

"Possessed," Jill repeated. "Why should I believe this horse shit?"

"Remember the cook at Dim Sum Delight?" Dan asked. "The one who said a magician kidnapped him? He was possessed. So was Jada Morales."

"Then Dan was," I added. "Remember when he called out sick for all those days? Possession."

"A cook, a random woman, Dan, and now Chief." Jill frowned. "Actually, that makes sense." She looked at me, and asked, "How is all of this tied to you?"

"I'm a seer," I replied. "I've lived in the supernatural community almost all of my life. There's a lot of stuff going on around here that most mortals don't notice."

"I'm not most mortals," Jill said. "What do you need me to do?"

"Just keep an eye on Renault, and let us know what he's up to," I replied. "But don't interfere. If you see him acting in an off way, or dealing with unusual people, stay clear. These people are dangerous."

"Dangerous how?" she asked. "Can they possess me, too?"

"Yes," I said, and her eyes widened. "They can also torment you so badly you'll wish you were dead."

"Observe but don't engage," Jill said. "Got it." Dan and I turned to leave. "There's one thing that's been bugging me for a while. That case at fifty-four Suffolk Street, where we found the body poisoned by oleander?"

"What about it?" I asked.

"Was he really dead?"

"Yeah. He was."

"But, we identified that body as Jacob Allwood. I see him walking around town like he's still alive. Is he a zombie?"

I took a breath, and debated how much I was willing to share with Jill. Gran had always advised honesty in all dealings with mortals, even when the truth was hard to bear. Dan trusted Jill, which meant I did, too. However, there was no reason to blow her mind all at once.

"I'll explain everything, but not now," I said. "It's a long story, and I don't really have time to tell it—but I promise I will answer all of your questions. I can tell you that Jacob is not a zombie."

"Not a zombie. That's good." Jill nodded, and repeated, "That's good. Okay, I'll watch Renault and call if anything gets hinky."

"And let us know when he leaves," I said.

Jill nodded. "I'll text you when he does."

"Thanks, Jill," Dan said. "I owe you."

"Add it on top of what you already owe me," Jill said. "Bring Eli around more often, and maybe that can go toward your debt."

"Will do."

"Thank you," I added, then Dan and I left Jill in her office and escaped out the station's side door. Once we were inside the car I took out my phone and looked up motels on Route Ten.

"Crap, there's six hotels and three motels on this road."

"Why'd you pick that street?"

"Believe it or not, my foresight told me to do it." I scrolled through the listings, making note of the addresses. "There are four close together. Want to have a stakeout?"

"Why'd you tell Renault I'm single?"

And now I knew Dan had observed the entirety of my short but meaningful interaction with the chief. "I meant as in not married. I was trying to rattle him, and it worked." When Dan said nothing, I asked, "Did I rattle you, too?"

"I don't rattle." Dan glanced at the clock on the dashboard. "Renault's usual shift ends at five, so we've got time to kill. Still want to go shopping?"

"Um, sure." The abrupt subject change caught me off guard, but I did that to Dan all the time. I was probably rubbing off on him in the worst way. "Do you even like shopping?"

"Not really, but I like you."

I smiled, because I liked him, too, but I wondered what he was hiding behind that brave face.

Chapter 3

Shopping and Secrets

We ended up going shopping at a nearby supermarket discount store. I usually avoided these sorts of places, but it would be easier for us to make one trip instead of running all over town. Speaking of running...

"Do you think they have running shoes here?" I asked as I grabbed a cart.

"This place has all kinds of stuff," Dan replied. "I'll head over to sporting goods and have a look."

"Okay. Meet me by the bubble bath."

I watched Dan make his way toward the tents and fishing poles, resisting the urge to tell him that running shoes would probably be in the shoe section. He obviously needed a few minutes alone with his thoughts, and I was more than willing to let him have them. I had a few things to think about myself. Namely, who in the world would have enchanted Chief Renault?

My gut instinct was to accuse my nemesis, Nathaniel Beauclaire, but as Nathaniel himself had said all too recently, I need to stop blaming him for everything bad that happened to me. In fact, I'd been so fixated on Nathaniel as the mastermind behind all of my problems, I hadn't considered any other suspects. Then Amir reentered my life and almost killed me, assuming that Amir had meant to kill me by blowing up my place. For all I knew, Amir had thought an explosion would be great fun. I'd watched him blow up bigger places for less.

There was also my curse, which Tess had located in my fricken' uterus, of all places. While I didn't doubt Tessa or her magic, I wondered why I'd never noticed the curse before. Maybe it was tiny? Programmed to enlarge on my thirtieth birthday? As I contemplated what was happening down there, I passed the feminine care aisle. I glanced at the brightly packaged products and decided to worry about the curse another day. The curse had been quiet for over twenty years, so I figured I had some time before things got too heavy.

Who was I kidding? Curses don't just evaporate, and I would need to deal with this sooner rather than later. I only hoped sooner meant not immediately.

I was standing in the hair care aisle reading the back of a shampoo bottle when Dan found me. "Hey," I said, as I dropped the shampoo into the cart.

"This is for you," Dan said, then he took my hand and pressed something small and metallic into my palm. A key.

"You got me a key?"

"It's a key to my place." While I stared at it, as the weight of what this small piece of metal in my hand really meant bearing down on me, he went on, "I know we're a new thing. I also know we're barely a thing at all, but you know how I feel. And you need some place to stay and I've got room. You can stay with me for as long as you need to. Or not at all. I can take you apartment hunting, or you can go alone. Whatever. It's your call." He paused for a breath, and I did the only thing I could do. I stood on my toes and kissed his cheek.

"Thank you," I said. "You're very good to me."

"Does that mean you'll stay with me?"

"Let's try it," I said, which was as close to commitment as I could get.

"You can even have your own room, if you want."

"I like your room." I stashed the key in my pocket, and turned back to the shampoo bottles. "I might end up taking up the entire shelf in your shower, though."

"We can move upstairs to the big bedroom, too."

I froze, for a moment unsure I'd heard him correctly. The upstairs bedroom and its adjacent bathroom were where Dan's wife, Charlotte, had slept. That room had been vacant since she died five years ago.

"Are you sure you want to do that?" I asked.

"The bedroom is made for two people, and I know you love that bathroom," he said, and it was true. I had dreams about lounging my cares away in that huge, jetted tub. "Or you can move up there by yourself, and I'll stay on the first floor."

"Why do you keep trying to stick me in my own room? Is this your way of telling me I snore?"

"Babe, you could snore like a buzz saw and it wouldn't matter to me."

After our shopping trip—where I spent way too much money on new clothes, toiletries, and all sorts of things for the master bathroom—we loaded up the car and headed home.

Home.

"Want to paint the upstairs?" Dan asked. "I always meant to redecorate the house, but I never got around to it. We can make the master bedroom our own."

"If you want." I'd never painted anything in my life, but I was always up for trying new things. "I like purple."

"Purple. As in, purple walls?"

Apparently, purple walls were a little too much for my straight-laced detective. "Maybe we can start with some new curtains."

He flashed me a smile. "Curtains it is."

My phone buzzed. I checked the screen, and saw a text from Tessa.

"Tessa wants us to go over so we can talk about my curse," I said. "And here I was having a great day."

"The day can still be great," Dan said, as he got into the turning lane. "You really can't feel the curse. Do you think it's why you don't have kids?"

I blinked, wondered how we'd segued from walls to curses to children in less than two minutes. "How would a curse keep me from having kids?"

"Where it is, for one," he said. "And, you don't have any."

"Neither do you. Are your balls cursed?"

He laughed softly. "Not that I know of. Also, I've been *single*," he said, putting extra emphasis on the word, "for five years. I can't really have kids by myself."

"Neither can I. I've only had one serious relationship in my entire life, and it ended two years ago." I stared out the window, remembering the few nights I'd spent with Amir. With the benefit of hindsight I realized that I'd never loved him, but man had it felt different at the time. I also remembered that Dan had always wanted a big family, something that had so far eluded him.

"Would that be a deal breaker for you?"

"Would what be? If you can't get rid of the curse?"

"No. If I really couldn't have kids."

Dan was quiet for so long I thought I knew his answer. I also thought his silence was the death knell of our nascent relationship, and wasn't that just par for the course with me? The moment I'd found something good, the moment I'd let myself acknowledge and appreciate that something not awful was happening in my life, my happiness crumbled to dust.

Once again, Dan surprised me.

"I'm not gonna lie. I've always wanted kids… But, I gave up on that dream a while ago." He glanced at me, then returned his attention to the road. "Charlotte couldn't have kids. She had a hysterectomy when she was really young, long before we'd ever met."

"Oh." I hadn't known that. "But, you wanted your house to be the Lyons Family Estate."

"You remember that? Well, for a while she seemed to be getting better, and we thought about our options. There's lots of ways to have kids, you know. There's fostering, adoption… Anyway, to answer your question, nothing about you would ever be a deal breaker for me."

You know that children's book, where the main character's heart grows three sizes? "You shouldn't let go of your dream. You'd be a great dad."

"You think so? I bet you'll be a great mom, too."

The thought of giving birth to and then caring for a baby literally terrified me. "Let's not get crazy. Maybe we can get a dog, instead."

He laughed. "You'd be a great dog mom, too."

When Dan pulled into Gran's driveway, I was still full of warm fuzzy feelings. I felt good about my relationship with Dan, I had some new things so I didn't feel like a drifter living out of a tote bag, and most importantly, I wasn't homeless any more. Dan and I had a home, together.

Holy shit.

"I've never lived with anyone I wasn't related to before, except Tessa," I said. "Are we going to split the bills fifty-fifty?"

He snorted. "We can worry about that later. Besides, my expenses are pretty low."

"Even your mortgage?"

"The house is paid for." We got out of the car, the gravel crunching underneath our feet. "Char had a life insurance policy. I used it to pay off the place."

"No wonder you don't care if you get fired." Dan followed me toward the back door. "What do you do with your salary? Or do detectives not make very much?"

"We don't, and I save most of it." He opened the back door of the house for me. "It's always been a dream of mine to retire by forty."

"You've got a lot of dreams."

He kissed my temple. "Some of them even come true."

We were still smiling at each other when we entered the empty kitchen. No Dad, no Tess, and no Feline Federation were there to greet us.

"Dad? Tess?" I called. "We're here."

Twelve paws thundered down the stairs, and the cats—Smokey, Pumpkin, and Muffuletta—burst into the kitchen to say hello. A bare second later my father appeared in the doorway.

"Eli, Dan," Dad greeted. "I didn't realize you'd get here so quickly."

"I told Tess we were on our way." I observed how he busied himself with organizing the coffee mugs on the counter, and avoided meeting my eyes. "Did we catch you in the middle of something?"

"No, no," he replied. "Not in the middle of anything. Coffee?"

"Sure."

I watched as my father fumbled around with the coffee grounds, which was just weird. As the seers' marksman he regularly tattooed others with such precision that the images were extraordinarily lifelike. His skills with fine manipulation didn't end there, because he was also capable of rewiring delicate electronics and other instruments. I'd once watched him take apart, and then rebuild an intricate pocket watch from memory. The fact that he could barely handle the coffee scoop was far out of the ordinary.

Then Tessa appeared in the doorway, and things became clear. Her normally well-coiffed hair was mussed, she was missing an earring, and she was barefoot. Tessa never went barefoot, not even at home.

I turned to Dan, my mouth gaping in shock. He raised an eyebrow, and sat at the kitchen table.

"Eli said you wanted to talk about the curse?" Dan asked Tessa.

"Yes. The curse." Tessa smoothed her hair, and indicated I should sit. Instead, I whipped out my phone and sent her a text. Her phone beeped a moment later. She withdrew it from her bag on the counter, and read my message.

Eli: Were you and Dad having sex?

Tessa: No. You arrived before things progressed.

"Progressed?" I said. Tessa glared at me, then she shut her phone off and put on the table, face down. I took a screen shot of our exchange and sent it to Dan. His phone beeped, and when he saw the message his eyes got so large they almost fell out of his head.

"Are you all right?" Dad said, seeing Dan's face. "Did you receive a message from your job?"

"No, not from work." Dan put his phone away as Tessa glared daggers at me. "So, about the curse."

Tessa and Dad shared a glance. "While I cannot be certain, I do believe that Christina is the one who cursed you," she said.

"Sounds about right," I said.

"Why can't you be certain?" Dan asked.

"I've never directly encountered her magic before," Tessa replied. "However, there were a limited amount of people who had access to Eli when she was younger."

"And since Christina distrusted anyone who used magic, that means she was probably the only witch near you," Dad said to me. "Unless you remember any other magic being used at home?"

"I don't remember much," I said. "Mostly, I remember being bored, and lonely. Mom wasn't really interested in parenting, or anything besides hiding in her room."

Dad's forehead creased. "Bug, if I'd know what it would be like for you—"

"It's okay." I did not need to deal with my father's guilt over my mother's bad behavior, not on top of everything else. "You had no way of knowing."

"It stands to reason that Christina is the one responsible," Tessa reiterated. "Dan, have you had any luck tracking her down?"

"Yes and no. Christina Lind is a somewhat common name, which may be why that name was chosen in the first place."

"Chosen?" Dad repeated. "How do you mean?"

"If the woman that gave birth to Eli is the same woman who was born at The Open Arms Center For Women And Children, it would appear Cecily Allwood had a hand in things," Dan said. "Perhaps

Cecily deliberately chose a common name to make tracing her even more difficult."

Dad rubbed his jaw. "Are you implying that searching for Christina has been difficult so far?"

"It hasn't been easy. I've got nothing but a name—which may or may not be the name she's currently using—and an address from twenty years ago. If you have any more information about her, such as a date of birth or a social security number, that would help tremendously."

"I never knew her birthday," Dad said, softly. "She made it seem like she didn't know, either, because the orphanage didn't keep good records." Dad blew out a breath, and stared at the table. "Would a picture of Christina help?"

I blinked, assuming I'd misheard him. "I didn't think there were any pictures of Mom."

"There's one." Dad left the room, and returned a few moments later with his marksman's kit. It was housed in an old leather satchel, the straps and edges burnished from years of use. It was the one item that went everywhere with him, no matter if he was crossing an ocean or running to the corner store. His kit was his prized possession.

We watched as Dad set his kit on the table and opened the top flap. There was a pocket sewn into the silk lining, the opening well-hidden against the pattern. From that pocket Dad withdrew a photograph of my mother.

"This is Christina," my father said as he handed the photograph to Dan. "It was taken shortly after we found out she was pregnant."

I scooted my chair closer to Dan's so I could examine the picture. There was my mother, blonde and blue eyed and smiling so brightly she could have outshone the sun. Standing beside her was my dad.

Their arms were wrapped around each other, and Dad looked happier than I have ever seen him.

"When was this taken?" I asked. "Why were you so happy?"

"We were happy because of you," Dad replied. "As soon as we knew you were coming we started planning what we would name you, where we would live, what kind of life we would give you." He leaned across the table and grasped my hand. "We couldn't wait to become a family."

I opened my mouth, closed it. As far as I knew my parents and I had never lived all together. "What happened?"

Eyes downcast, he replied, "She discovered she was a witch."

Dan used his phone to capture an image of the photo, then he turned it over and took a picture of the back. "Thank you, Alex," he said as he handed the photo back to Dad. "This will help."

Tessa, who hadn't said a word since Dad first mentioned the photo, glanced at it as Dad replaced it in its special pocket in his kit, then she rose and left the room. I heard the jangle of keys, then the front door opened and closed. Tessa, the most fearless person I knew, had let the memory of my mother and an old photograph drive her out of the house.

"She didn't even put on her shoes," I said, then I turned to my father. "You really need to do better with her."

"Keeping secrets in a relationship never ends well," Dan added.

"Yes, I know." Dad closed his satchel, his hand resting over the pocket that held the photograph of my mother. "All too well, I know." He closed his eyes for a moment. "If you two don't mind, I'd like to be alone with my thoughts."

"Of course," I said. "Call me if you need anything."

Dad patted my hand, then he took his satchel and retreated upstairs. The cats followed him in a single file, which was good. Even though he said he wanted to be alone, I worried about him when he isolated himself from the rest of the world. The cats would make sure he didn't get too lonely.

"For a straight up guy, Alex has a lot of secrets," Dan said.

"I didn't even know that picture of my mom existed." My phone pinged; Dan had sent me the picture. "I'd almost forgotten what she looks like."

"I'm going to send it in, and have it added to the search criteria." Dan hunched over his phone, I assumed to take care of submitting the picture. I left him to it, and wandered toward the solarium.

The solarium was next to the kitchen, which explained why the plants near the entrance were all culinary herbs. Once you got past the oregano and the plethora of basils, everything else in the solarium was poisonous. Some of the specimens in this room were decades old, and many had been nurtured from seed. My Gran, who'd been Matriarch of Seers—that title was a step up from mine, since Gran had held the position for so long—from her twentieth birthday until her death, had taken her poisons seriously.

I also took them seriously, now. When I was a kid it had been a different story. I came to live with Gran when I was eight, shortly after my seer abilities had manifested and freaked out my mother to the point that she abandoned me in a hospital. At first, coming to stay with Gran had been a party; finally, I had adults around me who wanted me to play and laugh and be happy. But kid me hadn't understood why I couldn't play in the wolfsbane patch, or why I couldn't hang out at the adult parties filled with witches, and I ended up sulking in my room more often than not. There was also the time I decided to pretty up the punchbowl, and added foxglove and pokeweed blossoms to the cups. That had not gone over well.

Gran had been patient with me, as was Dad whenever he was home, and in time I understood the responsibilities that came along with being a seer. By the time I was fourteen I was cultivating my own poison garden, and planning out my magical future. Back then I dreamed about following in Gran's footsteps.

Too bad a few nightmares had interfered with all of that.

By the time Dan found me, I was lost in thought. I came back to reality when he slipped an arm around my waist and kissed the curve where my neck met my shoulder.

"You okay?"

"Just thinking."

"This is a pretty spectacular house, but I like this room best."

"Really?" I twisted in his arms so I faced him. "Why's that?"

"It's where I found out how much you love me."

I smiled, and hid my face against his shoulder. I'd never said the words, but the acres of bleeding hearts that popped up all over town had expressed my feelings for me. According to everyone in the know, bleeding hearts appear whenever a seer finds love. "Then I guess I like your kitchen best."

"Guess so." He reached toward the potted plant next to the wall. "What's this called?"

"Thornapple." I moved a few of the leaves aside until I found one of the spiky fruits. "As you can see, it goes above and beyond to protect its seeds."

"Like a parent, protecting their kids."

I thought about my father who would move mountains for me, and my absentee mother who could barely stand to acknowledge my existence. "If only they were all like that."

Chapter 4

Amir

Iran, Ten Years Ago

"**S**o, this is Iran," I said, as we walked through the airport terminal.

Dad shook his head. "I will never get used to calling it that. To me, this land will always be Persia."

I could have pointed out that the planet at large had been referring to Persia as Iran for decades. Like, a lot of decades. But, Dad was as old fashioned as they came, and he'd already agreed to travel to the Iranian coven by air instead of a boat, and then a caravan across the desert, and I didn't want to push him. Therefore, Persia it was.

However, the plane could only bring us so far. The way I understood things, one of Dad's contacts would meet us outside the airport, and it would be a two hour drive from Tehran to the coven's headquarters. From there, who knows how long it would take to reach the portal in question.

"What happened with this portal, again?" I asked.

Dad sighed; while he was an excellent diplomat, he didn't relish these sorts of trips. "The portal leads to a dimension parallel to ours. Supposedly if you learn to navigate that dimension, you can time travel in this dimension."

"Real time travel? Like in the movies?"

"Real time travel has serious consequences, so no, not like the movies."

"You said supposedly. Has anyone ever pulled it off?"

"Yes, and it ended badly. In fact, every story I have ever heard about a witch or seer using time travel has ended badly." Dad stopped walking and faced me. "Promise me you won't ever enter this portal, not for any reason."

"I won't," I said, and I meant it. The last thing I needed was to go looking for more trouble.

Outside the airport we saw a man holding up a piece of cardboard that had "Moore" written across it in black marker. He was tall, with very shiny dark hair, and deep brown skin. When he spotted Dad and me, he smiled.

"Mr. Moore," the man called. He had a British accent, which surprised me. Then again, this was my first time outside my hometown, so I guessed a lot of things would surprise me. "Alexander Moore?"

"Yes," Dad said. "Were you sent by the coven?"

"Yes, sir, I was," he replied. "I didn't know you'd be arriving with a traveling companion."

"This is my daughter, Eliza." I waved. "Should we be going?"

"Yes, sir, let me load your luggage." The man stowed our bags in the back of the Land Rover, while Dad and I settled in the back seat of the hot, stuffy car.

"Please tell me this thing has air conditioning," I grumbled.

"Not a fan of the desert?" the driver asked. Mortified, I slunk down in my seat. "Neither am I. Let's see how cold we can get it in here."

With that, the driver turned on the air, and we set off toward the Iranian coven, and the portal that was causing all the trouble.

We bumped along the desert road until we reached a village nestled at the foot of a mountain, filled with flat-topped houses and tidy stone streets. Bright gauzy curtains hung in the open windows, and carpets were draped over stone walls, whether for cleaning or decoration I didn't know. As I sat mesmerized by the village, we turned down a long paved driveway that led to an absolute mansion.

"Here's our stop," the driver said, then he parked in front of a large house made of pinkish stone. The windows and balcony were covered in stone latticework, and arched mosaics topped the windows. The ground in front of the house was paved with octagonal stones, and matching octagonal planters held a riot of blooming plants.

"This is not what I expected," I whispered to my father.

"Witches like to live comfortably, no matter what part of the world they're in," he replied. Dad nodded toward a man standing next to the front door. "That's the coven leader, Mehrded."

"Is he nice?"

Dad smiled down at me. "He is. He's one of the best men I've ever met."

I relaxed a bit at that, not that I'd really had any doubts about this coven in the first place. My father would never bring me someplace where there was a chance I could be harmed, but we were seers. That meant we regularly dealt with some of the most dangerous people on the planet; namely, witches. Our ace in the hole was that one regular seer was more dangerous than ten witches. A seer like my father could take out a hundred witches, no problem. My grandmother, the Matriarch of Seers, could wipe out an entire clan without breaking a sweat.

And then there was me, a young, weakling seer, and the reason I was here with my father was because witches had overpowered me.

"Alex, it's been too long," Mehrded said as he approached us. "Is this your famous daughter?"

"Famous?" I squeaked. Merhded smiled.

"You're only famous in that we know Alex has a daughter, and he refuses to share anything about you, other than your name." He offered a shallow bow. "Eliza, welcome to my home."

"Thank you," I said. "This place is amazing."

"I look forward to giving you a tour of all we have to offer you during your stay with us." He turned to Dad. "I see you have already met the seer at the heart of this incident."

Dad blinked. "Who—our driver?"

"Hello again," the driver said, as he extended his hand. "Amir Hassan. I'm afraid all of this has gotten a bit blown out of proportion."

"It has not," Mehrded said. "Amir, please show Alex and Eliza the rooms they will be staying in."

Dad and I ended up with an entire suite to ourselves. We had separate bedrooms, thank all the gods, a private bathroom, and a large sitting room. The only thing missing from this almost paradise was a mini fridge in my room.

The next morning, I woke up when someone sat on the edge of my bed. Fearing the worst, I gasped and sat straight up, ready to fight or scream or maybe just cry loudly enough for someone to come see what all the noise was about, but it was just my father.

"I wish you would knock first," I grumbled, irritated with myself for overreacting.

"I did, but you were in such a deep sleep you didn't hear me," Dad said. "Bug, I want to talk to you about what will happen today."

"We're going to the portal, right?"

"Yes. And that portal is within a very deep, very dark cave." He went to the windows, and beckoned me to his side. "You see the base of that mountain? And the bright blue house? The entrance to the cave is just beyond."

I swallowed hard. It was just a cave. I'd been in caves before. Nothing bad had ever happened to me in a cave. But I heard everything he left unsaid. "And, it would be very bad if the marksman came all the way out here to judge whether opening the portal violated any treaties, and his daughter has a panic attack in the cave." I faced him, and asked, "Why did you even bring me if I have to hide in my room?"

"I brought you here because you wanted to come," he replied. "Also, you don't have to hide. You are more than welcome to accompany me to the cave. I only wanted you to be aware of what the cave will be like."

I blew out a breath. "I know. I just hate being so skittish. I want to put everything behind me, but it's so hard."

"You will put it behind you, but it takes time. Be gentle with yourself. And Bug, you are not skittish. You are one of the most fearless people I've ever met, and I love and admire that about you."

"Am I more fearless than Tessa?"

Dad smiled. "I don't know about that."

Later, after my father, Mehrdad, and a few others went off to see the portal, I wandered the grounds by myself. In addition to the lush gardens, there was a reflecting pool, a man made pond, and a swimming pool. I'd never expected to find so much water in the desert.

I sat on the edge of the reflecting pool, and dipped my fingers in the pristine water. As much as I'd wanted to go to the portal with the rest, Dad was right. The damp, dark cave might be too similar to the damp, dark basement I'd been held captive in, and even though that nightmare had ended almost a year ago, I had barely moved on. The last thing I needed was for whatever was in that cave to destroy the small bit of progress I'd made.

I clenched my fist in the water. This wasn't fair.

"Going to fight the fish?"

I looked up, and saw Amir walking towards me. "The fish are in the other pond," I said, as I relaxed my hand. "Aren't you supposed to be at the portal with everyone else?"

He sat next to me, and frowned. "I'm not allowed to attend the viewing of the portal. Mehrdad seems to think I'll influence your father's decision."

"Will you?"

"Maybe," he admitted, then he smiled. "Why didn't you go?"

"Caves aren't my thing." This person did not need to know about my trauma, no matter how nice his smile was. "I like it better out here, in the sunlight."

Amir's smile widened. "Me, too. Perhaps, a bit later, we can have lunch together."

Having lunch outside in the sunlight sounded like exactly what I needed. I would beat the darkness back, and it would never ensnare me again. "I'd like that."

CHAPTER 5

MERMAID COVE

"Something's not right with Alex and Tess," Dan said, as he drove us to his place. I mean our place. Dammit, I've got to start calling it our place.

"That is the understatement of the century."

"Hear me out. Alex is head over heels in love with Tessa, and I'm pretty sure if she dropped her Italian princess act it would be obvious that she feels the same way. You said they met when Alex was in his twenties?"

"Yeah. Tessa had been staying with family in Europe, and hadn't even known Gran had a child. By the time she came back, he was an adult." I remembered all the stories my grandmother used to tell me about my calm, level headed father, and how Tessa's arrival had driven him nuts. "From what Gran used to say it was love at first sight with those two."

"They adored each other then, and they adore each other now," Dan continued. "That begs the question, how are you here?"

Dan pulled into the driveway and parked. I thought about his question as I grabbed some of the shopping bags from the back seat and followed him to the front door.

"What do you mean, how am I here? I was born, that's how."

"But if Alex was in love with Tessa, how did he even notice Christina?" Dan unlocked the front door. "Want me to carry you over the threshold?"

I gave him a look. "Maybe after dinner."

From behind us, someone trilled, "Hello, you two!"

"Hi, Gretchen," Dan and I responded in unison. Gretchen lived across the street from Dan, and she was the stereotypical nosy neighbor. According to Dan she knew everyone's business, whether they associated her or not. She would probably make a great detective.

"I'm surprised to see you here, Eliza," Gretchen said. "I saw a dark haired woman leaving last night, and assumed you were out of the picture."

Even though I knew she'd seen Tessa, I couldn't resist giving her a bit of her own medicine. "You had a woman here?" I asked Dan. "In our house?"

"You were here, too," Dan said.

"Cheating on me while I was asleep," I screeched, then I stalked inside. "This is the last straw, Dave!" I yelled over my shoulder.

"Who's Dave?" Dan demanded. "Is that who you were with last week?"

Gretchen gasped, and I was all I could do not to fall over laughing. Dan made some kind of excuse to Gretchen, then he followed me inside.

"She's harmless, you know," he said.

"Harmless yet annoying," I said. "If she was a weed I would torch her."

"Good thing you don't have a flamethrower." We set the bags on the coffee table, and continued our conversation from before the busybody interrupted. "You were telling me how your parents met."

"When I've asked Dad how he met my mother, he's always said that one day he turned around and there she was. They weren't even together that long before she was pregnant."

"See, that doesn't make any sense. If Alex was already with Tessa, why be with Christina at all? It's not like he fell out of love with Tess. Not only that, he's a thorough, meticulous man. Getting someone he just met pregnant doesn't seem like his style." Dan sat on the couch next to me. "What are the odds of Christina pulling something over on Alex?"

"You mean, like a love spell?" I shook my head. "Those are rare, and they usually backfire. In fact, they're rare because they backfire."

"This one definitely backfired. If it hadn't your mother probably wouldn't have acted the way she did." He put his arm around me, and said, "I had another idea, too."

"Wow, you're full of ideas. Okay, tell me."

"Ever since you put this on me," he held out his arm so I could see the lock I'd tattooed on his wrist in my attempt at giving him a seers mark, "I can sense magic. Maybe, since we know where the curse is on you, I can check it out?"

I looked up at him. "Based on where this curse is located, I have to assume you have an ulterior motive."

"Me?" he asked with feigned innocence. "Never."

"You are sneaky," I replied, and his smile widened. That smile of his had very nearly won me over, when my phone vibrated. I answered the call without checking the number, assuming is was Tess. "What's up?"

"Is this Nine Lives Investigations?"

"Um, yeah." I untangled myself from Dan. "This is Nine Lives. How can we help you?"

"I-I need to hire an investigator."

I'd heard that waver in a client's voice many times before. "You called the right place. How soon do you need one?"

"Is tonight too soon?" She paused, and added, "I think my husband is cheating on me."

"I'm so sorry." I took a step toward my desk—and remembered that my desk had exploded along with the rest of my apartment. I mimed writing to Dan, and he went to find a pen and paper. At least, I hoped that was what he was looking for. "Why don't you tell me what you know so far, and we can figure out what our next steps should be."

"He used to come home right after work, but he doesn't anymore," she began. "Now he comes home in the middle of the night, and I get so worried. He won't talk to me, either. I tracked his phone's location, and he's been spending his nights at a motel. Why would he be going there?"

"I don't know, but we can find out." Dan returned with a notebook and pencil. "Can I have your contact information?"

She rattled off her name and phone number, along with the name of the motel her husband was frequenting: Mermaid Cove. Interesting name for a place situated over a hundred miles inland. "Got it. Can you give me a description of your husband?"

"He's five eleven, has dark hair with gray on the sides, no facial hair." She went on, giving me such details as the make and model of his car and even his license plate number. I was impressed.

"I can go by this motel tonight for a bit of recon," I said, after I'd filled two pages with details about the wandering husband. "I will call you tomorrow at ten o'clock with the results."

"Thank you so much. Should I stop by your office with a check?"

"My office is under construction and not safe for clients right now," I replied. "Why don't we see what I find tonight, and take it from there?"

"Thank you, Miss Moore. You're a lifesaver."

I ended the call, looked up at Dan, and grinned. "I got a case!"

"I see that. What's your first move?"

"I'm going to try and surveil her husband—crap, we're supposed to watch Renault tonight."

"I can handle Renault," Dan said. "Go, work you case. I'll follow the chief."

"You're sure?"

"Believe it or not, I do know something about following suspects." He sat next to me, and draped his arm around my shoulders. "We can divide and conquer."

"Look at us. It's like we're partners, or something."

"Partners." Dan kissed my temple. "I like that."

Dan and I had a late lunch, then he went to the police station while I headed to Mermaid Cove. According to my client, Virginia Parker, her husband normally worked until five, and per his phone's data he went directly from his job to the motel. I thought her tracking her husband via his phone was a bit disingenuous; then again, his erratic behavior had more than likely given her probable cause to do a little snooping. Now that I was on the case, the truth would come out soon enough.

As I drove toward the motel, I wondered if I would ever have similar suspicions about Dan. While our romantic relationship was only a few weeks old, we'd known each other for more than two years. Dan had proven he was an honest and straightforward man without a deceitful bone in his body long before we'd ever kissed. If anything, Dan proudly wore his heart on his sleeve. I couldn't imagine him cheating on me, or anyone

My mind wandered toward memories of Amir, as it often did while I was distracted by boring things like driving or picking up trash. Amir had never acted like he was cheating on me, but he'd never behaved as if he loved me, either. If anything he'd only been going through the motions of a relationship, and I was so affection starved I went through those motions with him. All in all, it had been two years of empty promises and an even emptier relationship.

Dan had come through on every promise he'd ever made to me.

I was smiling as I turned onto Piper Lane and pulled into the motel's back parking lot, but dialed it down as I found a parking spot. My theory was that if Mr. Parker was cheating on the regular, he would be using the back door as opposed to walking through the main entrance. I scribbled a note, reminding myself to check into any possible video surveillance at the hotel, and ask about credit card records. My pencil's tip broke, and I swore.

"And this is why I need a keyboard." I picked up my phone to check the tracking number on the new laptop I'd ordered, when another portion of my notes caught my eye. Mrs. Parker had specifically mentioned that she hadn't taken her husband's surname. In my haste I'd written down his name, but it hadn't actually registered in my mind. I read it now, and gasped.

My target's name was Louis Renault.

Dan's boss's name was Chief Renault.

"It can't be the same guy," I muttered, then I looked toward the main road. I was in the back lot, but the motel faced Route Ten.

"What are the odds," I began, then I saw Dan's white rental car pull into the front parking lot. "Odds are good."

I started my car, then I drove into the front lot. There was a space open next to Dan, so I parked in it, got out of my car, and hopped into his.

"What the—" he said, when I opened the passenger door.

"You should really lock your doors," I said. "Especially while hanging out near seedy motels."

"You're not wrong," he said. "Let me guess, Renault is your client's husband?"

"One in the same."

"I don't suppose your foresight is in the mood to offer up any additional clues?"

"Sorry. It's my least helpful gift." I slunk down in my seat and checked out the front of the motel. The roadside sign boasted a pink and blue neon mermaid, with an animated tail and the requisite bare breasts. "Did he act like he was doing anything shady while he was leaving?"

"Nope. He left the station, got in his car and drove here, then he walked in through the front door like it was no big deal." Dan drummed the steering wheel. "He didn't act like he was cheating, or doing anything wrong. Just a guy going about his day."

"Well, if it turns out he's not cheating on his wife that'll be a good thing." I refocused my attention from the sign to the actual motel. The motel was a standard two story building, but the rooms didn't appear to have private entrances. "Is the front door the only way in? I only saw a fire exit around back," I added.

"Seems so. Want to rent a room?"

"Seriously? Now?"

"I mean, want to rent one so we can get inside?" He shook his head. "Really, Eli, what else could I have meant?"

"Yeah, I forgot how innocent you are."

He gave me a lopsided smile, then he faced the motel. "This place is buzzing with magic."

"Really? Just where Renault is, or everywhere?"

"Not sure yet."

"Okay, now we have two reasons to get inside." I counted the number of windows, figuring one window per room. "This place has at least twenty-four rooms, maybe double that. Even if we did rent a room, someone's bound to notice us skulking about the place."

"I can talk to the front desk clerk," Dan began, but I shook my head.

"Let's try something a bit stealthier." I closed my eyes, and summoned my best ghostly friend, Prudence.

Prudence had lived and died in my now-demolished apartment about a hundred years ago. She was a morally upright champion for children's welfare, mostly because seven of her own children had contracted polio in the days before the vaccine was widely available. While Prudence did not approve of my lifestyle, and thought I was far too old to still be unmarried, she'd helped me out with my cases more often than not. In fact, if not for her timely warning Dan and I might not have escaped my apartment before Amir's spell blew it to bits.

A familiar sensation of disdain mingled with curiosity let me know when Prudence's spirit had joined us. "Hey, Pru," I said, turning around so I could see her in the back seat. "You remember Dan, right?"

Pru looked down her nose at Dan. "Have you finally come to your senses and married him?"

"Not yet."

"But you intend to?"

"Yeah. I guess." I held out my wrist to Dan, so he could touch my seer's mark and therefore see and hear Prudence. He glanced at my arm, and shook his head.

"I can see Prudence just fine. How are you, ma'am?"

Dan and Prudence said their hellos, while I sat frozen in my seat. I knew that the mark I'd tattooed on Dan made him able to sense magic, but I hadn't expected him to be able to interact with Pru. Now, Dan had heard what Pru said to me. Even worse, he'd heard my response. Since I could not deal with any of that at the moment, I took a deep breath and turned my attention to the situation at hand.

"Pru, we need to know what room a certain man is in," I said. "Could you go in and have a look around?"

"Why should I do that?" she countered. "What's this man done?"

"Actually, it's what's being done to him," Dan said. He pulled out his phone and called up a picture of Chief Renault. "This man is my boss, the chief of police. He's got an excellent record spanning several decades. Now, someone's laid a spell on him, and that's not right. We need to find whoever's messing with his mind, but more importantly we need good men like Chief Renault. He's helped many people over the years, but now he needs our help. Can you help us help him, ma'am?"

Dan's speech moved Prudence so much her eyes welled up. "Very well. I'll go inside and see what I can find for you."

Prudence dematerialized, set on her task. "Good job, getting Pru on your side so quickly," I said. "She usually makes me work for her help." When Dan remained silent, I glanced at him. His face was thoughtful, and in a rush I remembered why.

"Listen, I know you heard what she said," I began. Dan took my hand, and rubbed his thumb across my palm.

"I did. And, I know that if I say anything about what you said to her you'll clam up and then you won't talk to me about anything."

"I don't clam up."

"Fine, you'll clam down." He glanced up from his examination of my hand, and smiled. "For now, it's enough for me that you said it."

"For now?"

Dan kissed my knuckles. "For now."

Prudence reappeared in the back seat. "Now that I see you with Mr. Lyons, I can understand why you've waited so long to accept a man's offer," she said approvingly. "I must say, Eliza, his values and manners are without reproach."

"Thank you, ma'am," Dan said, beaming.

"Enough, you two," I said, smiling. "Did you find him?"

"I did. He is in room two one four, and," Prudence leaned close and whispered, which was just hilarious coming from a ghost, "there is a young lady in the room with him."

"Thanks, Pru," I said. "We'll take it from here, and do our best to preserve everyone's virtue."

Prudence sniffed. "See that you do, Eliza." With that, she was gone.

"Now what?" Dan asked, as he stared at the empty space Prudence had just been in.

"I think we should wait for Renault to leave, then we can sneak up to the room and see who he's meeting. Want to watch a movie on my phone until then?"

Dan turned the right way around, then he jerked his head to the door. "Chief's on the move."

I watched as Louis Renault exited the motel, got into his car, and drove away. Based on his wife's descriptions he was out all night after work. I wondered if these motel visits were always so quick, and where else he was off to.

"Think one of us should follow him?" I asked.

"Nah. We know where to find him. Let's see what we've got going on here."

We entered the motel's lobby, and as luck would have it the front desk was vacant, unless you counted the basket of shiny red apples next to the call bell.

"This place is... Odd," Dan said.

I took in the striped orange and yellow wallpaper, and avocado green rug. "It could use a makeover."

"Not that. The magic is much stronger in here."

"Really? Where's it coming from?"

He shook his head. "It seems to be coming from everywhere, all at once."

"Great." We made a beeline toward the elevators, and wouldn't you know it one of the employee's intercepted us. Based on his nametag, he was Bryce the Manager.

"You're not guests here," Bryce said.

"We're visiting someone," I said. "She's in room two fourteen."

The manager scoffed. "That girl gets a lot of people. Any more show up, and I'm adding them to her bill."

He stepped aside, and Dan and I entered the elevator. "How do you bill for visitors?" I wondered.

"Five bucks a head?"

I laughed, then the elevator doors opened. We went down the hall to room two fourteen. Dan put his hand on the door knob, and tested it.

"Unlocked," he said. "What do you think?"

"Let's do it."

"Me first." Dan drew his gun, then he gently opened the door. "Police," he announced. "Coming in."

He went a few steps inside the room, then he stopped dead. "Eli, you've gotta see this."

I entered the room, and gasped. Sitting on the bed was Jada Morales.

CHAPTER 6

FOUND HER

"What the hell are you doing here?" I demanded.

"This is my room," Jada retorted. "What are *you* doing here?"

I looked around the tiny motel room, half expecting someone like Amir or Nathaniel to jump out of the bathroom. The room had barely enough space for the bed, dresser, and side table, but it appeared to be clean and well-maintained. Those orange drapes hadn't been in style in several decades, and they clashed with the mustard yellow bedspread, but at least there weren't any obvious stains. I wondered what secrets the brown carpet was hiding.

"Everyone's been looking for you," Dan said in his even toned police detective voice. "We've all been pretty worried. How did you escape from the hospital?" When Jada remained silent, he added, "Did someone take you?"

"No one took me," she said. "I didn't want to be there anymore, so I left. That place was boring, like getting sent to my room except when finally I got to go outside again, I only had that hospital to walk around in." Jada pulled her knees up to her chest, reminding me that mentally she was still a little girl. "It was so cold and lonely."

"Jada, I'm sorry," I said. "I didn't realize how unhappy you were."

"It's okay," she said brightly, her mood shifting on a dime. "I told Nathaniel how I was scared that the new place they wanted to send me to would be worse than the hospital, so after I got out, he brought me here." Jada spread her arms wide as if she wanted to hug her motel room, twin bed and all. "This place is awesome! And there's three vending machines in the hall!"

I glanced at Dan. He holstered his gun, then he withdrew his phone and called up a picture. He showed the phone to Jada, and asked, "Is this Nathaniel?"

Jada grinned from ear to ear. "Yes! Do you know him?"

"We're acquainted." Dan tilted the phone's screen toward me. He'd shown Jada an image of Amir that had been caught by his home surveillance cameras.

"Does Nathaniel come by every day?" I asked.

"No," Jada said, pouting. "He's very busy. But he gave me an important job to do." She rolled to the other side of the bed, grabbed a notebook, and rolled back. "He sends his friends by to tell me things, and I write it all down. See?"

I glanced at the top page. On it was a summary of Chief Renault's interrogation of me. "I'm impressed."

"You are?" Jada beamed at me. "That's awesome, Ellie."

I bristled, since the only person who'd ever called me Ellie was Amir. Well, until he told Jada about my hated nickname. Now two people called me Ellie, and that was two too many. Dan put his hand on my arm, and asked, "Does Nathaniel have you do anything else?"

"Yeah, but it's kind of weird."

"Weird how?" I demanded.

"Well, I told him about these dreams I have," Jada began. "They're old fashioned, like I'm living hundreds of years ago, like a pioneer or something. Anyway, I told Nathaniel, and he asked me to write them down." She reached across the bed and grabbed a different notebook. "So, every morning I write down my dreams. It takes a while."

"I'm sure it does," I murmured. We'd suspected Jada had retained Sarah Allwood's memories, and now we had proof. "I used to keep a dream journal, too. Maybe we can compare them sometime."

Jada grinned. "That might be fun!"

"Speaking of fun," Dan began, "would you like us to take you anywhere?"

"No. Why would I?"

"Just asking." Dan squeezed my arm, then he reached toward Jada's notebook. "Is it okay if I write down my and Eli's numbers?"

"I still owe you a lunch date," I added, as I wondered where Dan was going with this.

"Okay," Jada said. "That's cool. I mean, I still get bored sometimes."

"Yeah? Me, too." Dan handed the notebook and pen back to Jada. "It was great seeing you, Jada. If you need anything, give us a call."

"Bye," Jada and I said in unison. We laughed, and waved, then Dan and I retreated to the hall. On our way out I swiped the Do Not Disturb door hanger.

"Why did you steal that?" he asked, after Jada's door shut.

"Why are you just letting her stay here?" I countered.

Dan put his hand on the small of my back and guided me toward the elevator. "Jada is an adult, and claims she's here of her own free will. She's also not doing anything wrong. If we forcibly remove her, that's kidnapping."

I jabbed at the elevator's call button. "She admitted escaping from the hospital."

"From where she was due to be discharged from, anyway." The elevator arrived and we stepped inside. "We know where she is, and that she's safe. We can keep an eye on her."

I glared at our reflection. "Can't you remover her for her own good? Don't the police do that?"

He laughed softly. "Do me a favor, find me a single incident of that happening where the cop doesn't going to jail in the end."

I sighed. "I guess I like you better out of jail. Hey, since you found Jada does that mean you can have her case back?"

He scoffed. "Probably not. Besides, I don't know if I want to report her as found until we know what's up with Renault."

"That's smart." The elevator doors slid open. "See the manager anywhere?"

"Coast is clear."

I frowned. "I wanted to get another look at him. He's not right." I showed Dan the door hanger. It was a dull orange, and it was printed in a curly disco-style font. "Like you said, none of this is right. This looks like it came from the seventies."

Dan looked around the lobby, his gaze steady. "Just because the decor isn't up to date doesn't mean there's magic involved. Who's to say this isn't one of those retro places?"

"That's a possibility, but what if Amir used a time slip here?"

Dan's brow pinched. "I thought Tessa bound him to the present."

"She did, but what does that mean for all the time slips he already cast? Do they just go away, or do they stick around?"

"That is a question for your pal, Jacob." We got to the rental car, and Dan swore.

"You really don't like this car, do you?"

"I do not," he replied. "I want my check from the insurance company, and I am going to take it and buy the exact same truck I had before. In fact, maybe I'll go out and buy a new truck tomorrow, and the insurance company can play catch up."

"Or you could just return the rental, use my car, and relax." I leaned against my car's fender. "Or get creative. Leave the rental here, say it was stolen."

"You are bad," he said, then he pulled me close and kissed me. "Race you home?"

Every time he said the word home—as in, the home I now shared with him—my heart did a somersault while the butterflies in my stomach did a little dance. "I'm going to check on Tess. She likes to be alone when she's upset, but I don't want her to wallow for too long."

"If you need anything while you're there, call me." Dan kissed my forehead, then I slid out of his arms. "Tell Tessa I'm always ready to defend her honor."

"She'll like that." We stared at each other for a moment, then I said, "Okay. See you soon."

"Okay."

I got in my car and Dan entered the hated rental, then I waved a last goodbye and pulled out of the back of the parking lot. It was such a new and confusing feeling to be officially living with Dan, and that even though we were going our separate ways now within a few hours, we would be together again. And tomorrow, and next week, and for who knows how long. There was a lot of togetherness in our future.

Oh, boy.

Chapter 7

Oranges and Truth Spells

Eli: **In the mood for a visitor?**

  Tessa: Just you.

Eli: Be right up.

I dropped my phone into my bag and pulled into the parking lot of Tessa's luxury condo complex. Tessa was the only witch I'd ever known of who chose to live in such a place, rather than her own estate, with a legion of servants seeing to her every need. But Tessa had been born into royalty, and frequently said how she'd long ago grown tired of having people around her at all times of the day and night. She was at a point in her life where her solitude was something to be protected. Also, the complex had a really nice pool.

I swung by the pool, but wasn't surprised when I didn't find Tessa sunning herself. Being that I was still a bit freaked out from the motel's retro aesthetic, I took the stairs to the penthouse in order to give myself a few extra moments to compose myself. Technically, this complex had three condos on every floor, but Tessa owned the entire top floor of her building. She was cultivating solitude, along with her privacy.

I knocked on the door. When no one answered after a few moments, I let myself in. "Tess?"

"Out here."

I followed her voice out to the balcony. It was decorated with shady nooks and all sorts of plants, though it wasn't a poison garden like

Gran's solarium. Tessa's balcony was packed with potted herbs and dwarf fruit trees, and in the summer months it reminded me of Italy. Actually, it reminded me of Italy year round. Tessa had cast a weather spell on her balcony, thus ensuring her tender herbs would never get frostbitten.

I found Tess reclining on a deck chair by the citrus trees, an unopened book on her lap, and an untouched drink on the side table. She was wearing a black strapless swimsuit and oversized sunglasses, and wouldn't have looked out of place in a World War II pinup calendar.

"Hey." I sat on the deck chair opposite from her. "Working on your tan?"

"You know I don't tan. I do, however, enjoy the sun." Tessa lowered her sunglasses, and I saw her pink, swollen eyes. "I always hope it will burn away some of my more painful memories, but that's yet to happen."

"I'm so sorry," I said. "I don't know what Dad's problem is. It's like he's doomed to always say or do the wrong thing around you."

"Yes. Well." Tessa opened the book and closed it. "Did you know about the picture?"

"I had no idea it even existed." Tessa's jaw tightened, and she picked at the book's cover. "Why did a simple picture upset you so much?"

"It's not the picture," she began. "Not really. It would be foolish of me to assume Alex had eradicated all traces of Christina, especially since she gave birth to his only child. It's just..." Tessa set the book aside and covered her eyes with her hand.

"Every time I let myself get close to Alex again, she comes between us. I never wanted to feel this way about him or anyone, not after..." She cleared her throat. "Not after Tomas."

Tess had told me many stories about Tomas. He was a past lover of hers who had lived and died over two hundred years ago. "He was mortal, right?"

"He was, but he may as well have been a witch for how he took my heart with him when he died. Did I ever tell you that he loved oranges?"

I glanced at the dozens of potted orange trees on the balcony. "Yeah. You told me he grew them."

"His family had orange groves. It was the most beautiful life, living and working among the trees, breathing in the scent of the blossoms... But he was mortal, and he died."

"How old was he?"

"I never really knew. Records weren't very well kept in his village, but we were together for more than fifty years. Fifty glorious, warm, wonderful years. After Tomas passed I mourned him, but I didn't despair. He lived a good life, and I wanted to honor him by continuing to live mine. Many of my clan had come to this area, so I did as well." She blew out a breath. "Eventually, I became friends with your grandmother and oh, the adventures we had! Then Helena met Adesh, and bearing his child became her mission."

I blinked. I hadn't expected a story about Tomas to segue into one about my grandparents. "How was it a mission? Did Gran have problems?"

"She did, but not of a medical nature. Adesh wasn't certain that taking up with a seer was in his family's best interests. Helena spent many, many days and nights convincing him otherwise." Tessa gave me a look, and added, "As you know, they never married."

"I feel like you're about to delve into stories I'd rather not hear."

Tessa shook her head. "No, nothing like that. Helena once told me that she'd had a vision, and she knew that Adesh needed to father the next generation of seers."

"And that was my dad," I said, and Tess nodded. Then, she held out her hand.

For as long as I could remember Tessa and I had an agreement: when we held hands we could tell each other anything, no matter how embarrassing or awkward, without judgement or shame. Usually I was the one who initiated these moments. Now, I moved from my chair to perch on the edge of Tessa's, and grasped her hand as tight as I could.

"When I met Alex, he was perfect," she began. "I am not exaggerating. He had Adesh's dark eyes and skin, and Helena's wit and charm. He was brilliant, and fun, and his smile warmed me in a way no one's had since Tomas. I think I fell in love with Alex the moment I saw him." A tear splashed onto Tessa's leg. "I used to think he loved me, too."

"Dad does love you," I said. "He's an idiot about it, but he does. I'm sure of it."

"Then why was he ever with Christina?" Tessa asked. "Why did he have a child with her, if he loved me?"

"I don't know. Have you ever asked him?"

"That's the thing. He doesn't seem to know, either. It's as if he decided to have a fling without considering the consequences." Tessa gasped, and said, "Eli, I don't mean to imply that you are anything other than a much wanted child. You're the center of Alex's world."

"It's okay. I often wonder why he shacked up with my mother, too." I'd wondered about many things in my life, but I'd never doubted that Dad loved me. Even though he was gone for much of my youth, I'd never felt like I was a burden to him. For all of his faults, he was a great father.

I thought about some of those faults, and how some of mine mirrored his. "Dad isn't great at showing people how he feels. He's fine with saying stuff, but then he runs off and acts like he left his brain behind. I... I think I might be like that too."

"I don't know about that. Aren't things going well with you and Dan?"

"I guess. He gave me a key to his house."

"Oh, so you're living together now?"

"Jealous I'm not living here with you?"

"Not hardly. I had enough of living with you after our time in Paris."

"Maybe I had enough of you, too. My point is, Dad loves you. I can't explain his strange behavior, but love is behind it. Maybe we can cast a truth spell on him and make him spill his secrets once and for all."

Tessa hugged me. "Eli, you always know how to make me feel better. Let's get working on that truth spell."

"Wait, that was a joke."

CHAPTER 8

ONE NIGHT AT THE LOUVRE

PARIS, ALMOST FIVE YEARS AGO

"I can't believe we're doing this," I said. "I've never snuck into a place after-hours before."

"You've never been twenty-four before, either," Amir said. Tessa and I had arrived in Paris just last week, and this morning Amir showed up at our apartment with a bouquet of flowers and a birthday cake for me. I couldn't believe he'd come all the way to Paris to see me, or that he remembered it was my birthday. We'd spent the day together, and at some point I mentioned that I wanted to see the Mona Lisa.

Now we were sneaking into the Louvre.

"Is this really a good idea?" I pressed. "We don't have to do this now. We can just come back tomorrow."

"What, and spend the day surrounded by tourists?" he scoffed. "This is how true art aficionados take in the greats."

I didn't quite believe that, because why would art experts want to see paintings in a dark building? But I was having fun, and I didn't want to go home just yet.

We crept down the motionless escalators, wandered through the gift shop and down a wide red corridor, and came upon two curved staircases surrounded by white marble columns. "Those are Corinthian columns," I declared, flush with knowledge from junior year art history.

"Very good," Amir said. "Our girl's this way."

We descended into a vaulted corridor lined with sculptures, which looked extra creepy thanks to the darkness. Amir led me in and out of a few more rooms—I think we made two complete circuits of the place, but since it was dark, and I'd never been to The Louvre before, I couldn't be certain—until we finally came to the room the Mona Lisa was in. The sign at the door said we should keep our visit short and sweet.

"Just like you, Ellie," Amir said, with a nod toward the sign.

"Come on," I said, and we stepped inside the room. The walls were lined with large paintings, but Mona herself was in her own glass case.

"She's so much smaller than the rest." Since there were no guards to tell me not to, I got right up to the glass—I guess there was a benefit to breaking and entering an art museum—and looked her in the eye. "Amazing how she's a tiny little thing, but she's the most important person in the room."

"Again, just like you." Amir slipped his arm around my waist, and we contemplated Mona's famous face.

"I wonder if, when she sat for this portrait, she had any idea we'd still be looking at her hundreds of years later," I mused. "Immortality bestows strange and random gifts, but you have to know where to look."

"Mehrdad used to say that," Amir mused. "You're a sharp one. If you've had your fill of staring at Ms. Lisa, there's something else I want to check out."

Amir led me out of the portrait gallery, and after a few turns we were in the Egyptian room. In a small alcove in the rear of the room was a mummy.

"Isn't this more interesting than a painting?" Amir asked as he strode up to the mummy.

"I guess." Even though I was a seer, and regularly worked with the dead, I thought displaying human remains was in bad taste. If I had things my way we would let everyone stay at rest and in their graves as they were meant to, but we weren't living in the world according to Eliza. "Why did you want to visit him? If it is a him."

"It's a him." Amir set his hand on the mummy's foot, and closed his eyes. "He's the only mummy in the museum. I thought it best to pay our respects."

"Well, they're paid. Let's get out of here before we set off an alarm."

"Whatever you say, birthday girl."

CHAPTER 9

CURSES

Tessa and I relocated from the sunny balcony to her living room, and sprawled across her snowy white and incredibly expensive sofa. It was softer than the highest quality featherbed, and whenever I was on it I closed my eyes I pretended I was laying on a cloud. We had the television on, but the sound was muted. Tessa's favorite movies were old black and white romantic comedies, and she'd seen them so many times she had all the lines memorized.

"What if Dad really is cursed?" I asked, out of the blue.

"Cursed with what, exactly?"

"Not sure, but hear me out. You say that whenever you two get close again, something pops up about my mother. After the thing with her picture earlier, and you stormed out in a huff—"

"I was not in a huff!"

"You left your shoes behind." She frowned, and gestured for me to continue. "Anyway, after you left Dad was all out of sorts, and he went upstairs to lay down."

"You came to check on me, before your own father?"

"He's got the cats. You were all alone. My point is, he seemed off, like cursed off. Add to that the fact that Dad can't even really explain why he was ever with my mother. He's always said they met and it was a whirlwind, but he has no actual details." I tapped my chin with my forefinger. "But, that doesn't explain why Gran didn't detect the curse."

"Curses are hard to find, especially if you're not looking for them," Tessa said. "Take yourself, for example. I never knew about your curse, yet it's there all the same." She swung her legs around and sat up, her jaw set. "If Christina cursed both you and Alex, we can probably cure both of you at the same time."

"Great! How do we do that?"

"Well, it certainly won't be easy," Tessa said. "We still don't know what the curse is supposed to do, or if Alex is truly cursed. Our first step should be to determine if anything magical was done to Alex."

"And we have to figure out why my mother cursed him in the first place," I said. "Although, Dad claims she didn't know she was a witch until after she was pregnant. What if... What if Amir used a time slip to give her the curse?"

Tessa shook her head. "Eli, that's a bit far-fetched."

"I don't think it is." Something had been nagging at me about the picture of my parents, other than the fact it existed. I pulled out my phone and brought up the picture, then I enlarged it and passed the phone to Tessa. "Check out the necklace she's wearing."

Tessa pursed her lips, but she accepted the phone. When her brow pinched, I knew she saw what I saw. "It looks like the sapphire necklace you lost in Paris."

"What if it is the necklace I lost in Paris?" I asked. "What if Amir took it, and then he went back in time and gave it to my mother? What if the curse my mother put on Dad—and the one she put on me—originally came from Amir?"

"Let's put aside the rampant speculation for a moment," Tessa said, as she set the phone down. "Exactly what would Amir's purpose be? Why would he want to curse Alex?"

"I don't know," I said. "Maybe to make sure my mother cursed me, so he could make a play for the seers?"

"That would demonstrate a great deal of forethought. Or, perhaps foresight. All seers have foresight, correct?"

"In theory," I replied. "It's pretty useless."

"Nothing is useless. You just need to learn how to use your skills appropriately."

"Speaking of skills, how does that temporal binding work on Amir? Could we somehow use it to track where he's been, time wise?"

"Perhaps. Though I must say, this whole business would be easier if the elders would talk to me, and explain how Amir abducted them in the first place. But no, they enjoy shunning me."

"Maybe they're under the same curse."

"You can't use a possible curse as the answer to all of our problems," Tessa said. "The more likely explanation is that they feel like fools for letting Amir capture them in the first place. Witches are quite prideful, you know."

"Really. I had no idea."

Tessa retreated to her bedroom so she could mediate on Dad's possible curse, but I thought she was psyching herself up to talk to him again. I meant what I'd said—Dad adored Tess, so much so he would move mountains for her. The fact that he'd jeopardized his relationship with Tessa for a woman he'd just met was out of character, and downright weird. Maybe, cursed weird.

As I drove home, my mind swirled with images of curses, time slips, and that damn sapphire necklace. That necklace had been the first thing I'd bought in Paris. I'd never bought myself something so expensive before, but I had birthday money and figured it was time to splurge. The necklace was a heart-shaped sapphire set in white gold, and the chain was the perfect length to let the gem rest in the hollow of my throat. I'd worn that necklace every single day, until it disappeared.

Never before had I wondered if Amir had taken it. Keeping mementos from past lovers wasn't his style, and he didn't have a penchant for sparkly things. Now, I wondered what else I hadn't noticed about him.

I pulled into Dan's driveway, and sat in the car staring at the house. I lived here. With Dan. Even though I'd been staying here for the past few nights, I'd only had a key for a few hours. This was new, and strange, and I didn't quite know what to think.

I spied movement through the living room windows. Dan must have seen the headlights when I pulled in. Since I didn't want to spend all night in the driveway, I got out of the car and went in the house. The front door was unlocked; my new key's debut performance would have to wait.

"Dan?"

"Right here." He stepped out of the kitchen and smiled, and all of my uncertainties melted away. "How's Tess?"

"Sad, but she's sad with a plan." While Dan made coffee, I told him about my visit with Tessa, my theory about the curses, and my missing sapphire necklace.

"You like sapphires?" he asked as he poured the perfect amount of milk into my coffee.

"It's my birthstone." We went out to the living room, and sat on the couch. "I like this. Talking with you at the end of the day."

"I like listening." He set his empty mug on the table. "Although, we might overdo it on caffeine."

"What, it's before midnight. We can totally handle another pot."

He laughed. "I thought about ordering one of those cup at a time coffee makers, but I hear they're not good for the environment."

"A French press works just as well, and doesn't use plastic." I finished my coffee, and set my mug next to his. "Have you lived with a lot of people?"

"Other than family, and one disastrous college roommate, no," he replied. "You?"

"Same, except for the couple years I spent in Paris with Tess."

"Got cold feet already?"

"No! But, I like that this is new for you, too."

Dan leaned back against the couch and extended his arm. I took the invitation and snuggled up against him, my arm around his waist and my feet tucked under me. "Do you like new things?"

"This time, I do." I reached for my mug, and pouted when I remembered it was empty.

"With our drinking habits we should probably look into getting one of those home delivery coffee subscriptions."

I stared at him, mouth agape. "You can subscribe to coffee?"

Chapter 10

Foresight, Again

The next morning, my alarm woke me for my usual pre-dawn run. Instead of getting out of bed, I rolled over and grabbed my phone, then I checked the tracking number on the new pair of running shoes I'd ordered; the shoes, along with my new laptop, were only a few towns away. With any luck they'd get delivered to Gran's today, and I could have my run tomorrow.

Once I'm awake I have a hard time going back to sleep, so I left Dan in dreamland, got dressed, and went down to the kitchen. I ate a banana while the coffee brewed, then I took my mug out to the garden. Dan's wife, Charlotte, had kept a poison garden, and I was itching to get my hands into the soil.

Her reasons behind keeping a poison garden differed from mine. Whereas I'm a seer, and I work with poisons to amplify and enhance my inborn abilities, Charlotte had been bespelled by the worst seer in history, also known as Amir, who then compelled her to grow an assortment of baneful herbs. She kept the garden in two parts: an outdoor raised bed, and a greenhouse.

The greenhouse was mostly empty, except for a few old pots and a huge castor bean plant, which is where ricin comes from. I decided to leave that beast alone for now, and sat on the grass next to the raised bed. Charlotte had been gone for years, yet the plants in the bed were well cared for, and the soil was weeded and mulched. Dan didn't have a green thumb, and while he had a lawn service come by every few weeks I doubted they were looking after the raised beds, too. All these healthy plants coupled with a lack of care led me to one conclusion: this bed was enchanted.

But, enchanted by what? And by whom?

Fun fact, I have a lot of tattoos. I'm far from being a contender for the next Illustrated Woman, but I definitely carry around more ink than the average person. All of them were designed and applied by my father, and almost all of them had a magical significance; when I was eighteen I'd begged him to tattoo a charm bracelet around my left ankle, and after much cajoling he agreed to it. The bracelet was a thing of beauty, and it was so realistic most who saw it thought it was an actual piece of jewelry.

As for the rest of my tattoos, they all had varied functions from warding off diseases to sending me a warning shock if they were touched by someone who meant to harm me. My seer's mark, a lapis lazuli-colored bit of line work on my left wrist, had the added benefit of being able to detect magic. It wasn't a reliable magic detector, and now that I knew I was half witch I wondered if my witch blood was somehow interfering with the mark's innate properties. Then again, being that I'd only recently learned I was part witch, maybe I needed to lean into that side of my heritage a bit further.

Hmm. I wondered what my witch blood could tell me about these plants?

I blew out a breath, and surveyed the front line of plants in the bed. The specimen in the far left corner was white snakeroot, which was so poisonous that if a cow ate it, and later on you drank that cow's milk, you'd still die. I made a mental note to get a marker and maybe a fence for the snakeroot, and focused on the three plants in front of me.

The plants were foxglove, aconite, and belladonna, all planted in a pretty little row. All were poisonous to varying degrees, and all were lovely plants. Foxglove and aconite were commonly sold in nurseries, on account of their long lasting flowers. Belladonna was a less forgiving plant, and was treated as a weed more often than not. That was a shame, since its purplish flowers and fat black berries were gorgeous.

The belladonna specimen in front of me was especially well kept, which was another irregularity in this very irregular bed. It was full and lush, as if someone had known exactly how to care for this specific strain of belladonna—and since this was Dan's yard, I was certain no one had cared for it beyond watering, and the occasional dose of plant food. I fluffed its leaves, hoping it would trigger my seer's mark, and got a flash of foresight instead.

Or rather, hindsight.

I was transported back two years ago, and Tessa and I were sitting in my car. We were in Forge Heights Assisted Living Center's parking lot, and I was checking out two large and healthy belladonna plants that framed the center's front entrance.

I gasped and released the plant, and took a few deep breaths while the vision dissipated. The incident at Forge Heights had been my first case after I'd opened Nine Lives Investigations. It was also the first time I'd ever acted as a seer after my gran passed, and used my gifts to help people. That case also led to me meeting Dan.

This poison garden was here two years ago. When Forge Heights' activities director, Marianne, had gone looking for belladonna, this plant—a plant which had been cultivated years earlier by Dan's now-deceased wife—would have existed. We'd already established that Amir had compelled and possibly possessed Charlotte, and had her plant every single specimen in this bed. Thanks to my foresight, I now knew that the plant in front of me was identical to the belladonnas at Forge Heights.

Somehow, some way, Marianne had obtained a cutting of the belladonna growing in Dan's yard. And here I was, dealing with the same plant two years later.

I'd ended up exactly where Amir wanted me.

As my father said, Amir liked to play the long game.

"But, why?" I asked the plant. "Why would Amir want me to meet Dan? Or, was us meeting an unintended side effect?"

I grasped a leafy stem, and asked, "May I?" The belladonna didn't object, so I snapped off the stem, thanked the plant for its gift, and went inside to put the stem in some water. My plan was to head over to Forge Heights, check out the belladonnas at the center, and hopefully come away with a few answers. Before I could act on any of that, I got a text from Jill. I glanced at the kitchen clock, and saw it was just before eight. I'd been sitting in the garden for over two hours.

Jill: Are you with Dan?

Jill: Renault's on the warpath.

Eli: Is Dan in trouble?

Jill: Yes.

I set my phone on the counter, and went back to the bedroom. Dan was still sleeping, and I would have given anything to let him rest. However, experience had taught me that it was better to get these things over with as soon as possible.

I gently shook his shoulder. "Dan? Dan!"

"Wha—" He blinked himself awake, then he focused on me. "Why are you all dirty?"

I glanced at my hands, still dusted with soil. "I was in the garden. Jill texted. She said you should go in right away."

"Chief's pissed?"

"The word she used was warpath."

"Great." Dan flung the comforter aside, then he sat up and rubbed his eyes. "I wonder what I did this time."

"You really don't know?"

"Could be anything. Chief and I have butted heads a few times." I nodded, then I went into the bathroom and washed my hands. When I returned I started gathering clothes together. "What are you doing?" he asked.

"I'm getting dressed so we can go." When Dan only stared at me, I added, "Listen, we know the chief's either possessed or enchanted, or maybe both. While you talk to him, I'll talk to Jill, and maybe we can figure out what's really going on." I turned away, and added, "And maybe I'm moral support, too, you know? We are partners, after all."

Dan got out of bed and stood behind me. He moved my hair to the side, and kissed the back of my neck. "Partners to the end, babe."

"Are you going to tell me about it?" Dan asked.

We were in the rental car, and on our way to the police station. I'd been staring out the passenger window, but now I refocused on Dan. "Tell you about what? I only know what Jill texted me, which isn't much."

"Not about that. About whatever's swirling around in your head."

I debated denying everything, since whatever was happening with his job was much more important... But, what if it the belladonna from years ago really was connected to what was happening now? That was important, too. "While I was in the garden, I had a vision."

"Foresight again?"

"Yeah."

He grunted. "That's never a good sign."

I wanted to argue with him, but he had a point. My foresight only gave me snippets information, and it was never about anything specific. I'd never once figured any of my visions out until after the events had already happened. But, this time the vision might have shown me at least part of the answer.

"Remember the belladonna incident at Forge Heights?"

He reached over and squeezed my knee. "How could I forget the bonkers case that led to me meeting you?"

"When I had my vision, I leaned that the belladonnas at Forge Heights were grown from cuttings of the belladonna growing in your yard."

He opened his mouth to speak, closed it. "I was going to ask how that's possible, but I feel like we're in the realm of anything's possible."

"Tell me about it." I dropped my gaze to my hands in my lap. "I was thinking about going up to Forge Heights later on, to have a look around."

"What do you think you'll find?"

I shrugged. "Maybe nothing, maybe something."

He laughed. "Yeah, that sounds like one of our plans. Do I get to tag along?"

"You can be my backup."

"Sounds like a plan. Wait, you're in charge? I'm the one with the badge."

"I can talk to ghosts! And work magic! And—"

"All right. You've got me there."

We pulled into the parking lot, and entered the station a moment later. The door to Jill's office was open, so we went to her first.

"Bad news first," Dan said in lieu of a greeting.

"It's all bad," Jill said. "I don't think I can help you, not this time. Chief says you were following him last night?"

"That was sort of my fault," I said. "I got a new case yesterday. Chief Renault's wife hired me to surveil him."

Jill stared at me, then she faced Dan. "You do recall that he doesn't have a wife?"

"Yes, he does," Dan said. "I remember meeting her."

"When was that?" Jill demanded. "When you first came here? She divorced him."

"Did he remarry?" I asked.

Jill shook her head. "He did not. Dan, you must remember this. It was about five years ago."

"Five years ago, I was—" Dan began, then he glanced at me and his face crumpled. Five years ago, he'd been wrapped up first with Charlotte's illnesses, and then her death.

Since I didn't want him to dwell on the past, I said, "So I got duped by a woman pretending to be Renault's wife. Awesome."

Before anyone could say anything, Chief Renault yelled, "Is Lyons here yet?"

Dan grimaced. "Be right back," he said, then he left Jill's office, leaving the door ajar behind him. I watched him leave, then I faced Jill.

"Is this his last straw?"

"Maybe," she replied. "But, this time it might not be Dan's fault."

"And the other times were?"

Jill smiled ruefully. "That man of yours is a hothead. He's gotten in fights—verbal and otherwise—with every single person in this station."

"He's not my man," I muttered. "We've only been together a few weeks. This is all new."

Jill shook her head. "He's been yours for a while, you just never noticed until recently."

I decided to deal with Jill's rather astute deduction later. "Have you ever fought with Dan?"

"Oh, yeah. Many times. When he first came up from New York he thought his way was the only way, we were all backwards country cops, stuff like that. I let him know that I didn't care what his opinions were, and he could keep them out of my office."

"You two seem like friends now."

"I don't know if we're friends, but we have an understanding. My wife's an RN, and the first time Charlotte got rushed to the hospital after she moved here, she ended up in Angel's ward."

"Your wife's name is Angel?"

"Angelique," Jill said, her cheeks going pink. "I call her Angel. Anyway, I went to bring Angel dinner, and there was Dan in the waiting room. We didn't talk that day, but ever since my wife took care of his, he's had my back."

"Dan's loyal to a fault," I said. "It's one of the first things I noticed about him."

Jill laughed. "Take it from me, don't waste too much time. I spent a long time rationalizing away my feelings for Angel when this perfect woman was right there in front of me."

"She sounds awesome."

"She is." Jill reached for her bag, maybe to show me a picture of Angel, when Chief's door banged open.

"Go," Jill said. "Get Dan out of here. I'll see what I can find out. Talk soon."

"Thank you," I said, then I went out and found Dan stalking toward his desk, cardboard box in hand. I noticed that his badge wasn't on its usual place on his belt, and his holster was empty.

"Hey," I said.

"Hey." He looked at me, then he set the box on the floor. "Let's go to Forge Heights."

"Okay. Should we pick that up?"

"Leave it."

I nudged the box to the side so no one would trip over it, then I followed Dan out of the station and back to the car. Dan started the car, then he threw it into reverse as if the gearshift was his mortal enemy.

"So. I'm suspended."

"What? Why?"

"It seems that the station received an anonymous tip regarding Jada Morales's whereabouts," he began. "When surveillance footage from the motel was reviewed, they clearly saw me in the lobby, and entering her room. Therefore, it would appear that I not only aided her escape from the hospital, but that I also concealed her current location."

"But, Chief was there, too! We saw him!"

"I know, but as you said there's some kind of a spell on Chief." Dan paused, then added, "He didn't mention you being there, either."

"But, I was right next to you."

"You were, which furthers my theory that you were right all along."

"I was?"

"You were. Chief's under a spell, or something, and that motel is hinky. Once we figure it all out and break the spell, everything will go back to normal."

As if breaking a spell—any spell—was ever that easy. "Jill said she'll call if she learns anything."

"Jill's a good egg. Do you want to go straight to Forge Heights, or stop for breakfast first?"

Chapter 11

Fate, Evil or Otherwise

We ended up stopping for breakfast.

I was hungry, and Dan hadn't eaten yet, so stopping wasn't a bad thing. I was also confused as hell, both by what had happened back at the station and by Dan's behavior. He was acting as if him being suspended was no big deal. Personally, I thought it was a very big deal, but he had mentioned how he'd never really wanted to be a police officer. Maybe he saw this as his way out of an unwanted career.

The diner near my old apartment had the best breakfast in town, so that was where we went. Thankfully, it hadn't been damaged by the explosion that destroyed my apartment building, which was proof that the food gods were watching over it. Dan and I grabbed a booth in the back, and he immediately put a few coins in the table side juke box.

"Dinner music," he explained, when I raised an eyebrow. "What should we get?"

"Pancakes." As if pancakes weren't the only acceptable response. "I talked with Jill earlier. I didn't know she was married."

"Jill's wife, Angel, is just that. She's an absolute angel," Dan said. "Sweetest woman you'll ever meet. How she ended up with Jill is a mystery to me."

"Fate?" I offered, though I honestly didn't know if I believed in fate, unless it was evil. "Gran used to talk about fate all the time."

"Yeah? Think it was fate that someone impersonated the chief's wife to you?"

The server arrived with our coffee and took our order. "You know, maybe it was fate," I said after she walked away. "Let's call the number she gave me and see who answers."

I set my phone in the center of the table, put it on speaker, and called Mrs. Parker. She picked up on the first ring.

"Miss Moore?" she said. "Did you learn anything?"

"I learned that Louis Renault got divorced five years ago and hasn't remarried," I replied. "Is there anything you'd like to share with me?"

"Yes. Watch out." And with that, the line went dead.

"That was enlightening," I said as I put my phone away.

"Did you recognize the voice?"

"No, other than it seemed to be the same person I spoke to yesterday." I tapped the table with my fingertips. "But the voice did sound familiar."

"Familiar how? As in, someone you know?"

"Not sure." I spied the server walking toward us with two sets of cutlery in her hands. "Let me think on it."

After breakfast, we went straight to Forge Heights Residential Care Center. Dan parked in the center of the visitor's lot, which gave us an unobstructed view of the front entrance.

"I still can't believe this was my first case," I said. "I had no idea what I was doing."

"I remember you handling everything like a champ," Dan said. He hadn't worked the case with me, but he'd taken my statement after the fact. "Think us meeting was part of Hassan's plan?"

"I'm not sure. It would be smarter to keep us apart, what with Charlotte growing poisons for him."

"Why did he need Char at all?" Dan wondered. "You can get that stuff anywhere. Wouldn't it have been easier for him to buy his own stuff instead of hassling Charlotte?"

"There you go, thinking like a mortal again," I teased. "For ritual use it's best to have herbs grown in local soil," I explained, and then I realized how callously I was discussing Charlotte's possession.

"Dan, I'm so sorry about what happened to her, and to you," I said. "If I'd had the slightest idea of what Amir was doing to her, I would have stopped it."

"Hey. C'mere." He stretched out his arm, and I leaned across the center console and let him hold me as best he could. "None of that was your fault. You've got to stop seeing everything and everyone as your responsibility."

"Says the guy who carries the actual weight of the world on his shoulders."

"Only for you." He kissed my hair, and asked, "What's our next move? Do you need to check out the plants?"

"Actually, I thought I would talk to Marianne." Marianne Richardson was the activities director at Forge Heights, and she'd planted the belladonnas. "I want to find out if she remembers where she got the plants."

"Sounds like a plan." I straightened, and Dan's hand reflexively went to where he normally wore his badge. "I, uh, don't have any credentials to get us through the door."

"It's okay. I can get us in." We exited the car, and I faced him across the roof. "I've kept in touch with Marianne. I'll just ask for her at the front desk."

Dan shook his head. "Look at you. You don't even need me."

"That is not true," I said, then I turned and walked toward the front entrance. A moment later, I felt Dan's hand grasp mine.

"I need you too, babe."

I gave our names at the front desk, and a few minutes later Dan and I were sitting with Marianne in the courtyard. It looked just the same as it had the day we'd exposed Spencer Cortez as a serial killing dirt bag, right down to the big, shady tent a few residents were playing cards underneath.

"I'm glad you got to keep your position here," I said. "They weren't too harsh with you?"

"On the contrary, they lauded me as their savior," Marianne said. "I was told that you, Detective Lyons, had a hand in that."

Dan smiled tightly. "No detective, just Dan to you. And I'm glad I could help."

"Well, Dan, you have my eternal gratitude," Marianne said. "You do, too, Eli. If you ever need anything, just ask."

"Actually, I have a question for you," I said. "Do you remember where you got the belladonna? Was it a cutting?"

"It's funny you say that, because initially I tried to grow them from seed," she began. "As you can imagine, that didn't go well. One day I was at the garden center, and a man approached me in the parking lot and asked if I wanted any of his belladonna cuttings."

Dan called up Amir's picture on his phone. "Was this him?"

"Yes," Marianne said without hesitation. "He gave me a half dozen cuttings, and they all grew well."

I looked around the courtyard and saw three belladonna plants among the landscaping. "So these belladonnas are all from those cuttings?"

"Yes, every one of them."

"Why are they still here?" Dan asked. "I remember the center specifically being told to rip out the poisonous stuff."

"That's another odd thing," Marianne said. "They took them all out, several times, in fact. The plants have always grown back."

"That's strange." I went to the closest belladonna and claimed a stem. It seemed like an ordinary plant, but based on what Marianne said, something else was clearly going on here.

I returned to my seat, and asked, "Have you seen any other unusually robust plants around here? By robust, I mean staying green well into winter, coming back after being mowed, stuff like that."

"I haven't, but I haven't been looking for that stuff, either." Marianne leaned closer, and asked, "Is there another serial killer?"

I glanced at Dan. He said, "There is an individual we suspect of growing and distributing poisons, but I wouldn't call him a serial killer at this time. He seems more of a nuisance than anything else, but you can't be too careful these days."

Marianne nodded, eyes wide. "No, you really can't be. I still look over my shoulder, expecting Spencer to come out of the physical therapy room."

I grasped Marianne's hand. "Don't worry about him. He went away for a long, long time."

"Eliza?" came a voice from underneath the tent. I turned and saw Martha Pickford waving at me. "Eliza, come over here and say hello!"

"Be right back," I said to Dan and Marianne, then I went to visit my favorite living resident of Forge Heights. If it hadn't been for Martha's husband, Frank—who was my favorite resident on the spiritual side—we might not have caught Spencer.

"How are you?" I asked, as I bent over to hug her. Martha looked great, which made me hope the techniques I'd given her for contacting Frank's spirit were working out just fine. "Keeping out of trouble?"

"Not on your life," she replied. "Who's the hunk?"

"Martha! What would Frank say?"

"He's the real nosy one, so he'd wait to hear your answer."

How could I fault that logic? "His name's Dan. He's a detective." I almost mentioned his suspension, but I bit my lip instead. Martha didn't need to know the gritty details about Dan's job.

"Are you two working on another case?"

"We sure are. Why? Want to be my assistant?"

Martha laughed and swatted my forearm. "Work is a four letter word to us retired folk, but I'll let it slide this one time. Are you tracking another killer?"

"Not this time." Since I wanted to give Martha a truth, even if it wasn't our most pressing concern, I said, "We're looking for my mother."

"Really? Is she lost? Hurt?"

"No. Maybe. I don't know. She left when I was eight, and for the longest time it wasn't a big deal... But now, I need her."

Martha patted my hand. "Family can be awfully inconvenient at times, but if you're looking for her, I know you'll find her."

Frank materialized at my shoulder. "What's her name?" he asked.

I held out my wrist, and Martha grasped it and my seer's mark. "I see how it is, Frank," she teased her husband. "We start talking about girls, and suddenly you appear."

"I have my priorities, Martha." Frank leaned over and kissed his wife's forehead. Based on her smile, she felt it. "I also need to help Eli whenever she needs me. What's your mother's name?"

"Her name is Christina. Christina Lind."

"We know some Linds," Martha said. "Frank, why don't you check in on them?"

"I surely can," Frank said, then he dissipated.

"Wow, he's fast," I said.

"Who's fast?" Dan said, as he joined us. "Hello, ma'am."

"Hello, detective," Martha said, with an exaggerated wink at me. "I hear you've been helping our Eliza."

Dan grimaced when Martha said detective, but he didn't miss a beat when he replied. "I handle whatever Eli needs doing."

Martha patted my hand. "He's a keeper." She looked beyond me and frowned. "They're getting ready to round us up for lunch. Don't be a stranger, Eli!"

"I'll come visit soon," I said. "Promise."

Dan and I said our goodbyes to Martha and Marianne, and we made our way out to the parking lot. I visited each of the five belladonnas on site, and thus verified that they were all cloned from the one in Dan's garden.

"I'm surprised you told Marianna that Amir's just a nuisance," I said, when the silence between us got too heavy.

"No need to worry her," he replied.

"I also never knew you put in a good word for Marianne."

"Yeah, well." Dan started the car and backed out of the parking space. "You said she hadn't hurt anyone and that she's a good person. I guess I believed you."

"You're a good person, too," I said. "We'll get this whole business with the chief straightened out."

Dan paused, and said, "You know what? You're right. We will handle it."

He leaned over and kissed me. I'd never been kissed so much in my life as I had been these past few weeks with Dan, and I loved every minute of it. In the midst of our public display of affection, my phone chirped.

"You gonna get that?" Dan asked.

"I have voice mail."

Eventually, the ringing stopped... Only to start up again thirty second later. "Maybe it's a client," Dan said.

"Hopefully a real one, this time." I fished out my phone, and answered it. "Nine Lives Investigations."

"Eliza Moore, please."

"This is Eliza." After a pause, I put the call on speaker, and asked, "Is there something I can help you with?"

"Eliza, this is Melinda Howe. I need you to come to my estate. Immediately."

Dan shifted into drive. "Of course she does."

Chapter 12

A Witch's Debt

The Howe Estate was similar to the Allwood Compound, while also being completely different. Only a witch could pull off that level of nonsense.

Like the Allwood Compound, Melinda Howe's home was a large house set far back from the road on spacious grounds. Instead of being perched on the crest of a hill, like Jacob's home, the Howe Estate was on more of a plateau; Dan thought it was a manmade berm, but either way, the house was raised above the surrounding landscape. The home itself was long and flat, stretching out into wings on either side of a prominent central edifice, in contrast to the Allwood Compound's tall and commanding four floors. At both estates, the grounds were guarded by a stately gate, and a long driveway brought you to the house. However, the biggest difference was that literally everything about the Howe Estate was in poor repair.

The front gate was rusted and hung open, and a few hinges looked ready to give way at any moment. The guard stand was vacant, and the intercom was covered in a rather aggressive moss. Dan drove past the creaky wrought iron gate and onto the lumpy, cracked pavement of the driveway. When we got closer to the house, we saw broken window panes, and a hole in the west wing's roof. Add to that the flaking paint, loose shingles, and hedges that could really use a trim, and Melinda's home made it look like her clan had come into hard times.

"I guess being a witch doesn't pay well," Dan said.

"This is really strange." We pulled into the parking area, which had actual weeds poking up through the concrete. "If Jacob saw this, he would be appalled."

"Maybe, what with the poisoning, she's got bigger things on her mind than landscaping."

"Even so, what about the staff?" When Dan raised an eyebrow, I added, "Witches always have staff, especially the important witches. It's in the rule book."

He shook his head. "Sometimes, these smartass comments of yours actually make sense."

"My comments always make sense," I said. "There isn't really a rule book."

"I get that," he said. "But you're right. What about the staff? They couldn't have all up and left at once, could they?"

I took in the estate, which looked more like a haunted house than the home of a powerful member of the community. "If they did, that makes me wonder where they went."

We left the car and approached the front door and were greeted by an actual liveried butler. That answered Dan's question about the staff's whereabouts. The butler was very polite, even if his immaculate suit was out of place in the run-down house, and he showed us into the parlor. There we found Melinda Howe herself seated in a red velvet armchair caked with a year's worth of dust.

"Eliza, thank you for coming," she said. "I see you've brought your mortal."

"His name is Dan, and I actually do not own him." Melinda made a face, letting us know how she felt about mortal-supernatural relationships. Luckily, I didn't care about her opinion one way or the other. "What's this about? On the phone, you made it seem urgent."

"Time is of the essence." Melinda indicated the chairs across from her. "Please. Sit."

Dan and I sat, and sent up little plumes of dust from the upholstery in the process. I glanced around the parlor, and saw that the room's cleanliness issues extended far beyond dust. The silver was tarnished, the curtains were faded, and the fireplace looked as if it hadn't been swept out in ages.

"Random question, but is the house under a curse?" I asked.

"Ah. You noticed." We were interrupted by the butler, who brought in a tea service on an ornate silver tray. He set it on the central table, bowed, and left without uttering a single word.

"Forgive Humbolt his silence," Melinda said. "He's quite unnerved by the situation. Tea?"

"Sure," I said.

"Tea would be lovely, ma'am," Dan said, doing his best to cut through the tension between Melinda and me. "Would you like me to pour?"

"No, thank you." Melinda poured the tea, and handed out cups. The rim of my cup was chipped so deeply I wondered if it would cut my lip. I briefly wondered if she wanted me to cut myself so she could use my blood in a spell, and drank from the other side.

After we'd sampled and approved of our tea, Melinda said, "To answer your question, the house itself is not under a curse. However, the estate and my entire clan are dependent on my health and vigor, and as you know I have been poisoned."

Melinda paused, whether for dramatic effect or to wait for me to offer my assistance I didn't know. What I did know what that I'd already publicly offered my help, and she and three other clan elders had snubbed me in favor of Amir. What's more, I'd reached out to all four elders again multiple times, and gotten the cold shoulder. While I wouldn't go so far as to hold a grudge, neither was I in a mood to play games. If Melinda wanted my help, she could come right out and ask for it.

Dan, however, he was definitely holding a grudge. "Have you brought your concerns to Hassan?" Dan asked. "After all, he's the seer you all chose to lead you."

Melinda pursed her lips. "He is not inclined to assist me. I was hoping you would feel differently."

"It's not that I don't want to help you," I began, "but I don't see how I can. You said Amir brought you and the others to a different time and poisoned you, but you don't know when that was, or what type of poison was administered to you and the others. Is that correct?"

"Yes, I'm afraid it is."

"Exactly how do you know that whatever he gave you was poison?" Dan asked. "He might not have been forthcoming about what the substance really was."

"He... he said it was, and he is a seer," Melinda replied. "Everyone knows that seers deal in poisons."

"Yes, but Amir also deals in lies." I glanced at Dan, and he nodded. "Why don't you tell us exactly what happened, beginning with when Amir first time shifted you." When Melinda grimaced, I added, "Dan's a detective, and I'm a private investigator. We solve cases for a living. Give us the opportunity to solve yours."

"You're a seer, not a mortal problem solver," Melinda huffed.

"Us mortal problem solvers have a pretty good track record." Dan opened the notes app on his phone. "We can begin whenever you're ready."

Melinda looked like she swallowed a bug, but she relented and told us her story. "I can't speak as to how the others were abducted, as I didn't witness it. As for my own abduction, somehow, Amir Hassan gained entry to my home and my bed chamber, and spirited me to an unknown location while I was sleeping. When I woke, I was in a room with the rest of the elders, save Jacob Allwood and Nathaniel Beauclaire. The others were also unaware of how they'd arrived in the room."

"What did the room look like?" I asked.

"It was all white," she replied. "White walls, white floor and ceiling. White, and very bright."

"What else was in the room?" Dan prompted. "Windows, doors, furniture?"

Melinda shook her head. "There wasn't anything else in the room besides us. It was four walls, a ceiling and a floor, and four witches."

"Interesting," I said. "Did any of you attempt to escape?"

"We all did, multiple times," she replied. "Nothing we did affected the room. I went so far as to conjure fire, and it neither burned the walls, nor left a mark."

"What happened to the smoke?" Dan asked.

Melinda blinked, as if she was shocked Dan questioned her. "It dissipated. Why?"

"If the smoke cleared out, it means the room wasn't airtight," Dan replied. "That information helps us narrow down the type of place you were held."

I smiled at my sneaky detective, who managed to gather clues and show Melinda how good he was at his job in one move. "How did Amir deliver the poison?" I asked.

"He appeared in the room with a pitcher of water and four glasses. Normally I wouldn't accept food or drink in such a situation, but I had never been so parched in my life. As soon as I tasted the water I knew it wasn't right. It tasted bitter, like rue." Melinda frowned, and averted her eyes. "I know you must think me foolish."

"I don't," I said. "Since Amir had shifted you to a room that was obviously meant to disorient you, you might have gone without food or water for days. Also, the room could have been wrapped in a compliance spell."

Melinda clasped and unclasped her hands. "That's kind of you to say. I... I do regret refusing to follow you, Eliza."

"It's all right," I said. "You were under duress. Hell, we were all under duress. However, we can still make things right."

"That sounds like something your grandmother would have said." I looked away, since I did not want to discuss my grandmother with Melinda. Her intentions were questionable at best, and the last thing I needed was for her to play a sympathy card, and me to fall for it. As always, Dan came to my rescue.

"May I ask a question?" Dan asked.

"Please." Melinda gesture for him to continue. "Ask what you'd like."

"You say your poisoning is affecting this house, and your entire clan," Dan began. "Does the health of all elders affect their respective clans?"

"Why, yes," she replied. "It's one of the reasons we began building these large estates, so we could keep our elders safe."

"Elders," I repeated. "So if one was unwell, the rest of the elders in an individual clan could potentially pick up the slack?"

Melinda shrugged. "I suppose. It would depend on how strong each elder was, and what they were afflicted with." She leaned forward, and asked, "Since we last spoke, have you made any headway on your curse?"

"Yes and no," I replied. "We may know who cursed me, but we still don't understand why I was cursed, or what the curse's purpose is."

Melinda regarded me. "I meant what I said before. I cannot follow a cursed seer. However, I also cannot allow my clan to rot while I wait for Amir's poison to either kill me or leave my body once and for all."

"Then what do you propose we do?" I asked. "And what will your help cost me?"

"I don't care for owing others, and I suspect you don't either. Helena certainly never let herself be put in a witch's debt." Melinda rose and picked up a small silver box from the mantle. "I can reverse your curse, but in order to do so, I need the item you were cursed with. Bring it to me, in this box, and I will do away with whatever you've been afflicted with."

"Thank you," I said. "And what will I do to even the scales?"

"You will draw this poison out of me."

I stood and accepted the box. "We have a deal."

Dan and I said our goodbyes to Melinda, and Humbolt the butler showed us out. Once we were in the car, Dan said, "You know there's magic dripping off that box, right?"

"Oh, yeah." I could feel whatever the box was imbued with poking at my skin, clawing and grabbing and trying to find purchase. I set in on the car's floor, and said, "Can we go somewhere away from people, so we can get a better look at this thing?"

"Will do."

Dan drove toward the west side of town, past the neat shopping areas and orderly housing developments, and straight into farm country. He pulled off the main road and took us down a dirt stretch, and parked behind an old tobacco barn.

"This farm's been abandoned for years," he explained. "Sometimes, we get calls to come out here and break up parties."

"Nothing like a kegger in the woods." I got out of the car, grabbed two leaves from a nearby maple tree, and used those as a barrier when I picked up the box.

"Here, give me that," Dan said as he took the box from me. "Why don't you want to touch it?"

"Whatever's in there is trying to latch on to me," I replied. "It's not doing that to you?"

"Not yet." Dan swept his gaze across the property, then he walked toward the barn. "Think we should do this inside?"

"Might as well."

The inside of the barn was an empty rectangular room. The barn's purpose had been drying tobacco leaves, so it had probably never been used to store farm equipment or other sundries. That was great, since the last thing we needed was to step on an old, rusty hunk of metal.

Dan set the box on the dirt and backed away from it. "You said whatever's in here was trying to latch on to you?"

"Yeah. Whatever's in there was poking at me, like it was looking for an opening." I walked around the box in a slow circle. It was a small, round box, and the lid did not appear to be hinged. "Think we should open the box, see what's in there?"

He rubbed his chin. "Is it a spell, or an entity?"

"I... don't know." I reached out with my senses, and didn't feel any sentient beings in the barn besides Dan and me. "If it's an entity, it has a pretty rudimentary brain."

"What if something leaps out at us?" Dan countered. "Maybe we should call Tessa."

I thought about Tess, already hard at work trying to figure out my curse, if Dad was also cursed, and if she could somehow undo the temporal binding she'd placed on Amir. "I think Tessa has enough on her plate. Let's just watch it for a minute, see if anything happens."

"Okay." We stared at the box, which just sat there, as boxes do. "Something Melinda said has been bothering me."

"Was it the line about the clan elder's health affecting everyone else?"

"Yes," Dan said. "If that's true, why isn't Jacob's death affecting the Allwoods in the same way?"

I tapped my chin. "We have two possible answers. Either Melinda lied, or Jacob isn't the head of the clan. And if Jacob's not the clan head, that leaves—"

"Cecily," Dan finished.

Cecily Allwood was Jacob's sister. She'd been working with my archenemy, Nathaniel Beauclaire, for years, and had been behind my abduction when I was seventeen. Their plan had been to put the spirit of Nathaniel's deceased wife into my body. Thankfully, that hadn't happened, but I'd only gotten out of that situation by the skin of my teeth.

Years later, Cecily made an inter-clan power play, which resulted in Jacob's death. I'd ended up feeding Jacob enough spiritual energy to make him appear like a living person, and he continued leading his clan. As for how long he'd be able to do that, no one could say. He could revert to spirit form tomorrow, or a hundred years from now.

"What if, when Jacob died, clan leadership automatically went to Cecily?" I asked. "What if she's been the one in charge all along?"

"What if it's someone else entirely?" Dan asked, then he approached the box and kicked off the lid.

"Why'd you do that?"

He shrugged. "I was bored." Dan crouched in front of the box and peered inside. "Got your witchfinder on you?"

"Always." I fished the cracked amulet out of my pocket and dangled it first over the lid, and then inside the box. The witchfinder remained cold, but I saw a familiar blue grit in the bottom of the box.

"This looks like Amir's magic," I said, tilting the box so Dan could see the residue. "Which means that either Melinda's working with him against me, on purpose, or she's working against me without him in a desperate attempt to save herself."

"Neither one of those options seem particularly good." Dan went to the back of a barn, and rummaged around in the corner. "You know, this isn't the first time we've been in a barn together."

"Hopefully there aren't any skeletons in this one."

"Agreed." He returned carrying a shovel. "I think we should bury this, for now."

I frowned. "What if there's a clue in it?"

"If there is, we can always come back and dig it up," he said. "However, you said it's trying to latch on to you. Until we know more, I want whatever's in this box far away from you."

"I can't argue with that."

Dan dug down about six inches, then he used the shovel to put the lid back on the box, and the whole thing went into the hole. After he'd buried it and tamped the dirt down nice and flat, he laid the shovel over the top.

"Where to, now?"

"I... I don't know," I admitted. My head was swimming, and the last thing I needed was to add more scenarios to my already crowded thoughts. "I think I need some time to process everything that's happened. Maybe we should go home."

"All right, then. Home it is."

Chapter 13

Boxing Lessons

Once we got back home, Dan and I reverted into a semblance of domestic bliss while we both avoided what was really eating at us. He kept pretending to not check his phone for updates from Jill, while I obsessively tracked every package I'd ordered over the past few days; he needed answers, and I needed my new laptop and running shoes. After dinner Jill hadn't texted, none of my stuff had been delivered, and I was so over everything I took a shower and went to bed.

A few hours later, I woke up alone. Wondering what Dan was up to, I slipped out of bed and padded around the first floor. He wasn't in the living room, or the kitchen, but the basement door was ajar, and the light was on. My curiosity got the better of me, and I went to see what he was doing.

I'd only gone down to the basement a few times before, and that was to do laundry. This time, I didn't find Dan sorting whites and colors. He was on the far side of the basement, working out with the punching bag.

I hopped up on the dryer and accidentally knocked over a box of soap powder; the top flap proclaimed that the scent was apple blossom fresh. I righted the box, then I watched Dan for a moment. He was in great shape, and having a front row seat to his latest exercise session was just the distraction I needed. He must have been down here for a while, and his damp tee shirt clung to his well-muscled back and shoulders in all the right places.

"I know you're back there," he said, after a minute or so of my spying.

"I thought I was being sneaky." He laughed, but didn't let up on the bag. "Do you always work out in the middle of the night?"

"You know how I said I didn't care if I got fired?" He landed another punch. "Turns out I care." He landed another hit, and the bag swung wildly. "Apparently, I care a lot."

"But you said your expenses are low, and you have savings," I said. "Besides, I have money, too. We'll be fine."

He steadied the bag, then he faced me. "I can't expect you to help out with my bills."

"Why not? Earlier, you were all about helping me with mine."

Dan grunted, then he pulled off his shirt and used it to wipe his face. "I've always paid my own way. I don't like loans, or handouts. I like being the breadwinner."

"No one's offering you a handout, but if I'm going to live here, I want to pay my share." When he didn't respond, I asked, "What, you don't like having a woman pay for you?"

"It's not that," he said. "If I lose my job, everything from my old life will be gone. The only thing I had left from Queens was being a cop. If that goes, I'll have failed at everything."

"You are not a failure," I said. "Everything happening with Chief Renault is way out of your control, and this isn't over, not by a long shot. We're still working our case."

"Yeah, I guess we are." Dan gave the punching bag a halfhearted shove. "You ever box?"

I blinked. "I don't think I've ever hit anything in my entire life."

"Then what do you do for exercise?"

"I run," I replied, a bit bewildered because Dan already knew that.

"But what else do you do?" he pressed. "I like to vary my workouts. I run, box, lift weights."

And that's why we called him Officer Muscleman. "You're under the impression that I run to stay I shape, or maintain a certain weight. I could care less about being thin or fat—but what I do care about is keeping up my endurance. I've been chased by some really gnarly beasts, and me having the ability to outrun them could be the difference between life and death."

"When you were kidnapped, did they chase you down?"

I shuddered, the memory having chilled me. "They did, and I didn't get very far. Maybe fifteen, twenty feet, and they had me."

Dan approached me, and stood between my knees. "I'm sorry. I don't mean to bring up bad stuff."

I draped my arms over his shoulders, and rested my forehead against his. "Don't be sorry. I got out, and now I'm the fastest seer alive."

Dan chuckled. "If your goal is endurance, that's all the more reason you should vary your workouts. Besides, on the off chance someone does catch you, you want to be able to fight back." He grasped my waist and lifted me off the dryer, then he set me on my feet in front of the punching bag. "Go ahead. Hit it."

"Um, okay." I made a loose fist and hit the bag. It didn't even budge.

"All right, let's start with learning how to make a fist." Dan stood behind me, reached around my torso, and repositioned my fingers. "Always keep your thumb down."

"Why?"

"So you don't break it."

"Oh. Okay." I threw a few test punches into the air. "I feel much fistier now."

Dan chuckled again, and his warm breath on my neck made every hair on my body stand on end. "Fistier's good. Very good. Okay, now we need to work on your stance." He adjusted my arms, and nudged my feet farther apart. "You want a wide base, so you can swing from your hips."

"My hips?" I said. "I thought I was punching with my new fists."

"You are, but your strength comes from your core."

I threw a few more test punches. Dan observed, then he tried adjusting my hips but my body didn't move the way he'd intended. "No, like this," he said, then he slid his hands underneath my long tee shirt. He paused, having discovered I was only wearing that shirt, then he pushed my right hip forward while the left one moved back.

"What are you doing?"

"I'm trying to align your right hip with your right hand."

"You could have just said that." I moved so my right foot side was closer to the bag.

"Good," he said. "Keep your feet shoulder width apart, hips low and heavy. Go on. Give it a try."

"Are you going to back up?" I asked, since his hands were still on my hips.

"Nah. I'll be fine."

I hesitated, since he was in imminent danger of getting an elbow in the gut, but he seemed unconcerned. I stared down the bag, pictured Melinda Howe's face, and hit.

Man, that felt good.

"Wow," Dan said. "Did you imagine you were hitting Hassan?"

"Melinda, actually," I said as I gave the bag another round of hits. "How dare she first refuse to acknowledge me as Mistress of Seers—which was humiliating, by the way—and then have the audacity to ask for my help? And lie about needing my help all so she could stick a magical whatever on me. Who does she think she is?" I dropped my arms, panting. "This is exhausting."

"It is, if you do it right." Dan wrapped his arms around my waist, and kissed the curve where my neck met my shoulder. "You did great."

"I feel like I ran a marathon." I felt Dan's cock pressing against me, but when I tried to turn around he slid his hands up my torso and cupped my breasts. "You really like boxing."

"I really like you."

I twisted around so we were facing each other. "I like you, too." I pushed down his shorts and he pulled my shirt up and over my head, then we tumbled down to the mat. My butt had barely touched the floor when Dan grabbed my waist and pulled me toward him, then he thrust into me in one smooth stroke.

It was hard, and fast, and amazing.

Afterward, we laid on the mat together. My shirt was balled up into a makeshift pillow beneath my head, and Dan lazily kissed my neck while I pushed the punching bag with my foot.

"You always get like this after a workout?" I asked.

"Never once, which was a good thing. Would have made things awkward at the gym."

"You go to a gym, too?" He had so much exercise equipment in the house a gym membership seemed like overkill.

"I used to, then I met this hot brunette that likes running. I've been hanging out with her." I giggled, then Dan raised himself up on his elbow, and said, "I have a confession to make."

"Confess away. I'm in a mood to be lenient."

"You're not faster than me."

"Yes, I am. I have beaten you every single time we've raced."

"I had a very compelling reason to stay behind you," he said, then he slid his hand underneath me and squeezed my butt.

"You mean to tell me you only raced me so you could ogle my butt?"

"Not at first," he said. "And you did beat me, the first time. All the others, well..." He squeezed harder, and I laughed. "Let's just say I kept it slow."

"Kept it slow," I muttered. "As soon as my running shoes get here, it's on. We're having a rematch, and you are going to eat my dust."

"Whatever you say, babe."

CHAPTER 14

NED BURROUGHS

"Eli? Baby, wake up."

Dan was shaking my shoulder. I was still exhausted and sore from our boxing practice the night before, and everything that came afterward, and not in a mood to be awake.

"Don't wanna," I mumbled into the pillow.

"Tessa called. There's something you need to see."

Dan sat next to me, and held his phone in front of my face. On the screen was a picture of a man wearing dark trousers and a white button down shirt, complete with suspenders. He was sitting on a concrete staircase, and his ashen, sweaty face made him look like he had the flu.

"Who is that guy? He looks sick."

"She said he's one of the clan elders, and he's dying."

The man in question was Ned Burroughs, and the concrete staircase he was sitting on was the entrance to City Hall. It took Dan and me about twenty minutes to get there, and by then Ned had amassed a small crowd of onlookers. Among them was my father, and Tessa.

"What's happening?" I asked, when we joined them. I wanted to ask if they'd reconciled after the picture incident, but figured we had more pressing matters.

"We think Ned is suffering from Amir's poison," Dad replied. Ned was lying on his back on the second step from the top, his expensive shirt soaked in sweat and vomit. "He's been here for over an hour, and his condition has steadily degraded."

"Why isn't anyone helping him?" I asked.

"We've tried, but no one can approach to him." Dad jerked his chin toward a group of paramedics. "Whenever anyone gets close to Ned they get burnt, as if by an unseen flame."

"So we're just gonna stand here and watch him die?" I demanded. As I spoke, a paramedic shoved up his sleeves and stalked onto the stairs. He went running back into the street a moment later, his bare arms red and angry as if he'd been in the sun for hours.

"As I said, we can't help him," my dad said.

"We can always help," I said. "We just need to figure out how."

"Can't we get to him from inside the building?" Dan asked.

"Apparently, the building is locked," Tessa replied. "No one can seem to find a key. And before you ask, I've already tried magically unlocking it."

"There's at least ten ways into that place," Dan said. "I'll get inside—I'll break a window if I have to—and see if I can get those doors open," Dan said, then he approached the side entrance and tested the door. When it proved to still be locked, he moved around to the back. While Dan searched for a mundane way onto the stairs, I thought about a magical way to help Ned. If people couldn't get up the steps, or through the doors, there was either a person we couldn't see guarding Ned, or there was some sort of repulsion spell in place.

"Tess, what are the odds of an invisibility spell being used?" I asked.

"In full daylight? None."

"So what's keeping everyone away from Ned?" I asked. Since no one offered up any suggestions, I approached the stairs. "Mr. Burroughs? Ned?" I called. "Remember me, Eliza Moore? I'm going to try to help you."

"Eliza?" Ned's head lolled toward me. "Eliza, I don't have much time."

"I know. I'm gonna work fast." I held out my wrist, using my seer's mark to detect where the magic began. When it hovered above the stairs the mark sizzled as if hot grease had splashed onto my skin. "Do you know what's keeping you isolated? Is it a spell?"

"Not... not a spell," Ned rasped. "It's another time. I have another time wrapped around me."

Another time... I spun around and asked Tessa, "How do I turn off a time slip?"

"I-I don't know," Tessa said. "I've never used one!"

"Who has," I began, then I remembered Jacob Allwood's warning about using time slips. I closed my eyes, and a moment later Jacob himself appeared beside me.

He was dressed similarly to Ned—must be a clan leader uniform—and had his glasses perched on the edge of his nose. "Eli, I wish you would call before you—" He saw Ned, and fell silent. "Oh, dear."

"I think he's being held behind a time slip," I said. "The steps are hot, like an inferno, but there's no reason for them to be so hot."

"And City Hall burned down a few decades ago, which would account for the heat," Jacob concluded. "You think this is more of Amir's handiwork?"

I nodded. "How can we get around it, and get to Ned? He needs help."

Jacob looked up at Ned, and frowned. "Yes, he does." Jacob cleared his throat. "In order to undo a time slip, you must bring the affected area back to the present time."

"Okay. How do we do that?"

"We need something that will put the area out of the slip, and into the here and now."

"That doesn't give me a lot to work with," I said, then I spied the bell tower above the main doors. It used to chime the hour, but people complained about the noise and it was silenced a few years ago.

If the bell chimed the hour, that would be pretty here and now.

I grabbed my phone and called Dan. "Yeah, babe?"

"Are you inside?"

"I am."

"Go to the tower and make the bell ring."

"How the hell do I that?"

"Figure it out!"

Dan ended the call. I turned to Jacob. "Are any of the other elders sick?"

"Not that I know if," he replied. "Do we know what Ned's afflicted with?"

"Not yet." I recalled the Howe Estate, and said, "I saw Melinda Howe yesterday. Her place has seen better days."

"Oh? Did she appear to be under attack?"

"An attack of dust bunnies," I muttered, then the bell rang in eardrum-splittingly loud peals. As always, Dan came through for me. The air above the steps shimmered, then went still.

"Do we think it worked?" I asked.

"Perhaps," Jacob said. "Want me to go first?"

"I've got it." Tentatively, I climbed the steps. When I didn't feel any heat by the fourth step, I ran to Ned and knelt beside him.

"Stay with me, Ned," I said as I took his hand. His skin was marked with red, angry blisters, and his eyes were watery. "We're going to help you."

"Oh, Eliza, we were foolish not to follow you," Ned rasped. "But you will stop him, won't you?" Ned rolled to the side and retched blood onto the stairs.

"Dad," I yelled.

"I'm here." Dad knelt behind Ned, and set his palm on his forehead. "It's ricin."

"How do you know that?" The paramedic who'd tried to reach Ned earlier had finally gotten up the stairs. He knelt opposite from me, and shone a light in Ned's eyes. "Are you sure?"

"I am," Dad replied, then he said to Ned, "There's no antidote."

The paramedic called for a gurney, and said they needed to bring Ned to the hospital and pump his stomach. Ned ignored him, and patted Dad's hand. "I know there isn't. He's using me as an example."

"I'm so sorry, Ned," I said, tears streaming down my cheeks and splashing onto Ned's arm. "Amir's only here because of me. I'm so sorry you got dragged into this."

"Don't blame yourself. Amir Hassan would have come back here eventually, regardless of where you were. Don't let him or anyone else blame you for his actions." Ned's gaze focused behind me, and he smiled. "Jacob, I didn't know you were dead. When did this happen?"

"Some time ago, I'm afraid." Jacob crouched beside me, and said, "There's not much keeping his spirit here."

"I'm holding on to him." I could feel his life force trying to flee his body. "Ned, do you want to go?"

"I think I do." Ned's fingers barely tightened on mine. "Thank you, Eliza, for easing my way." He gave my hand a final, weakened squeeze, and he was gone.

"I'll look after him," Jacob said, then he dissipated as well.

Then Ned's body instantly decomposed into a puddle of red, stinking goo.

"Holy shit!" I scrambled back from the steaming liquid. Dad grabbed my upper arms and hauled me down the steps and away from Ned's remains.

The paramedics started yelling about biohazard, and telling us to get away, but I couldn't stop staring at the puddle that used to be Ned. "Ricin does not do that," I said.

"Ned said Amir wanted to set an example, and he has," Dad said. "He just publicly murdered a clan elder."

I leaned against my father. "And I was powerless to stop him."

Chapter 15

Family Ties

The aftermath of Ned's death was awful.

Dad helped me navigate down the steps as paramedics and police officers rushed up them, only to stop and gawk and the bloody puddle oozing into the cracks. Sirens blared and a biohazard truck arrived, cordoned off the area, and took samples of Ned's remains. I acted like a little girl and hid my face against my father's chest, letting him shield me from the awful things behind us as we pushed our way through the crowd.

By the time we got to Tessa, Dan had emerged from the bowels of City Hall. The four of us stood together on the sidewalk and watched the first responders in chaos on the steps. Dan took my hand, and I leaned against him.

"It was Amir's poison," I whispered to Dan. "Dad said it was ricin."

"Is it contagious?" he asked, as people in protective suits taped off the steps and shouted orders at one another.

"It's not," I replied. "But it's good that they're being careful."

There was another commotion behind us. We turned and saw that the mayor had set up a podium at the park across the street from City Hall; it was already surrounded by reporters. As soon as the cameras were rolling, he gave a speech about how—if reelected—he would help curb violent crime. When one reporter asked what violent crime had to do with a man dissolving, the mayor was, for once, speechless.

"It starts like this," Tessa murmured. "Always like this. Something unexplainable happens, then people are scared and frantic and need someone to blame, and witches die." She shuddered. "Witches always die."

"Not this time," Dad said, then he wrapped his arm around Tessa and held her close. "And not you. Never you, Isa."

I blinked; almost no one was given leave to refer to Tessa by her real name, which was Isabella, and even those of us who were allowed to refer to her as such still used her nickname. The fact that Dad had called her Isa, and she hadn't corrected him, made me hope they'd reconciled. I liked my dad and Tess being together.

"Nothing's going to happen to you, either," Dan said to me, then he stiffened. I followed his gaze, and saw a few police officers taking statements from people in the crowd.

"I don't want you near the cops," Dan said. "Let's get out of here."

"Aren't you a police officer?" my father asked.

"Actually, I got suspended yesterday," Dan replied.

"I forgot to tell you, the police chief's under a spell," I added. "Where should we go?"

"Go to the Allwood Compound," Dad said. "Jacob will protect you." He blinked, and said, "My foresight told me to say that."

"All right. Allwoods it is." Dan withdrew his keys. "You two coming along?"

"We'll find our own haven," Tessa replied. "Talk soon."

With that, Tessa snapped her fingers and cast an obfuscation spell on her and Dad; no one would recognize them or remember their features, for around twenty minutes. Just long enough to make a getaway.

"Can you do that?" Dan asked.

"Unfortunately not."

Dan's phone started ringing. He silenced it, then pointed toward an alley. "This way."

The ringing started up again, then my phone rang as well. "What the hell," I muttered.

"Give me your phone." I did, and Dan dropped both of our phones into a roadside mailbox.

"Why'd you do that?"

"In case they're tracking us," he replied, as he scanned the sidewalks. "We need to lay low for a bit."

"What about the rental car?" I asked, then a black limousine with tinted windows pulled up alongside us. The rear window rolled down, and inside the car I saw Jacob's assistant, LeClerc.

"Jacob sent me," LeClerc said. "Get in."

I almost declined. We didn't really know LeCLerc, and him appearing in the middle of a busy street with a getaway car was far too convenient for my suspicious mind. But the police had already closed off one end of the street, and Dan and I were rapidly running out of options.

Therefore, we got in.

"How much do you know?" LeClerc asked, once we were seated and the limo was in motion.

"How much do I know about what?" I shot back. Now that we were inside Jacob's luxury limousine, I knew it had insanely comfortable black leather seats and came complete with a wet bar. What it did not have was one Jacob Allwood, whom I desperately wanted to talk to.

"About why Hassan is targeting you," LeClerc replied. "Has Jacob told you everything?"

I glanced at Dan. LeClerc divulging Jacob's secrets without him present didn't feel right. "He's told me enough," I hedged. "Where is he?"

LeClerc studied his fingernails. "He's with Burroughs, helping him transition to the spirit plane."

"You and Jacob have a history," Dan said. LeClerc frowned, and looked away. "Or, Jacob and Burroughs do."

"Both of those statements are true," LeClerc admitted.

"But, Jacob's a spirit so you can't be with him, and now Ned can," I concluded. "Does that make this ride part of a revenge scheme against Jacob?"

"I would never betray Jacob," LeClerc said. "After Burroughs passed, Jacob came to me, and requested I get you out of the downtown area as soon as possible."

"I'm glad you're loyal," I said. "I would never betray him, either."

"Loyalty's great and all, but you mentioned that Jacob knows why Hassan's targeting Eli," Dan said. "Care to enlighten us?"

"The Allwoods are no strangers to time travel," LeClerc began. "Most witches aren't, especially not the older ones. However, time travel is a fickle business, and it goes wrong more often than not. Hassan is one of the few in this era who have mastered time slips." LeClerc shook his head. "Imagine, a seer mastering what a witch could not."

"Amir learned how to time travel because of a portal he found," I said, and LeClerc nodded. "But, the portal got closed down. The Iranian coven collapsed the cave. I saw it happen."

"Unless there's another way into the cave," Dan said.

"Astute deduction, but the portal you mention remains closed to this day," LeClerc said. "However, if one set up a network of time slips—interdimensional time tunnels, if you will—before the collapse, those would remain open regardless of the portal's condition."

I swallowed, contemplating all of the destruction Amir could accomplish with an actual network of time tunnels. "Tessa bound him to this plane," I began, but LeClerc held up his hand.

"She did, but the network still exists," he said. "Anyone who knows how to access the tunnels can use them."

That was not good. "Who knows?"

LeClerc shrugged. "Any number of people, I assume. Time slips aren't exactly a secret."

"What does this have to do with me?"

"Jacob's sister, Cecily, bred you to be an ideal companion for Hassan."

All at once, I felt my face go hot and my stomach twist into knots. "Bred me?" I demanded. "What am I, a fucking German shepherd?"

"Witches breed people all the time," LeClerc said, unaffected by my outburst. "Mates are selected based on strengths and flaws, to ensure the next generation is strong. While mortal royalty interbred across Europe, we watched how that weakened their families, and we did the opposite. Mortals used their children for power, but we made sure our children would be able to carry on our legacy, and to forge legacies of their own."

Until that moment, I hadn't realized LeClerc was a witch. "I'm only half a witch," I said. "Seems like the breeding plan went awry."

"It did," LeClerc said. "Around the time your mother came of age, Cecily's assignment was altered."

"Assignment," I repeated.

"How much of this assignment were you privy to?" Dan asked.

"Not much," LeClerc admitted. "Cecily and Jacob weren't close, and she hid a lot of her dealings from him. It wasn't until after she'd incapacitated him that the clan began investigating her, and her true nature came to light."

"She is a sneaky bitch," I grumbled, then I remembered that Cecily herself wasn't all that far away. "Dan, is she still in the women's prison on Route 202?"

"As far as I know, yeah."

"Change of plans, LeClerc. You are taking me to that prison, and I am going to interrogate Cecily myself."

Witches hate mortal prisons. It was why we pushed so hard to get Cecily into one. Like most of the supernatural community, witches preferred to fly under the mortals' radar, so to speak, but they also liked to use their magic often. It was hard to be an undercover witch when you're constantly being watched by guards, and all the other prisoners.

In the end, Cecily wasn't charged with murder, even though that was what she was guilty of. Jacob's robust spirit walking around town had put a damper on that. But she was charged with kidnapping her brother and denying him much needed medical care, along with some technical charges like money laundering and tax evasion. She was still waiting for her trial, and knowing how slow the courts moved, she might be waiting for another twenty years. However, due to the seriousness of her charges, she would spend all of that time waiting in prison.

Not to be outdone by a mundane court system, Tessa had cast a dampener spell on Cecily, which held her magic in check. In her current state, Cecily wasn't capable of conjuring a puddle in a rainstorm. Tessa claimed the dampener wasn't permanent, and should wear off in a decade or so. That meant that even if Cecily could find a moment of solitude so she could flex her magical muscles, those muscles were in effect frozen.

Normally, I'm a sympathetic person. Not this time. After all the things Cecily had done, I hoped her magic atrophied and never returned.

When we got to the prison, its cold and bleak exterior matched my heart. My bred for optimal characteristics heart, that is. "How do we do this? Do I ask for her by name, or prisoner number?" I asked.

"Usually there's a list of people who can access each prisoner," Dan said. "If I had my badge, I could get us in, no problem."

"Use these." LeClerc presented us with two laminated identification cards on lanyards. "They're enchanted to allow you access to whomever you wish to see. How are you with truth spells?"

"Um, truthful?"

"Okay. Give me a moment."

LeClerc rummaged around the wet bar, and after he mixed a few liquids together, he handed me a stoppered vial. "Anoint Cecily with this oil," he said. "Once it soaks into her skin, she will be compelled to speak only the truth."

"Thank you," I said as I tucked the vial into the front pocket of my jeans. "I appreciate all of this, but why are you helping me? I know Jacob asked you to, but this seems above and beyond."

"What Cecily did was wrong," he replied. "And Jacob really was unaware of Cecily's actions until recently. He wouldn't have allowed these things to happen to you."

"I believe you," I said, then I looked at Dan. "I guess we should go."

"I'll have a car waiting for you when you emerge," LeClerc said. "Be safe."

Dan and I exited the car, then the limousine drove away. I wondered if Jacob had given LeClerc other tasks to handle, or if he just wanted to get away from the prison, and Cecily, as fast as possible.

I watched the limousine disappear down the road, then I turned around and stared at the prison. "You may not believe this, but I've never been inside a prison before," I said.

"Really? Well, I've been here plenty of times. Follow my lead."

"Okay." I scuffed the pavement with the toe of my boot, and froze. Some of Ned's blood was on my boot.

Ned Burroughs was dead, all because I couldn't save him.

I started shaking and wrapped my arms around myself. Dan embraced me and held me for a few moments before he spoke.

"Talk to me, babe," he said, his lips against my forehead.

"Ned's gone," I said. "I was helpless against whatever Amir did to him. There was nothing I could do."

"There's plenty you can still do," he said. "We can start by talking to Cecily, and learning more about Hassan's plans. We can protect the rest of the elders. And we can kick Hassan's ass." He tightened his arms around me. "I know this is tough. It's goddamn awful, but we can't break down. Not yet. Let's get this done, then we can mourn Ned the way he deserves."

I squeezed my eyes shut, and willed my heartbeat to calm down. "I didn't even know him."

"You're the most badass seer that ever lived. You can still get to know him, by summoning him. And once we avenge him, you two will be the best of friends."

"You're right. I'm not just a seer. I'm the Mistress of Seers, whether these stupid witches want to acknowledge me or not." I stepped back from Dan and wiped my cheeks. "Let's go talk to the evil sister."

Getting inside the prison was a dance between automatic doors and creaky old turnstiles, as if those spokes could really keep anyone in—or out—of the building. Once we were past all of that, Dan and I showed the front desk clerk our magic lanyards. They worked like a charm, and an officer led us into a waiting room, where we sat at a table and were told Cecily would be right out.

"I thought you talked to prisoners through bulletproof glass panels," I said. "On a little phone."

"This place is minimum security," Dan said. "It's for people who aren't considered violent offenders."

I stared at Dan. "How is Cecily not violent? Jacob's dead because of her!"

Dan shrugged, then the door buzzed open and a handcuffed Cecily Allwood was led to the table. The last time I saw her, she had perfectly coiffed hair and was wearing designer clothes. Now, Cecily's blonde hair was restrained in a basic ponytail, and she was wearing a prison issued tan jumpsuit. I had to admit, in her present state she looked pretty nonviolent.

The officers that escorted Cecily into the room ordered her to sit, then they fastened her handcuffs to a metal loop on the table. Once they were confident she was secure, they left the three of us alone in the room.

"To what do I owe the honor, Mistress?" Cecily asked. "Have you come to poison me?" Instead of answering, I took out the vial of truth spell and poured a few drops on Cecily's wrists. "What will this do, send me into convulsions?"

I wanted to fire off a smart comeback, but I decided to conserve my energy. Her threats were meaningless, in more ways than one. "How did you meet Amir Hassan?"

"Ah." The handcuffs rattled as Cecily folded her hands on the table. I guessed that meant the truth spell was taking effect. "I was wondering when you would ask me about him."

"Looks like I'm asking now."

"The better question is, when did Amir Hassan meet Sarah All-wood?"

I blinked, then I glanced at Dan. "Does that mean Amir's older than he appears?"

"Actually, I have no idea when he was born. He's very careful when divulging information about himself, as I'm sure you already know."

"I assume he used a time slip to meet Sarah?" I asked.

Cecily nodded. "He did. Amir wanted to find the most powerful witch in this area, and lo and behold, Sarah was the winner. Unfortunately for him, she lived well before this century."

"Does that mean Amir is from this time?" Dan asked.

"Whether he is or not—and as I said, I don't know where or when he was born—this is the era he prefers to live in," Cecily replied. "Initially, that was a problem. You see, Amir didn't want to copulate with a witch from what he considered a primitive era, and Sarah, well, she didn't want to be with him at all. But she was powerful, and she was crafty, and she figured out a way to give Amir what he wanted while also getting her own needs met."

"Wait," I said, holding up my hand. "You said copulate."

"That was Amir's initial plan," Cecily said. "He was wandering through time, looking for a suitable mate."

My jaw dropped. "Was he successful?"

Cecily shrugged. "Based on the lengths he's gone to in order to secure a partner, I am guessing he's had very little success."

I recalled my lackluster romance with Amir, and agreed. "So, how did Sarah help him? What does any of this have to do with me?"

"Amir wanted a powerful witch as a mate, but he also wanted her to live in this century. Sarah agreed to help him breed a mate who would be of a suitable age during this time period. She enlisted me to assist her, and a few decades ago, your mother, Christina, was born."

"At the Open Arms Center for Women and Youth," I said, remembering the halfway house Dan and I had visited. "She was born in an orphanage."

"Yes, exactly. We liked to keep potential breeders isolated from any family, so we could test them early. We were looking for naturally powerful witches, and when your mother was born, and she exhibited such innate talent alongside her attractive appearance, we knew finally had someone who was as powerful as Sarah, as well as someone who would appeal to Amir."

"But my mother didn't know she was a witch."

"Of course not. We couldn't let any of our subjects learn how powerful they were. They might have rebelled against the program and we would have lost years of work."

I flopped back in my chair, struggling to comprehend what Cecily was telling me. My mother had been bred to be a super witch by Sarah

Allwood and Amir fucking Hassan. The worst part of it all was the since Cecily was under a truth spell, I knew these were all facts.

"How does Eli's father figure into all of this?" Dan demanded, since it was obvious my mind was too blown to ask any coherent questions.

Cecily frowned. "That was not supposed to happen, but as I said, Christina is a beautiful woman. When Alexander crossed paths with Christina, things happened quickly, and we had to change our plans."

"So Amir lost out to Alex," Dan said.

"He did, but we gained an even more powerful girl." Cecily beamed at me, as if I was a prized pumpkin at the state fair. "Once we learned that Christina's child was to be a girl, we realized a witch-seer hybrid would be a far better mate than an orphan witch."

I turned to Dan, my mind swirling with what Cecily had told me. "I'm a hybrid. Like a one of those cars with the electric engines. Am I even a person?"

"Of course you're a person," Dan said, then he refocused on Cecily. "Then what? You all hung around waiting for Hassan and Eli to meet?"

"No, we arranged for Amir to relocate to the Persian coven, and cause an incident that meant Alexander Moore would need to travel to him," Cecily replied. "When your father brought you along, it was a bit of serendipity."

"Well, that serendipity had a shelf life," I said. "Amir and I broke up years ago, and I'll never go back to him. He knows this."

"And what about Beauclaire?" Dan asked. "Why did he kidnap Eli?"

"And why did Sarah try to possess me when I was a kid?" I added.

"Those were separate situations," Cecily replied. "As for the possession, Sarah and Amir had a falling out, and as such, she decided to possess you herself. When the possession didn't pan out, Nathaniel had you abducted with the intent of finally installing Jemima's spirit in you. Those actions were also outside of our agreement with Amir," she added.

"They were trying me on like a hat," I said. "That's... I don't even have words for that."

"I do," Dan said.

"Careful, mortal," Cecily said. "I won't be powerless forever."

Dan ignored Cecily's vague threat. "These plans to manipulate Eli are zero for three," he said. "What's Hassan really after?"

"Why, power and control," Cecily replied. "He wants both witches and seers under his thumb. He wants to be an emperor."

I shook my head. "He's as crazy as you are. There's no way a witch or a seer could run the world. Mortals outnumber us a hundred to one. Maybe a thousand to one."

"If he gains enough power to reanimate and control dead mortals, the living will do whatever he wants," Cecily replied.

"That was Beauclaire's plan," Dan said. "Did he steal all of Hassan's ideas?"

"Actually, this plan isn't original to either of those losers," I said. "Witches are always trying to get their claws into seers, one way or another. It's why the lineages are kept, and why a seer who's part witch can't be in charge." My voice caught at the end, and Dan squeezed my hand.

"Maybe it's time for those rules to change," he said.

"Many witches have sought to change the rules, as you put it, for some time," Cecily said. "Just ask your Uncle Jacob."

My stomach dropped. "My what?"

"My dear, we're related," Cecily said. "Where do you think Sarah found all of those witches willing to be bred? She didn't have to look further than her own family."

After Cecily dropped that bombshell, I was done. Dan dealt with the guards and had Cecily returned to her cell, then we left the prison and walked out to the visitor's lot.

"Car's not here," Dan said. "And we have no phones. I guess we're walking home."

"You know what I hate?" I demanded. "I really, really hate how everyone in the goddamn world knows more about me, and my family, than I do."

"Do we believe Cecily?"

"She was under a truth spell."

"Yes, but that means Cecily told us what she believes to be true," Dan said. "No offense, but this whole magical community seems to be built on lies and misdirection."

"You're not wrong." I linked my fingers behind my neck and stared at the sky. "Do witches really breed their children for certain powers? That seems barbaric."

"And witches live a long time. Why bother breeding for anything? Why not just work on your own magic, and become more powerful that way?" Dan shook his head. "Something's not right. Maybe we should meet up with Tessa."

"No. Tessa is probably still with Dad, and I really don't want to see either one of them right now." I glanced at Dan, then toward the forest that surrounded the parking lot. "I realize that if all or part of what Cecily said is true, everything that has happened was way beyond their control. Still, I'm not in the best headspace right now and I don't want to lash out at them."

"What you need to do is go a few rounds with the punching bag again."

I glanced at him, saw his grin. "You'd like that, wouldn't you?"

"You know it." Dan looked at his watch. "Before we get to punching, we should get moving. There's a diner about a half mile down the road. We can call a cab from there."

"Hang on." I closed my eyes, and said, "LeClerc, I'll take that car now." When I opened my eyes, a shiny black SUV that was an exact match to Dan's destroyed truck was idling in front of us.

"Whoa." Dan opened the driver's side door, and found the keys in the ignition. "If you're really related to the Allwoods, I gotta say it's not a bad family to be part of."

"They flash one car at you, and your morals go out the window." I got in the passenger side, and saw a note on the dashboard. "Check this out." I held it up, and Dan and I read it together.

The car is yours for as long as you need it, be it a day or a decade. It is paid for, and registered and insured to the family. Call if you need anything – LeClerc

"This is very generous," I said. "I know Jacob's wealthy, but who gives someone a whole car?"

"That's a problem for later on." Dan put the car in drive, and headed toward the main road. "We've got our wheels, and we're not going to Tess or Alex. Want to hit that bag for a while?"

"Actually, I think we should pay Bennet a visit."

"Bennet it is."

Chapter 16

Poor Pacheri

Paris, Almost Three Years Ago

"Admit it," Amir said. "This was fun."

"I don't know if I'd call it fun." We'd gotten into the habit of walking through Père Lachaise, which was one of the largest cemeteries in Paris, once or twice a week. Earlier today, we'd stayed after closing, and Amir got the idea to sneak into the Aux Morts ossuary. One thing Amir loved to do was get inside anyplace that was closed or forbidden. The more off-limits it was, the more he liked it.

We emerged from the ossuary, and I halted. Tessa was standing on the walkway in front of the steps, arms crossed over her chest and murder in her eyes.

"Get down here," she said. "Now."

"Hey, Tess," Amir drawled. "We were just—"

Tessa made a catching motion with her hand. She'd grabbed Amir's voice from the air, and held onto it. "You are not to speak. Eliza, what in the name of Hecate do you think you're doing?"

"We heard there was an enchantment on the door and wanted to see if we could break it." I'd never seen Tessa so mad, and an angry Tessa was terrifying. "We broke it, so that's good, right?"

"How in the world is this a good thing?" she countered.

"It shows that my spell worked!"

"It also leaves evidence. Evidence that is very, very hard to hide." Tessa looked up at the entrance to the ossuary. When we broke the enchantment, we also broke the door, and an arm off of one of the statues. "Witches and seers need to blend in with mortals. That's how we stay safe."

"Why do we need to hide?" I asked. "We're stronger than mortals."

"Are we?" Tessa took a step toward me. "If we're so strong, why are the history books filled with stories of suspected witches being burned at the stake? And hung? And killed in all manner of gruesome ways? If we're so strong, why were we the ones persecuted, run out of our homes, had our children stolen from us? Why?"

"I-I don't know," I said, tears streaming down my cheeks. "I'm so sorry. I didn't think. I'm so, so sorry. I-I'll fix this."

The anger bled from Tessa's face, and she pulled me into her arms. "I'm sorry, too. I don't mean to be so harsh, but I've lost too many people to misguided witch hunters. I don't want to lose you, too."

"You won't," I said. "Gran would kill both of us."

Tessa gave me a last squeeze before she released me. "She would. Let's go home. Amir, take care of the door."

Amir flailed his arms as his mouth opened and closed, but no sound came out. "Are you going to give him his voice back?" I asked.

"The spell will wear off," Tessa replied. "Eventually."

The next morning, I was up early and one of the first in line at the boulangerie. By the time Tessa got out of bed, I had a selection of pastries set out on the kitchen table, and fresh coffee and juice.

"Is this an apology breakfast?" she asked.

"It's an 'I'm a dumbass breakfast'," I said. "I don't know why we went snooping around the ossuary last night. It was a dumb move."

"It certainly wasn't one of your better ideas." Tessa turned on the radio on the kitchen counter, and poured herself some juice. "Or was this another one of Amir's schemes?"

"I don't know if I'd call it a scheme," I said. "He always says he's looking after the dead."

"But why is he looking after the Parisian dead?" Tessa wondered. "He's British, and his family has lived there for a long time. These aren't his people."

I shrugged. "Maybe he's looking after them because this is where he is?"

Tessa held up her hand, and cocked her head toward the radio. "That's odd," she said.

"What's odd?" I asked.

"At the Louvre, they were doing some routine maintenance work, and someone noticed something off about the mummy. Honestly, I didn't even know the museum had a mummy."

"I did," I said. "His name is Pacheri."

"Well, Pacheri's foot looked odd, so they had the mummy x-rayed, and all of the bones from his left foot were gone."

I remembered going into the Egyptian room with Amir, how he'd touched the mummy's foot. That had been two years ago, on my twenty-fourth birthday. "Maybe he lost his foot before he died," I suggested, but Tessa shook her head.

"The mummy was x-rayed a few years ago, and at that time all bones were present and accounted for. Somehow, some way, the foot bones were extracted from the body without damaging the wrappings."

I strained my ears, but the announcer was speaking very quickly, and my French wasn't nearly as strong as Tessa's. "Could you cast a spell to move bones through wrappings?"

"I suppose," Tessa said, then she froze. "Why do you ask?"

"When Amir and I went to the Louvre, he touched Pacheri's foot."

Tessa clenched her fist, then she muttered something in Italian that sounded like a particularly brutal curse. "Did he take anything else from the museum?"

"What? No! Why would anyone..." My voice drifted off, as I remembered the other places we'd broken into, just to "have a peek' as Amir put it. "We were at the Louvre after hours, just like the ossuary. And we've gotten into the Catacombs—a few times, actually—a bunch of cathedrals, and..." I looked at Tessa. "This is really bad, isn't it?"

She shoved back from the table and stood. "It's stupid, and I'm putting a stop to it today."

When we got to Amir's apartment, he wasn't home. Tessa magicked the lock open, and we let ourselves inside.

"Where does he keep the bones?" Tessa asked.

"I don't know," I said. "I've only been here a few times."

Tessa's gaze slid toward me. "You've been together for almost two years now, yet he's still keeping you at arm's length?"

I frowned at the floor. When Amir had first come to Paris, he was romantic, and attentive, and showered me with affection. Now, he only came around when he needed me to pick a lock. "Maybe I'm keeping him at arm's length."

"If he's going around stealing from tombs and reliquaries, we shouldn't associate with him at all. Can you feel the bones, and their spirits?"

I reached out with my seer abilities. "I can feel a few bones, but there aren't any entities here, or at least no one nearby is connected to the bones he took. If he took them."

Tessa gave me a look. "At the very least, he has the mummy's foot."

I toed the carpet with my boot. "I guess."

"Let's just find the bones. We'll worry about Amir's motivations later."

We moved further into the apartment, Tessa searching with magic while I looked around the old-fashioned way. We didn't find anything in the front room, and while Tessa checked the bathroom, I stood in the doorway of Amir's sparse bedroom.

The room had a bed, a table, and a chest of drawers. There wasn't any art, or mementos, or other personal items on display. For all I knew, Amir didn't own anything personal. He wasn't nostalgic, and had no interests outside of honing his seer abilities.

No, that wasn't quite right. Amir was also interested in honing my seer abilities.

Every break in and heist we'd been involved in was all about Amir testing my skills. He'd present me with a spell, and make a game of teaching to me. When I mastered the first set of tricks, he heaped so much praise and attention on me, I felt like the queen of the world.

Then the attention faded, until I mastered the next trick, and the next. It wasn't long before I was learning complex spells just to win his approval.

A hot tear escaped my lashes. I ground it away with my fists. I did not like being this pathetic girl, seeking his approval the way a dog begs for scraps. I am a Moore—I am Eliza goddamn Moore—and no matter how many cheap tricks he stuffs up his sleeve, Amir will never be as powerful as me.

"Eli," Tessa called from the kitchen. "Come see this."

I gathered my dignity and joined Tessa. "Did you find something?"

Tessa pointed toward the open cabinet doors. Amir didn't have anything like boxes of pasta or tins of tea in the cabinets. Instead, there were clear plastic bags full of bones.

"I..." I stared at Tess, slack-jawed. "I had no idea."

"Now we know why he didn't invite you over more often." Tessa flicked her hand, and the bones floated out of the cabinets. There were long arm and leg bones, tiny finger bones, and everything in between. And there were three skulls.

Human skulls.

"We're going to have to return everyone," Tess said, to me as much as to the bones. "Do you have a list of the places you've been to with Amir?"

"No, but I can make one." I leaned closer to one of the skulls. It had a bit of gilding on it, like a saint's relic. "How much bad karma has Amir generated by stealing all these bones?"

"A fair bit, I'd say. But, think of all the good karma we'll create by putting them back where they belong." Tessa frowned, and added. "Everyone, except for the mummy's foot. If those bones miraculously re-appear, that will make things even worse."

"Poor Pacheri."

It took us about a week to return the bones to their rightful resting places. As it turned out, most of the bones were from The Catacombs and a few public cemeteries, so it was easy to put them back. A few, like the gilded skull, were actual saint's relics, and Tessa called in a few favors from the Paris coven so those bones could be returned respectfully, and quietly.

The amount of favors Tess called in, coupled with the fact that we'd suddenly come into possession of a large number of relics we had no business associating with, meant that as soon as all the bones were replaced we made plans to leave Paris. The coven had readily believed Tess's explanation, and that Amir was the bone thief in question. However, we still didn't know what Amir's ultimate plan was, and Tess thought it best to put an ocean between us and whatever that was.

The day before we left Paris, I was out running errands alone, when Amir stepped into my path. "Hey, Ellie," he said. "I've been looking for you."

"I'm not hard to find," I said. "You know where I live. You could have called."

He swallowed hard, and I wondered if he'd kept his distance out of fear of Tessa. For all her frivolities, she was one of the most powerful witches in Europe. "I thought you might be mad, after the ossuary," he said at last.

"Why would I be mad?" I asked. "Just because you tricked me into helping you break into yet another place, why would that upset me?"

"If you're not mad at me, why did you take my bones?"

"First of all, none of those were yours," I said. "You stole them. You dishonored the dead—multiple times—which goes against everything a seer stands for."

"How dare you," he seethed. "How dare you, a pathetic child, scold me? You were born into power, and all you do is run from it. Here I just want a few crumbs for myself, yet you deny me."

"Deny you?" I demanded. "Power isn't something you hand out like candy! Skills are learned, and there aren't any shortcuts."

"As if the Moores never took any shortcuts," Amir snapped. "Why are you people in power, anyway?"

"Probably because we're better than you," I said, then I turned on my heel and stalked away. I hadn't gotten far before Amir grabbed my arm.

"You are nothing compared to me," he hissed in my ear. "We'll meet again, Ellie, and you will regret how you've treated me."

With that, he was gone.

The next day, I went by the café Amir liked, and a few other places he frequented. I don't know why I wanted to see him so badly; I didn't want to apologize, or rekindle our lame romance, but I couldn't let an argument be our last interaction. Even though I wanted our time together to end, I didn't want it to end on such a bad note.

Having exhausted all other options, I went to Amir's apartment and picked the lock. When the door swung open, I gasped. The apartment was completely empty.

I went into the kitchen, the bathroom, and finally the bedroom. All of Amir's meager possessions were gone. Stunned, I slid down against the wall and sobbed. I hadn't been in love with Amir, but I'd loved being with someone. And now, the only real boyfriend I'd ever had had effectively disappeared from my life. It was like he'd confirmed my worst fear: I would be alone forever.

Everyone who loved me ended up leaving.

CHAPTER 17

WIZARDS ARE REAL?

Bennet Carrington was called a shepherd, but he didn't own any sheep. In the supernatural community shepherds were the ones who maintained records for just about everything of note. Those records included births, deaths, treaties, and even when certain clans originated and where they were currently located. I liked to think of them as librarians dialed up to eleven.

I hoped Bennet's librarian sized brain would be able to give me some answers.

Dan parked in Bennet's driveway, and pocketed the keys. "Think the truck will still be here when we come out?"

"I don't see why it wouldn't be." I looked at Bennet's house, which was as close to an English cottage as you could get in Northeastern America. It was a cape style home with dormer windows and a covered porch, and the front walk was bordered with roses and lavender. "Hopefully, Bennet's home."

"We'll know soon enough."

We stepped onto Bennet's quaint little porch, and knocked. A few moments later, a bewildered Bennet opened the door.

"Eli, Dan, how lovely to see you," he said. "Do we have an appointment?"

"We don't. We would have called first, but we mailed our phones," I said. "Do you know what happened earlier, at City Hall?"

Bennet's face darkened. "Sadly, I do. Please, come in." He stepped aside, and we entered Bennet's cozy, cluttered home. "I'll just put the kettle on, then we can talk."

Dan and I sat on the couch. "He sure has a lot of stuff," Dan said, eyeing the packed bookcases and overflowing desk.

"He's responsible for a lot of information." I left off the rest of my thought, which was that hopefully Bennet would be able to dig up more information about my family tree. "And he's the only local shepherd."

"Why is that, I wonder," Dan mused.

"It's because traditionally all of the shepherds were located in Ireland," Bennet said as he entered the room with a teapot. He set it on the table, then he ducked back into the kitchen and retrieved three teacups and saucers. "While most of Europe lost a great deal of information during the early medieval periods, that which was held in Ireland's monasteries remained largely intact. When those in power realized this, our operations were centralized to the western portion of the island."

"Interesting," Dan said. "Then how did you end up here?"

"The Carringtons have always looked after the Moores," Bennet replied. "When Helena's ancestors relocated to the New World, mine did as well."

"Have you ever looked after any witches?" I asked. "Looked after to the point where you'd know if a certain clan was breeding for desired characteristics?"

"What, as in cultivating roses for a certain scent?" Bennet shook his head. "Why would anyone seek to do that? Here, have a biscuit."

"Thanks." I accepted the shortbread cookie, and dunked it in my tea. "According to Cecily Allwood, my mother is the result of generations of witchy breeding."

"That... That may have a basis in fact. Hang on." Bennet set down his teacup, and disappeared through the stacks of books into an adjacent room. I knew from prior visits to his house that room he'd ducked into was an office. I also knew I didn't want to go in there with him, mostly because the room was so packed there wasn't enough space left over for two people.

"What's he looking for?" Dan muttered.

I shrugged. "I have no idea."

Bennet emerged carrying what looked like an old school accounting ledger. After we rearranged the teacups and cookies, he laid it on the coffee table and cracked it open.

"One thing that we—we being myself and certain other shepherds—have always found odd is that witches will come and go from public life, and no one ever seems to know why," he began. "They always disappear for around a year, and then return to their former lives as if nothing ever happened."

"Maybe they're just on vacation," I offered, but Bennet shook his head.

"Those who vanish are always women, and particularly powerful women, at that." Bennet indicated a few names in the ledger. "It's the lack of information surrounding their disappearances that's odd—normally, those of prominent families are well documented. However, something else stands out."

"And that is?" Dan prompted.

"About half of these women end up taking in a ward a few years after their return," he replied. "The ward is always treated as a natural child, and indeed, they all turn out to be witches."

"How unusual is it to come across an orphaned witch?" Dan asked.

"An orphaned witch with no other family to care for them is a rare occurance," Bennet replied. "These facts, coupled with Christina being born in an orphanage and supposedly unaware that she was witchborn, do lend a bit of credence to Cecily's claims."

I worried my lower lip as I stared as the lists of names and dates that made sense to Bennet, but to me were just a jumble of letters and numbers. "Cecily claims Sarah Allwood was breeding witches to create a powerful—" I had to squeeze my eyes shut before I said the word, "mate for Amir."

"Did she?" Bennet leaned back in his chair. "I suppose that's a possibility. But that would make you part of the Allwood clan." He rubbed his chin. "That would explain a few things."

"Such as?" Dan prompted.

"Jacob Allwood's continued presence upon this mortal coil, for one," Bennet replied. "Eli, when you described how you summoned the Allwood ancestors to assist you, you never indicated any resistance on their part. Is that correct?"

"Yeah. I asked for help and they gave it," I replied, and I realized what Bennet was getting at. "They complied because they're my ancestors, too."

"It would seem so," Bennet said. "And perhaps that familial bond is what made you able to reanimate Jacob to a certain degree."

"Reanimate," Dan said. "Sounds like zombies."

"That's me. The Zombie Queen." I grabbed another cookie and dunked it in my tea. They had caramel centers, and were very tasty. "Have you already recorded Ned's death?"

"I've begun the process," Bennet replied. "It was poison, yes?"

"Ricin, according to Dad," I replied. "I don't know how Ned came in contact with it, or when. I don't even know how he got to City Hall."

"Do you believe someone poisoned him?" Bennet asked.

I glanced at Dan. "Amir had Charlotte grow castor bean in her greenhouse. The plant is still there, and it's healthy."

"Ah." Bennet made a few notes. "Are you planning on summoning Ned in order to confirm how he received the ricin?"

"Should I?"

"That depends." Bennet removed his glasses and polished them with his handkerchief. "When Helena had questions about how one had passed on, she had no qualms about summoning them and asking all the questions she needed to."

"That's the thing. I don't know if I need to do anything." I ran my hand through my hair, and tried to purge the image of Ned in his death throes from my mind. "I feel like I should let Ned rest, at least for a little while. He's been through a horrible ordeal, and I don't want to prolong it."

"Then rest he shall," Bennet said. "Eli, you're the Mistress of Seers. If it's your will to leave him be, it will be done."

I swallowed, and stared at my hands. They were shaking, so I clenched them into fists. "Thanks, Bennet. And thanks for seeing us. I'm sorry we barged in on you like this."

"My door is always open for you. Both of you," Bennet added, nodding toward Dan.

"Thanks. Again." I stood. "I guess we'll get out of your hair now."

"One more thing," Dan said. "Melinda Howe. What do you know about her?"

"Only the basics, I'm afraid," Bennet replied. "She's been the head of her clan for around seventy years, and while she appears powerful the Howes are also quite secretive. Melinda also was one of Helena's strongest supporters." Bennet paused, and asked, "Has something happened with Ms. Howe?"

"She gave me a silver box that had some kind of a spell in it," I replied. "I don't know what the spell was supposed to do, but it kept trying to latch onto me."

"Interesting. Do you have the box handy, so I could examine it?"

"We buried it in a tobacco barn."

"As one does. Well, then, I shall endeavor to learn all I can about the Howes."

"Thank you, Bennet." I smiled. "Is that the third thank you, or the fourth?"

"You're quite welcome for all of them."

Dan and I left Bennet to his research, and got back into the truck. "You know what's interesting?" Dan asked.

"Tell me."

"Bennet's practically soaked in magic, but there's nothing magical in his house, at least not in the rooms we were in."

"What'd you expect? He's a shepherd, not a wizard. He has no reason to hoard magical artifacts."

Dan's gaze slid toward me, then he backed down the driveway. "Is that your way of telling me wizards are real?"

"Maybe."

Dan shook his head. "Be nice to the mortal. I'm new at this, re-member?"

"Aren't we all." I watched the neighborhood go by through the side window. "What should we do now?"

"Up to you, but I do have some thoughts."

"Please, regale me with these thoughts."

"Sooner rather than later, the police will want to question us, espe-cially you. You were right next to a man who publicly expired on city property."

"So was my dad." I reached for my phone, and remembered that Dan dropped it into the mailbox. "Why did you get rid of our phones?"

"They can be tracked, and I don't want you talking to anyone before you're ready."

"Isn't that evading the law?"

"We aren't evading if they haven't asked us to come in yet. It's a technicality, but one that will work in our favor for a little while."

"Can't they just go by your house?"

"Yeah. They can. This is why I think we should get a room and lay low."

"Let me guess, you want to get a room at Mermaid Cove."

Dan glanced at me and grinned. "You got it, babe."

CHAPTER 18

AWFUL WITH A PURPOSE

When Dan and I got to Mermaid Cove, the place was just as weird as before. The seventies vibe in the lobby remained strong, thanks to the abundance of wood paneling and orange carpets. The same manager, Bryce, was working the front desk, and wouldn't you know it, he recognized us.

"Hey! Great to see you two again," he said as he checked us in. The bowl of apples on the counter was present, and the fruit looked as if it had been freshly shined. I could practically see my face in the apple skins' mirror sheen. "I could tell how impressed you were by our establishment."

"Very much so," Dan said, as he accepted the room keys. "Thank you, sir."

We walked down to our room, which was on the first floor and on the other side of the building from Jada's. That was good, since I didn't want us to spook her by being too close. Once we were inside the room I kicked off my boots, sat cross legged on the bed, and looked up at Dan.

"So. Why are we here?"

"This place is steeped in magic," Dan replied. "The walls are buzzing with it. There's as much magic here as there is at your grandmother's house, maybe more."

"Really?" I rolled across the bed toward the wall and placed my wrist flat on the geometric patterned wallpaper. My seer's mark heated up, which was a sure sign of spell work. "You're right. But who would enchant a motel?"

"No idea, but Amir put Jada here for a reason," Dan said. "Maybe he enchanted it?"

I shook my head. "This doesn't feel like his magic. This is older, and more sophisticated. Whoever wove these spells together saw magic as an art. Amir sees magic as a tool, no different than a hammer or a wrench."

Dan grunted. "How do you see magic? Is it a gift you celebrate, or just something to get the job done?"

"That is a great question." I walked the perimeter of the room, dragging my hand along the wallpaper. "Many older witches see magic as something refined, elegant, even. They don't view magic as a series of spells and charms."

"How do they view it?"

"As an extension of themselves."

"Isn't that what seers think about their abilities?"

"Pretty much." I bumped into the other side of the bed, which meant my circuit of the room was complete. "So, how is a seer different than a witch?"

"If you ask me, you're more alike than different, but what do I know? I'm the mortal." Dan flopped back on the bed. I sat on the opposite side of the bed and mimicked his position, so that while our feet remained on the floor our heads were next to each other. He glanced at me, then something on the ceiling caught his eye. "There is a mirror over the bed."

"What?" I looked up, saw our reflections, and burst into laughter. "Is there an award for the cheesiest motel in town?"

"I don't know, but this place is a contender." We laughed for a moment, then Dan turned to me. "Hey. How are you feeling?"

"Awful, but awful with a purpose, if that makes any sense."

"It does." I watched in the mirror as Dan smoothed my hair back from my face, then he leaned over and kissed my forehead. I closed my eyes, and focused on the sensations of being warm and comfortable and loved. Not so long ago I was a miserable, lonely person, and while I've never been the sort to think I needed a man to complete me, I had to admit that almost everything about my life was better now that I was with Dan. Even though my apartment had blown up, and I was hiding out from the police and Amir in a cheesy motel, I wasn't alone. Finally, I had someone to talk to, and lean on. Granted, I talked to Tessa all the time, and leaned on her way more often than appropriate, but with Dan it was better. Different.

With Dan, things were good.

"I'm glad we're here," I said.

"If I'd known how much you'd like it here I would have gotten us a motel room months ago," he said, and we laughed.

"I meant, I'm glad we're together."

He kissed my forehead again. "Me, too." When I opened my eyes, I was focused on the reflection of the room's awful carpet.

And realized that the carpet had a pattern.

"Dan, look up at the mirror," I said. "See the carpet?"

"That ugly thing?"

"Yeah. There's a pattern in it." I sat up, scrutinizing the reflection. "It's... familiar."

Dan looked up at the mirror, then he stood and tracked the pattern in the carpet. It wasn't a printed design so much as cut into the pile itself. "It's some kind of branches, with flowers on it? Or is it fruit?" He got up on the bed and surveyed the floor from his vantage point.

"Babe, whatever the elegant old magic is in this room, it's strongest in those branches."

"Someone made a brown shag carpet into a power source?" I got down on my hands and knees, and traced the cut pattern. Much as it had felt in the walls, the carpet's magic seemed older, and more refined than modern spell work. My fingertips grazed one of the rounded images alongside the branches, and a protection tattoo on my leg flared.

It was the same tattoo that warned me about Nathaniel Beauclaire, back when he worked with Bennet at the college's greenhouse, and was pretending to be Jada's older brother.

"I need to summon Nathaniel," I said.

"Beauclaire again?" Dan demanded. "Why do you always go running back to that prick?"

"I do not run to him," I snapped back, and that was when the police officers in riot gear broke down our door.

Chapter 19

None Of This Is Right

According to the officers, Dan and I were being arrested as accessories to the murder of Ned Burroughs. This information was gleaned as they threw us against the wall, searched us, and put us in cuffs. Oh, and apparently Jada saw us enter the motel, and she was the one who turned us in because she thought we were there to spy on her. Awesome.

"They didn't even read us our rights," I muttered as they marched us out of the room and through the lobby. Dan remained silent, and I realized he hadn't said a word since he accused me of running to Nathaniel at the first sign of trouble. "Are you mad at me?"

He shook his head slightly. "Not here."

Since Dan wasn't talking, I let the officers manhandle me out of the motel and into the back of a police van. They tossed Dan in after me, then shut and locked the rear doors. We sat on the cold metal bench seat next to each other in the quiet, dark van. The officers hadn't let me put my boots back on, and my toes were like ice cubes.

"What's with the silent treatment?" I asked, as I stretched my toes.

"This isn't right," Dan said, as he scoped out the interior of the van. "None of this is right."

"What should be happening?"

"First of all, how are we accomplices to a murder?" he began. "Ned was in distress long before we got there. Being present when a person dies doesn't equate to you murdering them. Second, why did a SWAT team come after us? This sort of response is used for dangerous threats, like hostage situations or suspicion of weapons, not for regular people like us with no records."

"I did think this was a bit excessive," I said. "What else isn't as it should be?"

Dan met my gaze. "I don't know any of these guys. I've been in this department for eight years. Where did these people come from?"

I scooted closer to him, and pressed my arm against his. "When I said I need to summon Nathaniel, it was because I recognized his magic in the carpet. He's got something to do with this. And I'm pretty sure that pattern in the rug was apple tree branches."

"Which means Sarah Allwood."

"Who apparently had a falling out with Amir around the time my parents met. Maybe he somehow seized her properties after she possessed Jada."

"For us to get hauled into a van like this, we must be close to the truth." He rested his forehead against mine. "I'm sorry about what I said."

"It's okay. I should have explained myself instead of dumping information on you." I rattled my cuffs. "My lock picks are in my leather jacket. Which blew up with the rest of my apartment," I added.

Dan blew out a breath. "We've got to get you out of here." The van's engine started, then it lurched into motion. "Where do you think they're taking us?"

"Nowhere fun." Something was tugging on my awareness, something that had always been there, but I'd never paid attention to.

Something familiar.

"You've got foresight face," Dan said.

"I can go to the Allwoods." I opened my mouth and the words just tumbled out. "I can go, because we're family."

Dan nodded. "Okay. You go, and I'll stay here and see where these guys are based out of."

"I can't leave you!"

"This is a golden opportunity for us to learn more about what Hassan's up to."

"It is, but they could hurt you."

"I'm not exactly helpless. Besides, you'll come rescue me, right?"

"This isn't funny," I said, but Dan had a point. Splitting up was a good idea. I turned so my back faced him. "There are three razor blades sewn into my waistband."

"I remember this trick." He turned so his back was against mine, and investigated the inside of my jeans. I heard the fabric tear as he claimed two of the blades. "Got anything else?"

"Unfortunately not. I need to restock my supplies." I turned around, and pressed my cheek against his. "As soon as I'm out, I'm sending people after you."

"I'm counting on it." He kissed me. "Be careful. I love you, baby."

"Please be safe," I whispered, then I pictured Jacob Allwood's office, and the world went hazy.

A moment later, I was sitting on his office floor, barefoot and in handcuffs, while a room full of people stared at me. "Eli, what is the meaning of this?" Jacob demanded.

CHAPTER 20

THAT'S THE SPIRIT

I got to my feet as Jacob cleared everyone out of his office, and apologized to his guests for the unexpected intrusion. That was me, usually unexpected and always intruding.

Once most of the people were gone, LeClerc approached me. "That didn't happen in the jail, did it?" he asked, nodding toward my handcuffs.

"This bit of fun happened afterward. They have—" My voice caught, so I cleared my throat and started over. "Fake police officers rounded us up and tossed us into a van. They have Dan."

"I'll find him," LeClerc said, then he left the room and shut the door behind him. That left me alone with my possible relation, Jacob.

"Where did these people accost you?" Jacob asked.

"Are you my uncle?" I countered.

"I take it you and Cecily had quite the discussion." He touched my handcuffs, and they unlocked themselves and fell into his hands. He placed them in a wooden bowl on a side table, then he sat behind his desk. "Please, sit. Would you like a drink? I feel alcohol may be in order for this conversation."

"No alcohol. I want to remember everything that happens."

"Suit yourself." Jacob retrieved a bottle of water from the bar and set it in front of me, then he poured himself a healthy portion of

Scotch. "The way I understand it, we're more cousins than niece and uncle."

"Oh." Any joy I felt over confirmation that Jacob and I were family was overshadowed by the fact that if Cecily was right about this, she was also right about other things. "Why didn't you ever tell me?"

"Honestly, I only recently learned of it, myself. After you and Dan came by asking about the Open Arms Center, I looked into the business. I was curious as to why Cecily, who was not a charitable sort, had invested so much time and effort into the center. You can guess what I found."

"Yeah." I looked at the door LeClerc had left through. "Will he really find Dan?"

"He will. LeClerc always accomplishes what he sets out to do." Jacob drank. "What happened? Why were you handcuffed?"

"We needed answers, so Dan and I went to see Cecily. Then we went to the motel where Amir stashed Jada—it's on Route Ten, by the way—and we got arrested for Ned's murder." I paused, remembering the kind man I'd only ever spoken to right before he died. "How is he?"

"He's settling in to his new form," Jacob replied. "I felt how you helped his spirit transition out of his body. That was good of you."

"It's what I'm supposed to do. Witches protect life, seers protect death. We hold the line."

Jacob smiled sadly. "Helena used to say that. And before you ask, no. Helena did not know what Cecily was doing. If she had, she would have put a stop to it."

"But, after my mother's powers manifested Gran went to the orphanage," I said. "She didn't figure it out then?"

"It would seem that she did not." Jacob took a deep breath. "Things certainly have escalated, haven't they, Mistress?"

I scoffed. "I'm not the mistress of anything. The witch elders either won't follow me or want to bespell me, and this whole town has gone to hell in a handbasket."

"This town went to hell a long time ago," Jacob said. "And it's only the living elders you need to convince. Ned and I are your staunch allies. Who tried to bespell you? Nathaniel?"

"Ironically, no," I replied, and I told him about my meeting with Melinda Howe, and the creepy silver box that wanted to be my best friend. When I mentioned the dilapidated house Melinda lived in, and her claim that her health affected her entire clan, Jacob frowned.

"First, the health of the clan is not tied to the health of the leader," he said. "I'm non-living proof of that. Second, you say the spell was trying to latch on to you?"

"It felt like a burr. Prickly, like it was looking for a loose bit of me to grab. The magic was similar to Amir's."

Jacob rubbed his chin. "It sounds like it was a compliance spell. But the question remains, what was Melinda, or Amir, attempting to make you do?"

"What he's doing is driving me nuts." I remembered the motel room's carpet. "I think Sarah Allwood is trying to contact me."

"Oh?" Jacob leaned forward. "What makes you say that?"

"I keep seeing apples everywhere. Bowls of apples, patterns with apples. Apple blossom scented detergent showed up in Dan's basement. At the motel the carpet had a pattern of apple tree branches. When I touched the branches, it felt like the magic from Stone Creek Orchard. Initially, I thought it was Nathaniel's magic, but the more I think on it, I feel like it's Sarah." I faced Jacob. "Cecily told us that Amir and Sarah had a falling out. Maybe Sarah is trying to get me on her side, against him."

"Interesting. You do realize that Amir wants something, quite desperately, and I don't think it's you. No offense."

"None taken, but you're right. He's after something here, in this town or nearby, and he's done an awful lot of planning to get it." I realized Amir wasn't the only person who liked this area so much. "Why are the witch clans here?"

"When we began coming here from the Old Country, most of us settled in and around Boston," Jacob replied. "After the trials at Salem, many of us sought to relocate, and we came here."

"But, that's it. Why here?" I tapped my chin. "I bet Sarah knows why, and I bet she knows a bunch of other facts that can help us put Amir, well, elsewhere."

"Elsewhere may not be a good enough solution," Jacob said, "but we can leave off such discussions until they're needed. How can we summon Sarah? According to Nathaniel, her bones were destroyed when the police investigated the orchard."

"Nathaniel's a liar," I began. "And since she's the one trying to contact me, her bones must not be an issue." All of the facts I'd recently learned swirled in my head, one of which was that Sarah and I were related.

"We're Sarah's descendants. We can summon her." I frowned. "Have you ever summoned anyone?"

"I haven't, not on my own, but I suspect you'll be an excellent teacher."

"I'll do my best. Do you have any apples?"

Unsurprisingly, the dead witch didn't have a ton of produce lying around. What he did have was a very efficient staff, and after they made a quick run to the grocery store, we had an assortment of apples heaped in the center of Jacob's desk. Jacob drew the curtains, then I set a white candle in the center of the apples, and snapped my fingers to ignite the wick.

"Sarah Allwood," I said. "Sarah, do you want to talk to us?"

A form coalesced in the chair next to mine. "I have a few things I'd like to say."

Once she was fully formed, I faced Sarah—and did a double take. The woman next to me was dressed in old-fashioned but very fine clothes, had shining dark hair carefully combed back from her face, and perfectly trimmed nails. If I hadn't summoned her myself, I would have thought this woman was one of Tessa's contemporaries, not the witch described in local folklore as the old hag who lived on the edge of the woods and poisoned children with fruit pies.

"We're ready to listen," I said. "Does what you want to discuss have anything to do with Amir Hassan?"

"That snake," Sarah snapped. "He reneged on every agreement we had. In my day, a man's word meant something. Amir's promises are so much dust."

"No arguments there," I said. "When he first reneged, was that when you possessed me?"

"Yes," Sarah said. "Are you surprised at my forthrightness? We are above lies, you and I."

"I appreciate that," I said. "So, you tried to possess me, but ended up possessing Jada Morales for twenty years. Why did you stay in the wrong person for so long? Why didn't you just leave Jada's body?"

"Because I was trapped," Sarah said. "Amir placed the mirror I used to leap into Jada. At the time, he referred to his help as a peace offering, but that was another lie. He somehow enchanted the mirror, so when I entered her body, I was tethered to it. Only your exorcism set me free. Thank you, for that," she added, with a tip of her head.

"You're welcome," I said, my mind reeling as the pieces fell into place. "You're saying that Amir can send a spirit into a particular body, and keep it from leaving? That's..." I glanced at Jacob, who was as wide eyed as I surely was. "Unprecedented."

Sarah nodded. "It is. In my many, many years, I've never known another who could do such a thing, be they witch or seer. Supposedly, he learned these tricks in his time portal."

"That portal's closed... Or is it? He's still using his time tunnels, isn't he?"

"He never stopped," Sarah replied. "The only reason he caused such a ruckus in Persia was to attract Alexander's attention. He wasn't expecting to meet you at the same time."

I bristled when Sarah mentioned my father, but I kept my angry comebacks to myself. "And why is Amir here now? Why have witches and seers and gods know what else been drawn to this area for centuries?"

"Why, the nexus of power, of course." When all I did was stare at her, she continued, "You, the scion of the Moore line, didn't know about the nexus? Well, Helena died when you were still fairly young. She probably never got around to telling you. Not that she was a very good teacher."

"That's enough," Jacob said. "You will not disparage Helena, not on this plane or the spiritual."

"You're still carrying a torch for her," Sarah said. "How does unrequited love feel in death?"

"Probably the same as it does when you're alive," I said. "Tell me about the nexus."

Sarah's eyes narrowed. "You're not going to order me to speak nicely about your grandmother?"

"I can't make you have good manners," I replied. "Besides, Gran's also a spirit. If she takes issue with what you say about her, she's perfectly capable of dealing with you herself."

Sarah threw back her head and laughed. "I like you, Eliza. It's a shame your fire ended up in the Moore house, while we Allwoods were burdened with Cecily. About as powerful as a wet dishrag, that one, but she takes orders well."

I wished I'd accepted that glass of Scotch from Jacob. "You were about to tell us about the nexus."

"Ah, the nexus. We all wanted it, but the seers found it first. They've been guarding it for centuries, and no matter what witch or mortal tries to knock them off the mountain, they dig in and remain rooted in place." Sarah paused. "You really didn't know."

"I really did not. What's so unusual about this nexus?"

"Why ask me when you can learn about it? You should, really, since it's your heritage. As a show of good faith between us, I will give you the key to the nexus. It's all in my spell book."

"Spell—you mean the cookbook?" I asked, and she nodded. "What will Amir do if he gains access to this nexus?"

"What won't he be able to do?" she countered. "He will be able to reanimate forms, but he will also gain the ability to put spirits into bodies of their choosing. He could put Jacob in you, for instance."

"Is that why he's kept the Morales girl close to him?" Jacob asked. "Supposedly, she has retained all of your memories."

"Has she? Isn't that interesting." With that, Sarah disappeared. I looked at Jacob, and shook my head.

"Well, shit."

"Can I use your phone?" I asked. "I haven't checked in with my father or Tessa since this morning, and after what just happened with Sarah..." My voice trailed off, but Jacob wasn't the sort to not own up to what he'd done.

"You mean how I gave our most powerful enemy a piece of knowledge that might give her a significant advantage?" he finished. "Yes, warning Alexander and Tessa is a wise move." He pushed his desk phone toward me. "Please."

I picked up the receiver and dialed Gran's house number, visualizing the old rotary phone on the kitchen wall screaming to life and scaring the crap out of the cats.

"It's about time you called," Tessa said when she picked up.

"How did you know it was me?"

"Perhaps you've heard of witchcraft?"

The edge in her voice told me how stressed she, and probably Dad, had been since the scene at City Hall. "What happened after we left?"

"The area was suddenly swarming with police, who began questioning everyone they could get their hands on. My spell kept Alex and me from being targeted, but only just."

"What were the police asking about?"

"They were asking about you. Not asking who Ned was, or why he died, none of that. They wanted to know where you were." Tessa paused. "I have your phones."

"You broke into a mailbox? That's a federal offense." When Tessa sighed in concert with Jacob, I said, "Okay, not the point. Thank you for grabbing them."

"You're welcome. Anyway, Alex and I remained in the downtown area for a time, but it when it became clear we weren't going to learn anything, we came here."

I imagined the two of them hiding out together and almost smiled. "Well, Dan and I went to talk to Cecily in prison, then we got taken by fake police officers and they still have Dan, but I escaped and now I'm here at the Allwood Estate with Jacob. We summoned Sarah Allwood."

"Who took you and Dan?"

"We're not sure. LeClerc went to rescue him." I felt my lower lip tremble. Jacob reached across the table and placed his hand on mine. "I'm an Allwood. Did you know that?"

"Are you? I had no idea. Wait... That means Christina—"

"Was bred by Sarah Allwood to be a mate for Amir, but she met Dad first and, well, here we are."

"Here we are, indeed." Tessa didn't speak for a moment, and I heard her moving. I imagined she was getting as far away from the kitchen as the phone cord allowed. "Would you like me to tell Alex?"

"If you want. Actually, it would probably be good, since it proves Dad wasn't in his right mind when he met her. She probably used her Allwood magic to put a spell on him."

"Eli—Actually, we can discuss that later. Did Sarah reveal anything useful?"

"Apparently, all of Amir's nonsense is over a power nexus somewhere around here. And she knows Jada has some or all of her memories."

Tessa groaned. "Wonderful."

"Yep. About the nexus, have you ever heard of such a thing?"

"Oh, yes, everyone has. Well, everyone in the supernatural community. Who knows what mortals hear?"

"Sarah said her cookbook has information about how to access the nexus. Is it still in the solarium's bookcase?"

"If it is, I'll find it. Aside from all of this, you have a bunch of messages on your phone from Marianne, at Forge Heights." Tessa read me the phone number.

"Really? Okay, I'll give her a call. Are you and Dad staying put?"

"For now, yes. Call if you need us."

"I will."

With that, I ended the call. "How much of that did you hear?" I asked Jacob.

"All of it," he replied. "This spiritual hearing is excellent." He patted my hand. "LeClerc will find Dan."

I nodded, because I needed to believe in LeClerc, and Jacob's faith in him. "He's more than just your assistant, isn't he?"

"At times, he's been everything to me, but now..." Jacob gestured at himself. "Now, who knows? I certainly don't."

"That's one thing we have in common. Most of the time, I have no idea what's happening, either to me or around me." I ran a fingertip around the buttons on the phone. "Do all witch families really do that? Breed for certain traits?"

"Certainly not," Jacob replied. "Coercing two individuals to bring a child into the world, only to place that child in an orphanage while you determine if they will or will not fit into your plans, is truly despicable. In fact, I've begun researching Cecily's files to determine if any more such children are out there, alone in the world. We do not leave family behind."

I smiled. "Maybe being an Allwood isn't so bad. Most of you are pretty good people."

"Why, thank you. Would you like to return those calls to Marianne now? I recall Forge Heights being important to you."

"Might as well," I said, and I dialed Forge Heights's number. After a few transfers, Marianne picked up.

"Eli, you're not going to believe this," Marianne began.

"Try me," I said. "My suspension of disbelief has been stretched to the breaking point lately."

"You know how you asked about any strange plants popping up? Well, the belladonnas are bigger than they've ever been. I cut all of them down to the ground after you and the detective came by, and they're all two feet tall again."

"Weird." I wondered if Amir using his magic nearby accounted for the belladonnas' growth spurt. "Is that the only reason you called?"

"Oh, no. Martha Pickford wanted me to give you a message. She says Frank found someone you were looking for, a Christina Lind."

My jaw went slack and my mind went blank. "She's alive?" I whispered.

"Apparently so. I have an address, if you'd like it."

Marianne read off the address. I didn't write it down, because I was certain I would never forget it.

My mother, who I hadn't seen or heard from since she left me in a hospital bed twenty years ago, lived a few miles away from where I was sitting in Jacob's office.

After Marianne and I said our goodbyes, I faced Jacob. "My mind has been blown so many times today, I don't think I have any brain matter left." I shook my head. "My mother is alive, and living a town over. Why is she so close?"

"Family," Jacob said. "I don't know if it's the same for seers, or mortals, but witches feel a strong pull toward their kin. It's why we have these large estates and bury our ancestors nearby. We need to remain close."

Close. "How close? If one witch was taken over, say, by a rogue seer, would it affect the entire clan?"

"I suppose it's possible," he began, then his eyes lit in recognition. "The Howes."

"And the Burroughs." I stood. "Is there another car I can use? I think we need to pay a few visits to our witchy friends."

"Of course," Jacob said as he stood. "Follow me."

Jacob led me to an underground garage that was filled with enough cars to open his own dealership. "Exactly how much money does this family have?" I asked.

"We're quite comfortable," he replied, then added, "That includes you, too."

"You believe Cecily's claims that we're related?"

"I believe Sarah," Jacob said. "And Cecily... Cecily has always had a tendency to get swept up in the schemes of others. Why do you think no one wanted her to lead the clan?"

"Because Allwoods have good taste?"

Jacob chuckled. "I suppose we do. Which car would you like to take?"

I surveyed the rows of sports cars, trucks, and sensible sedans. "I guess a sports car is out of the question. Let's take one of the sedans." I approached the closest one, and found it unlocked with the keys in the ignition. "You aren't afraid someone will steal the cars?"

"Who in their right mind would steal from a witch?" Jacob countered. "Besides, we have security cameras."

"Cameras for the win." I started the car, put it in drive, and we headed toward the Howe Estate.

When we pulled up to the rusty gate, Jacob gasped. "I hadn't thought it was this bad."

"It's much worse than it was a few days ago."

When Dan and I had visited Melinda Howe, we'd both been shocked by the deplorable state of her house. As Jacob and I drove past the gate, I realized it hadn't been so bad. Then, it had looked as if the maintenance staff had taken an extended vacation. Now, it looked like the house had been abandoned years ago. Many, many years ago.

The area in front of the house could no longer be called a lawn. If anything, it was an old field dotted with dead trees and knots of brambles. The road that led to the main house was uneven, with weeds pushing up through the broken pavement. The house itself was the color of dust and mildew, and the western wing's roof had collapsed. Many of the windows were broken, while the others were either missing glass or so filthy they no longer reflected the light.

"This looks like a horror movie," I declared. "If I was watching this in a theater, I'd be yelling at the characters to get out of here."

"But they always go inside the spooky house, don't they?"

I sighed, and shut the car off. "Well, at least if I die here, I can hang out with you and Ned in the afterlife. He seemed nice."

"That's the spirit."

I gave Jacob some side eye, but based on his pensive face the pun was unintentional. We got out of the car and approached the Howe Estate. Much like the gate, the front door hung open and somewhat precariously from its rusty hinges. When I touched the doorknob, it came off in my hand.

"Oh, dear," Jacob said. "I have never seen anything like this."

"Great." I stashed the doorknob in the corpse of a potted plant, and pushed the door open. We were met by a gust of stale, dry air. At least it didn't smell like anything had died recently.

"Hello?" I called. "Melinda? Humboldt?" When no one answered, we moved further into the house. "I can't feel any spirits."

"Neither can I," Jacob said, then he paused. "I do hear someone."

"What are they doing?"

"Breathing. It's quite labored."

"That can't be good."

I let Jacob lead the way, and as we navigated around the buckled floorboards and sun bleached drapes, I looked for clues as to what had happened. I didn't find anything, not a literal or figurative smoking gun. All of my instincts told me that this house had sat empty for a very long time.

Well, almost empty. Jacob's spiritual hearing led us to a small bedroom behind the kitchen. There was an elderly man lying in the narrow bed, and even though he'd looked to be about forty a few days ago, I recognized him.

"Humboldt?" I asked. "What happened here?"

Slowly, his eyes opened. "Eliza Moore?" he gasped. "I haven't seen you since you refused to help us."

"When did that happen?" I asked, then I remembered the silver box Melinda had given me. "What was in the box?"

"Melinda couldn't ask for help, not from you or anyone," he replied. "Hassan would have killed her, and the rest of the family. So, she put her plea into a spell, then she put the spell into a box and handed it to you."

I remembered how the spell had been desperate to get my attention, and latch onto me. "I'm sorry. I didn't realize what the spell was. I thought it was trying to hurt me."

"Melinda wouldn't hurt a fly," Humboldt said. "But that was a long, long time ago. Why are you here, now?"

I took in Humboldt's wrinkled face, his snow white hair and beard. "How long has it been?"

"Fifty years next summer," he replied. "He took Melinda first, Hassan did, and one by one, he claimed the rest of the clan as they tried to rescue her. I was only left alive because I'm not a Howe."

I placed my hand atop Humboldt's. His spirit was weak and would be moving on soon. "Jacob, I hate to ask for more help," I began.

"Helping people is what we do," he said, then he took out his phone and sent off a few messages. "Humboldt, if it's all right with you, I'm going to have a few people from my clan come to help you. Would you like to stay here, or relocate to my estate?"

"I like it here," Humboldt said. "I've always liked it here." His eyes fluttered closed, and he drifted off to sleep. Jacob and I stepped out of the bedroom.

"Amir moved the entire fricken' house through time," I whispered.

"And he seems to have claimed the entire Howe clan," Jacob added. "We should go to the Burroughs' Estate next. Without Ned to protect them, the same might happen to that family."

I looked at the closed door. "Will he be okay?"

"He's been surviving here for the last fifty years, and my people are on the way," Jacob said. "We've done what we can for Humboldt. Let's see if we can stop this from happening to anyone else."

Since Jacob was right, we returned to the car and headed off the Howe property. As we approached the main road, Jacob's phone trilled.

"LeClerc has Dan," Jacob said, as he read the message. "He's safe, and unharmed."

I blew out a breath, feeling like I might melt with relief. "Thank you, Jacob. Thank LeClerc for me, too."

"I shall. Apparently, Dan had a litany of things he wishes to say to you."

I smiled to myself. "Tell him to wait until we're together. I'm sure LeClerc'c got better things to do than transcribe Dan's thoughts and feelings."

"They're going to—Eli, do you know a woman called Sanders?"

"Jill Sanders? She works with Dan."

"Apparently, LeClerc and Dan are going to her home."

"Think we should meet up with them after we check out Ned's place?"

"I think that's a very good idea."

Chapter 21

Secretive, Even For Witches

"Eli, may I make a somewhat straightforward comment?"

My gaze slid toward Jacob. We were traveling from the Howe Estate to the Burroughs Home, and I for one couldn't wait to see what surprises Amir had left for us. I was sure each would be worse than the last. "Have we ever not been straightforward with each other?"

"Good point." He studied me for a moment, then said, "Your witchcraft isn't very refined."

"How could it be? It's not like I've ever trained, and I've only known about my half witch status for a short time."

"Yes, true."

"But," I prompted, when he was too quiet.

"But you shouldn't need training in order to feel your power," he said. "Consider your seer's gifts. You didn't need training to speak to the dead, did you?"

"No," I admitted. "Gran taught me a lot, but it's as natural as breathing for me."

"And if you'd been away from your family—say, if you were left in an orphanage—when your abilities manifested, you'd be labeled as a psychic, or a medium," he continued. "A mortal that can see the dead."

It was a known fact that mortals who had a bit of magical ability were descended from the supernatural community in some way. But

Jacob was right; except for the few small spells Tessa had taught me, my witchcraft had lain dormant for almost my entire life. "What are you getting at?" I asked.

"You have been saddled with a curse of unknown provenance or intent," he replied. "I believe its purpose is to hold your magic in check."

"Really? But I'm pretty powerful," I said, and it wasn't boasting. My seer abilities were as strong as Gran's were, had been since I was young.

"You are," Jacob conceded, "which makes this all the more puzzling."

"Melinda offered to remove my curse, in exchange for me curing her from whatever she was poisoned with," I said. "Do you think she could have done it?"

"I'm not sure. Removing a curse is a tricky business. If you don't understand the curse's exact purpose, pulling it out willy-nilly could cause more harm than good."

I frowned, and kept my snarky comments to myself. Jacob was only trying to help, but he'd reminded me that I had a mysterious curse doing mysterious things to me. For all I knew, it was also a time bomb, just waiting to explode and cause even more chaos.

We turned off the main road onto the access road that led to the Burroughs Estate. It was a narrow gravel driveway that crept around a mountain. "This is a rather remote estate."

"It is. Out of all the local clans, Ned's home is currently the most remote."

"Currently?"

"The Beauclaire estate is—was—on the other side of the ridge." Jacob glanced at me, frowned. "I'm sorry. I don't mean to remind you of anything you'd rather not think about."

"It's fine… But now that I do think about it, I don't remember how I got to the Beauclaire house, or very much about it at all. It was less than an hour from when they grabbed me to when I was in their basement, but how did we get there so fast?"

"Where were you abducted from?"

"The shopping area near the center of town. I was leaving the grocery store." It was my father's birthday, and even though he'd been traveling and wasn't home to celebrate with us, Gran and I planned on baking a cake. When my attackers grabbed me, I dropped the bag of sugar, and after it burst open, the crystals stuck to my black jeans. My pants had sparkled until they were ripped off of me.

Jacob shook his head. "It would take at least two hours to drive from the town center all the way out to the Beauclaire house. You're sure about the length of time?"

"Absolutely. I was wearing a digital watch, and after they threw me into the trunk it was the only light I had. I stared at that watch the entire time." I coughed, my throat suddenly thick. "They grabbed me just after two in the afternoon. The car's trunk opened again at two fifty-eight."

Jacob grunted. "Here's the estate."

I pulled onto a cul-de-sac, and parked in front of the roundabout in front of the Burroughs house's gates. Intimidating wrought iron gates must come with the witch starter pack. I didn't see any guards, which was just as well, since I didn't feel like explaining why we were gawking at the house. As for the house itself, it was large, and well maintained, and everything appeared to be in order.

"Ned's house looks fine," I said. "Want to swing by what's left of the Beauclaire house?"

"Yes, I feel we should do that."

It took us another forty-five minutes to reach the Beauclaire Estate's grounds. Jacob was right; there was no way my abductors could have gotten me all the way out here in less than an hour.

"This place is desolate," I said as we approached what was left of the house. All that was left was a burned-out shell, and the deep, dark cellar. Even the grass hadn't grown back. "Remote and desolate."

"Is this the first time you've been here since you were rescued?"

"Yeah. I didn't see much of the area, even after Tess got me out. I remember her wrapping me in a blanket and bringing me outside, and not much else." I parked the car and shut off the engine. "Let's see what there is to see."

We got out of the car, and picked our way across the scorched earth. "The soil is dead," I said, marveling at the barren earth. "What caused this?"

"Unless I'm mistaken, your father is responsible for all of this," Jacob replied. "Alexander was in a state when you were taken, and he swore vengeance on those responsible. As you can see, he made good on his word."

My gentle, artistic father, the man who looked more like a grad student than the seers' legendary and feared marksman, had effectively destroyed the Beauclaire legacy. "What else did my father do? Did he kill anyone?"

"He did not. He made sure everyone was alive and awake, so they would be as terrified as you were."

Cold fingers shivered up my spine. "What happened to the Beauclaires?"

"A tribunal of elders judged them," Jacob replied. "Those who physically abducted you and held you captive were executed. The rest of the Beauclaires were ordered to disperse. Until a year or so ago, the only Beauclaire that remained in the area was Tessa."

"Because she was a Beauclaire by marriage, but she had to cut ties with them," I said, remembering the terms Tessa had agreed to in the aftermath of my kidnapping, and Jacob nodded. "Were you on that tribunal?"

"I was. If I'd known you were an Allwood, I would have executed those responsible myself."

I smiled, because having family at your back was one of the best feelings in the world. "I appreciate that. So, how do we think I got here so quickly?" I turned in a complete circle, and didn't see any roads except for the one we'd traveled on. "Was this area more accessible in the past?"

"No. The main reason this site was chosen was for its remoteness. The Beauclaires have always been secretive, even for witches."

"I guess you wouldn't want to broadcast your evil plans," I began, then I noticed a set of doors flush against a small rise. "Is that a receiving vault?" I asked, since it looked like a cold storage area common in northern cemeteries. It was where they held those who passed over winter, when the ground was frozen and therefore too hard to dig graves.

Jacob followed my gaze. "It certainly looks like one, but the Beauclaires did not inter their deceased on site. They have a family cemetery a few miles west of here."

"If they weren't burying people nearby, why did they need the vault?" I mused. Witches had no need of cold storage or any other sort of embalming, since they could quite easily preserve a corpse with magic. Add that to the fact that I couldn't feel a single spirit on site, and this vault was definitely out of place.

I approached the doors, which were heavy wood and at least ten feet wide. "Also, why would a vault need to be so big? Was someone burying giants?"

Jacob placed his hand on it. "It's locked. Give me a moment." He closed his eyes, and a few moments later, the hinges rattled and the doors creaked open. We each pulled a door open, and stared inside the vault.

Or should I say, we stared inside the tunnel.

"I think we know how you were brought here so quickly," Jacob said, gesturing toward the tire tracks worn into the dirt. "It seems this area wasn't as inaccessible as the Beauclaires would have had us believe."

"It's not just a tunnel for cars." I crouched down and examined a bit of blue grit near the bottom of the doors. "This is Amir's magic. I think this is one of his time tunnels."

"Gods below," Jacob muttered. "He was here under our noses all this time." Jacob gazed at the doorframe and took a step back. "Please don't think me cowardly, but I don't think entering the tunnel is wise."

"Agreed." We shut the doors, and faced the remains of the house. "I was not expecting to find this."

"Nor was I," he said, then he asked, "Have you ever considered summoning Jemima Beauclaire?"

"Nathaniel's wife? No, why would I?"

"We've learned so much from so many, but no one has heard her side of things. We know that she was manipulated first by her mother, and now by Nathaniel, but no one knows Jemima's side of the story."

"True. All I know is that Nathaniel loves her, and has been trying to put her into a new body ever since she died. I wonder what she wants."

Jacob cracked his ethereal knuckles. "Let's ask, shall we?"

Chapter 22

Jemima

I found a blanket in the car's trunk—these Allwood vehicles came well-stocked—and after I spread it on the ground, Jacob and I sat across from each other. Summoning spirits outside in the harsh light of day wasn't my favorite method, since the sunlight tended to bleach them out and make them harder to see, but it could be done.

My eyes closed and my spine relaxed, and I thought about Jemima. Unlike the charlatans with their crystal balls that kept booths at carnivals and near boardwalks, I didn't need any fancy equipment or spooky vibes to make contact with the spirit plane. The only thing I needed to summon a ghost was me.

I cracked an eyelid and glanced at Jacob. He was a spirit, but the bright sun wasn't washing him out in the slightest. If anything, he looked more vibrant than he did indoors.

"How do you feel?" I asked. "Spiritually, I mean."

"Honestly, I feel almost the same as I did when I was alive," he replied. "I must admit, I was a bit nervous when I collected Ned and helped him across. I wasn't sure I'd come back, but here I am."

"I'm glad you're here. I don't know if I could do this without you." I took a deep breath and shook out my hands. "Do we know if Jemima ever lived here?"

"I don't believe so, but Nathaniel did for a time, after her death."

"Then her spirit will find this place familiar." I closed my eyes, and concentrated on a woman I knew nearly nothing about. "Jemima, would you like to talk to us?"

"Do I have a choice?"

I looked to my left, and the only thing that kept me from gasping aloud was the many years of experience I had of being caught unawares by spirits. Jemima had lived and died back when this state was still an English colony, and I'd expected her to present as a simple woman in a bonnet and homespun dress. Instead, she lounged on her side wearing a toga worthy of an empress, with her shining black hair caught up in a gold fillet.

"Of course you have a choice," I said. "Everyone does."

"You always were a righteous one." My confusion must have been plain on my face, since she said, "Eliza, we have met before."

I glanced at Jacob. He, unhelpfully, shrugged. "Have we? I'm sorry, I don't remember."

She pursed her lips. "You will."

I left that ominous statement for another time. "I'm sure I will, but that doesn't change the fact that no one's forcing you to be here."

Jemima made a small harrumph noise, and plucked at her skirt. "That's where you're wrong. I was supposed to move on years and years ago, but I've been trapped in this in between state ever since."

"I thought Nathaniel was trying to find you a body, so you two could be together again."

Her shrill laughter was unexpected and unnerving. "Is that what he told you? How could we be together if I was in another woman's body? Why does he think that is in any way a good idea?" She frowned, and stared toward the burnt remains of the house. "I'll tell you why he thinks that. My mother refuses to let go of this life, so she convinced him that he could keep my spirit here."

"Why won't Sarah let go?" Jacob asked.

"The only thing my mother has ever loved is power," Jemima replied. "She didn't love me, or my father, or anything else. And because of that love of power, she is afraid that if she moves on, she will lose it all."

"Perhaps Nathaniel can't let go of you, because he's afraid of losing you," I offered.

"Perhaps. Or, perhaps if he truly loved me he would let me go, and trust that I would wait for him in the next world."

"Does he love you?"

"Once, I thought he loved me more than anything. Now, I'm not so sure."

Jemima's lower lip trembled, and my heart went out to the poor spirit woman. Her natural life had ended hundreds of years ago, but she'd been kept in limbo ever since, denied the opportunity to move on. It must have been exhausting, and upsetting on a level I could hardly imagine.

"I thought Sarah was still holding you captive," Jacob said. "If that's the case, how was Eli able to summon you?"

"She only held me captive from Nathaniel," Jemima replied. "That, and I'm captive to her essence. While she remains on this plane I'm tethered to her, but any seer could have summoned me at any time. Seers have always been stronger than my mother, much to her chagrin, which is why she wanted to possess one so badly."

"You know, your mother tried to possess me once," I said. "She missed, and ended up possessing the girl next to me."

Jemima giggled. "I remember. Mother was furious to be trapped inside a small child." Her laughter died, and she said, "I am aware of exactly who you are, Eliza Moore, and I know what my family has done to you. I do offer my deepest apologies, worthless though they are."

"Your apology means quite a lot to me," I said. I looked at Jacob, my spiritual friend who became my relative, and hoped he would back me up on my latest idea. "Jemima, if you want to move on, I can help you."

She gazed at me, her head tilted to the side. "Yes, I expect if anyone could, you could," she murmured. "What will your help cost? I'm sure you understand why I'd rather not owe you, in this world or the next."

"I understand." I wracked my brain, wondering what I could ask of Jemima in return, and figured I should go for broke.

"Your mother mentioned a power nexus in the area," I began. "One that is so large it's been attracting witches and seers since the beginning of time. What do you know about it?"

Jemima's eyes widened. "That's what you want to know? You're not already aware of the nexus's location?"

"Um, no."

"It's at your house," she replied. "The Moore seers came to this land centuries ago, long before they were called Moore, and have guarded the nexus ever since." Jemima regarded me, her face thoughtful. "I understand you have witch blood. Perhaps this is why you were never told?"

"That, or my father is very, very forgetful," I replied. "Thank you, for that knowledge." I reached for her hand, but Jemima drew back.

"That was not enough to balance what will sit between us once I have ascended," she said. "Therefore, I offer you a second piece of knowledge. Amir Hassan, he who walks through time and who would rule the nexus if given half a chance, is not from this era. He was born centuries before I was, and befriended Nathaniel before either of them came to the new world."

"Amir is that old?" I shook my head. "I had no idea. He must use more magic than I realized to keep his body so youthful."

"It is not magic he uses, but time," Jemima said. "He has learned how to not only move through time, but he can also move time through his body, and the bodies of others."

I remembered Humboldt, who had been forty one day, and ninety a few days later. "Do you know how he does such a thing?"

"I don't, but I do know that the secret is kept within his tunnels."

"Thank you, Jemima." I reached for her again, and this time she took my hand. "Are you ready?"

"I daresay I've been ready for some time." Jemima cradled my hand in hers, rubbing her thumb across my knuckles. "Oh, Eliza. It's been so long since I've touched another. Thank you for this most generous gift."

"You're very welcome," I said, then I gave her spirit a gentle push. The golden cords that bound her to this plane unraveled, and she was gone. I took a moment to ensure her spirit found its way, then I turned to Jacob.

"The answer is in the tunnels." I said.

"And the nexus is under Helena's house," he added. "What are the odds of the tunnels running all the way to the nexus?"

"It would explain why my family set up shop there," I began, then a bolt of lightning struck the ground between us. The force flung me away from Jacob and onto my back. When the smoke cleared, Nathaniel was standing over me.

"What have you done with my wife?" he growled.

CHAPTER 23

ALEX WAS NEVER CURSED

I lay sprawled on my back in the dirt, my ears ringing from the lightning strike. Disoriented, I tried to push myself up to a sitting position. Nathaniel struck me at the base of my neck. I saw stars as I fell back again. As I gasped for breath, he planted his hand under my throat and held me flat against the earth.

"What did you do?" Nathaniel ground out.

"Get your hands off me." I punched him over his heart, putting all of my nascent boxing skills into the hit. He stumbled back from me, but he'd only moved because I'd caught him by surprise. I wouldn't get so lucky a second time. "Jemima wanted to move on, so I helped her."

"She wanted no such thing," he spat. "She wanted to be with me!"

"But you don't want to be with her, do you?" Jacob asked; as a spirit, he was immune to Nathaniel's physical attacks. That didn't mean he was safe. "If you did, you would have found a way to join her in the next world."

"Is that your quaint little way of telling me to kill myself?" Nathaniel spat. "I've done nothing but try to bring Jemima back!"

"But you can't," I croaked; my throat hurt from the punch and subsequent throttling, and every word felt like swallowing needles. "No matter what you do, no matter how much power you hoard, she's gone. Death is the one line we can't cross. Jemima will always be dead, now and forever, and you need to accept that." I paused, watching Nathaniel as emotions played across his face, and came to a realization. "Did you start working with Amir in order to return her to life?"

Nathaniel's eyes narrowed. "Would that it was that simple," he snapped, then he disappeared.

"That was quick, yet terrifying," I said. "Do we think he's gone?"

"I find it's best not to have an opinion on Nathaniel," Jacob said. "That way, you aren't shocked when the complete opposite occurs. I will say, it's unusual that he so quickly removed himself. Nathaniel is a man of vengeance, and you've put Jemima beyond his reach. He won't let this go unpunished."

"Then he must have left to work on a new plan." I stood and dusted off my jeans. "We should probably go to Gran's. If he's up to something, I want to be as close to my father and Tess as possible."

We'd debated taking the hidden tunnel back to town, since it had obviously been used for vehicle traffic in the recent past, but decided against it. We didn't know where the tunnel let out, or if there were any obstacles, such as a cave in or one of Amir's traps, between the Beauclaire property and wherever the endpoint was. So, we drove the old-fashioned way, down the mountain and across town.

A full three hours after Nathaniel throat punched me, Jacob and I pulled into Gran's driveway. When I heard the familiar sound of gravel crunching under the tires, I finally let myself relax. I was home, Dad and Tess were here, and everything was going to be fine. Hopefully.

"No matter who lives here, I will always think of this as Helena's home," Jacob said, as he gazed up at the house. "Even a hundred or a thousand years from now, it will always be Helena's home."

"Gran did have a way of making her mark on places," I said. "You miss her, don't you?"

"I do. Someday, perhaps, I'll amass enough courage to seek her out in the next world."

"You haven't yet?"

"Gods below, no. I'd hate to intrude upon her if I'm not wanted." Jacob left off the last bit, that he wasn't sure if Gran had ever wanted his company, even when they were both alive. It was amazing how a powerful witch and clan elder could still get his feelings wound up in knots over a pretty girl.

"Well, now that we know we're family, you have an icebreaker." The sun was dipping toward the horizon, and the back garden was filled with comforting orange light. "Let's get inside."

I led Jacob up the porch steps and through the back door. We'd barely entered the mudroom before the thunder of tiny paws came to greet us.

"You remember Gran's cats?" I asked. "They're our first line of defense." The cats preened at that, curling their tails and rubbing themselves against my legs. Then they focused on Jacob, and sat down in a line across the threshold, effectively barring our way to the kitchen.

"Funny, guys," I said, then I tried stepping over them. Muffuletta's paw shot out, and he almost scratched me. "Hey!"

"Quite the soldiers." Jacob went down on one knee and regarded Pumpkin. She gazed back at him in the unblinking way cats do. "These cats are not spirits. At least, they're not like me. They're more... guardians."

I picked up Pumpkin, ignoring her hiss. "You don't have to guard the house from Jacob. He's good. Promise."

Smokey and Muffuletta looked Jacob over, then they retreated to the kitchen. Pumpkin let me carry her, but she didn't take her eyes off Jacob. Since we were being allowed in, we entered the kitchen and I yelled a greeting to my father.

"Curious," Jacob said, as he watched the cats take up positions on either side of the solarium doors. "Do you think they're guarding the nexus?"

"Maybe." I heard footsteps on the stairs, so I set Pumpkin on her feet and turned to face my father.

"Eli," he said as he pulled me into his arms. "I've been so worried about you."

"I'm okay," I said. "Have you heard from Dan?"

"No, but his phone's here, along with yours. Tessa destroyed a postal box to get them, but it was for a good cause." Dad held me at arm's length, then he looked at Jacob over the top of my head. "Thank you, for looking out for Eli."

"It was my pleasure," Jacob said. "If anything, she looks out for me." Jacob glanced at the cats, and continued, "I'll return home to check on things there, and I will have LeClerc reach out to you with regard to his and Dan's whereabouts. If either of you need anything, please don't hesitate to summon me." With that, Jacob faded from view.

"He hung out with me for the whole drive back, when he didn't have to," I murmured, then I faced my father. "Where's Tess?"

"She's resting," Dad said. "Murdering mailboxes is hard work. How are you?"

"Did she talk to you about your curse?" I asked instead of replying.

Dad's brows lowered. "I'm not cursed."

"Maybe not now, but you were. Mom cursed you. She was a witch, and she cursed you—or enchanted you, or whatever—so you would leave Tessa for her."

Dad ran a hand through his hair. "Bug, have a seat. I'll make us some coffee."

I sat at the kitchen table and watched as my father went through the motions of making our favorite beverage, all the while wondering why he didn't seem happier. Wasn't it a good thing that he was cursed? That we now had evidence he hadn't wanted to be with my mother, and that Tessa was his true love? In my mind, this curse straightened out a lot of things.

Unlike my own curse, which was one big headache that steadily got bigger.

Once the coffee was done, Dad filled two mugs and sat across from me. "First of all, I'm not cursed. I never have been."

"Yes, you were," I insisted.

Dad held up his right arm, and pointed to a red tattoo on the inside of his elbow. "This is a ward against curses. I received it at least a decade before I met your mother."

I frowned at his tattoo. "But a curse is the only explanation."

"It's not, and the truth is far simpler." Dad stirred his coffee; he always left the spoon in the mug even after he'd added sugar. It was a wonder he hadn't poked an eye out. "Around twenty-nine, maybe thirty years ago, Tessa went back to Europe. She had business there—family business—and I didn't begrudge her going. However, I returned from an extended trip to Asia just as she left. The circumstances of our lives meant we hadn't seen each other for nearly two years."

"Yeah, you travel a lot," I said, wondering where this story was going.

"I was here, with no pressing matters for once, and I was alone," Dad continued. "I wasn't lonely, but…" Dad clenched his fist. "Tessa and I had never been exclusive, especially when we weren't together. We didn't talk about it much, but we had an understanding. I don't know what she did while she wasn't with me, and I never asked. It was none of my business… But I always remained faithful to Tess. What was a few months apart when we have our entire lives, I'd say to myself. Then we were apart for two years, and then two became three… And then I met Christina."

He drank some coffee, then he resumed his hypnotic stirring. "She was so beautiful, Christina was, and so intelligent and witty, and… And she was here. She was here, and I was lonely, and I gave her my number. As you can guess, she called." He met my gaze. "Eli, I wasn't cursed by your mother. Not for one moment. You were born of love, nothing else."

"Did you love Mom?"

"I did," he replied. "When Christina told me she was pregnant, it was the happiest moment of my life. All I could think about was giving you and your mother the best life I could."

"But that didn't happen," I said.

He shook his head. "No. It didn't. Christina couldn't reconcile her being a witch and me being a seer. She worried our child would be uncontrollable, filled with magic and abilities she didn't understand. I was worried she would leave, and I'd never find you. I ended up taking her to court to get joint custody of you before you were born."

"Really?" I asked.

"Turns out you can't do that before birth, since the courts want a paternity test," Dad said. "But Christina said no test was needed, and didn't argue against joint custody. She really did want the best for you."

"Yeah, she really went out of her way to be a great parent." Dad winced, and I regretted my outburst. It wasn't his fault my mother had been less than awesome, and for the eight years I lived with her, he'd never once missed an important event or a visitation with me. And after Mom abandoned me, he dropped everything to come home and become a full-time parent. Without my father, I don't know what would have become of me.

"I used to wish Tessa was my mother," I said.

He smiled, and squeezed my hand. "I understand, but I wouldn't change a thing about you. You're perfect as you are."

"You have to say that," I said, and we laughed. "Do you love Tessa now?"

"Yes. I do. Whether she'll ever love me again is up for debate, but that's something else I understand."

"Well, I'm glad you're not cursed like me, although it would have been convenient," I said. "It could have been a father-daughter bonding experience."

"Chalk it up to missed opportunities." Dad glanced into my mug. "Would you like more coffee? Or something to eat? You've been out all day."

"Yeah, I have," I said, and suddenly my exhaustion settled across me like a leaden weight. "I am pretty hungry, but I should probably go to bed."

"Eat first," Dad said, then he got up and started taking ingredients out of the fridge. While he made me a sandwich, I told him everything that had happened since that morning, from the prison, to the magic-soaked motel, to my field trip to what was left of the Beauclaire house.

"Great job destroying the house, by the way." I finished off my second pickle. "You can still smell the ashes."

"Good," Dad said. "Not only did I want to punish those who hurt you, I wanted to leave a very blatant reminder that the Moores are not to be trifled with." He ate a few potato chips. "I really wanted to kill them. All of them. It was difficult to hold back."

"How did you?"

"I didn't want you to have a murderer for a parent."

"You can kill Amir if you want," I said. "I won't mind."

"Gods willing, it won't come to that." Dad deposited our empty plates in the sink, then he faced me. "You're certain you're all right?"

"I feel better after eating," I said. "As for the rest, I don't know if I'm all right, but I'm getting there. It's just a lot, you know?"

"I do."

I stood, and hugged my dad, who was without a doubt the best man I'd ever known. "I'm going to go to bed. In the morning, we should probably look for the way into the nexus." Dad had known the house was on top of the nexus, but according to him, no one had accessed it in centuries. He wasn't sure if Gran had ever been inside it.

"I'll find that apple cookbook, since that apparently will tell us the way," he said. "Get some rest, Bug."

"Thanks, Dad. Good night."

I went upstairs, the sounds of Dad cleaning up the kitchen following me up the staircase. As I climbed the stairs I wondered which room Tessa was in, and if she and Dad had truly reconciled. I hoped they had. While I understood how my parents had fallen for each other, my father and Tess were made for each other.

My old room was the same as ever, as was the fancy Art Nouveau bathroom. After a scalding hot shower, I found an old tee shirt in the wardrobe, pulled it on, and flopped onto the bed, fully intending to sleep for a week. When I opened my eyes, Dan was lying next to me.

"Hey, babe."

Chapter 24

Sweet Rolls

"You're here!" I threw my arms around Dan and buried my face against his neck. He was so warm and solid and here that all of my lingering aches and stresses from the day before just melted away.

"I'm here," he said, then he kissed my forehead. "You really thought I wasn't doing everything I could to get back to you?"

"I didn't know what to think." His skin smelled so good, like soap and sunlight and him, and I didn't think I would ever get enough of him. "I was so worried."

"That LeClerc guy took care of everything. He's not half bad." Dan adjusted our position so he was above me, and cupped my cheek. "I missed you, baby."

"Missed you, too." I affected what I hoped was a very serious face, and said, "Next time, we escape together."

Dan smiled, then he leaned down and kissed me. Had I really been having doubts about living with this wonderful man who could turn my knees to jelly with one kiss? I was never letting go of him, not for anything.

"What's this?" Dan asked when we parted, his fingers gliding across my collarbones. I remembered seeing the bruise take shape in the mirror last night. It must have looked especially awful in the morning light.

"Oh, that?" I glanced downward, but couldn't see the bruise because of the angle. "Nathaniel throat punched me."

His forehead creased as he turned my chin from side to side, gauging how far the mark spread around my neck. "Does it hurt?"

"It's sore, but it feels better than it did last night. I can handle it."

His face darkened. "I'll kill him for hurting you."

"I punched him right back, just like you taught me."

The corner of his mouth curled up, but the concern didn't leave his eyes. "Good. Why was he close enough to hit you?"

"I summoned his wife, Jemima, so Jacob and I could ask her a few questions. She answered them, then she told me she was sick of being in between and wanted to move on. Since helping the dead get where they're going is kind of my job, I sent her on her way. Then Nathaniel showed up, and he was not pleased." Dan nodded, but he didn't stop tracing the edges of the bruise.

"Hey." I caught his hand, kissed his fingertips. "I'm okay. Promise."

"I know you are. It's just..." He gathered me against him, then shifted us so I was lying beneath him. I curled one of my legs around his waist, needing to be as close to him as I could get. "I wasn't there for you, and I should have been."

"It's okay. You got to have your own adventure," I said, then I kissed him. Dan cupped the back of my head and kissed me back so hard he stole my breath. He was wearing a plain black sweatshirt and matching sweatpants, and it took less than a minute to get them off of his body and on the floor. Then my tee shirt joined them, and I let Dan prove just how much he'd missed me.

Unlike the last time we'd—what? Made love? That was a term for soap operas and telenovelas, not something real people did—been together, this wasn't hard or fast. We took our time, and Dan showed me with every stroke and caress how much he cared for me.

Huh. Maybe we were making love.

Afterward, I laid with my head on his chest while his arm was tight around my shoulders. The morning had already gotten hot, but the windows were open and a breeze found its way into the room. Besides, there was no better feeling than snuggling under a blanket with your lover. It's not like we weren't already sweaty, anyway.

While Dan played with my hair, I recounted everything Jacob and I had been through the day before. Dan, of course, was fixated on Nathaniel's brief but memorable involvement.

"You should have seen his face after I told him Jemima wanted to move on," I said. "He was furious."

"I bet. You didn't know Beauclaire and Hassan were acquainted until Sarah Allwood told you?"

"Nope, but it's also not something I would have asked. Back when I met Amir I was deliberately not thinking about the Beauclaires."

"Still, if they've known each other for so long, and Beauclaire was so desperate to get Jemima back, why didn't he just have Hassan take him back to a time before she got sick in the first place?" Dan asked. "With modern medicine, he might have a good shot at actually saving her."

"Good question," I murmured. "Maybe Amir won't do it, or maybe he's got something on Nathaniel."

"That something would have to be pretty big," Dan said. "Might be worth figuring out."

I picked at the edge of the blanket. "If you could, would you try to go back for Charlotte?" When he didn't answer right away, I said, "I'm sorry, that's a really heavy question."

"Don't be sorry," he said. "It's okay. As to whether or not I'd want to go back, the answer is no. Even before I met you, and learned all about this magical nonsense, I wouldn't have tried a move like that.

Char was sick her whole life, so there's no way I could wind back the clock in order to have time with a healthy version of her. It was never in the cards for us."

I leaned against his shoulder. "I wish she hadn't suffered like she did. It's not fair."

Dan kissed the top of my head. "It's not, but neither is life."

"You said, even before you met me." I craned my neck around so I could see his eyes. "And now?"

"And now I know, more than ever, that some lines aren't meant to be crossed," he replied. "Char really is better off now. I'll always miss her, but she's in a good place. You helped me see that."

I settled back against him. "For a mortal, you're not half bad with all this magical nonsense."

"Hey, how about that?" he asked, clearly pleased with himself.

"So tell me what happened after I blinked out of the van."

"Not much, at first," he began. "Those fake cops brought me to the station, but when they got me out of the van, and you weren't in there with me, whatever spell was holding them snapped. I managed to slip away and observe from the edge of the parking lot, while the every officer in the station rounded them up and asked why they were impersonating the police. As near as they could figure, those guys were police officers, but back in the nineties. It was utter chaos."

"Holy shit!"

"Holy shit ain't the half of it. Anyway, Jill spotted me at about the same time LeClerc showed up, and, in an abundance of caution, the three of us left that circus behind and went to her house." Dan paused, then said, "Jill found something."

"Is it something about Amir?"

"No. It's video footage of you and your mother. It was taken in the hospital, right before she left you."

"Oh," I said, my voice shaky. "Remember Frank Pickford, Martha's husband? He found my mother's address. She lives nearby."

"Do you think all these instances are signs telling you to get back in touch with her?"

"I don't know." I rolled away from him and flopped onto my back. "I really don't want to. I've never wanted to get in touch with her, not even when I was younger. I've only ever wanted to move on with my life. I mean, she already moved on, so what good would it do to reach out?" I closed my eyes, and took a breath. "Did you watch the footage?"

"No. I thought it would be best for you to see it first."

"Thanks. Well, I guess we should get ourselves over to Jill's."

"No need. Her and Angel gave me a ride over this morning. They're here, and Jill brought the tape."

"What?" I bolted upright and stared at him. "You mean we've been laying around naked without a care in the world, and they've been downstairs waiting this whole time?"

"It hasn't been that long. Besides, it's not like they're bored. Angel's making breakfast."

I made a wordless noise of frustration, and after the shortest shower of my and possibly Dan's life, we got dressed and went down to the kitchen. I found Tessa and Jill seated at the table, while my father and a woman I assumed was Angel hovered over the stove.

"There you are," Tessa said. "I came downstairs and found strange women cooking. It was like that summer in Bruges all over again."

I looked at Jill and shrugged. "I see you've met Tessa."

"I have," Jill replied. "And that man who looks to be about twenty is your father?"

If I told Jill my dad's actual age, she might pass out. "That's Dad. And—"

"And you must be Eliza," Angel said as she embraced me. "Jill and Dan have told me so much about you! How are you, sweetheart?"

"I-I'm good, thank you." I glanced at Dan, who was grinning from ear to ear. "It's so nice of you to cook, but you didn't have to."

"It's nothing." Angel released me, then her gaze caught the bruises around my neck. "Dan filled us in on what you've been dealing with, and the last thing you need is to worry about is where your next meal is coming from. Lucky I came by to take care of you."

Angel grabbed a dish towel, then she opened the freezer, put a few ice cubes into the towel, and turned everything into a makeshift cold pack. "Here, sugar, the ice will help that ecchymosis on your neck." The oven beeped, and Dad moved to open it. "Don't you dare touch my sweet rolls," Angel warned.

"Yes, ma'am," Dad said as he backed away from the stove. "Is there anything I can do?"

"There sure is," Angel replied as she took the sweet rolls out of the oven, and set a casserole inside to warm. "You can set the table."

Dad did as he was told, and soon all six of us were enjoying breakfast. In addition to the sweet rolls, Angel had put together an egg and vegetable frittata, home fries, and a veritable mountain of bacon. All of it was delicious.

"Angel, will you come live with me?" Tessa asked after she'd finished her third sweet roll. "I can't imagine living the rest of my life without these buns."

"She has a pool," I offered.

"Thank you, but I would miss my Jill too much," Angel said, as Jill blushed at her plate.

"Bring Jill along," Tessa said. "Witches don't have nearly as many hang ups as mortals do. We can be a throuple."

"Really," Angel said. "Tell me more about this pool."

Jill dropped her fork. "Angel!"

"I'm only kidding," she demurred. "But we should talk about getting a pool."

"Speaking of a pool, what happened with the mystery SWAT team?" I asked in the worst segue way ever.

"Last I heard, it was a literal nightmare," Jill replied. "What's funny is that those guys weren't retired cops from the nineties—they were the actual guys from thirty years ago. Same gear and everything. Even the tags on the van tracked back decades." Jill eyed me as she munched a piece of bacon. "Think Hassan moved them through time?"

"He must have," I said. "Was the chief there?"

She shook her head. "He never came in to work yesterday."

"Great. I don't know what Amir's really after with dragging people and places through time, but this is getting messier by the moment."

"We know he wants the nexus," Dan said, "and we know the nexus is here. My thought is that he's creating chaos all over town to draw us away from the house, and claim the nexus for himself."

"Logical," my father agreed. "Bug, I found the cookbook."

"Cookbook?" Jill repeated, as Dad handed me the book. "Do we need that right now? I can't eat another bite."

"It's not for food," I said. "A few hundred years ago, a local witch hid her spells and maps to her treasures in a cookbook. Supposedly, one of the recipes is a way to access the nexus." I pushed my plate aside and set the cookbook in front of me. It was called Granny Apple's Magical Recipes from the Orchard, and had been written by Sarah Allwood herself.

I opened the cookbook, and frowned. "Tess, remember when you took the extra ink away from the recipes so we could read all the maps?"

"I do," she replied.

"Well, all that ink came back." I held up the book, which was open to a page for apple fritters. "So, how does one determine if a recipe is actually a spell?"

Angel held out her hand. "Give it here. I've been baking since I could reach the counter. I'll have a look and see if anything's out of place."

"Thank you," I said, as I handed the book over. Since things were going well, I figured it was a great time to kill the mood. "Dan told me you found footage of my mother?"

"I did," Jill replied. "Do you have anything that can play a video-cassette?"

"I do," Dad said as he pushed back from the table. "Follow me."

We got up from the table, and followed Dad out of the kitchen, behind the main staircase, and down to the basement. When he opened the door to the radio room, Jill gasped.

"Is this setup from the fifties?" she asked, as she entered the room. Near the doors were floor to ceiling vintage servers with built in television screens and hundreds of colored lights and toggle switches. "This must run on miles of tape."

"It did, at one time," Dad replied. "And the genesis of the room is much older than these machines." He gestured toward the rear of the room, the walls of which were covered with ancient switches and gauges. "Around the turn of the century, my mother began keeping company with a man who was somewhat of an innovator in radio waves. He built most of this for her. Over the years, we've added to it."

"You certainly have," Jill said. "Wait, you said the turn of the century. Which century are we talking about?"

Dad grinned, which made him look even younger. "The twentieth, of course. The videocassette player is over here."

He wheeled over a television on a cart, and after he navigated and plugged in a few cords, Jill put the cassette in the appropriate slot.

"Sure you want to do this?" Dan asked, as Jill fiddled with the controls.

"Yeah." My voice wavered, because I'd never been good at lying. "I mean, no, I don't, but I want to watch it so we can maybe learn something, and move on. Does that make sense?"

Dan took my hand. "It does."

Jill's gaze moved between Dan and me, then she grabbed the television controller. "All right. Hitting play."

The video cassette player whirred to life, and we watched as eight year old me slept in my hospital bed. "I'm so small," I said.

"I can't believe she left you there," Dan muttered. Jill's brows pinched, but before she could react further, my mother entered the frame.

"Is that her?" Jill asked.

"Yes," my father said. "That is exactly how Christina looked the last time I saw her."

I tightened my grip on Dan's hand. We watched as my mother approached me, and sat in the bedside chair.

"You remember any of this?" Dan asked.

I shook my head. "She brought me to the hospital and had me admitted, and I didn't see a single other person I knew until Gran came to get me out of there about a week later."

"Shit," Jill said. "That's horrible. But, your mother obviously went to visit you at least once. Why didn't she wake you up?"

"Is there any sound?" Dan asked.

"Yeah. Hang on."

Jill adjusted the controls, and my mother's voice filled the room.

"I'm so sorry, Eli," my mother said to my sleeping form. "I never meant for things to go this way. I... I only want you to be happy, but you can't be happy with me." She put her hand on my chest, or maybe it was my stomach. "I don't want you to ever, ever have to go through what I've endured, but I'm afraid there's no other way. At least, not for me."

"Pause that," Dan said, and Jill stopped the tape. "Can we enlarge this shot, and see if Lind passes anything to Eli, or otherwise introduces a foreign object?" Dan leaned closer to the screen, and continued, "And we need to know what kind of flower she has in her hair."

"You think her hair accessories harmed Eli?" Jill asked.

"Could be poisonous," Dan said.

"It is." I tapped the screen, right over my mother's freeze framed head. "It's a thornapple blossom. It was her favorite flower from Gran's solarium."

Dan rubbed his chin. "That stuff grow wild around her?"

"Yes, but I've never seen a wild specimen around here with a purple flower. Gran's thornapple flowers are purple."

"That flower's fresh, not wilted at all," Jill said. "That means your mother was at your grandmother's house—here—no more than a day or so before this was recorded."

I frowned at the television screen. "Yeah. It does." I turned toward my father. "Did she often wear thornapple blossoms?"

"Not that I recall," Dad replied. "And if she had ever worn thornapple in her hair, that's something I would remember."

"Then why was she wearing it then? Why would she even come here, alone? It's not like she got along with Gran, and wanted to pay her a visit." I stared at that flower, and felt my foresight spark at the base of my skull.

"She came here for the thornapple," I declared, then I turned on my heel and made a beeline up the stairs and to the solarium. The thornapple was in its usual place against the back wall, large and lush and laden with its pretty spiral flowers alongside the spiky green seedpods.

"Why did my mother wear your flower?" I asked the plant. "What did you offer her that nothing else could?" Gently, I touched the leaves, running them through my hands, willing a leftover shred of her essence to give me a hint as to her motivations. When I grazed a seed pod, I jerked my hand away.

I paused, then I grasped the seed pod, feeling the many thorns press against my skin. The thorns protected the seed. The plant protected its babies.

My mother had wanted to protect me.

Wracking coughs overtook me, the dry hacking shutting out the rest of the world until I was on my hands and knees. Jill and Dan tried giving me water, but Tess kept them back. She knelt beside me, and watched as I coughed up a thornapple seedpod.

"Eli, this is your curse," Tessa said, marveling at the seed pod. "It's the same shape, and it's prickly like the curse was. Why didn't I realize it was a thornapple seed?"

"How could you?" I said, the coughing have made my already hoarse voice even rougher. "She must have had the thornapple in her hair to try and make a protection spell, but she didn't know what she was doing. Instead of protecting me, she cursed me to not know my witchcraft." I wiped my eyes, found my father with my bleary gaze. "She did the best she could."

Dad went down on one knee and hugged me. "I have always believed that."

CHAPTER 25

CATS AND CROSSBOWS

As soon as I recovered from my coughing fit, and could breathe again, we moved back to the kitchen. Dan and Jill washed the myriad dishes and pans that had been used for breakfast, while Tessa, Angel and I sat at the table. Tessa scrutinized the seed pod I'd hacked up while Angel flipped through the apple cookbook, and I slowly drank milk hoping it would soothe my much abused throat. As for my father, he was rooting through a broom closet looking for the house's blueprints.

"This doesn't make sense as a protection spell," Tessa muttered. "Or as a curse."

"What is thornapple used for?" I asked.

"Mostly as an oracle," Tessa replied. She blinked, and faced me. "Perhaps the thornapple in your system is why your foresight never seemed helpful. Its prophetic abilities could have disrupted your natural talents."

I eyed the seedpod that had been magically hibernating inside me for the last twenty years. "Maybe. I'm just glad it's out of me."

"Found them," Dad called out from the closet. We watched him back out from behind the door, his arms laden with folders and rolled up papers. He brought them to the kitchen table and started rifling through the house's building plans.

"This is the oldest plan," Dad said, carefully setting a coffee mug on the paper so it wouldn't re-roll up. The paper was so brittle I worried the mug's weight would leave a hole in it. "However, there was a house here long before this was drawn up."

"Do you know when the original was built?" Jill asked, from the sink.

"I don't think anyone does," Dad replied. "Maybe Ma did, but she never told me."

"Or me," I said. I leafed through the less fragile plans, and unrolled one on top of the ancient parchment. "This one seems newer, but with more details."

"And it's labeled in a language I can read," Angel said. She still had the cookbook in hand, but eyed the plans over the top of the pages. "What was that other one written in?"

"Occitan," Tessa replied. "It's spoken in southern France, and a few other places."

Angel's gaze slid back to Dad. "Is your family French?"

"No, no," Dad replied. "Historically, the Moores—my mother's family, the ones who built this home—hail from northwest England. Lancashire, thereabouts. My father was Indian."

"No French, then." Angel set down the cookbook, using her finger to hold her place. "Were these English and Indian ancestors architects?"

"They weren't, but trades mean very little in our community," Dad replied. "With magic on your side, one can accomplish almost anything."

"Jacob says something similar," I murmured, then I jerked my chin toward the cookbook. "Find anything nexusy in there?"

"Not a thing," Angel replied. "These are all standard recipes for cakes, pies, what not. I have to say, even though the illustrations are line drawings, they're positively mouthwatering."

"I wonder if Sarah drew them." I squinted at the building plan, willing them to tell me something. They remained frustratingly silent. Jill wiped her hands on a towel, then she stood behind Angel and examined the plans.

"This house had five floors at one time?" she asked. "What happened to the top two?"

We all looked at Dad, and he shrugged. "Perhaps there was storm damage?" he suggested.

"Wait, I don't think it's really five," I said, tracing the room layouts with my fingertip. "This floor is really the basement, along with the wine cellar, radio room, and all the other stuff down there."

"You have a wine cellar?" Jill asked.

Tessa winked at her. "They do, and it's magnificent. I would be happy to take you and Angel on a tour."

"Then here's the first floor, and second," I continued, ignoring Tessa's flirting with an entire married couple, "which seem like the second and third because of how the basement's labeled. The third floor—fourth on the plans—isn't much of a living space. It's more of a weird lopsided attic. What looks like the top floor is the cupola."

"What's in the cupola?" Jill asked.

"We don't go up there," was my rote reply, then I felt a bit of magic loosen and fall into place inside me, like a key fitting into a lock. I looked at my father, and asked, "Why don't we go up there?"

"It's where I go when I need to defend the house," he replied, then he tugged the plans toward him. "See this big room on the second floor? It's the library, and these are the spiral stairs that lead up to the tower. Along the staircase there are cabinets packed with weapons, should I need them."

"What kind of weapons?" Dan asked, finally coming to join us. I guess that meant the dishes were done.

"Crossbows, mostly," Dad replied. "I also have slings for throwing spells and other types of missiles."

"No guns?" Dan asked.

"Alex doesn't need a gun," Tessa said, with a hint of pride in her voice. Great, now she was flirting with half of the room. "His accuracy is legendary."

Dan grunted. "You're a marksman in more ways than one."

"I suppose I am," my father allowed, ever the modest one. "And everyone is allowed into the cupola. The only person Ma or I ever told not to go up there was—" Dad blinked. "Christina. Ma asked Christina not to go back up there."

"Back up?" I repeated. "Why did she go up there in the first place?"

"For a very short time, Christina lived here," Dad replied. "She put a few boxes of her things in the tower room, thinking it would be a good spot for storage. Ma worried the boxes would be in the way, and asked her not to do that. As far as I know, the boxes are still up there."

"You haven't been up there in almost thirty years?" Jill asked.

"We haven't been attacked in that time," Dad replied. "Don't worry, the cabinets remain stocked."

"While I think it's great that you could wage war on the neighborhood," Angel began, "according to this plan, the tower has two floors."

Dad, Tess and I looked at Angel, then we turned as one and regarded the plan of the cupola she was pointing to. "That's just the cupola," I began, but Angel shook her head.

"What about this staircase in the back of the room?" she asked. "It's on the other side from the spiral staircase, and it doesn't go below the tower. It goes up."

"But, there isn't another room," I said. "You can tell when you look at the house from the outside. The cupola is freestanding, with a three hundred sixty degree view. Nothing is adjacent to it, not even the attic."

"Could it be roof access?" Dan asked. "Maybe there's a hatch?"

"Or maybe it's the nexus," Tessa said. We all looked up at the ceiling.

"I thought it would be underground," I said. "Since Amir's building tunnels, and all."

"So did I," my father murmured. "Could an all-powerful portal have been hovering over our heads all this time, and we never noticed?"

"It's easy to not notice things you aren't looking for," Dan said. "Gotta keep an open mind when you investigate. Eli knows," he added, flashing me a smile.

"But what about the cats?" I blurted out, and the tingling at the base of my skull told me why I'd said that: foresight. I turned to Angel, and asked, "Does that cookbook have any recipes that mention cats?"

"You know, there is one." Angel opened the cookbook to the page she'd marked earlier. "It's not in the name, or the ingredients—thank god—but there are three cats in the illustration." She handed me the book. On the page was a towering apple cake set on a pedestal. Around the base of the pedestal were three cats: a gray, a tabby, and a calico. "I noticed it, because who would let cats up on the table with their baking?"

"Someone who needed them to guard something," I said, then I handed the book to my father. "Where did Gran get the cats?"

"These were your grandmother's cats?" Jill demanded. "Is everyone immortal around here?"

"The cats are spirits," I replied, then I faced Dad. "I remember her telling me they were hers when she was little. Where did she get them?"

"Ma had the cats her whole life," Dad said. "I don't know where they came from."

"They were here before Helena was born," Tessa said. "I remember when I first came to the area with the rest of the Beauclaires. The cats followed Helena's mother, Elizabeth, around constantly."

I looked at my father, and we turned as one toward the solarium doors. There, seated in a neat row across the threshold, was the Feline Federation.

"We've always called them our first line of defense, but they're really the last line," I said, my foresight sparking all sorts of connections that I would have made years ago but for the thornapple's spines impeding me. "You guys are here to guard the nexus, aren't you?"

Pumpkin padded over to me, so I picked her up. She purred, and put her paw on my cheek. "You've all done a great job. Thank you."

"Okay, so we've got cats for guardians and crossbows for defense," Dan said. "What's next? Do we go have a look at this nexus?"

All three of the cats hissed. "He was just asking," I admonished them. "Being that we don't know exactly what the nexus is, other than powerful, I think we should stay away from it for now."

"Agreed," my father said. "As long as Amir is in play, we need to concentrate on defending it. I'm not even sure if we can enter the nexus, so let's leave that debate for another time."

"Then what do we do now?" Jill asked.

I stroked Pumpkin's head, and said, "I think the first thing we need to do is check on Chief Renault."

CHAPTER 26

MAGIC ON THE ROOF

Dan, Jill, and I were chosen to go to Chief Renault's place to figure out how he fit into everything. It made sense, since Jill's car was already here, and she was also concerned about her boss. My father and Tessa were going to continue checking over the house for signs of nexus-like activity, whatever that was supposed to be, and look through some of Gran's old paperwork for additional clues. As for Angel, she was going to stay behind and bake stuff from Sarah Allwood's cookbook, because she loved baking and hated Chief Renault.

"I wouldn't say she hates the chief," Jill said, as she pulled away from Gran's house. "They just don't see eye to eye."

"Yeah, when she screamed at him at the Christmas party a few years back, they were hardly eye to eye at all," Dan said. "More like nose to nose, and at each other's throats."

"Ooo, what happened at the party?" I asked from the back seat. I'd been relegated to the rear of the vehicle because I'm short, and Dan supposedly needed additional legroom in the passenger seat. Whatever. He was so riding in the back on the return trip.

Jill sighed. "To this day, I'm not really sure. Chief had had a few beers and made a joke, and Angel called out his crude behavior."

"Is Chief often crude?"

"Not usually, but he had a rough few years after his divorce," Jill replied. "He's much better now. Or rather, he was until this whole enchantment deal started up." She met my gaze in the rearview mirror. "Think he'll be okay?"

"I honestly don't know," I replied. "There are a lot of factors in play here. We don't know who enchanted him, or how. It's entirely possible he got roped into this situation because of some other bargain he struck, and now he needs to deal with the consequences."

"A bargain?" Jill repeated. "Like, a deal with fairies?"

"Basically," I replied. "If he accepted help from something or someone supernatural, whatever he's doing now could be him keeping up his side of the deal."

Jill glanced at Dan. "Have you made any of these bargains?"

"I let Eli do the talking in supernatural situations," Dan replied. "The last thing I need is to end up as some goblin's bitch for the next hundred years."

We laughed, then Jill asked, "Eli, can you tell me how old your father is?"

I hesitated, wondering why she wanted to know something so specific about my father. Then again, my dad and I appeared to be about the same age, and I could understand how that was off-putting to mortals. I mentally ran down a list of age-related spells, and decided that sharing the truth with Jill wouldn't harm Dad.

"He's one hundred and seventeen years old," I replied.

"Shit, really?" I could see Jill's eyes widen in the mirror's reflection. She was blinking rapidly, and I wondered if she should pull over before she had a traffic accident. "Wait, you're an only child, right?"

"Um, yeah."

"So he was in his eighties when he had his first kid?"

"Yeah."

Jill and Dan shared a look. "That's wild," she said.

I shrugged. "Want to know how old Tessa is?"

"No," Jill replied. "Let me get my head around this factoid before you barrage me with others."

Jill turned into Renault's apartment complex. "It's so weird that he has an apartment, and not a house," I said. "Imagine living a few doors or floors away from the chief of police. That's got to be stressful."

"After the divorce, he wasn't doing well financially," Jill said as she parked. "He was thrilled to get this place."

"Did his wife take it all?"

"No, they separated as amicably as possible, but they didn't have much to begin with. And half of not much is hardly anything at all." We exited the car, and Jill pointed toward the far building. "That's his building. Second floor."

Dan clapped his hands together. "All right, let's move." He took two steps, then he swiveled and turned toward at the building closest to us.

"What is it?" I asked.

"Magic on the roof," he said. "A lot of it. Feels like the same magic from the motel."

I blew out a breath. "Okay, let's check it out."

"What if it's unrelated?" Jill asked.

"Then we move on," I said. "You're right, whatever's going on up there could just be a few witches performing a harmless spell and have nothing to do with what we're after. But, it could also be whatever's powering the enchantment on Renault."

Jill nodded. "Okay. Up it is."

We climbed up the fire escape, me in the lead and Dan taking the rear, since there was no reason to barge through the building and disturb the residents. When we got to the top of the ladder I situated myself on the roof, and waited for Jill and Dan to join me. Once we were all safely on the roof, I asked Dan, "Where's the magic coming from?"

He jerked his chin toward a jumble of structures that appeared to house the building's heating and cooling systems. "Behind all of that. Follow me."

Dan's hand reflexively went for his gun, but of course it wasn't there, and he clenched his fist in the empty air. Once all of this was behind us, I needed to talk to Jill about getting Dan his badge back. He might claim he didn't care about losing his job, but he was born to help people. Dan approached the far side of the air conditioning unit, then he stopped dead and raised his hands.

"It's okay," he said. "I'm unarmed. Are you okay, Jada?"

Jada? I pointed to the far side of the unit. Jill understood my meaning and circled around behind. While she did that, I approached Dan. When I saw what he was staring at, I almost choked.

Chief Renault was tied to a wooden chair, his head and shoulders caked with dried blood. Jada stood over him brandishing a broken glass bottle and a scowl that could curdle milk.

"You're here, too?" Jada said when she saw me. "Of course you are. It's your mission to ruin my life."

"It's not," I said. "What happened to Renault? Did you come here to protect him?"

"Did he hurt you?" Dan asked.

"He was bothering me," Jada shrieked. "Every day, barging into my room and telling me all about the stupid, stupid things he did. Why did he think I cared about any of that? I don't!"

"I thought you were writing stuff down because Nathaniel asked you too," I said. "Weren't you also writing down your dreams? Or was it your memories?"

"That was stupid, too." Jada glanced at Renault, and wrinkled her nose. "And the worst part is that Nathaniel hasn't even been by in days, and I was so bored and then Renault came over after you got arrested yesterday." She shrugged. "Sorry about that."

"Don't worry about it," Dan said. "We're good. So, what happened after Renault showed up?"

"I told him I didn't want to write anything down, and he yelled at me," Jada began, her voice going shrill. "He yelled at me! Then I told him Nathaniel wouldn't like him talking to me that way, and he called me a dumb girl, and I hit him!"

I recalled my session with the punching bag. "You hit Renault hard enough to knock him out?"

"No, it wasn't hard at all, but it did something to him. Short-circuited his brain, or something. After he stood there drooling for a while, I told him to take me to Nathaniel. He brought me here, to the roof, and Nathaniel hasn't come by at all!"

"Not coming by is a dick move on Nathaniel's part," I said, and Jada nodded furiously. "So you tied Renault to the chair?"

"I had to," Jada shrieked. "He said he was going to leave, but he won't tell me where Nathaniel is! Someone needs to tell me something! I am so sick and tired of everyone treating me like a baby!"

"We're not going to treat you like a baby," Dan said. "You're a grown woman. I'm sorry if others treated you badly, but we won't. But we do need to get Renault some medical attention."

"He doesn't deserve it!"

"That's not for us to decide," Dan said. "I'm no doctor, and neither is Eli. Let's call in some experts, and get him some help."

While Dan did his best impression of a hostage negotiator, I scanned the area. We seemed to be on a regular roof that topped a regular apartment building, but something had to have drawn Amir to this location. Enchanting Renault was a good way to infiltrate our lives, but there must have already been some sort of an inroad.

Amir made grand plans, but he was lazy. He'd always liked to have a significant portion of his work done by others.

There's something here, but what? In the far corner of the roof was an old wooden pigeon coop; apparently someone used to keep birds up here. It was little more than a heap of weathered wood and rusted chicken wire, but something within the coop shone. I moved to the side, and confirmed it was the same bright blue as the other globs of Amir's magic we'd found around town. Before I could investigate further, Jill reached Renault.

"He's alive," she said, her fingers having found the pulse in his neck. "I'm calling an ambulance."

"Don't you dare," Jada shrieked as she spun around toward Jill. While her attention was on Jill, Dan stepped forward and grabbed the broken bottle from her hand.

"We only want to help him," Dan said, as he tossed the bottle behind him. "We can help you, too, if you let us."

"I don't need your help," Jada screamed. "I am so sick of everyone helping me!" She paced back and forth, her hands tearing at her hair.

"Jada," I said, as I took a step toward her. "I'm sorry."

"This is all your fault," she screamed, then she charged at me.

Dan pulled me out of the way, and Jada sailed past me toward the edge of the roof.

Her foot hit the raised edge at full speed.

She was moving too fast to stop herself, and she went over the edge.

I screamed and tried to follow her. Dan held me back.

"Stay here," he ordered. "Sanders, how long on the paramedics?"

"On their way," she replied.

Dan went to the edge and looked over. He closed his eyes, then he herded me away from the edge. "Don't look."

"I have to!"

"No, you don't."

"You two need to get out of here," Jill said. "I'll say I came by to check on Renault, and found him up here with Morales. My story will check out, but you're already in too much trouble."

"We can't run," I said. "This is all my fault."

Jill took my hand, and used her other sleeve to wipe my cheek. "It's not. I know you feel responsible for her death, but she was troubled. I've seen it often enough to recognize the signs. She did what she did of her own free will, not because of anything you said or did." A siren wailed in the distance. "Go. If you talk to Angel before I do, tell her I'm all right."

"We will," Dan said. "Eli, is there any other way off this roof?"

My gaze landed on the pigeon coop, and my foresight sparked. "This way."

Chapter 27

Tunnels in Time

D an flung open the front of the pigeon coop and we rushed inside. Jill was right; if Dan and I were found at this crime scene, after having also been present at Ned's death and subsequently arrested at the motel, it wouldn't look good for either one of us. We were innocent, but how would we convince the mortal authorities of what really happened?

And, I wasn't totally innocent. Not about Jada.

"Dan," I began, but he held up a hand.

"Where are we?" he demanded.

"The pigeon coop," I replied, but the words died on my lips. We'd walked into the pigeon coop, but we weren't surrounded by any bird nests or feathers. Instead, we were in a tunnel.

An underground, dirt-walled tunnel.

Dan touched the dirt walls. "How…" he began, then he shook his head. "Did you know this was here?"

"Obviously not," I said, because who expects the entrance to a tunnel to be attached to a rooftop pigeon coop? I sure didn't. "I thought there might be some stairs in here leading back to ground level."

"We're at ground level, all right." Dan turned back the way we came, and we saw paramedics and firefighters burst onto the roof and crowd around Jill and Renault. "Let's get moving before anyone tries to follow us."

"We don't even know where this tunnel goes," I said, remembering the gloomy tunnel at the old Beauclaire home Jacob and I had specifically avoided.

"At this point, it's better than getting arrested," Dan said, then he turned toward the darkness.

I grabbed his arm. "Is this even safe?"

"You tell me." When I remained rooted in place, he cupped my face with his hands. "I'm not going to let anything happen to you."

"I'm more worried about something happening to you." I saw myself reflected in his dark eyes, and said something that broke my heart, even if it was for his own good. "You should stay away from me."

"How am I going to do that when we're stuck in a tunnel together?"

"Dan." I turned away from him, and crossed my arms over my stomach. "Everyone who comes near me ends up hurt or dead. Just stay away."

"No." He put his arms around me. When I struggled he tightened his arms, keeping my back pressed against his chest. "No. I am not going to stay away from you, and no, everyone around you does not end up hurt or dead."

"They do," I wailed. "Ned, Jada, Jacob... everyone near me gets hurt." Even though I'd told him to stay away from me, I clutched Dan's arms as if he was my lifeline. "I can't let you get hurt, too. Not again."

"Nothing that happened to those people was your fault," he said, his mouth close to my ear. "You didn't even know Ned or Jacob before they died. You were a kid when Jada got possessed. And nothing that ever happened to me was your fault. None of this is your fault." Dan turned me around, forcing me to look at him. "Even if you were somehow to blame, it doesn't matter. I'm not leaving you. Never, not for any reason."

I pressed my cheek against his throat. "Why are you so stubborn?"

"I could ask you the same question." We stood there, holding each other for a moment. "Why do you want to get rid of me so badly? Was giving you a house key too much, too soon?"

"Yes. No." I took a breath, and started over. "I love and appreciate the key so much. So, so much... But you've already been through so many awful things. If anything more happens to you, it'll kill me." I stood on my toes, so my eyes were level with his. "I don't want you to go, but I want you to be safe. If you being safe means you have to be far away from me, then that's what I want."

"Baby, no one's safe," he said. "Not a single person is getting out of this existence alive. Living is a risk, and there's no one I'd rather risk it with than you."

Fresh tears flowed down my face. "Okay. I guess you can stay. But be careful!"

"I'll be as careful as you are." He pulled me closer, and let me cry against his chest. The rational part of my mind understood that I was freaking out over Jada's sudden and violent death, and the injuries she'd inflicted on Renault. The rest of me wanted to wrap Dan in cotton wool and keep him hidden away from the monsters of the world.

A tiny part of me wondered if I was one of the monsters.

"I'm so sorry," I said at length. "You must think I'm a mess."

"Be messy, if that's what you need." He kissed my hair. "However, we should probably get moving before someone decides to look inside this pigeon coop."

I glanced over my shoulder, and saw all the first responders milling around the roof. "Jill seems to have things under control."

"Jill knows her stuff."

I stepped back from Dan and wiped my face, then I looked down the tunnel. "I guess we should see where this goes."

"Lead the way."

We headed further down the tunnel. "I think this is one of Amir's time tunnels."

"It's definitely magical, and not just because technically we're thirty feet above ground." Dan gestured toward the walls. "Notice how it's not very dark?"

I hadn't noticed, but Dan was right. While the tunnel was gloomy, I had no problem seeing what was around me, and what was ahead of us. "The tunnel at the old Beauclaire house seemed to go underground. I wonder if Amir built all of these, or he just took advantage of tunnels that already existed. It also explains how Renault got involved in all of this."

"How so?"

"If a tunnel already existed near Renault's home, then it would be easy for Amir to enchant him. I've been wondering how Renault got drawn into all of this, since he's a wild card, and I bet he was just in the wrong place at the wrong time." Dan brought my hand to his mouth and kissed my knuckles. "What was that for?"

"We made a deal, remember? I let you tattoo me, and I get to kiss you whenever I want," he said, referencing the one and only tattoo I'd ever given anyone, which happened to be the mark that allowed Dan to sense magic.

"And you wanted to kiss me now, while we're walking down a tunnel that might lead to actual hell?"

He shrugged. "What can I say, I like kissing you. If we end up in hell, I'll kiss you there, too." He jerked his chin toward an opening in the side of the tunnel. "What's that?"

"It looks like a room." We stepped into the space, and saw that it had the same dirt floor as the tunnels, but the walls and ceiling were stone. Dan dropped my hand, and touched the gray walls.

"Remember when I was possessed, and my mind was sent elsewhere?" he began. "I was in a room like this, only it was closed. All walls, no exit."

"I wonder how many of these rooms there are down here," I said. "When Amir kidnapped the witch elders, he might have put them in one." I glanced at Dan, saw his rigid posture. "Let's get out of here."

"No arguments here."

We continued on, me clutching Dan's hand so we wouldn't get separated. That, and I was still on edge, and craved physical contact with him. I didn't like being so needy, so I limited myself to holding his hand and resisted wrapping my arms around him while we walked. Once all of this was behind us, I planned to lie on top of his chest for a week.

After we'd walked for what felt like half of an hour, he said, "It's lighter up ahead."

"It's... it's a garden." A gap in the side of the tunnel opened up onto a well-maintained green lawn. Directly in front of us was a raised bed, and the front row of plants were aconite, foxglove, and belladonna. The back corner of the bed had a gigantic white snakeroot looming over the neat border. "Dan, we're in your backyard."

Dan shook his head. "No, it's not. That's my yard."

He pointed toward an image that hung in the air like a magical projection screen, and he was right. The image was his backyard, and we were standing in his backyard's twin.

"Someone made a copy of your yard," I murmured, but as I scoped out the area I realized it wasn't an exact copy. There was no stockade fence, and the stone pathways and batting cage were missing. The only real similarities were the raised garden bed with the poisonous plants, the shed that Amir had used as a portal, and the greenhouse.

"Amir mimicked your poison garden," I said. "Charlotte grew the plants, but he harvested their essence. That must be why he bothered enchanting Charlotte in the first place. He got the benefit of having baneful herbs grown in local soil without having to do the work." I shook my head. "Tess always said his biggest flaw was his laziness."

Dan crouched next to the corner of the raised bed, thankfully not on the side with the white snakeroot, and poked at the mulch. "What's this," he mumbled, then he dug something shiny out of the soil. "It's... a necklace?" He held his find out to me on his palm, and I could hardly believe what I was seeing.

"It's my necklace." I picked up my sapphire necklace that I hadn't seen for over three years. "I bought this when I lived in Paris, and wore it every day until it went missing."

"Looks like Hassan stole it," Dan said. "But, why?"

"Probably to maintain a connection with me." I stuffed the necklace in my pocket, then I turned toward the image of Dan's yard. "That image appears to be a portal."

"By portal, you mean we could theoretically step through it, and into my actual yard."

"Theoretically, yes." I shrugged. "I've never actually seen one of these before."

"Me neither." Dan shook out his arms, then he reclasped my hand. "Okay. Let's do it."

"Shouldn't we follow the tunnel, instead?"

"If it's a portal, won't it work from both sides?"

"Um, sure. I guess."

"Then we can always come back."

I blew out a breath. "All right. Let's go to your place."

We stepped through the portal, which was as underwhelming as walking from the living room into the kitchen. Dan let go of my hand and walked further into the yard, gaping at everything around him.

"This isn't right," Dan said. "My yard never looks this beat." He scuffed the tall grass with his shoe. "It looks like this place hasn't been mowed in a month."

"It's not just the grass," I said, pointing to all the fallen leaves. I turned around in a circle, and noticed how the trees that had been green just yesterday were covered in yellow and gold. "Wait. I think we're in the past. Or maybe we're in the future. It's autumn."

Dan gazed at all the fallen leaves and dry grass, and frowned. "Does that mean we've been walking through that tunnel for a month?"

"Your guess is as good as mine." Dan moved toward the kitchen door, but I grabbed his arm. "What are you doing?"

"I'm going inside the house."

"I don't think that's a good idea. We don't know if we're a month on from when we were, or a few years. What if someone else lives here?"

"When we were." Dan shook his head. "Okay, what do you suggest?"

"You're asking me as if I have experience in time travel."

He grinned. "Let's face it, this is more your wheelhouse than mine."

In spite of everything, I returned his smile. "Maybe we should go back to the tunnel, and try to find our own time."

"This is rapidly turning into the plot of a bad science fiction movie."

"Are there any good science fiction movies?"

He gave me some side eye. "Because I love you, I am going to forget you said that."

I looped my arm with his, and kissed his cheek. "Come on, before anyone spots us."

We went back through the portal and into the tunnel, and walked away from Amir's poison garden. The tunnel kept its eerie blue glow, and aside from our footfalls, it was deathly quiet.

"I do not like it here," I said, just to hear something.

"Me neither," Dan said. "Is walking through here like going through one of those forbidden time slips?"

"I know almost nothing about time slips. If we ever get out of here I'll have to ask Jacob."

"Can you summon him? We could probably use his help."

"I don't know if that's a good idea, what with him being a spirit. He could end up trapped here." The light increased up ahead. "Look, I think it's another portal."

"This ought to be interesting."

We stepped through the portal, and blinked at the bright sunlight. While my eyes adjusted I realized that it was hot, which meant we were in summer. I just hoped it was our summer, not summer ten or a hundred years from now.

"Where are we?" I asked.

"Cemetery." Dan indicated the headstones. "Looks like we're in time for services."

A group of mourners was assembled around an open grave. The priest stood at the front, giving a speech about how tragic it was when a life was cut short. Floral arrangements surrounded the coffin, and I could hear people weeping.

"There aren't very many people," I said; the last funeral I'd been to was Gran's, and hundreds of people had turned out to pay their respects. There were barely a dozen people present at this service.

"Could have been an older person, who didn't have a lot of family left," Dan suggested, then a woman turned and I saw her profile.

"She looks familiar," I murmured, then I realized why I recognized her. She looked like an older version of Jada. I was looking at her mother.

"Dan, those are Jada's parents," I said. "This is her funeral."

"Then we're only a few days, maybe a week from where we're supposed to be," he said. "We must have gone back in time after we left our backyard." Dan pulled me toward the portal, but I remained rooted in place. "Eli, we've got to keep moving."

"Shouldn't we pay our respects?" I asked. "Shouldn't I tell her parents I'm sorry?"

"If it was a bad idea to go inside our house, then it's a bad idea to get involved here."

I nodded. "You're right. Let's go."

We turned back toward the portal. I was almost all the way through when someone yelled my name.

"Don't look," Dan said, but I'd already turned back.

Amir had spotted us.

"Ellie Moore, false Mistress of Seers," he yelled. "Using time slips, are you? Can't follow your own rules?"

"Ignore that asshole," Dan said as he pulled me farther into the portal.

"I'll have you banished," Amir shrieked. "I'll have you tried and executed for Jada's murder! I'll end you, Ellie!"

Dan and I jumped through the portal and ran.

CHAPTER 28

IT'S A MAP

We ran away from the cemetery and deeper into the tunnel, heedless of where or when we were going. For all we knew, we'd end up somewhere worse than Jada's funeral, but we had to take our chances. We knew what was behind us, and that was enough reason to run.

Eventually, we needed to rest. We found a small offshoot from the tunnel that appeared to be blocked by a cave in. It was dark, and quiet, but most importantly it was just Dan and me; no Amir, no mourners, no accusers. For the moment, we were safe.

"That was bad," I said, after I caught my breath. "Very, very bad."

"I don't think anyone followed us," Dan said.

I looked back the way we'd run. Even though the tunnel emitted an eerie glow, the way we'd come from was as black as the tomb. "Amir was waiting for us."

"How could he do that?" Dan demanded. "I thought Tessa bound him to one time."

"He's been bound and reprimanded numerous times, and he's always found a way around it," I said. "He's slippery like an eel."

"No argument there." Dan took my hands. "What else has he done? He's got you beyond freaked out."

"When we were in Paris, Amir collected bones," I began. "Tessa thought he was amassing the residual energy and power from the dead, but some members of the Paris coven thought he was trying to raise an army."

"An army of skeletons?" Dan shook his head. "What happened to those bones?"

"Tessa and I returned them." I remembered the dozens of trips Tessa and I had made to cemeteries and churches in order to return all the bones Amir had stolen. Some of the caretakers appreciated us putting things right. Many thought we were part of the problem. "But that was years ago. Since then, he could have collected more. And we just saw him in a cemetery."

Dan grunted. "We should keep moving. You good, or you need another minute?"

"I'm good."

I let Dan pull me to my feet, and after an all too brief embrace, we continued on through the darkness.

"I wish we had a map," I grumbled.

"I wish we knew if we were moving backward or forward in time," Dan said. "Time in this place isn't moving in a linear fashion like it's supposed to. It's like Hassan shook up the days and weeks like a cup of dice."

"I wonder if that's on purpose," I mused. "Maybe we're not the first to stumble into these tunnels. If he lures people in here, maybe he's using these out of order days and weeks to disorient them."

"It's working," Dan said. "Seeing our house all run down like that freaked me out, and I hate being freaked out."

"You didn't seem upset."

"I didn't want to upset you." He held out his arm, and I slid my own arm around his waist as his came around my shoulders. "There's very little I have to offer in these situations. All I can really do is keep you focused and protect you from physical threats."

"That is not true," I said. "I don't need a bodyguard. I need you." He squeezed me against him. "I'm serious. If you weren't with me, I think I'd be hiding behind Tess right now."

"Not true," he said. "You were kicking ass and taking names long before I started tagging along. I read all your old case files, remember?"

My face warmed at the memory of a stubborn police detective who would not stop sticking his nose into my business. "I remember." I wracked my brain, trying to think of what I could say to Dan to make him understand how much he meant to me, but I've never been good with words. He wasn't either, since the act that had convinced me of how much he loved me—besides the bleeding hearts popping up all over town—was when he'd let me tattoo him.

Dan's tattoo...

"Can you still sense magic in here?" I asked, and he affirmed he could. "Has it changed?"

"It comes and goes," he replied. "The tunnel itself seems like it's seen a lot of magic. It lingers, almost like a cooking odor."

"Are you saying Amir's magic is like when you microwave fish?"

"Yeah, stinky and unwanted." He laughed, and I wrinkled my nose. "But now that you mention it, when we step out into the real world—assuming these scenes really are the real world and not some other form of mind fuckery—there's no magic. It's all in here."

"Huh." I untangled myself from Dan and approached the tunnel walls. I was no expert, but they seemed like regular packed dirt. "How are these dirt walls not collapsing? Something must be shoring them up."

"Magic?" Dan stood behind me, his chest warm against my back, and touched the wall. "Yeah, it's in there."

"Interesting." I put my hand on top of Dan's, and visualized old, peeling wallpaper. Moments later, the topmost layers of dirt peeled away from the wall, leaving behind a network of colored lines.

"Did you do that?" Dan asked.

"I did. I asked the tunnel to show me the magic that lay beneath."

Dan leaned closer to the wall. "This looks like a map of the subway system."

"You're such a New Yorker," I began, then I paused. "What if this is a map? What if we can follow the lines wherever—whenever—we want?"

He trailed his fingertips over the rainbow hued lines. Some of the lines were hair thin, and some were wider than his thumb, and some sparkled like glitter glue. "Which one should we follow?"

"Which is the most powerful?"

"This one." Without hesitation, he tapped a reddish orange line. "Wherever this leads, it's somewhere important."

"All right. Lead the way, magic man."

Dan kissed my temple, then he followed the line while I peeled away the top layer of earth; even though Dan was tracking it magically, I wanted to know if the line suddenly broke, or met up with any other lines. Magic has a tendency to be sneaky, but the orange line continued strong. Eventually, it led us to yet another portal.

"Ready?" Dan asked.

"As I'll ever be."

We clasped hands, and stepped out of the tunnel.

And almost fell into a charred pit.

CHAPTER 29

LET'S GO BACK TO WHEN IT ALL BEGAN

"**G**et back," Dan said as he looped his arm around my waist. "That's got to be fifteen feet deep, maybe twenty. Is it a mass grave?"

I shuddered, assuming Amir had taken his bone collecting and grave robbing to a new and awful level... Then I realized that this place was familiar.

"This is a cellar," I said. "It reminds me of what's left of the Beauclaire house."

"Whatever this place was, it burned recently." Dan pointed at some glowing red pockets in the hole. "It's still smoldering."

"What could have destroyed a house so thoroughly," I wondered, then I looked at the area around the charred bits. Behind the hole was the rose garden with its stone benches, and the carriage house that had been converted into a garage. Horror threatening to choke me, I looked down.

Dan and I were standing on Gran's gravel driveway.

"This is Gran's house," I whispered. "What's left of it. We're still in the future, and Amir must have come for the nexus."

"Does this mean he won?"

"No. If my father couldn't defend the house, he would have destroyed it." I swallowed, and returned my gaze to the smoldering cellar hole. "This is his work. When he destroyed the Beauclaire house, this was how he left it."

"But that was an act of revenge," Dan said. "Wouldn't Alex be trying to protect his family's house?"

"What he did to the Beauclaires was protection, too. He was protecting me from them ever coming after me again."

Dan snorted. "No offense, but if that's the case, why is Nathaniel still after you? It's like him and Hassan have been fighting over you for decades."

I blinked, and faced Dan. "What if they have been fighting over me? Well, not me exactly, but what I can do?"

"Or maybe, what you represent," Dan said. "Hassan wants power, and he thinks you're the ticket to him ruling seers and witches. Nathaniel also wants power, and not in a very different way."

"And he used Jemima as an excuse to get to me," I said. "Let's see if these tunnels can show us how this all started."

Dan's brows pinched. "You don't think we should look for Alex or Tess? Or the cats?"

"This is the future we want to prevent," I said. "I order to do that, we need to know exactly how we got here."

"Wait, when do you want to go?"

"I want to talk to Jemima, before she died."

Despite that I'd come up with the dubious plan of traveling back in time over three hundred years, Dan was all for giving it a try. We really needed to have a talk about him being more critical of my ideas.

After a bit of trial and error, we found the colored line in the tunnel wall that felt older than the rest. We followed it for a time, and eventually it brought us to a portal. We stepped out of the tunnel and into the middle of the eighteenth century, which was when Nathaniel's wife, Jemima Allwood Beauclaire, was still alive.

At least, I assumed she was still alive. We were just going to have to see for ourselves.

"Where are we?" I asked, once we were outside the tunnel.

"We're in the center of town," Dan replied. "Look, that's Main Street, and there's Pleasant Street."

I followed his gaze, and realized that the dirt roads were the bones of what would later become the bustling downtown I was used to. The city I looked at now was hardly more than a trade outpost, with the area that had been home to my apartment and my favorite coffee shop little more than a few wooden and brick structures surrounded by dirt roads. That moment was when it hit me: we'd done it. We'd gone back in time.

In the next moment, I realized that our twenty-first century clothing was going to cause some problems.

"Crap, I forgot about our clothes." Dan was still wearing his black sweats, which were out of place but workable. I, on the other hand, was wearing jeans and a fitted tee shirt. In other words, I had on less clothing than the town prostitutes. I retreated to an alleyway, and said, "I need to steal a cloak, or a dress."

"Why can't you just make yourself blend in, the way Tessa does?" Dan asked.

"I've never tried."

He took my hands. "Try now."

"Okay." I closed my eyes, and thought about how Tessa cast her obfuscation spell. She'd cast the same spell so many times it only took her a moment to focus her intent, but I took my time. After all, I needed this to work. Who knows how the locals would react to the sight of us in our modern attire.

Finally, I squeezed Dan's hands, and declared, "Unseen."

"Is that it?" he asked.

I opened my eyes, saw his brow creased with concern. "It should be. I guess we'll find out."

"Stay behind me," Dan said, and we ventured onto the street. There were several people going about their day, which meant plenty of opportunities for us to be discovered. "I'm going to walk toward that building." He pointed to a structure about a hundred feet away. "If anyone notices us, or says anything about you, I want you to run behind one of these buildings and hide."

"What about you?"

"I'm more worried about what could happen to you," he replied, and he was right. As an underdressed woman, I could be thrown in jail or the stocks for public lewdness, or perhaps labeled as a witch. Which, of course, would be accurate.

Dan walked down the street with purpose, while I crept along in his shadow. After he passed a storefront, and then a public house, I let myself relax. We'd gone by a dozen people and not one of them had batted an eyelash at us.

"Are we invisible?" Dan asked, as we approached the bank.

"I honestly have no idea." I could still see Dan, and when we passed by another storefront our reflections were visible in the window. That was reassuring. "My theory is that we're not invisible, so much as we're unnoticeable. We're blending in to the background, so no one is paying attention to us."

Dan raised an eyebrow. "So your spell is making the world ignore us."

"Do you have any better explanations?"

"I do not. How long will this blending in last?"

"Not long," I replied. "Tessa can only hold it for around twenty minutes."

"Then we need to get moving." He looked up and down what would become Pleasant Street in a hundred years or so. "Since the Beauclaire place is a few hours outside town, we need to borrow some horses."

"I'm not sure the Beauclaire house is where we need to go," I said, leaving off that I hadn't ridden a horse in at least fifteen years, and hadn't missed the activity at all. I bet the horses didn't miss me, either. "Sarah Allwood lived at the edge of the village, near the woods but still close enough to hand out candy to the kids."

"Was that candy poisoned?"

"Probably. Anyway, I remember reading that after Jemima and Nathaniel got married, they lived with her."

"I thought Sarah lived in the apple orchard."

"She owned the orchard, but she didn't live there."

"All right, looks like we're going to Sarah's. You know where this happy home is?"

"It's on the south side of town, near Gran's. Near the nexus." I started walking in what I hoped was the right direction. "You know, Sarah might have already died. She passed a few years before Jemima did. It was how Nathaniel got the idea to catch his own personal seer and stick Jemima in their body."

"If Sarah's a spirit, do you think you should you summon her, and ask a few questions?"

Ice prickled the back of my neck. "My foresight thinks that's a bad idea."

"Now that the thornapple's out of you, your foresight seems to be much more helpful."

"It does," I said, then I frowned.

"What is it?"

"I'm not really sure, but the whole curse couldn't have been the thornapple, could it? It wasn't really impeding my witchcraft; I didn't know I was half witch, so I never leaned into that part of myself. And it wasn't really impeding my foresight, either. That talent is notoriously fickle in witches and seers."

"But, your foresight does seem to be sending you clearer messages now that the curse is over with."

"It does. Or maybe I'm just paying better attention to what it's telling me." I faced Dan. "I'm beginning to wonder what she really meant to accomplish with the thornapple. It definitely wasn't a curse."

"You think your mother was trying to help you, and whatever spell she cast went haywire?"

"Maybe." I wasn't at a point where I could consider my mother doing anything for my benefit, but there was the fact that the thornapple had been inside me for twenty years, and I'd suffered no ill effects. "She wasn't trained as a witch, either, so it would make sense if she screwed up one of her first spells."

"Sounds like you two have more in common than you realized."

I didn't know what to say to that, so I asked a question instead. "Is your mom still around?"

"She is. She's back in Queens with the rest." He glanced at me sidelong, and continued, "Don't freak out, but I have a pretty big family."

"Why would I freak out?" I asked. "Just because I come from a long line of only children doesn't mean I'm scared of relatives."

Dan snorted. "After you meet my brothers and sisters, you might change your mind."

We continued on to Sarah Allwood's house, with Dan telling me crazier and crazier stories about all the trouble he and his siblings used to get into. There were seven of them—which I had to admit was a lot of kids—and Dan was the youngest boy.

"So you're the baby," I said.

"No." He made a cutting motion with his hand. "That honor goes to my sister, Alicia. You see, the youngest has dish duty."

"That's mean. What was your chore?"

"I, ah, delegated my stuff to the others."

I bumped my shoulder against his. "You mean you scammed the rest into doing your work for you."

"Hey, now, that's some accusation." A house came into view. "Is that it?"

"Should be." At the end of the path was a tidy brick cottage. The area around the cottage was well tended, and I could see a kitchen garden in the back. I wondered if Sarah and Jemima grew vegetables alongside their poisons.

"All right," Dan said. "Let's see what everyone's up to." We approached the window, and peeked inside. Seated next to the fireplace was Jemima.

"That's her," I said to Dan. "Jemima. I recognize her from when I summoned her spirit."

"She doesn't look good," Dan said, and he was right. Jemima was reclined in a chair and had her feet propped up. She had several blankets spread across her lap, a shawl wrapped around her shoulders, and a bonnet on her head. Her skin was pale, and her movements were weak, but despite all of that, her voice was strong.

"Nathaniel, I don't want this," she said. "Why would you try to put my spirit in someone else's body? My mother only tells you these things to confuse you. Get me a doctor, and once I'm healed, we'll find a seer and help Mama's soul move on for good."

"Don't you see what we could become?" Nathaniel said, as he crouched next to his wife. "We could become the most powerful witches in the New World. You could be my empress."

"I don't want to be an empress." She touched his cheek. "I only want to live with you, but if this illness takes me, I want to move on. Don't you dare trap me, like a ghost in a bottle. I won't be your pet."

"It won't be a trap," Nathaniel said. "It will be salvation."

"He let her die," I whispered to Dan. "He refused to get her a doctor, then he did exactly what she didn't want him to do. He trapped her spirit on this plane."

"At least you helped her move on."

"Hundreds of years later," I muttered, then Dan held up his hand. We heard the door open and shut, and someone entered the cottage. The man strode into view, and I gasped.

It was Amir.

"Nathaniel, who is this man?" Jemima demanded.

"This is my friend, Amir," Nathaniel replied. "We met in Antioch."

"Antioch," Dan muttered. "That's in Turkey. What were they doing there?"

"Probably nothing good," I said, then I returned my attention to what was happening inside the cottage.

"Yes, we met during the Crusades," Amir was saying; I heard Dan suck in a breath. Someday he was going to have to get used to rubbing elbows with very long lived people. "Mistress Beauclaire, it is a pleasure to finally meet you. Nathaniel has told me so much about you."

"I haven't heard a thing about you," Jemima snapped. "Are you a doctor?"

"I've done my share of healing." Amir set his bag on the table, and began removing small lidded jars and organizing them in groups. "In fact, Nathaniel has shared with me that you've been ill. Is that correct?"

Jemima narrowed her gaze. "I thought my husband didn't want me to recover."

"Of course I do, beloved." Nathaniel knelt next to her, and took her hand. "I want you to remain with me, always. Will you let Amir prepare a tonic for you?"

My skin turned to gooseflesh as I watched Amir open some of the jars and begin measuring out ingredients. "He poisoned her," I said. "Nathaniel poisoned his wife, and he had Amir make the potion."

"This guy is a real piece of work," Dan said. "No wonder none of the Beauclaires follow him."

"I think they're terrified of him." I clutched the wooden window sill until splinters poked underneath my fingernails. Jemima was about to die, and I couldn't look away. "I wish we could save her, but there's nothing we can do."

"What can't you do?" came a male voice from behind us. Before I could turn around, everything went black.

CHAPTER 30

FOXGLOVE TEA

When I came back to myself, Dan and I were inside Nathaniel and Jemima's house. We were sitting in the middle of the front room's floor, and tied up back to back. Jemima was dozing in her chair, and the three of us seemed to be the only ones in the room.

"Dan? Dan," I whispered.

"I'm awake," he said. "This is an awful lot like what happened when Nathaniel tied us up in his basement. I guess he repeats his crimes every couple hundred years or so."

I was about to list the many ways this scenario was different, when I noticed the heaps of dried foxglove lying near the hearth, and the cauldron set over the fire. Swap out Jemima for Jada, and the gang was all here.

Plus Amir, of course. He always had to put himself in the middle of other people's drama, just to make himself feel important.

"Do you think this was Amir's bargain with Nathaniel?" I asked. "To lure me, or any seer, to Jemima's deathbed so he can stick her spirit into their body?"

"I'm not dead yet," Jemima said, as she roused herself. "You must be Eliza."

I nodded, remembering how when I'd summoned her spirit, she told me we'd met before. Apparently, we were very old friends. "Jemima, I believe Amir is here to poison you."

She sighed. "That would not surprise me. When Nathaniel gets a plan inside his head, it is very, very hard to divest him of it." She eyed me, and then Dan. "At the risk of stating the obvious, you two are not from this time, and I suspect that you, sir, are not witchborn."

"You are correct, ma'am," Dan said. "I'm as mortal as they come."

"We won't be born for more than three hundred years," I said. "There is a network of time tunnels in and around this area. The tunnels are how we came to be here."

Jemima closed her eyes and took a shaky breath. I didn't know what she was sick with, but she was very weak. It wouldn't take very much poison to do her in. "I wonder if this Amir also arrived by way of those same tunnels."

"If you don't mind my saying so, you sound like you're from our era," Dan said.

"Witches are no strangers to time travel," Jemima said. "There are such portals all across the land, and easy enough to find if you know where to look. As a result of contact with many eras other than our own, we are excellent communicators."

"No arguments here," Dan said.

I wanted to ask Jemima about the nexus, but she was so ill I worried we didn't have much time. Therefore, I told her the truth. "What Nathaniel's doing now, trying to send your spirt into another body," I began. "It doesn't work."

Jemima closed her eyes and nodded. "No, I imagine it wouldn't. Being that you're the most powerful seer to walk this soil for a thousand years, are you willing to help me?"

I blinked. "N-No, I'm not that powerful. You must be thinking of my grandmother."

"I am not, Eliza Moore," Jemima said. "You are the most powerful seer to exist for a full thousand years before your birth, and for another thousand after your death. Those who cast augers have been aware of your coming for some time. They refer to you as the seer who traveled to the past in order to save the future. Since Nathaniel has brought this Amir to our home, and you followed so soon afterward, I can only assume that Amir is also familiar with these predictions. Perhaps you're the reason why he used these time tunnels in the first place."

"You might be right," I said, glad that she'd changed the subject from my supposed power level to Amir's shady dealings with the tunnels. "Jemima, I do help you move on. It doesn't happen today, and it won't be for a while. But in the end, I help you."

She smiled. "Thank you, Eliza. I'm sorry you've gotten dragged into Nathaniel's schemes."

"I'm sorry for what's happened to you, too." I looked at the cauldron, and the empty mug beside it. "If he hasn't given you the poison yet, maybe we can help you."

Jemima frowned. "I don't think that would be wise," she said. "Don't misunderstand me, for I do not wish to die. However, I have a touch of precognition, and it tells me that I must drink the poison." She frowned, and looked at her hands. "Will it hurt?"

"Foxglove affects your heart," I said softly. "You'll probably feel lethargic, maybe a bit nauseous. Your heart may beat very fast. And, I don't know if he added anything else to the cauldron." A tear slid down my cheek and splashed onto my shirt. "Please don't let him kill you."

"Eliza, dear, I am much older than you," she began. "I believe that I have done what I was put on this earth to do, and now this illness has meant the end of my time here. I need to take the next step, but don't mourn for me. As you know, death is merely a door we all must walk through, eventually."

"But you should walk through when it's your time, not when someone else decides," I said, and she shook her head.

"My time is now," she said firmly. "There are witches and seers walking among us who must be stopped. I can best assist my brothers and sisters from the next world. And, you said you help me move on. Let me help you now, so you may return the favor to me one day."

Jemima flicked her fingers, and the ropes fell away from Dan and me. We stood, stretching the feeling back into our limbs. "Thank you, ma'am," Dan said, with a nod toward Jemima.

"You are quite welcome, sir. Now, the foxglove, if you would."

I went to the cauldron, and ladled some of the foxglove tea into an earthenware mug. The heat seeped through the pottery, the warmth welcome to my chilled fingers.

"It's hot," I said, as I brought her the mug. "Blow on it."

Jemima smiled, her eyes twinkling. "You are a caretaker, aren't you, Eliza? I am so very glad we've met."

"May I ask a question?" Dan asked.

Jemima lowered the mug. "Please. Ask me whatever you'd like."

"You said you're much older than Eli, but how do you know that?" he asked. "All of you supernaturals don't age much after you reach adulthood. For all you know, Eli could be a thousand years old."

"What a brilliant mortal," Jemima murmured. "I know that Eliza is currently less than thirty years of age."

I took a step back. "Wait, how do you know that?"

"Because, everything changes when you reach your twenty-ninth year, and are anointed as the Mistress of Seers," Jemima replied. "Perhaps we'll speak again, after the occasion."

"Perhaps," I mumbled, then Jemima drank the foxglove tea. "No, wait! We still don't know if this is a good idea."

"It is." Jemima put her hand on mine. "Trust me, Eliza. It is."

Jemima's eyes fluttered shut, and her pale skin took on an ashen sheen. Dan took the mug from her limp hand, and set it on the table. "I don't think she has long."

"She doesn't want to stay," I said. "Her spirit wants to go."

Dan grasped my hand. "Are you helping her?"

"Yeah." I squeezed his hand. "I am."

And she was gone. Jemima Allwood Beauclaire, one of the loveliest people I've ever met, drank poison from the cup I'd handed her, and passed on. Her spirit floated free from her body, and she smiled at me from above. She was right; it had been her time, and she was finally at peace.

Then she screamed.

Chapter 31

In the Cottage

Jemima's ethereal face contorted in pain, transforming her spirit from a vision of serenity into a shade from my worst nightmares. Her scream echoed through my mind, and I clapped my hands over my ears. It didn't help, since her scream was spiritual. I heard her not with my ears, but with my mind.

"What is it?" Dan demanded. "What happened?"

The pain was too much for me to bear, and I went down to my knees. Dan pressed his palm against my seer's mark, and gasped when he saw Jemima's spirit.

"Jemima, what's happening?" Dan asked. "Someone, talk to me!"

"I'll be glad to explain what's happening," Amir said as he reentered the room. He was holding a blue glass bottle that had an inch or two of liquid on the bottom. "As a seer, I can keep her spirit on this plane. I'm told the process is somewhat unpleasant, but only if the spirit resists."

Dan put his mouth close to my ear. "Can you fight him, and get Jemima out of here?"

"Maybe if I had a month to prepare." I had no idea how to keep a spirit on the earthly plane against their will, and I didn't know how to counteract what Amir was doing. "I don't know how to stop Amir, or help Jemima."

"But you do help her, in the future," Dan said, then he faced Jemima. "Ma'am, right now, we have to let you go. I'm sorry, but we will be back for you."

Jemima nodded, then her wailing ceased as she drifted toward the bottle. Amir uncorked it, and it sucked Jemima's essence inside, trapping her exactly where she didn't want to be. As her spirit passed me, I felt her caress my cheek.

Amir replaced the cork in the bottle, and his smarmy grin was more than I could bear.

"You're a monster," I snapped.

"Am I, or am I a man who gets things done?" Amir asked as he stoppered the bottle. "You can't evade me, Ellie. No matter where you go, or when you go, I will always be several steps ahead of you. The only time you ever surprised me was when we met, in Iran."

"You surprise me constantly," I spat. "Whenever I think you've hit rock bottom, you go lower. All you ever do is sink lower into your own muck."

Amir laughed. "You won't always feel this way, and you—"

Dan withdrew a gun from an ankle holster and shot Amir in the shoulder. His arms windmilled as he fell back, then he struck his head on the edge of the hearth and knocked himself out.

"You've had a gun on you this entire time?" I demanded.

"It's Jill's. I grabbed it from her glove box." He lowered the weapon and approached Amir. There was a lot of blood, but he was still breathing. "We know he doesn't die here, although that would be convenient. Should we take the bottle?"

"Leave Jemima here." I grabbed the bottle from Amir's limp hand, and set it on the table. "We know that Nathaniel takes care of her. She's safe here with him, and we don't know where we might end up."

"Speaking of Beauclaire, let's move," Dan said.

I caressed the bottle's neck, much as Jemima's spirit had caressed my cheek. "Thank you. I won't ever forget you, and I will help you move on. I swear it."

We heard noise at the front of the house; Nathaniel must have returned. I grabbed Dan's hand and we went the opposite way through the cottage, and escaped through the kitchen door. We crossed the kitchen garden and ran into the woods, and found a trail that led uphill.

"Gran's house is uphill from where the cottage was," I said, remembering the old town maps I'd studied when I was first trying to glean information about the Allwoods. "We should go there."

"Is that your foresight talking?"

"Nope. Just me."

"Good. Let's move."

We followed the trail, but I hardly noticed my surroundings. First, Jada fell off a roof to her death, and now Jemima had died right in front of me. I understood that Jemima's spirit was safe, but what Amir had done unnerved me. And, I had no idea what sort of potion was in the bottle he'd trapped her in. I hoped Jemima wasn't in any pain.

We rounded a bend in the trail, and saw Nathaniel standing in front of us. Dan drew his gun, but I blocked him from advancing. "He's wearing modern clothing," I said, noting Nathaniel's button-down Oxford shirt and modern wing tip shoes. His khakis even appeared to be freshly pressed.

"He's still dangerous," Dan said.

"You're right. He is." Louder, I said, "Is there something I can do for you?"

"I am here to do something for you," Nathaniel replied. "I have known Amir for centuries, but it wasn't until after Jemima's death that I understood what a truly villainous person he is." Nathaniel met my gaze, and I saw pain and regret in his eyes. "Jemima didn't have to die."

"No, she didn't," I said.

"You're aware of Amir and Sarah's schemes?" he asked, and I nodded. "Well, you've one upped me yet again, Miss Moore, because I was not aware of them for a long time. A very, very long time. Sarah double crossed Amir many times, and used myself and Jemima as her pawns."

"What was Sarah's goal?"

"She wanted control of the Beauclaire and Allwood clans," he replied. "As you know, that has never quite worked out for her."

"And what does Hassan want, besides Eli?" Dan demanded.

"Amir wants power, and he believes he can get it through you, Miss Moore." Nathaniel sighed. "I really only wanted my wife returned to me."

"You must understand that what you wanted is impossible," I said. "Even if Jemima had possessed me, it wouldn't be her returned to you. Not in the way you wanted."

"Yes, that became clear after Sarah possessed the girl." Nathaniel looked past us. "The prior version of me is tracking you, and will overtake you momentarily. Go. I will keep him from following you."

"Why should I trust you?" I asked.

"Because thanks to you, my Jemima is finally at peace."

"Why do you suddenly—" I paused, because there was only one way Nathaniel would know the state of Jemima's spirit. "You made contact with her?"

"I did, after our most unpleasant discussion at my former estate," Nathaniel replied. "Thank you, Miss Moore, for having the courage to do what I could not. You are a worthy successor to Helena."

I bristled, but for the first time I not only agreed with Nathaniel, I knew he was correct. I am a worthy successor to Gran, and I am the

Mistress of Seers. All I had to do was convince whatever witches were still alive in my time that I was, too. At least I would have Jacob, and probably Ned Burroughs, on my side.

Nathaniel would probably be on my side if I asked it of him, but I didn't. All I wanted him to do was stay out of my way.

I glanced at Dan, and tilted my head toward where Gran's house would someday be. "Let's go."

"You trust him?"

"No, but we have work to do."

Dan and I walked past Nathaniel, none of us making eye contact as we did so. We remained silent until we were a ways down the trail, then we heard sounds of fighting from behind us.

"Think he's fighting himself back there?"

"Probably. Amir must be woozy from all that blood loss." I glanced at the gun he still held, lowered but at the ready. "I'm surprised you didn't shoot Nathaniel."

"Believe me, I thought about it," he said. "But you're right, we've got work to do. I can settle my scores with him at another time."

Time. We suddenly had an abundance of it, what with time tunnels spread out around us both in the air and beneath our feet. I wondered if we should head straight back to our time, or if we should make stops in other eras. Perhaps we could amass powerful artifacts, and learn new types of spellcraft, and—

"Eli?"

"Yeah?"

"That your gran's place?"

I followed his gaze, and saw that the trail led to a meadow. It was definitely the location where Gran's house would one day stand; I recognized the gentle slope down to the stream, and the raised area in the center had a sturdy wood-framed house upon it. Dad had said there was a house here long before the sprawling mansion that currently occupied pride of place in the neighborhood, and this was the beginnings of Gran's home.

"The cupola's there," Dan said, jerking his chin toward the roof.

"I wonder if it's always been here."

"Ah, babe? We've got company."

"We do?"

He pointed toward the greensward in front of the house. Sitting in a row were the three biggest cougars I had ever seen.

"Shit."

CHAPTER 32

VERY LARGE COUGARS

"Those are... Those are cougars," Dan said. "Very, very large cougars."

"Why are they just sitting there?" I did not know much about wildlife, but I did know that cougars were not supposed to be as big as horses. That meant these were magically altered cougars. Great. "Do cougars eat people?"

"These cougars eat whatever they like," came a voice from the direction of the house. "If they want to, they'll eat you, too." Standing in the open doorway was a woman wearing a navy blue dress, her bright white shawl and apron in stark contrast to the dress's deeper hue. Her brown hair was pulled back from her face, and she watched us with curiosity rather than fear.

I, however, was terrified.

"You're not scared of them?" I asked, nodding toward the cougars.

"I am not," she replied. "I will say that they aren't scared of you, either."

"How can you tell?"

"You're still breathing."

I gulped some air and tried to coerce my foresight into giving me a hint. Of course, it ignored me. While I was literally freaking out, the woman's skirts moved, and a tiny face peeked out at us.

"Now, Elizabeth, you stay inside," the woman said to the child.

"Elizabeth?" I repeated. "Elizabeth Moore?"

The woman's face went hard as stone. "Why did you say that?"

"Your daughter," I replied. "Her name is Elizabeth, isn't it? That makes you Katherine."

Katherine folder her arms across her breast. "Stranger, you will tell me how you know such things."

Dan leaned closer to me, and asked, "Eli, mind cluing me in here?"

"Elizabeth Moore was my great grandmother. Gran's mother. I'm named after her." I regarded the cougars, and how they sat in a perfect row like a trio of sphinxes. Or, a trio of terror.

"Dan, these are the cats," I said. "The nexus's guardians. Pumpkin!"

The central cougar tilted her head to the side, then she padded toward me. Dan tried to shield me with his body, but I waved him away. Pumpkin would never hurt me.

"Hey, fluff," I said to the cougar. "I don't know what you're called now, but by the time I come along, everyone calls you Pumpkin. Do you like that name?"

The cougar—Pumpkin—sat directly in front of me and sniffed my feet. Satisfied with where I'd been walking, she moved on to my legs, then my hands, and finished by dragging her enormous, sandpapery tongue across my cheek.

"I love you, too," I said as I wound my arms around Pumpkin's massive head. Smokey and Muffuletta approached us, and I did my best to bestow the mandatory scritches. I had to stand on my toes to reach the good spots behind their ears, but we managed. "You guys haven't changed in three hundred years, you know that?"

Smokey bumped her head against Dan's shoulder. He was a big man, but the impact almost knocked him over. "Whoa, kitty," he said. "Be gentle."

While the Feline Federation let Dan and me know we were loved in any time, Katherine had approached us. "The guardians know you," she observed.

"In my time, they're housecats," I said. "Can they change shape now?"

"It is said that they alter their forms as needed, though they've always been cougars for me," Katherine replied. "They're not usually so large, though."

"They were probably being cautious, until they knew who we were." I held out my hand. "I'm Eliza Moore. Your descendant."

Katherine went pale. "And you?" she asked Dan.

"Daniel Lyons," he replied. "We're not related."

"Thank all the gods for that," Katherine muttered.

"Forgive me for being blunt, but you don't seem all that shocked to meet people from a different time," Dan said.

"This is not the first time I've encountered travelers such as yourselves," Katherine replied. "We'd best get inside and talk. For the two of you to have come all this way, something important must be happening."

We followed Katherine into the house, though she shook her finger at the cougars when they tried to go inside. I pressed my forehead against Pumpkin's and thought about the fluffy calico I knew her as.

"Could you be little cats?" I asked. "Just for now? Then you can come inside for a bit."

Pumpkin purred deep in her throat, and a moment later I was holding an eight-pound calico cat.

"Kitty," Elizabeth exclaimed, and I handed Pumpkin to her. Smokey and Muffuletta similarly changed shape, and slipped past us into the kitchen. Katherine just shook her head.

"Now they'll never go back out," she said, then she shut and barred the door. "I'll put the kettle on, then we shall speak."

After the tea was made, and Elizabeth served us slices of cake dotted with candied fruit, we sat around the polished dining room table. I did little more than stare into my tea, my thoughts still reeling with everything that had happened within the last few hours. Dan, however, was the king of making small talk.

"Then Jemima Beauclaire has passed," Katherine said, once Dan had finished recounting everything that happened to us since we arrived in this time. "I did not sense her spirit."

"She was trapped, in a… Eli?"

Dan's question roused me. "Yeah?"

"How was Jemima trapped?" he asked.

"Amir had a glass bottle," I replied. "There was a liquid in the bottom. I don't know what the liquid was, but somehow he drew her spirit into the bottle, and then he stoppered it."

"It was probably salt water," Katherine said. "The salt weighs down the spirit, and keeps them on this plane. It's an evil thing to do to one who has passed."

"That's Amir. Evil." I cleared my throat. "Is there anything we can do for Jemima?"

"Once the water is gone and the salt dries up, she will be free to move around," Katherine replied. "Then, we can look to helping her move on."

"I do free her, but not until my time," I said, my guilt over leaving Jemima behind having made my voice small.

"That was good of you, to help her as you did. Do. Perhaps things have happened the way they were always meant to." Katherine regarded me for a moment, then asked, "You're my descendant?"

"Yes. You're my great-great grandmother. I'm named for Elizabeth." I pushed some cake crumbs around with my fork. "My name was supposed to be Elizabeth, but my father says I was so small when I was born he worried I couldn't carry around such a big name. That's why I'm just Eliza."

Katherine reached across the table and grasped my forearm. "My dear, I highly doubt you are just anything. For you and Daniel to have navigated through the eons, only to end up exactly where you need to be, is quite a feat."

I smiled, because I could see a lot of my gran in Katherine. "Thank you."

"Now tell me, how may I help the two of you?"

"In our time, Amir—the seer who trapped Jemima—wants to take over the nexus," I began. "We know that the nexus is here, at the house, but no one has entered it in so long, we kind of forgot how to get there."

"My home is still standing in your time?" Katherine asked.

"The core of it is there," I replied. "The root cellars are intact, and this room becomes the front parlor. New kitchens get added on at some point, adjacent to the solarium."

"A solarium off the kitchen," Katherine murmured. "I would like that. And out of all the seers that must exist in the twenty-first century, none of you remember how to access the nexus?"

"There aren't a lot of us left in the area," I said. "There's only my father, who is the current marksman, and me."

Katherine blinked. "They you must be the Mistress of Seers."

I shook my head. "I'm not. My mother was a witch, so the witch elders won't follow me. They chose Amir, instead."

"Who cares what the witch clans think?" Katherine demanded. "Are they seers? No, they are not. Our business is none of their concern, and they'd do well to remember that."

"But, but someone with witch blood can't be Mistress of Seers," I said, looking to Dan for affirmation. "Sarah Allwood engineered this whole—"

"Sarah Allwood is a liar and a troublemaker," Katherine said over me. "Don't you dare believe one word out of that old hag's mouth. She's as rotten as her unkempt apple orchard."

I couldn't help it, I burst out laughing. "She does seem awful," I said. "Did you know her before she died?"

"I did, and believe me when I say that this world is a better place without her."

"That's exactly what I said." Dan picked up our empty plates and set them on the sideboard, then he kissed the top of my head before he reclaimed his seat. "That Sarah's got a way of working herself inside someone's head, and makes them doubt everything they know. She's insidious."

"That she is." Katherine nodded approvingly at Dan. "Normally I would not tell a single soul how to access the nexus, or even confirm its existence. However, since you are, both by blood and by rights, the true Mistress of Seers in your day, I see no reason not to share my knowledge with you."

"Want me to leave the room?" Dan asked.

"You may remain," Katherine said. "All true Mistresses have their partners, and it is plain that you and Eliza belong to each other." Dan squeezed my hand. "As for entering the nexus, it is the guardians that must bring you."

"The cats?" I said, glancing toward where the three of them lounged in a sunbeam in the far corner of the room.

"The cats," Katherine confirmed. "It is for them to show you the way."

"That makes so much sense, I feel like we should have known," I murmured. "Can they take us now?"

"As you know, they keep their own counsel," Katherine said, which was a polite way of saying that the cats weren't going to interrupt their nap time for me or anyone. "However, I would like to propose something to the two of you."

I glanced at Dan. He shrugged. "Um, okay. What can we do for you?"

"It's more of what I can do for you," she began. "You're both exhausted, both in body and in spirit. Soon, we'll be laying out supper. Stay with us tonight, rest and eat. I can offer you each a room, and fresh garments."

I glanced down at my jeans. They were a bit dusty. "That's very kind of you."

"I haven't gotten to the crux of my proposal yet," Katherine said, and her eyes twinkled just like my grandmother's once did. "The day after tomorrow is the equinox, and we shall host a gathering of all the local seers. I would very much like both of you to attend."

When all I did was stare at her, Katherine continued, "You seem to have a small community in your day, and while I don't know what led to that, I want to remind you of what a rich heritage we seers have. We were meant to work together in all things."

I remembered the gatherings Gran used to hold when I was younger, extravagant and decadent parties that sometimes lasted for days. After I'd been kidnapped by the Beauclaires, tensions between my family and the witch clans were high, and the parties became little more than meetings, and gatherings that used to occur weekly dwindled down to monthly, and eventually they stopped happening at all. I wondered if fracturing the community was part of Sarah's plan to destroy us, so she could pick up what was left and keep it for herself.

Not on my watch.

"I would very much like to attend your equinox celebration," I said, and Katherine beamed. "I was shocked because when we left our time it was August, and now... Wait, it's September thirteenth?"

"Why, yes."

"We've been gone for a month," I said. "My dad and Tess much be worried sick about us."

"Eli, we used time tunnels," Dan reminded me. "We can probably work it out to have them put us back on the same day we left."

"Oh, okay." I faced Katherine. "Can we do that?"

"You know much more about these time tunnels than I," she replied. "I only see those who travel through them, and end up here. I've never set foot in one myself."

"They're rather easy to navigate, if you ever find yourself in one." I turned from Katherine back to Dan. "What do you say? Want to go to a party in two days?"

Dan grinned. "I'd love to. Ma'am, how can we be of help?"

Chapter 33

Cider and Rabbit Stew

Katherine insisted that there was absolutely nothing Dan or I could do to help and sent us off to wash up and change for supper. I suspected part of her invitation was intended to get Dan and me out of our modern clothes and into something that wouldn't require so much explaining.

The housekeeper, a seer named Hettie, led us upstairs, and put us each in a room where we could rest for a little while before dinner; I noted the separate rooms, but didn't mention anything. I supposed it was standard to put unmarried couples in separate rooms. Then I stepped inside my allotted room and momentarily forgot how to speak.

It was my room from when Katherine's home becomes Gran's house.

"This really is the same house," I mumbled, not that I'd had any doubts. The front room was exactly the same, though the actual bedroom was a bit smaller than the one I'd grown up in. I assumed it would get enlarged when the bathroom was added on, which wouldn't happen until indoor plumbing came into vogue a few hundred years in the future. The bed was even in the same place against the wall, facing the east windows. I promptly undressed, washed up, and lay down for a nap.

Hettie woke me up several hours later to tell me dinner was imminent. She also brought me some clothing. I declined her assistance in dressing, since I didn't plan on putting on most of the items. It was a warm day, and it wasn't like anyone was going to check to see if I was wearing all of those undergarments, right? After I was dressed and sitting at the vanity brushing my hair, someone knocked on my door.

"Come in."

Dan poked his head inside and smiled when he saw me. "Aren't you pretty?"

"I look like I'm dressed up for Halloween, or one of those medieval fairs," I said, ignoring how my face heated.

He stepped inside the room, and I saw his outfit of a loose white shirt, black waistcoat, and black knee breeches with the accompanying hose and shoes. Before I could tell him that he really did look good in those old-fashioned clothes, he took my hands and pulled me to my feet. "You look amazing," he said, then he touched the gem at my throat. After I'd managed to get the dress on, I put on my sapphire necklace. "You decided to wear it?"

"Why not?" I countered. "I used to wear it every day."

"It suits you," he said, then he drew me close and kissed me. "How did Katherine manage to have a dress that fits you so perfectly?"

"This is hers," I replied, smoothing my hands over my skirts. The dress was similar in style to what Katherine was wearing, but mine was chocolate brown. "I guess being this size and shape runs in the family. And check out these pockets!" I showed him the absolutely huge pockets that were accessible through a slit in the overskirt. In them I'd put everything I brought with me from the future, except for my clothes. I wasn't worried that anyone in the house would steal my stuff, but the last thing I needed was to leave my cell phone behind in pre-Revolutionary America and cause an incident with the timeline.

I also put the thornapple seedpod in my pocket, all the while marveling that only I would get so attached to an item that had cursed me. But it had been with me for the last twenty years, and I wasn't ready to give it up just yet. I figured carrying it around a little bit longer would hurt, so in the pocket it went. I hope it doesn't scratch my phone's screen.

"Out of all this it's the pockets that impress you?" Dan asked.

"Have you seen the pockets in modern women's clothing?" I countered. "That's right—you haven't, because they're almost nonexistent."

"If you like the pockets, I like the pockets." He offered me his arm. "Ready to eat?"

"Let's go," I said, and we descended to the dining room.

Unlike most households in colonial Massachusetts, where the last meal of the day tended to be served around four in the afternoon, Katherine served supper relatively late. I supposed that was a habit she'd held onto from her time in England. Whatever the reason, we were soon seated around the enormous polished table again, and Hettie and her flock of maids handed out bowls of rabbit stew with crusty bread, along with tankards of cold cider.

"These apples didn't come from Sarah's orchard, did they?" I asked, glancing dubiously at the pale liquid I'd been given.

"They absolutely did not," Katherine said. "You'll be glad to know that I source my apples from an orchard far from hers. Whenever Montgomery is in town, he obtains a few barrels for me."

"Who's Montgomery?" I asked.

"He's our marksman," she replied, and I noticed the pink cast on her cheeks. "He's also Elizabeth's father."

"Must be where Alex gets his gifts from," Dan said.

"Alex?" Katherine repeated. "Who's that?"

"Alexander Moore," I replied. "He's my father, and the marksman in my time. He travels an awful lot."

"As does Montgomery," Katherine said, then she asked, "Do the two of you have children?"

"We do not," Dan replied, when I just sat there opening and closing my mouth like a fish. "To be honest, we haven't been together long enough for anything like that."

"But we've known each other for years," I said. "Dan was the first mortal I brought into our community."

"I was?" he asked.

"Um, yeah." That admission felt heavier than I'd intended, which sent me into full-on over sharing mode. "If you look at his wrist, he's got a mark. A seer's mark. I gave him that."

"You gave a mortal a seer's mark?" Dan extended his arm toward her, and Katherine peered at his mark. "Does it allow you to interact with spirits?"

"It does," Dan replied. "I can also sense magic."

"What kinds of magic?"

"All of it, I think."

"Fascinating." Katherine's gaze moved from Dan's mark to me. "I am shocked, not only that you devised such a wild notion, but that you also executed the mark correctly. Most marksmen train for decades. Did your father assist you with Dan's mark?"

"Um, no," I replied. "I found his kit and did the work, then I told him about it afterwards."

"Was he angry?"

"No. He wasn't even mad."

She nodded. "That's good. That means he understood that the mark was right and necessary, no matter that it was applied to a mortal. No offense, Daniel," she added.

"None taken," he replied. "Believe me, I understand what a privilege it is for me to be included in your community."

"I don't know if I would call it a privilege, but I imagine we have a set of quirks mortals rarely encounter." Katherine signaled to the servers, and they began removing our empty plates and bowls. "Shall we adjourn to the parlor for bit of madeira?"

"Oh, I don't know," I said. "I'm already exhausted. If I have any wine, I might fall asleep in my chair."

"Come now, we should celebrate. It's not every day my descendants come by for a visit. And another thing," Katherine said as she stood, "tomorrow is laundry day, and everyone is expected to do their share."

"Laundry day," I muttered. "How interesting could that be?"

CHAPTER 34

LAUNDRY DAY

L et me tell you, laundry day was no joke.

We were woken up before dawn by Elizabeth jumping on the bed. After I got dressed and tied back my hair, Elizabeth grabbed my hand and dragged me outside. Behind the house, which in my time was a tangle of roses and brambles, were three enormous wash tubs. The tubs were set on stands over fires, and that was when it hit me: we were about to do the entire household's washing, by hand.

I will never disparage a modern laundromat ever again.

"Grab a bucket," Katherine ordered when she saw me. "I trust you know where the creek is?"

I did, and I got in line with the rest of the household as we filled our buckets and hauled water back up the hill and into the laundry tubs. While we filled the tubs, others sorted the laundry into piles, while another group set out supplies and hung the drying lines.

"Should we start adding soap?" I asked, once the tubs were full and fires were lit underneath them. Apparently, we were going to boil the dirt out of our clothes.

"Oh, no," Katherine said. "The laundresses will do that. We won't be needed again until the first batch is ready to rinse. After the rinsing we'll wring them out and hang everything to dry."

I gazed at the heaps of clothing, tablecloths, bedclothes, and other fabrics waiting to be scrubbed clean. "How many batches will there be?"

"Several." I sighed, resigned to my fate in laundry hell. Katherine laughed at my plight, and looped her arm with mine. "Come with me. I've been told that Hettie has just set out some lemonade."

I followed Katherine to the opposite side of the yard. Near the outdoor ovens, a second set of people were handling the day's baking.

"Running this place is a full-time job," I said.

"It certainly is." We stopped at the refreshment table, and Katherine poured us each a mug of lemonade. "How many staff to you keep on in your time?"

"We don't have any staff," I replied. "One of my ancestors got a witch out of a pretty big jam. As a thank you, he spelled the house to never need cleaning." I paused, remembering that the ancestor in question was my great-great grandmother. Katherine. I glanced around, and wondered if that witch was here now, helping out with the wash. "No one's cleaned the windows in decades, but the glass sparkles like diamonds."

"That must have been a rather delicate situation that witch found themself in."

I gazed out at the legions of servants, each one of them working hard and knowing exactly what was expected of them. "It must have been."

"I've told the rest you're my cousin from Virginia," she said. "While that statement isn't exactly truthful, it is a much easier, and I daresay better, explanation, at least for the time being."

"Yes, I imagine it is," I said, wondering if people would think Katherine was insane for believing Dan and I came from the future, or if the mundane townspeople would want her burned as a witch. There were some answers I didn't need to know.

A chorus of giggles rang out from behind us. We turned, and saw a group of women smiling behind their hands, and stealing glances at something beyond the ovens.

"Ladies, what is so funny?" Katherine asked. When the giggling only intensified, we went to investigate. When I saw what had caught their attention, I gasped.

They were watching Dan chop wood.

Shirtless.

"Oh, my," Katherine said. "Eliza, I do not know what one does when you're from—"

"Which is Virginia," I interjected. "That's where I'm from."

"Yes, Virginia, where you're from, but around here, we typically keep our clothes on during the day." The women chittered among themselves. "All of our clothes. Daniel's habits seem to be a distraction," she added, with a well-meaning glare toward the rest.

"I'll talk to him," I said, and I left Dan's ever-growing group of admirers—which now included Katherine—and approached the merry woodsman.

"Hey," I called. He paused mid swing and smiled at me. "I have lemonade."

"You are the greatest woman in the world," he said, then he claimed my mug and drained it in one gulp. "I needed that."

"You also need to put a shirt on," I said. "You have a fan club."

"I do?" Dan glanced over his shoulder, his eyes widening when he saw the group of women checking him out. "Hello, ladies," he said with a wave.

"Stop. You'll make them swoon." I picked up his discarded shirt and shook it out. "What were you thinking? People are quite literally puritanical in these times."

"Chopping wood is hot work," he said. "Besides, I was all alone over here when I started."

"Yeah, well, news of Officer Muscleman's hotness spreads fast in any century."

"Officer... what?"

I froze, and debated running. If all of those skirts weren't weighing me down, I would have made a break for it. "That's what Tess calls you."

"You mean to tell me that Contessa Isabella della Scala refers to me, a lowly mortal, as Officer Muscleman?"

"Mortals aren't lowly," I said. "And don't get too excited. It was something she used to say back when she was trying to get me to date you."

"Tessa tried to talk you into dating me? When?"

"Um, a while ago." I looked around, desperate to change the subject. "Do you think this is enough wood to get everything started? I'll grab some kindling." I walked away from him and picked up a few dry sticks, then Dan grabbed my waist and hauled me out of sight of the others. I dropped all the wood I'd collected as he set my back against the rear wall of the bakehouse and glowered at me.

"How long ago?" he demanded. "Like, a few months ago?"

"N-No. More like two years ago. Right after the Forge Heights case."

"Two years." Dan grasped my wrists in one hand and pinned them over my head, while his other hand rested on my hip. "All that time, when I was desperately trying to get you to hang out with me, you and Tess were checking me out and giving me nicknames?"

"It was all Tessa," I insisted. "I kept telling her she shouldn't call you that."

Dan adjusted his grip on my hands, and laced his fingers with mine. It was an old agreement that I had first with Tessa, and now with Dan. Whenever we were holding hands, we could tell each other anything without embarrassment or judgement. "What did you think of this nickname?" he asked.

"I thought it was appropriate." I loosened the hand that wasn't holding his, and stroked his well-toned chest. "Then there was that time in the Allwood basement when I had to take your shirt off you, and that was one of my better plans."

Dan grinned. "You could have taken the rest off. I wouldn't have minded."

"Do you have any modesty?"

"Officer Muscleman isn't burdened with such petty emotions." He squeezed my hip, then he released me and pulled his shirt over his head. "C'mon, babe. You can put your own pretty muscles to use helping me haul wood."

I batted my eyelashes at him, "Yes, Officer."

We brought the fruits of Dan's labors to the main woodpile, and watched as the three fire pits were stoked and the washtubs came to a boil. Two people stood over each tub, one who added clothes and other linens to the water, while the other stirred everything with a wooden paddle.

"How often do you do the laundry?" I asked Katherine.

"This will likely be our last big wash before winter," she replied. "Once it gets too cold to use the big tubs, we wash a bit a time in the kitchens. Then, come spring, we'll be due for another big wash."

"I bet." I scanned the crowd, and saw Dan talking to a few of the men near the woodpiles. He caught me watching him, and grinned.

"I see Daniel has decided to cover himself," Katherine said.

"For now, at least. Who knows what he'll get up to later on."

"He seems like a good man."

"He is. He's one of the best people I've ever met."

"Based on the way he watches you, he feels the same," Katherine said knowingly. "He keeps calling me ma'am."

"Oh, that's a term of respect in our time, like mistress. Should he call you goodwife instead, or Goody Moore?"

Katherine snorted. "I'm no one's wife, and many would say I'm not very good, either."

"Even Montgomery would say that?"

She narrowed her eyes. "Montgomery would do well to remember that I am Mistress of Seers, whereas he's my marksman."

"I bet he knows how to hit the mark."

"Eliza!"

Before I could make Katherine blush any redder—although that was fun—a cart drawn by two horses approached. The man driving the cart hardly had time to set his reins down before he was swarmed with others shouting greetings and offering to help him unload his wares, and see to the horses.

"This guy seems popular," I said. The driver stood, and I saw he was tall and easily as well-built as Officer Muscleman. He had shoulder length brown hair brushed back from his face, and deeply tanned skin. Even though I was certain I'd never seen him before, this man seemed uncannily familiar to me.

"Who is that?" I asked.

"That, my dear, is Montgomery." Katherine's gaze slid toward me. "I suppose I should introduce you to your grandfather."

"Should we tell him who I am?" I asked. "As in, who I really am?"

"Yes, but not here," she replied. "Too many eyes and ears." We started toward the cart, then Katherine put her hand on my arm. "Please don't mention how I blushed when you teased me about him."

"You really like him," I said.

"I have something to tell him," she said, and rested her hand on her belly. I gasped, partly because Katherine was pregnant. I also knew that Elizabeth Moore had been an only child, which meant this baby was doomed.

However, Katherine didn't need to know what I knew. "Maybe you two can celebrate in the barn," I say, waggling my eyebrows as Katherine's cheeks went even darker.

"Look what you've done," she said, pressing her palms to her cheeks. "I can't possibly approach him like this!"

Before Katherine could hide or find herself a cold compress, Montgomery spotted her from his perch on the cart. He leapt down from the cart, navigated through the crowd like a quarterback rushing toward the goal line, and grabbed Katherine's hips. She squealed as he spun her around, while he gazed at her like she was his world.

"I missed you, Katie girl," he said. Katherine swatted his shoulder as if she was embarrassed, as if it wasn't obvious that she'd missed him just as much.

"Monty, we have a visitor," Katherine said, as she straightened her bonnet, and then her apron. "This is Eliza, my cousin from Virginia."

"Virginia?" Montgomery's brows pinched. "I didn't know you had kin in Virginia. Whereabouts are you from, Eliza?"

"Um, Fairfax?" I replied, since that was the first Virginian town I thought of.

"Fairfax," he repeated. Katherine pinched his arm, which must have been some sort of code between them, because his disbelieving face was replaced by a wide grin. "Yes, lovely area. Pleasure to meet you, Eliza."

"The pleasure is all mine," I said, then Elizabeth shot through the crowd and jumped into Montgomery's arms.

"Papa," she cried, burying her face against his neck.

"There, there, my Lizzie," he soothed. "I missed you, too."

"Well, then," Katherine said, smoothing her hair underneath her bonnet, "now that we've all been introduced and reunited, let's see what Papa has brought us."

The four of us made our way toward the cart, which was still being unloaded. Dan was helping, and was issuing orders and organizing the rest as if they were his own little police department.

"Who is that?" Montgomery asked, jerking his chin toward Dan.

"That's Eliza's Daniel," Katherine replied. "He's also from Virginia."

"Ah," Montgomery said. "Fairfax?"

"Yes, Fairfax," I replied. "We're all from Fairfax."

Before I could babble away my and Dan's true identities, a group of Native tribes people arrived. "Who are they?" I asked.

"They are from the nearby Pocumtuc tribes," Montgomery replied. "Their seers usually attend our celebrations."

"I thought we were more closely aligned with the Abenaki," I began, then I shut my mouth with a clack.

"The Abenaki are somewhat farther north," Montgomery said, his brows lowered as he regarded me. "You're from Virginia, yet you're knowledgeable about our people?"

"There was an Abenaki village on this site long before the Moores came here from England," I said, reciting a story Gran had taught me long ago. "They were always in contact with us, then they sent word that they needed to move north, but a seer was still needed here. And so we came across the ocean, and here we are now."

Montgomery set down Elizabeth, and whispered for her to go play with the other children. Once she was out of earshot, he grabbed my arm, and demanded, "Who are you?"

"I-I'm Eliza Moore."

He leaned closer. "Not your name. Who are you? Why are you here, at my home and talking to my people? How do you know such things?"

"Hands off, buddy," Dan said as he shoved himself between me and Montgomery.

"I was asking the lady a question," Montgomery said.

"You ask with your voice, not your hands." Dan turned to me. "You okay? Who is this guy?"

"It's fine," I said. "Nothing's wrong."

"He looked like he wanted to rip your head off!"

"He won't," I said, rather desperately as I searched the crowd for Katherine, or Hettie, or anyone who might intercede.

"Katherine tells me your name is Daniel," Montgomery said, and Dan nodded. "Are you also from Virginia?"

"Virginia? No, I'm from New York," Dan said, before I could stop him.

Montgomery's face hardened, and I felt a lick of fear. As the seers' marksman, he would kill us where we stood in order to defend the Moore legacy. "You need to leave. Both of you. Now."

"Okay," I said, nodding furiously. "We'll go. I'm sorry."

"Montgomery." Katherine approached us, smiling at those who'd noticed Montgomery's displeasure. "Eliza is a Moore. She, and Daniel, belong here with us."

"Katie, they're telling lies," he protested.

"Because they cannot openly speak the truth," Katherine said. "The guardians know them."

Montgomery paused. "Both of them?"

"Yes. They shifted form when Eliza requested it."

"Did they?" Montgomery's gaze shifted back to me. "Tell me the truth. Where are you from?"

"Here," I replied, then I extended my left arm and showed him my wrist. "I got my seer's mark here, in this house."

Montgomery scrutinized my wrist. "It's quite well done. Who gave it to you?"

"My father, Alexander Moore."

He nodded, then he speared Dan with his gaze. "And you?"

"I really am from New York," Dan said, then he revealed his own mark. "I also got marked here. Hurt like hell."

"Your mark is unusual," Montgomery observed, because of course he would notice that. "This is not the work of the same person who marked Eliza."

"It's not," Dan said. "Eli did this."

"Are you a marksman?" Montgomery asked me.

"No. I've only ever given one mark."

Montgomery blew out a breath. "I do not understand where you came from or why you're here now, but you both speak the truth. If Katie has faith that the two of you belong, then so do I."

"Thank you," I said. "You don't know what that means to me."

Montgomery smiled. "I can imagine. As a gesture of good faith, I offer you a bit of knowledge: there are no Abenaki in Virginia."

"I know. I just got so flustered. I'm not very good at lying."

"That in itself is a good thing." Montgomery faced Dan. "Care to assist me with the rest of the supplies?"

"Absolutely," Dan said. "Lead the way, sir."

While Dan helped Montgomery unload supplies—and hopefully used his natural charm so Montgomery didn't have a change of heart and decide we were the enemy again—Katherine and I tackled more of the laundry. We hauled the clean clothes out of the water and into the rinsing tubs, then we pulled them out, ran them through this hand-cranked machine called a mangle, and hung them up to dry. By the time we'd done all of that, the second batch was ready to come out of the washtubs.

"I have never worked so hard in my life," I declared, as we finished hanging up the second batch of linens. "You must have abs of steel."

"What of steel?" Katherine asked. Right, colonial women probably weren't that concerned with their abdominal muscles, especially since they were covered by a hundred layers of clothing.

"You must be very strong," I amended

"I suppose I am," she said. "One needs to be, in order to manage a household of this size, not to mention the rest of the community. Look, more of our seers have arrived."

Whenever Katherine referred to the seer community as "ours" my heart swelled and my throat went tight. "Already? I thought the gathering wasn't until tomorrow."

"That's correct, but many travel great distances to attend our gatherings," she replied. "Most will arrive today, and we'll begin the celebrations shortly before dawn tomorrow."

"Before dawn? After all this work, won't you be too tired to get up that early?"

"Eliza, dear, I will be far too excited to sleep." She glanced toward the washing tubs. "The others can handle that last batch. Come, let's get you introduced to more of our people."

Katherine introduced me to the rest, always as her cousin, and every single seer greeted and accepted me as one of their own. I'd never met so many seers at once; in fact, I didn't think there were this many seers in the area. There certainly weren't in my time.

I wondered how, and why, our numbers had been reduced so drastically.

"I can't get over how kind everyone is," I said a bit later, as Katherine and I were setting out food and drinks for everyone.

"Why wouldn't they be?" Katherine asked. "You're one of us. You belong here just as much as I do."

"I guess," I mumbled. "Jemima sad something strange to me, just before she died."

"Really?" Katherine wiped her hands on her apron and faced me. "And it's been bothering you."

"My entire interaction with her has been bothering me," I began. "She said that according to some auguries, I would be anointed as Mistress of Seers on my next birthday."

"She said that? If you don't mind my asking, how old will you be?"

"Twenty-nine."

"You're not yet thirty?" Katherine asked, and I shook my head. "I had no idea you were so young, and also so isolated. You are strong, Eliza. Most of your age would hide from such things."

"I tried running, and hiding, but it didn't work. One thing I've learned the hard way is that you can't run from what you are, no matter how fast or far you travel."

"No, you certainly cannot." Katherine tucked a length of hair that had escaped from my cap behind my ear. "As to what Jemima said, who were these auguries?"

"She didn't say," I replied, leaving off how she'd also claimed I would be the most powerful seer for a thousand years. That was just nuts. "They're witches, I guess. But why would they want to know anything about me?"

"While I do not know the specific answer, I can speculate. Jemima's mother craved information, and I wouldn't put it past her to divine a seer's family tree many centuries into the future. As to whether these dates Jemima mentioned have any bearing on us, when is your birthday?"

"September twentieth," I replied. "Six days from now. But I'm here, and I honestly don't know if I can get back to where I'm supposed to be before then."

Katherine nodded. "I do have a solution, and a simple one, at that. Remain here until the twentieth. I shall anoint you myself."

"You can do that?"

"Of course I can. I am the Mistress of Seers, and as you know, it is our right to name our successor. Granted, you will not be my immediate successor, but that shouldn't be an issue."

I threw my arms around Katherine and hugged her. "You're brilliant, you know that? I'm so glad you're my new grandma."

She patted my back. "I am more like your very old grandmother, but thank you just the same." She drew back, and held me at arm's length. "Yes, six days from now will be good. Most of the others will have returned home by then, which will mean fewer explanations all around. Then we can have a small ceremony, just you and I, Montgomery, and your Daniel."

"And Elizabeth," I added. "I need my namesake."

Katherine smiled. "Of course, and Elizabeth, too. We'll have Hettie bake one of her cakes, and after the ceremony is complete we'll celebrate your birthday. It will be wonderful, Eliza."

I smiled at Katherine. "It really will."

The rest of the day was a blur of laundry, meeting people and trying to remember all the names and relationships, and food. There was so much food and drink; pies, cakes, mounds of apples, and bowls of cherries. And according to Katherine, there would be even more tomorrow.

It was near sunset when I finally caught up with Dan. "Hey," I called, when I found him near the edge of the fire pit that was set up for tomorrow's cooking.

"Hey, yourself." Dan leaned forward as if he would kiss me, but checked himself at the last moment. Others had commented on how affectionate we were with each other, and after his shirtless wood chopping, I wanted to tone things down. The last thing Katherine needed was a bunch of rumors springing up about her strange cousin from Virginia.

"What do you think?" Dan asked, nodding toward the fire pit. Since the main course would be a roasted pig, Dan had built a spit that would cook porky to perfection.

"It's quite the contraption," I said. "Are they only roasting the pig tomorrow? No chicken?"

"Only you would want chicken when roast pork is on the menu." Dan pulled me beyond the edge of the firelight and slid his arms around my waist. So much for toning down the public displays of affection. "I know pork's not your favorite. I looked through all the carts, but I couldn't find any cereal or bananas."

I hid my face against his throat as I laughed. "Are bananas even in America at this point? Not that it's America yet."

"If memory serves, bananas don't get real popular until the late eighteen hundreds." He kissed the top of my head. "Sorry, baby."

"You've got to stop kissing me all the time," I said, doing nothing to pull away or otherwise stop him. "People nowadays think it's unseemly."

"That's me, Unseemly Lyons."

I twisted around in his arms so I could see the rest of the gathering. Despite what I'd said about Dan being too affectionate for this time period, people were pairing off and escaping into the darkness. Across the clearing, I saw Katherine sitting next to Montgomery. His arm was wrapped around her shoulders, and little Elizabeth was fast asleep on his lap.

"Montgomery reminds me of my father," I said.

"I can see that. Although, Alex was never half as suspicious of me as this guy was."

"It's his nature as a marksman," I said. "He's our first and last line of defense. And believe me, if you'd said anything even remotely shady when you met Dad, he would have reacted in exactly the same way."

"Glad my mother taught me to be honest."

"Me, too. So, Katherine had an idea," I began, and I told Dan all about Katherine's plan to anoint me as Mistress of Seers in six days.

"What do you think?" I asked, when I'd shared the entire plan with him. "Should we stay in the past for another week?"

"Up to you, babe," he said. "But I have to say, I like it here. Maybe we should stay here permanently."

"We can't do that. People are depending on us."

"Maybe you can send them a magic message, so they know we're all right," he said, his mouth against my neck. "Or we can take the tunnels to our time, kick Hassan's ass, and come back here."

I leaned back against him, one of my hands holding his while the other reached back to tangle in his soft, curly hair. "What about the Lyons Family Estate?"

"Who's to say it can't be here?"

"Who's to say." I had to admit, I loved being surrounded by so many seers. Katherine was right in that I'd needed a reminder of just how amazing and vibrant our community was. However, as much as I loved living in the past, I wanted to rebuild this sense of community in our own time. As Mistress of Seers, it was my duty.

I clutched Dan's hand. For the first time, I felt like I really was a leader. Like I really could do this.

"What is it?" Dan asked. "You okay, babe?"

"I'm fine." I turned around, slid my arms around Dan's neck, and kissed him. "I'm perfect."

"Yeah, you are." He tucked my head underneath his chin and angled us so we were both facing the bonfire, and we held each other as we watched the flames dance up toward the stars. "So, speaking of Montgomery? He told me he'll be performing handfastings at dawn."

"Handfastings?" I repeated, ignoring the waver in my voice. Handfastings were a type of marriage ceremony where the bride and groom's hands were bound together, and they said their vows before a few witnesses. "Marksmen do that?"

"This one does. I guess the equinox is a good day for them, since each person is an equal partner in their relationship. What do you say?"

I drew back and regarded him, this straight-laced mortal that completed me in ways I never thought anyone could. "Is that what you want to do? In the morning? Tomorrow morning?"

"If you do, yeah. Or, we could ask if he could do one now."

"Now?" I shook my head. "You get some crazy ideas, Lyons."

"What can I say, Moore? I'm a man in love."

"We haven't even been together an entire month!"

"I've been in love with you since the moment I saw you," he said. "And, you told Katherine I'm the first mortal you brought into all of this. Does that mean anything?"

"Yeah. It does." My heart was beating so fast I worried I would pass out. "Okay. What do we do?"

"Okay?" Dan repeated, then his face was split by the widest, happiest grin I've ever seen. "Okay! We, um, I have no idea what we do. Wait, I don't have a ring."

"I don't need a ring." I caressed his cheek. His beard was coming in, and I liked how his stubble felt against my fingertips. "I only need you."

"I only need you, too." Dan lifted me off my feet and kissed me. "I love you, baby."

I heard thunder in the distance, and was momentarily worried the celebration would get rained out. The sound intensified, I realized it wasn't thunder, but a team of horses at full gallop. They barreled through the crowd and straight into the fire, sending sparks and hot coals everywhere. As we were pummeled by red hot projectiles, I heard Amir yell my name.

CHAPTER 35

BONES

"Ellie!" Amir screamed. "Where are you, Ellie? I know you're here!"

I scrambled back from the fire and into the darkness, dragging Dan with me. Once we were behind a hedge, I heard him groan.

"You're hurt," I whispered, feeling the singed patches on his shirt. When the horses galloped across the fire and sent burning wood flying in all directions, Dan had spun us around, shielding me from the worst of it.

"Some of the wood hit me," he said. "I'm okay."

"No, you're not!"

"I'm okay enough to deal with this asshole." He sat up, wincing as he did so. "I can handle it, for now. This is gonna need more than aloe, though."

I wanted to strip off his shirt and examine the burns, but Dan was right. We had to get out of this alive before we would have the luxury of licking our wounds. I peered toward the fire through the hedge. "Why did the horses run into the fire?" I muttered. "Wouldn't they have stopped, or gone around?"

"You didn't see them?" Dan asked. "They're not living."

"What?" I crept around the edge of the hedgerow and got my first full look at what had crashed our party. Amir was driving a black carriage that looked straight out of a horror movie, and it was being pulled by two massive horse skeletons.

"I can't believe it," I whispered. "He's using bones again."

"Again?" Dan said as he crouched next to me.

"That's been his thing for a while," I said. "He would raid museums and cemeteries for bones. Sometimes he robbed graves, but more often he would take from public museums or excavated tombs. I've never seen him raise an entire skeleton before."

"He stole bones from museums?" Dan asked. "Why there? Why not just dig them up?"

"An open grave attracts attention, but people don't check artifacts in museums very often," I replied, remembering how Amir's theft of Pacheri's foot bones was only discovered when the museum received a grant to x-ray the mummy. "He stole from a bunch of holy relics in Paris, too."

"Every time you tell me a story about this guy, I like him less," Dan said, then he grabbed my arm. "He's got someone with him. A woman."

"Is it Jemima?" I wondered, because I would not put it past Amir to reanimate her so soon after her passing. Then I heard Katherine scream.

"Melinda," Katherine yelled. The woman on the cart turned toward the voice, and I gasped.

Melinda Howe was sitting next to Amir.

"Shit," I muttered. "Does he have all the clan elders in that carriage?"

"I don't think that's our Melinda," Dan said. "Katherine knows her, and like you always say, witches live a long time."

"Yeah. They do." I debated summoning Tessa, since she was one of the few witches I knew of who was powerful enough to fight off Amir and a clan elder. But while she was alive during this time, she didn't come to North America for at least another century. If I summoned her out of the blue, that would cause even more problems. "What do we do?"

Dan jerked his head toward the edge of the clearing. "Montgomery has a plan."

Montgomery strode into the remains of the firelight, his crossbow trained on Amir. "Leave my home, villain! You are not welcome here, nor are you wanted."

"Give me Ellie, and I'll gladly leave this hovel," Amir snapped. "And I will have her. I will kill a seer every minute until you hand her over!"

"No," Montgomery said. "You'll get nothing here."

"You'll regret this, marksman," Amir screeched. "Eliza Moore has much to atone for. Tell them, Melinda!"

Amir jerked his arm. Melinda was lashed to the carriage seat with lengths of bandages. I was again reminded of Pacheri, the mummy Amir had desecrated in Paris, and realized that I wasn't looking at a living version of Melinda. That was her corpse.

"When did you kill Melinda?" I yelled, as I moved behind the hedge, using it as cover as I went to the opposite side of the clearing from Montgomery. Since I was Amir's target, I hoped I could draw him away from the rest. "Is that our Melinda, or the one from the past?"

"You're a seer. Figure it out," Amir shouted. "Or use your witch blood. Do your precious Moores know about your tainted blood?"

"Yeah. They know." I stepped out from behind the hedge and into full view of Amir and the rest. "And, I'm not tainted. What I am is more powerful than you."

I clapped my hands together and focused on the horses. "Dissemble," I said, and the skeletons clattered apart into two heaps of bones. "Lost your ride, Amir."

"Don't need it," he said, then he raised his arms, and the bones flew at me as if they'd been shot out of a cannon. I dropped to the ground, but not before some bones pummeled my shoulder and arms. At least the skulls had missed me.

Amir cried out and fell back against the carriage. I raised my head, and saw a crossbow bolt in his shoulder. Montgomery fit a second bolt in place and fired again. Amir used Melinda's body as a shield, and the bolt landed in her throat.

I heard an explosion behind me, and Amir jerked back. Dan had shot him in the torso... Which was the same place he'd shot him in a few days ago.

"How did Amir heal from that other gunshot?" I yelled to Dan.

"No idea," he replied. "He shouldn't be able to move around like he is. Wait, the doors are opening." The doors to the carriage banged open, and hundreds of bones poured out and began assembling into skeletons.

"I guess the clan elders are elsewhere," I muttered, then I saw Katherine, crouched down with Elizabeth in her arms, and crawled toward her.

"You and Elizabeth need to get inside," I said. "We can't let him hurt you!"

"What about you?" she countered. "You need to get back to your time, and stop him for good."

"Maybe we can stop him here."

"I don't think we do," she said. "My foresight has warned me of such an evil event for some years now. This villain decimates us, but you avenge us."

I paused. "Avenge implies you're dead."

"We all are, by the time you come along." Katherine caressed my cheek. "I believe we are meant to hold Amir here, and allow you and your Daniel time to escape."

Another bolt struck the carriage. More screams and bones tore through the air. "I don't know if we can find the tunnels in the dark."

"Go to the nexus," Katherine said. "The guardians will take you."

"What can the nexus do?"

"I don't know, but my gut is telling me that's where you need to be." Katherine pressed her forehead to mine. "It's also telling me that we shall meet again. Go, now, while he's distracted."

"I will come back, I swear it," I said, then I turned to Dan. His face was creased with pain, and he held his right arm against his body as if it were broken. Katherine was right—we needed to get out of here, if for no other reason than to get Dan to a doctor.

"Can you walk?" I asked Dan.

"Yeah," he ground out, then he hauled himself to his feet. "What's the plan?"

"The cats are going to take us to the nexus."

"And?"

"And that's all we have." I took his hand. "We can figure out the rest, right?"

"We can." Dan looked to Katherine. "Take care of yourself, and Lizzie and Monty. We need you."

"I shall. And you take care of Eliza."

"Ma'am, she takes care of me, but I'll do my best." Dan patted Elizabeth's head, then he and I crept away from the field and toward the house.

"This is awful," I muttered. "I can't believe we're leaving them to be slaughtered."

"We know they're not slaughtered," Dan said, "and according to Katherine, this is the only way. Where are the cats?"

As if on cue, the cats melted out of the shadows. They were still house cats, so I picked up Pumpkin and held her close. "Katherine says you need to take us to the nexus. Can you do that?"

Pumpkin purred deep in her chest, and the other two cats wove in between our legs. As far as I was concerned, that was a yes. I turned to tell Dan, and was suddenly facing Amir.

"Got you, bitch," he sneered.

I screamed as Amir sank his bony fingers into my shoulder. My skin sizzled, and I felt my knees give way as he pushed me into the dirt.

Pumpkin hissed, and her paw shot out. Amir jerked away from me, holding his face as blood dripped between his fingers.

"Go," Katherine yelled. "Now!"

I held Pumpkin against my chest as Dan hauled me to my feet, and we ran toward the kitchen entrance. When we reached the house, I heard a roar and looked back. Smokey and Muffuletta were giant cougars again, and the cats were beating Amir's skeleton army apart with their massive paws.

"Where did all those bones come from?" I wondered.

"Later," Dan said, and he pulled me inside.

We ran up the stairs, up to the library, and then to the spiral staircase that I'd never once climbed. When we got to the tower, Pumpkin leapt out of my arms and ran toward the back of the room, and touched the wall with her paw. There, behind a false panel, was the second staircase.

"Where does this go?" I asked, craning my neck so I could see where the stairs led.

There was a crash behind us. "We'll know soon enough," Dan said, then he pushed me onto the stairs. Once we were both on the stairs, the panel slid shut behind us.

"Okay. Follow the guardian." Pumpkin flicked my nose with her tail, and she led me up the stairs. They went on forever, easily more stairs than the rest of the house had, combined.

Once, I looked back to check on Dan. He was there, and I sighed in relief. Then I looked past him and realized we were surrounded by a black void speckled with blue orbs.

"Don't look down," I said to Dan, then I faced Pumpkin again.

Eventually, we reached a platform. Pumpkin hopped off the top step and sat in the middle of the platform. I followed, then Dan fell onto the platform behind me. I ran to him, stumbling to my knees beside him.

"Just a little farther," I said. "Come on. Just a little farther, and we'll get you some help."

I grabbed his right arm, and he cried out. "That arm's pretty bad," he ground out.

"Okay. Other arm, then." I grabbed his left arm, and dragged him toward Pumpkin. Good thing the floor was smooth. Once we were there, I helped him sit up, then I asked Pumpkin, "Now what, fluff?"

"Eli, look," Dan said. The area around us was no longer a void, but a pulsating blue tunnel. "It's a pattern, like rays coming out from the center."

"I wonder what the pattern's supposed to be," I said, then the floor went from solid to thick and viscous like quicksand, and we slipped down into the void.

Chapter 36

The Letter

My back hit the floor first. It hurt, but not as much as my other injuries hurt. I rolled toward Dan, saw his chest rise and fall, and passed out.

Some time later, Pumpkin licked my face. I swatted her away, and went back to sleep.

Later still, there was shouting.

"Eli? Eli! Dan!"

I recognized Tessa's voice, heard her fancy shoes click-clack across the floor. "Alex! Eli and Dan are up here!"

She click-clacked back toward me, and I felt the rumble of someone charging up the stairs. I cracked an eyelid, and realized we were in the library. So that was why my back hurt. We were lying on the hardwood floor. I moved to my side to ignore Tessa's shouting, and get more comfortable. Then my father burst into the room.

"Eliza," he said, gently easing me to a sitting position. "Eliza, sweetheart, how long have you been in the house?"

"We fell," I mumbled. "Dan is hurt."

"You're hurt," Dad said. I blinked my eyes open, and saw Tessa help Dan sit up. She moved his arm, and he hissed in pain.

"Pretty sure that's broken," Dan said, then he opened his eyes. "Oh, hey, Tess."

"Hey, yourself. How did you break your arm?"

"Got hit with a horse femur."

"That must have been painful," she said. "I'm going to take your shirt off, okay?"

"He has burns," I said. "On his back."

"So do you," my dad said, then he opened his marksman's kit. Dad always carried burn cream. "It looks like... a handprint?"

"Handprint," I mumbled, and watched as he squeezed out a bit of burn cream and dabbed it onto my shoulder. The fabric of my dress had burned away where Amir touched me, leaving my shoulder bare. "That's where Amir grabbed me."

My father and Tessa shared a look, then she refocused on Dan. When she got his shirt off, she paused. "I haven't seen clothing like this in centuries," she said, then she noticed the monogram inside the shirt. "M.F.? Who is M.F.?"

"That's Montgomery's shirt," I said, remembering how Katherine had offered Dan and me some period appropriate clothes so we wouldn't stand out in our jeans and sneakers. "I don't know his last name. He was a marksman, like you, Dad," I added.

"Do you mean Montgomery Fletcher?" Dad asked, and I shrugged. Then I whimpered, because shrugging had aggravated all of my wounds. "Eli, where were you?"

"We were here, but three hundred years ago."

"More like three hundred and fifty, maybe three hundred and seventy-five years ago," Dan added. Tessa had grabbed the burn cream, and was applying it to his back. "We were... we were going to celebrate Eli's birthday."

"Hettie was going to bake a cake," I mumbled, then my mind caught up with what had happened. "What day is it?"

"September fifteenth," Dad replied. "You two have been missing ever since you disappeared off Chief Renault's roof."

"We went through a pigeon coop and ended up in a time tunnel." I faced my father. "Dad, there's a whole network of time tunnels around here. Amir's been sneaking back and forth for centuries. Through the centuries, too. I think all the tunnels lead to the nexus, and he's been siphoning power from it. And... and he's the one who made the poison that killed Jemima Allwood," I added, my voice cracking when I said her name.

"Let's get you two downstairs so we can take care of Dan's arm," Tessa said, as she helped Dan to his feet. "You can tell us everything while we do that."

"Shouldn't I go to a hospital?" Dan asked. "Get an x-ray, see an orthopedist?"

"We can deal with a small break at home," she replied, and they disappeared down the stairs. Dad helped me stand, then he pulled me into his arms.

"I am so glad you're home," he said. "I was so worried. No one could sense you, not Tessa or even Jacob. They even tried summoning you, but if you were in a different time, I can understand why that didn't work."

"I'm sorry we were gone so long," I said. "It didn't feel like more than a few days, but it was so confusing." Dad was holding me so hard it hurt, with my burns and bruises screaming in protest. I didn't care. Dad could squeeze me as hard as he wanted to. "I met Katherine Moore, and her daughter, Elizabeth."

"Your namesake," Dad said. "Are you a lot like her?"

"She was only about five," I replied. "But I also met her dad, Montgomery. He's a lot like you. Or, I guess you're a lot like him."

"Montgomery Fletcher is a legend." Dad said. "It's said he..." Dad drew back and regarded me. "It's said he defended the house from a siege by a rogue seer."

"I hope that means he survived Amir's attack," I said, remembering the flaming bones flying through the air.

"He died of old age," Dad said. "I'll get the records for you, after you get cleaned up. For now, let's take care of your shoulder."

We ended up sitting at the kitchen table. While my father made coffee and sandwiches, and Tessa practiced her magical first aid skills, Dan and I recounted everything that had happened to us since we set foot inside the pigeon coop that was definitely not a home for birds.

"Jill told us you went into the coop, but when we went to the roof to look for you, it was destroyed," Tessa said. She was confident she could heal Dan's fracture herself, and was spreading yet another ointment across his arm. "We could tell it was once a coop, but only a pile of old wood and wire remained, along with a few feathers. It may have been spelled to disintegrate after use, so to speak."

"We stepped off the roof, and into a subterranean tunnel. It was surreal." I cleared my throat, and said, "One of the first places it brought us to was Jada's funeral."

"Was that very far in the future?" Dad asked.

"You mean it hasn't happened yet? But she died weeks ago."

"Jada's alive and well," he replied. "She was injured in the fall from the roof, but not terribly so."

"How is that possible?" I turned to Dan, and asked, "I thought you saw her afterward?"

"She was lying on the ground and not moving, but that doesn't mean she was dead," Dan said. "I am happy to be wrong about that."

"Me, too," I said, as relief flooded me. "Where is she now?"

"She's in a higher security hospital," Dad replied. "Since she escaped from the last hospital, and kidnapped and held the police chief hostage, she's been undergoing a battery of tests."

"That's one death off my conscience," I said. "Do we know if Melinda Howe is dead? Maybe that wasn't her corpse alongside Amir."

Tessa set down her jar of ointment and wiped her hands. "No, but we can find out." She grabbed her phone, and sent a text. A moment later, her phone chirped. "Melinda hasn't been seen in public for several weeks. And no other members of the Howe clan have been seen, either."

"When Jacob and I went to the Howe estate, the place was a ghost town. Only the butler remained." I tapped the table with my fingertips. "I wonder if Amir has them all."

"Maybe that's where he got those bones," Dan offered. "Could be he emptied the Howe cemeteries."

"If he has their bones, he has their spirits, too," Tessa said. "And yet another very strong power source."

Dad refilled our coffee mugs, then he sat next to me. "What was it like inside the nexus?" he asked.

"Blue," I replied. "And, spiky."

"Spiky?"

"There were these blue blobs floating around, and they had lines shooting out of them," Dan explained. "Like sun rays."

"Or snowflakes," I said. "They were weirdly familiar, but I don't remember ever seeing anything like them before."

"Did the nexus pull you through to the tower room?" Dad asked.

"No, we landed on the library floor."

Dad grunted. "Then how did you get Christina's necklace?"

I touched the sapphire at my throat. "This is my necklace. We found it in the time tunnels."

My father frowned, then he stood and went upstairs. "Must be a dead ringer for your mother's necklace," Dan said.

I tamped down my smart comeback. Dan had a point, and it wasn't his fault I naturally bristled at the suggestion I was anything like my mother. Besides, Tessa had moved on to binding his arm, which meant he was already in pain. He didn't need me snapping at him, too.

Dad returned from upstairs, his appearance flanked by the cats. He set a necklace on the table, and I did a double take. It was a sapphire set in white gold, and it was an exact match to the one I was wearing.

"You can see why I was confused," Dad said.

"Yeah." I poked at the sapphire. It sparkled as if it had been newly polished. "It there a lot of her stuff up there?"

"A few boxes worth. You're welcome to look through them. Or, I could bring them down for you."

"Maybe later," I mumbled. "Do we know what Amir's been up to?"

"He's been rather quiet of late," Tessa began, "which, as you know, is unlike him. Now that we know he was in the past with you, I wonder if he's spent these past weeks tracking you through time."

"That's terrifying," Dan said. "Do we know what happened the day he attacked the house back in the seventeen hundreds?"

"Were there many casualties?" I added.

"There were," Tessa replied. "In the aftermath of the bone attacks, which is what that day came to be called, the local seer population was drastically reduced. Many had been mortally wounded, and many more left the area. For some time thereafter it was thought that living near the nexus was to invite danger. Eventually, only the Moores remained.

"However," she continued, just when I felt like my heart was about to hit the floor, "I have met both Elizabeth and Montgomery. They most definitely survived."

"What about Katherine?" I asked. "Did she make it?"

"I'm not sure," she replied. "Bear in mind, I came to this area almost a full century after these events. Anything could have happened in that time. Also, I had no reason to request an audience with the Mistress of Seers, and nor did Katherine have any reason to seek me out. Us not meeting isn't in any way unusual."

I nodded, because everything Tessa said made sense. Also, I now had confirmation that my namesake and her father survived Amir's attack. That, coupled with Jada's survival from her fall, bolstered my spirit.

"That's good news, but we need to plan our next actions," I said. "We can't just sit here and wait for Amir to attack again. We need to go to him."

"Agreed," Tessa said. "I'll put out some feelers, see if anyone has heard anything." She picked up her phone, and began typing.

"I will check the defenses, and the weapons cabinets," Dad said. "We need to be prepared in case he does attack."

"I'd like to help with that," Dan said.

"Shouldn't you rest your arm?" I said, since his right arm was incapacitated.

"I can shoot with both hands," Dan said, "and I do my best resting by being useful."

"All right, then. We'll be upstairs." My father and Dan went up to the tower, leaving me, Tessa, and the cats in the kitchen. I scooped Pumpkin onto my lap, and rubbed her ears.

"Thank you, fluff," I said, as she purred. "For everything."

I sat with Tess for a while, then she got embroiled in a situation with the clans; what with Ned Burroughs's recent death, and Melinda Howe apparently missing, the witch community was in disarray. I left her to it, and went into the solarium. Pumpkin went with me, and I followed her to the potted thornapple against the back wall.

"This plant certainly became significant," I said, as I sat on the floor in front of it. I had no idea how old this specimen was, but I was certain it was the same plant my mother had taken the flowers from to wear in her hair the day she abandoned me. What I did not understand was why she came here at all. Wouldn't it have been easier to avoid my grandmother's house completely, especially since she was planning on taking off after visiting me one last time?

From everything Dad had told me over the years, Gran had been livid when my mother allowed me to be admitted into the psychiatric ward. My mother knew I wasn't crazy, but instead of bringing me to Gran, who was more than capable of helping me with my nascent seer abilities, she allowed a team of mundane doctors to put a terrified child into a cold, unfamiliar place surrounded by strangers. And then she left me.

Just like that, she left me.

"I don't know if I can ever forgive that," I said to Pumpkin. "I get that she was scared, and confused, and way out of her comfort zone, but I was her child. Didn't that matter?" I picked up Pumpkin, and hugged her. "Didn't she ever miss me?"

Pumpkin rubbed her forehead against my cheek. At least the cats had always loved me. As I snuggled Pumpkin, I noticed something sticking out beneath the plant stand. I set Pumpkin down, and pulled out an envelope from beneath the thornapple.

"Weird." There had never been anything beneath this plant stand, save the floor. I'd moved it at least a dozen times over the years, either to prune it back or detangle the knot of vines on the trellis. But here in my hand was an envelope made of old, yellowed paper. I turned it over, and gasped when I saw who it was addressed to.

To My Cousin From Virginia

I carefully opened the envelope, and unfolded the letter within.

My dearest Eliza,

I do hope this letter finds you well. You mentioned that the solarium is still present in your day, therefore I assumed it was the best place to leave this letter. I hope you find it, and that it offers you some comfort.

The guardians—well, they don't say much, do they? But they have remained as small cats, and we have continued on referring to them by the names you gave them: Pumpkin, Smokey, and Muffuletta. Elizabeth finds great fun in that last name, though none of us have the slightest idea of what a Muffuletta could be. If you ever return, please do bring an explanation as to this unusual name's provenance.

I am certain you want to know what happened on the day you left. The attack was horrible, and the man responsible for all of that death and mayhem, one Amir Hassan, did escape with his life. However, he was gravely injured by Pumpkin, your Daniel, and my Montgomery. As I write this letter, it has been a full month since the bone attacks ended, and he has not returned. We now dare to hope he has succumbed to his wounds. Our community suffered many casualties, but both Montgomery and Elizabeth survived. I am forever grateful to you, Eliza, and to Daniel. If you hadn't been present when the attacks began, I truly don't know what would have become of us.

One thing that saddens me is that it is unlikely we will ever meet again. However, knowing that you will be there to lead us in the future gives me great joy. I wish I had been able to anoint you as Mistress of

Seers, but truly, you do not need me. You are strong, Eliza, and your mother's blood makes you stronger yet. I have no doubt you will lead us well.

Yours always,

Katherine

I clutched the letter to my breast, happy and relieved that Katherine and her family had made it through the bone attacks. I was on my third re-read of the letter when Dan joined me.

"I thought I'd find you here," he said, as he sat on the floor beside me. He was wearing one of my father's old band shirts, along with his knee breeches from three hundred years ago. It was quite the look. "What's that?"

"Katherine wrote me a letter," I said, and I passed it to him. "They survived the attack!"

"And they hurt Hassan," Dan said. "Hurt him a lot, based on what she included here. That's good news for us."

"How's your arm?"

"Sore as hell," he replied. "I still think I should go to a hospital, but I'm good for now. Tess knows what she's doing."

"She does," I agreed. "Are the defenses ready?"

"They are. Whenever this bastard shows up, we'll be ready for him." Dan stroked my cheek. "We were going to get married today."

"Handfasting's not the same as marriage," I said. "It's not legally recognized, and they're temporary. It's more like a trial marriage than the real thing."

"How long are these trial periods?"

"A year, I think. Or, a year and a day."

He took my hand, and rubbed his thumb across my knuckles. "Does this mean you've changed your mind?"

"Have you?" I demanded, momentarily terrified than Dan had finally had enough of my problems.

He didn't look up when he replied. "You know I haven't."

"I haven't, either." I moved closer, so my knee was aligned with his hip, and vice versa. "I've been thinking about you, and us, and I know I freak out a lot. I have baggage—like, a ton of baggage—and sometimes I can't feel anything except the weight of it."

"I'll help you carry it," he said.

"That's the thing. You do help me carry it, and you do so many other things for me. I don't know what I'd do without you." I leaned my head on his shoulder. He smelled like burn cream, and the herbal ointments Tessa had used on his arm, but underneath it all there was a whiff of Katherine's equinox fire. "I'm sorry I freak out so much. It's not you. It's all me and my issues."

"It's okay, baby." Dan cupped the back of my head, and kissed my forehead. "We've all got issues. You know I have plenty." He paused, took a breath. "Are my issues, coupled with yours, too much?"

"No. Never." I put my hand over his heart. "Like I said, I've been thinking, and I've figured a few things out." His body tensed. "Are you okay?" I asked, worried about his arm, and the burns on his back.

"Am I losing you?"

I placed my hand on his stubbly cheek. "Do you really think I'd give you up? I don't want to do this without you." His mouth twitched, but his eyes were concerned. "I love you, Dan. I'm pretty sure I've loved you my entire life, but when we met all my stupid baggage got in the way, and I couldn't see you around it. But you've always seen me, haven't you?"

"Always," he said. "I'll never forget the first time I saw you. You were like an angel sitting there in the station, waiting for me to take your statement. It was the best day of my life, and since then I've had better and better days. Every day I wake up is the best day of my life, because I get to spend it with you." He laughed softly. "That was pretty cheesy."

"I like cheese." I kissed him. "I like you, too."

"Wait, you like me? A second ago, you loved me. How'd I get demoted?"

"I can't like you and love you?"

"I guess that's okay." He looped his good arm around me. "What do you say we kick Hassan's ass, get you properly installed as Mistress of Seers, and then we can talk about us some more?"

"Can we talk about us in bed? Or, in a bubble bath?"

"Whatever you want, babe."

CHAPTER 37

NEW PLAN

The four of us reconvened in the front parlor. As far as I was concerned, our next order of business was charging our time traveling cell phones. My father was more interested in Katherine's letter.

"This is amazing." Dad had read the letter multiple times, and now he was examining the reverse side. "It was never there, and yet now that you've been to the past, it's always been here."

"Makes you wonder what else is different," I said.

"I'm beginning to see why all this time magic is forbidden," Dan said. "My brain hurts just thinking about this. How could anyone keep all of this straight?"

"They didn't, and mistakes happened," Tessa said, as she untangled the charging cords. "Here, Eli. These are all set."

"Thanks, Tess. I hope these still work," I said, as attached the cords and handed the phones to Dan. "There's an outlet behind that table."

"Let me," my father said, when Dan tried to plug the phone in with his injured hand. "I can't believe you had so much modern equipment with you. What did Katherine and Montgomery think of it?"

"Montgomery never saw any of it," I replied. I fingered the thornapple seed pod, which had made the journey to the past with us. It was the one thing I had on me that wouldn't have raised eyebrows.

"Although, he probably would have murdered us if we did. He was not a trusting sort."

Dad laughed softly. "Marksmen never are. We're more concerned with keeping our people safe than making friends."

"Good thing you trusted Dan when you met him."

"That was because you trust him, Bug. There is no opinion I value more than yours."

"Not even mine?" Tessa asked, with a coy glance. While she was binding Dan's arm, she told him that she'd spent almost every minute with Dad since we went missing. I hoped they had finally dealt with their own issues, and were ready to move on.

"You trust me, which automatically makes me question your judgement," Dad said, and they both laughed. "Other than being suspicious, Montgomery was a good man?"

"He was," I replied. "There were so many seers—they were gathering for an equinox celebration—and everyone respected him, but more than that, they liked him. He was a great leader. Also, his daughter just adored him. She was stuck to him like glue from the moment he arrived."

"A daughter adoring her marksman father," Tessa said. "Where have I seen that before?"

"Katherine adored him, too," I said. "She blushed every time he looked at her. Where have I seen that before?"

"I don't blush," Tessa said. "What were the plans for the equinox? I remember much business being conducted at those types of gatherings."

"Seemed like it was going to be a big party," Dan said. "That, and Montgomery was scheduled to do some handfastings. I guess people had been waiting for him."

"Why would anyone wait for him?" Tessa wondered. "Anyone can perform a handfasting. You bind the couple's hands together, they pledge themselves to each other, and then they consummate their new relationship. It's really quite simple."

"Then maybe you two should shack up," I said, looking pointedly from Tessa to my father. My phone powered up, and began beeping with a thousand notifications. Dan's started beeping a moment later.

"Well, we were gone a long time," I said, then I began scrolling through texts. "Aw, Tess, you were so worried about us."

"I now regret every drop of emotion I wasted on you," she said. "Is there anything useful in there?"

"Jada sent a text." I opened it, and read it out loud.

Jada: Ellie, I'm so sorry about what happened with the policeman. I didn't mean to hurt anyone, or scare you. I have all these images in my head, and while I know they're not real sometimes I get confused. I'm so, so sorry.

"Sarah's memories are driving her mad," my dad said.

"There's more," I said.

Jada: My boyfriend, Nathaniel, he told me some things, and I told the doctors but they just think I'm being nuts again. But I think he was serious! He told me that he's going to take the dead witch and teach the bitch a lesson. I remember, because witch and bitch rhyme. I don't know where he would get a witch, since it's early for Halloween, but the bitch is you. How does he know you? Anyway, please be careful!

I dropped the phone onto my lap. "Which dead witch do we think Amir will send after me?"

"Sarah Allwood?" Tessa suggested. "Although, it seems those two had their falling out some time ago. Ned Burroughs, maybe?"

"Or Melinda Howe," Dan said. "She seemed pretty dead when we saw her a few centuries ago."

"So he killed Melinda, and dragged her corpse through time?" Dad shook his head. "Why so much effort?"

"He wants me, but why?" I asked no one in particular. "Amir's goal is power, but he doesn't need me to get it. Hell, anyone can stockpile power."

"But Hassan wants all the power, and for him, that golden ring is the nexus," Dan said. "You've been through it, so maybe he thinks you're the key to him getting into it."

"You've been through it, too," I said.

Dan shrugged. "Yeah, but you're better looking. I'm sure he'd much rather hang out with you."

"That's the thing—Amir hates me," I said. "He has ever since Tess and I found his bone hoard in Paris, and put everything back where it belonged."

"Then perhaps it's not that he wants you to stand at his side," my dad said. "Perhaps this is more about revenge."

"He is a vengeful little man," Tessa said. "When you left him, he suffered a rather significant setback. Him plotting your demise along with his rise do power is the sort of drama he craves." Tessa was being kind when she said I left Amir. Actually, he'd all but vanished from my life. Not only was I devastated, I didn't even get the satisfaction of a final cathartic argument.

Instead of correcting Tessa, I said, "He is a drama llama." I appreciated her kindness. "Which means he's going to do something big and dramatic now."

"When criminals try to pull off something showy, that's when they mess up," Dan said. "They get so involved in making a statement, they forget details. That's how we'll stop Hassan, by looking for the flaws in his plan."

"We need to know what his plan is before we can find the flaws," I said, then I turned to Tessa. "Any luck finding him?"

She shook her head. "Not yet."

"Why don't we ask Jada?" Dan asked. "Arrogant bastard's probably still visiting her."

"Do you think we can get into the hospital?" I asked, then I looked down at my lap. I was still wearing Katherine's partially burned dress, and Dan was wearing colonial pants and shoes. "We need to change, and I don't know if I haven any clothes left upstairs." Dan definitely didn't have any clothes in my old room. That meant we needed to make a side trip to the house. "Tess, can you give us a ride?"

"The car Jacob gave you is here," Tess said. "We returned the rental a few weeks ago."

"I hated that rental," Dan grumbled.

"How did the car get here?" I asked. "We left it at that motel."

Tessa shrugged. "One morning I woke up, and it was in the driveway. The keys are in it."

I stood, and began gathering up my phone and other things. "Okay, new plan. We're going to go home to shower and change. While we're gone, can one of you get with Bennet, and find out how likely it is for us to get in to see Jada?" When everyone just stared at me, I asked, "What?"

"That was the first time you openly admitted you live with me," Dan said, then he grabbed his phone. "Alex, thanks for the shirt. I'll wash it before I return it."

"Keep it," Dad said. "Call if you need anything."

"We will."

I followed Dan out through the back door. Just like Tessa had said, the black SUV was sitting in the driveway. "I suppose you want to drive."

"You suppose right." Dan opened the driver's side door, then he jerked his chin at something behind me. "Your father."

I turned around; Dad had followed us out to the porch. "What's up?"

"I'm not going to ask if you're happy with Dan," he began in a rush. "I can see your happiness every time I look at you. But I want you to know that no matter what happens, you will always have a home with me, be it here or anywhere in the world." He frowned, and continued, "I don't mean to insinuate that someday you might not have a home with Dan. He can live with us, too, if he needs to."

I hugged my father. "I know what you mean, and thank you. You really are the best, Dad."

"I'd do anything for you, Bug." He gave me a final squeeze, then he released me. "I do regret not walling Amir inside that portal in Persia when we had the chance."

"Knowing him, he would have tunneled out, anyway." I stepped back, and took a moment to appreciate how awesome my father really was. Even though my mother hadn't been the greatest, because of him, I'd always felt like I won the parent lottery. "We'll get him."

Dad nodded. "We will."

CHAPTER 38

WE NEED A BIGGER GUN

Dan turned onto our street and swore. "What's wrong?" I asked.

"I don't have my keys," he said. "They're back in seventeen whatever."

"It's okay. I have mine." I reached into my giant colonial pockets and retrieved my keychain. "Remember, I stashed everything modern in my skirt?"

"You really are perfect," he said, then he brought my hand to his mouth and kissed my knuckles. "I have to say, of everything I had with me, at least only the keys got left behind. If I'd left Jill's gun back then, that might have had some consequences."

"Yeah, like Montgomery shooting Amir in the head," I muttered.

"I wonder if that would have done anything," Dan said. "When he showed up with the bone patrol, he didn't act as if I'd shot him the day before."

"You're right." Amir had moved and spoken freely, as if he wasn't in the smallest amount of pain. "I wonder if he used the tunnels to go off somewhere, heal, and then he came back to the same time he'd left us in?"

"I know you hit it off with Katherine, and you probably want to pay her a visit, but I'm thinking those tunnels should get filled up with concrete. Humans were not meant to time travel." Dan pulled into the driveway. "Let's see how bad the food in the fridge is."

I wrinkled my nose. "I hope the power didn't go out."

"Even if it did temporarily, it wouldn't stay off. The bill gets auto paid every month." I passed Dan the keys. He unlocked the door, then he faced me. "You realize I have to carry you over the threshold."

"You do not." He grinned, and I took a step back. "You can't pick me up with a broken arm!"

"You're little. I bet I can do it with one arm."

"Don't you dare!"

"Oh, I dare," he said, then he looped his good arm around my waist and lifted me off my feet. I squealed as he hauled me inside and set me down in the foyer.

"You're awful," I said, as I swatted his chest. He laughed, and squeezed my hip. "I'm going to water the plants."

The potted herbs that lived on the kitchen windowsill were pretty dry, but they had all survived our unexpected absence. I set them in the sink and turned on the sprayer, so they could have a good soak. Dan entered the kitchen behind me, and dumped an armload of mail onto the table.

"This is a lot of mail," he declared.

"Anything important?"

"Nah. Mostly junk." He left the mail behind, opened the fridge door, and closed it again. "Don't go in there."

"Believe me, I won't." I plucked off a few shriveled up sage leaves and set them aside. "Do you want to clean out the fridge before or after we handle the mail?"

Dan moved my hair to the side, then he kissed the back of my neck. "I can think of a few things I want to do before the mail." His arm slid around my waist as he pressed himself against me.

"Be careful," I said, wiggling toward his left side. "You'll hurt your arm."

"My arm feels great. Speaking of great, you really do look amazing in this dress." His kisses moved from my neck to my ear, while his hands roamed over the front of my dress. "How do I get in here?"

"Don't rip it!" I shut off the faucet, then I reached back and sank my fingers into his hair while he thoroughly explored my bodice. "What's gotten into you?"

"Feels like forever since we were in bed together." He nipped my earlobe, then he nuzzled the soft spot behind my ear. "Been three hundred years, at least."

"Technically, you're right. We should have snuck off to the barn, like Katherine and Montgomery did."

"Did they? I figured Katherine was too proper for something like that."

"Katherine couldn't wait to jump his bones."

Dan clenched his fist. "This dress is like Fort Knox. I'm getting the scissors."

"No!" I lunged in front of him. "You can't do that! Just ask nicely, and I'll take it off."

"Yeah?" He picked me up and sat me on the counter, then he slid his hand underneath my skirts. "Maybe you don't need to take it off."

I kissed him hard, more than willing to take the dress off, leave it on, or do any combination of the two, when someone knocked on the back door. I glanced out the window, and saw Dan's annoying neighbor, Gretchen, waving at us. "You've got to be kidding me."

"I'll get rid of her. Don't move." Dan went to the kitchen door as I smoothed my skirts into place. Gretchen did not need to know what we would soon be up to.

"Hi, Gretchen," Dan said as he opened the door. "Come on in."

"Oh, it's so good to see you," Gretchen said, then she saw me sitting on the counter. "And you, Eliza. What a lovely dress. What happened to your shoulder?"

"Barbecue accident," I replied. "What brings you by today?"

"I wanted you to know that I've been keeping an eye on your house while you were away," she said to Dan. "Not that I knew you'd be away, but I assumed it must have been last-minute police work."

"We were visiting family," Dan said.

Gretchen batted her false eyelashes at Dan. "Oh, you went back to Queens?"

"We were visiting my family, who live much closer," I said.

"But you were gone for weeks!"

"There are a lot of them."

She nodded, and turned her attention back to Dan. "Do you like Pink Floyd?" she asked, eyeing his tee shirt.

"Actually, it's Eli's father's shirt," Dan said. "Thanks for watching the house, Gretchen. I owe you one. Now, if you don't mind, we've got some unpacking to do."

"Oh, all right," Gretchen said, as Dan opened the door for her. "Speaking of unpacking, you did get quite a lot of packages delivered while you were away. I put them in the garage for you." She leaned closer to Dan, and stage whispered, "Some of them had her name on them."

"Great, thanks for letting us know," Dan said. "Have a nice day!"

He shut the door, and asked, "You didn't have anything delivered here, did you?"

"No. My default address on my credit card is Gran's." I hopped down from the counter. "So, what's in the garage?"

"Hang on." He went into the living room, and returned with his tablet. "Remember my surveillance cameras? I've got one in the garage. Let's see what's happening in there."

"Nice."

He powered up the tablet, and logged into the surveillance app. "I'll give you the password for this, if you want," he said. "I mean, I guess they're our cameras now."

I kissed his cheek. "You're sweet, but I don't need or want half of your stuff."

"You think I'm sweet?" The app pinged, and Dan brought up the image of the garage's interior. Sitting in the center of the floor was a pile of cardboard boxes.

"They're stacked up like a pyramid," I said. "Do we think Gretchen is branching out into box art?"

"It's not like she has anything else to do," Dan muttered. "Harassing the neighbors seems to be her sole hobby." He zoomed in on a few of the boxes. "She was right. Most of these are addressed to you."

"But who sent them?" I tapped my chin. "Do we want to open one and see what jumps out? Although, then we'll be in the line of fire."

"Can't you open them from here?" he countered. I was about to ask what he was talking about, when I remembered. Witchcraft.

"Okay. I can do this." I shook out my hands, took a breath to center myself, and said, "Open." The top box popped open. "Can you see what's in there?" I asked.

Dan adjusted the angle on the camera, then he sighed. "Those are socks, and I ordered them. Next box?"

"You buy socks online?"

"These are special socks, for running. Next box."

I gave Dan some side eye, but let the subject of his fancy socks drop. For now. I focused on the box to the left of the socks, and asked it to open. The tape popped and the cardboard flaps unfolded, then a bone clattered out onto the floor.

"Is that human?"

"No idea," Dan said. "Call Jill. This is her area."

I found my phone, and dialed Jill's number. She picked up on the first ring.

"Eli? Where are you? Where's Dan?"

"Dan's with me, and we're at his house. If I send you a picture of a bone, can you identify it?"

"Hang on. First, you need to tell me exactly what happened to the two of you, and where you've been all this time. I can't figure out how you got off Renault's roof without anyone seeing you."

"Hey, how is Renault?"

"Better. He'd like to talk to Dan, too."

"I bet." I moved the phone away from my mouth, and said, "Jill said the chief is doing better."

"That's good. What about this bone?"

"Hang on," I said, then I answered Jill's question. "As for how we got off the roof, we went through the pigeon coop and ended up in these weird tunnels, walked through time, and spent a few days at a gathering of seers and witches about three hundred years in the past. Wait, I have proof." I switched to video chat, and showed her my dress. "See? Old timey dress."

"Um, yeah. That's an old fashioned dress. Is Dan dressed like a Minuteman?"

"Only halfway." I turned the phone's camera toward him. He waved. I turned the camera back toward me, and asked, "Want more details, or can you look at the bone?"

"Show me the evidence."

I angled the phone so the camera could see the tablet's screen. "Can you see it? Dan, can you enlarge it?"

"I got it," Jill said. "That's a human scapula. What's in the rest of the boxes?"

"Socks," I replied.

Dan narrowed his eyes at me. "Babe, want to open a few more?"

"Sure." I focused my intent on the remaining boxes, and a few others opened. "Jill, what are these?"

"I can see a tibia, a calcaneus, and what looks like a pile of ribs," she replied. "How are the boxes opening?"

"Magic."

"Oh. Of course. Next questions, whose bones are these, and why do you have them?"

"We don't know," Dan replied. "Someone sent Eli a bunch of packages, and my neighbor put them in the garage. We're just now opening them."

"Your neighbor—wait, do you mean Gretchen?"

"That's the one." Dan glanced at me. "She doesn't like Jill, either."

"She only likes Dan," Jill said.

"I know, right?" I said. "Anyway, we have no idea who or where these bones came from."

"Have you called this in?" When neither of us answered her, she continued, "If you haven't, I should really report it."

"Yes, you should," Dan said. "Want to open a few more?"

"Sure."

"Wait," Jill said. "I should probably get over there first."

"Jill, I am going to overrule you," I said. "If these bones are spelled, they could hurt you."

"Can't they hurt you, too?"

I swallowed the lump in my throat; I wasn't used to having mortals worry about me. "Yeah, but this is what I do. I hold the line between the magical and the mundane."

"Sounds like you could use some help."

"That's why I called you." Before she could say anything else, I opened the next three boxes. "What're those?"

"There's another tibia, a clavicle... Are these all from the same body?" Jill paused, and I heard a pencil scratching. "Also, they look rather old."

"How old?" I asked.

"Not sure, but based on eyeballing these remains, they were buried for a significant amount of time before someone disinterred them."

I faced Dan. "It's one of Amir's tricks."

"What do we do?" Dan asked.

"Guys," Jill yelled. "That last box you opened is the skull."

Dan and I looked at Jill's image on the phone, then we turned as one and looked at the tablet. Jill was right. The last box I'd opened had what appeared to be a human skull in it.

"Jill, do what you need to do," Dan said. "We've got to go."

"Thanks Jill," I said, then I ended the call. "Want to open the rest?"

Dan nodded. "Do them all at once."

I clapped my hands together, and said, "Open." Then I gasped.

Bones poured out of the boxes; big bones, small bones, bones I was pretty sure weren't even human. They ran down the heap of cardboard boxes like rivulets of a stream, then they gathered in the center of the garage floor, swirling like a whirlpool. Before our eyes, the bones assembled themselves into a semblance of a human form.

"These are not all from the same person," I said. There were too many bones, and they weren't from the same sized body. A lopsided skeleton now lumbered across the garage floor, snarling and snapping at Dan's tool bench.

"What do we do?" Dan asked. "Eli, what do we do?"

"I-I don't know!" The skeleton paced the perimeter of the garage, then it clenched its bony hands into fists and slammed them down onto the table saw. The metal base shattered, and the saw blade skittered across the floor.

"Eli," Dan barked. "You can do this." I was about to say that I had no experience with skeleton monsters, when I realized they were just bones. Bones, I could handle. What's more, they would listen to me. After all, they were dead.

"I'll take it apart," I said, then I reached out with my ability and told the bones to return to rest.

They ignored me.

I increased my intent, threw everything I had toward them. They didn't budge.

"I can't affect the bones," I said. "They should return to rest when I order it, but I can't get through to them. It's like they're encased in something I can't penetrate."

"Hassan sent us a murder monster," Dan muttered. "Great. Shit!"

When Dan swore, I glanced at the tablet. The bone monster, apparently sick of being confined, had moved on from Dan's tools and was pounding on the garage door.

"We can't let that thing get out," Dan said.

"How can we stop it?" I asked, desperately. "Can you shoot it, make it fall apart?"

Dan passed me his handgun. "Take this. I'm going to get my shotgun."

"I've never shot a gun!"

"Just hold it!"

I heard a faint beeping as Dan unlocked his gun safe, then he emerged with a very large gun and a box of shells. He loaded the gun, and headed toward the door. "Let's kill this sonofabitch."

I followed Dan out the back door, through the side yard, and around to the front of the garage. The bone monster had pummeled the door until it was nothing but a misshapen sheet of metal. I glanced down the street, and saw Dan's neighbors standing in their yards and craning their necks in order to find out what was going on.

"People are watching," I said. "Lots of mortals watching."

"Can't be helped," Dan said, as he raised the shotgun and aimed at the door. "Keep 'em back, if you can."

The monster landed another hit, and the garage door ripped open like so much tinfoil. Sunlight struck the creature, and I realized it wasn't just human bones; a set of antlers was attached to its shoulders, and horns jutted off its spine. The creature's arm and leg bones were doubled up, which was probably why it was so strong.

I might not ever sleep again after seeing this beast.

"Get behind me," Dan ordered, then he fired the gun. It was a good shot, and hit the monster's upper torso. The onlookers screamed as bones splintered and rained down onto the driveway.

The bones stopped falling, and reversed course back to the monster's central form. In broad daylight in front of at least twenty mortals, the monster rebuilt itself.

"Shit," Dan said. "Shit, shit shit!"

"We need a bigger gun," I said. "Or a sledgehammer!"

"If I can get to the tools we can throw stuff at it," Dan said, then the monster stepped out of the garage, spotted me with its sightless eye sockets, and roared.

"It wants me," I said. "I can lead it away!"

"Get in the car," Dan yelled, and we jumped in the truck. The monster roared again, and took an unsteady step toward us. "At least it's not fast."

Dan got the engine started, and backed out of the driveway and down the street at breakneck speed. "Anyone in the road?" he asked.

"No." All of Dan's neighbors were wisely staying out of the street, even dumbass Gretchen. "What are you waiting for? Drive!"

"I'm gonna ram it."

"Dan! What if it wrecks the car? With us in it?"

"What if it stops it?" Dan turned to me, wild-eyed. "We gotta try. Even if it just slows it down, we can't let this thing run loose."

"Okay. Do it."

Dan leaned over the center console and kissed me. "My fearless girl."

"You're fearless. I'm scared of everything." We parted, and faced forward. The monster was in the middle of the street and heading right for us. "Hit the bastard."

Dan floored it, tires and onlookers screaming as we struck the monster head on. The monster broke apart on impact and the truck kept moving, so I guess that was a success. Dan paused, and looked through the rear window.

"It's coming back together!"

I spied bone fragments on the hood near the windshield wipers. "Some of the bones are on the truck, and they're not reassembling with the rest."

"Is that good?"

"The bones must need to be in range to attach to the rest. We can spread this guy out." The monster spotted me watching it, and roared. "Or maybe it just wants to kill me."

"We need to get this thing away from people."

"Go. It'll follow us."

"Okay." Dan drove down the street, leading the monster away from his house with me as the bait. While he broke all the traffic laws, I called Tessa.

"There's a bone monster following us," I said as soon as she picked up. "Someone mailed a bunch of boxes to Dan's and we opened them and now it's a bone monster. Also, it's after me."

"They're here, too," Tessa said. "Alex can't affect them, nor can my magic."

"Dan blasted one apart with a shotgun, but that only worked for a minute. Why are the bones immune to me and Dad?"

"No idea. I'm working on it."

"We're on our way."

I hung up and looked at Dan. "Bone monsters at Gran's."

"They know how to kill them?"

"Not yet."

"All right." Dan came to a stop sign, looked both ways, and turned toward Gran's. "Let's figure out how to kill them together."

CHAPTER 39

LITTLE SAND, LITTLE MAGIC, AND BOOM

Dan sped across town, flying through intersections and running red lights as if he was being chased by the cops. We were being chased, but not by anything living. Maybe it wasn't even dead. Since I had no effect on the bones, I was wondering if they were actually bones, or something else.

"Why won't the bones listen to you?" he asked.

"I don't know. If I tell them to return to rest, they should obey instantly. Not only that, I can't sense who they're attached to."

"Attached?"

"They all came from a person—or an animal," I added, remembering the antlers and horns, "that's now dead. Where are those spirits?"

"I'll tell you where they are. Hassan's got them." Dan stopped for traffic, his eye on the rearview mirror the entire time. "Why is it that this guy's so slow, yet he's never far behind us? It's like a horror movie."

"That is the least of our problems." Since we were stopped, I hopped out of the car.

"What are you doing?" Dan demanded.

"Finding out if these are really bones." I grabbed one of the bones that was stuck near the windshield wipers, and got back in. Now that I was holding a piece of the monster, I could confirm these were bones.

"They're real bones," I confirmed, as I traced the bumps on what I thought was a finger bone. "But why won't they listen to me?" I set the bone on my lap, but even with direct contact, I couldn't sense anything about it. It was like holding an inert rock.

"That thing telling you anything?" Dan asked.

"There is something on the bone." Whatever was coating the bone, it was clear and very thin, and appeared nonporous. "It's like he dipped them in glass."

"Didn't you meet this guy in the desert? Sand makes glass." We heard the bone monster roar behind us, then Dan turned left onto Gran's street. "Hassan probably bakes his collection in the sand for reasons known only to him. Little sand, little magic, and boom, he makes a monster."

"Glass bones that seers can't affect," I muttered, then Dan screeched to a halt.

The street in front of us was choked with bone monsters.

"They're not after you," Dan said. "They want the nexus."

"Look!" I pointed toward the house, where two cougars the size of elephants were beating the bone monsters apart with their massive paws. Even better, the bones they ground down to pebbles weren't reassembling. "The cats can destroy them!"

"Let's help them out." Dan put the truck into gear and floored the gas pedal. The truck bucked when he hit the first group as bones crunched underneath the tires. Then more skeletons got behind us and climbed onto the bumper. Their spindly fingers pulled at the edges of the window as they clawed their way inside the truck.

"Reverse," I screamed.

"On it," Dan said, as he shifted into reverse and backed over the monsters. Those creatures dealt with, he put it in drive again and slammed into the next group.

"Tire's out," he yelled when the truck dipped to the side. "Think we can make it to the house on foot?"

"We don't have a choice." I looked at the sea of bones. We weren't far from the house, but these monsters were relentless. "On three."

"Wait." Dan grabbed the shotgun from the back seat and loaded it with fresh shells. "I'll shoot, hopefully take some of them out. Then you run."

"What about you?"

"I'll be right behind you."

He reached for me, and I squeezed his fingers. "Okay. You shoot, then we both run."

Dan gave my fingers a final squeeze, then he opened the door, stood up on the running board, and fired. I opened my door the instant he shot and ran toward the house. The skeletons were numerous, but slow and stupid, and for about a minute I was in the clear. Then a wall of four skeletons blocked my way, and more crowded behind me.

A shot rang out; Dan had blasted the skeletons in front of me. He also hadn't left the truck yet. "Dan, come on," I shrieked.

"Working on it," he yelled back, then he used the butt of the gun to smack a skeleton out of his path. I was about to retrace my steps and drag him off the truck when Smokey galloped past me.

"Smokey," I yelled. "Help Dan!"

Smokey took her time approaching Dan. When I was about to scream at her for going so slowly, I realized she was methodically destroying the skeletons in Dan's path, and clearing the way for him to make a break for it. I trusted she knew what she was doing and ran the final twenty feet to the house.

I felt bony fingers on the back of my neck. Before I had time to scream, the skeleton had both of my arms, and it turned me to the left. There, in the middle of the monster packed street, was Amir.

"Ellie," he called. "You look out of breath."

"You look like shit," I yelled back. He was wearing the same tattered and bloodstained clothes from when he attacked the equinox celebration, but seemed to have healed himself from the gunshot and crossbow wounds. What hadn't healed was his eye, and he had a filthy bandage wound around his head. "That little cat scratch bothering you?"

"This?" He gestured toward the bandage. "It's nothing. Bring her here."

The skeleton tried dragging me toward Amir. I dug in my heels and tried to become so much dead weight—then the skeleton collapsed to the ground with a crossbow bolt through its skull. I looked toward the cupola, saw a flash of light. My father was up there, doing what he did best.

I shook off the remains of the skeleton and sprinted to the house. Pumpkin, leader of the guardians, stood just inside the fence, but she wasn't in cougar form. Instead, she was a tiger, her beautiful orange and black coat having re-patterned itself into deadly stripes. Pumpkin glanced down at me, then she turned toward the street and roared.

Every skeleton within twenty feet of the house collapsed. Unfortunately, more were coming in behind them.

"Where did Amir get all these bones?" I yelled.

"They're witches," Tessa yelled from the porch. "Amir raided the burying grounds and stole our ancestors. Come inside!"

"Not without Dan!"

No sooner were the words out of my mouth than Dan ran into the yard, with Smokey right behind him. Muffuletta took his position on Pumpkin's other side, and the three cats glowered at the monsters in the street.

"Let them do their thing," Dan said, then we rushed inside and bolted the door. The three of us stood there, panting.

"How long has Dad been in the tower?" I asked.

"Not long," Tessa replied. She moved back the curtain, and frowned. "Now we know why Amir wanted the clan leaders. With them under thrall, it was easy for him to steal our ancestors."

"When did you find out he emptied the graveyards?"

"Shortly after you and Dan left to change," she replied. "I received a barrage of text messages. You could say the witch community is in an uproar."

"Wait until they find out that there's something on the bones." I handed Tessa the bone I grabbed from the truck's hood. "Dan thinks the coating is glass. Whatever it is, I can't affect them."

Tessa picked at the bone. "Certainly appears glassine," she said, then she handed the bone back to me and frowned. "Alex is considering extreme measures to defend the nexus."

The image of Gran's house as nothing but a charred cellar hole flashed behind my eyes. "He wants to destroy the house!"

"If the house isn't here, there is no way to access the nexus," Tessa said. "Eli, I know it's awful, but we're running out of options."

We heard a crash from upstairs. "I'm going to help Alex," Dan said, then he and his shotgun went up to join my father in the cupola. Once he was out of sight, I faced Tessa.

"He cannot destroy the house," I said. "There have been seers on this land protecting the nexus for as long as there have been seers. Without this house, we have no gathering place. We lose our place in the world, and our sense of community."

"There hasn't been a community here for quite some time," Tessa said, and dammit, she was right. Even when I was small, Gran's gatherings were nothing like the equinox celebration Katherine hosted...

And the last big equinox celebration held at the house had been destroyed by Amir.

"This is the same thing Amir did to Katherine," I said. "He wants to split us up, so we would have no choice but to follow him. Only, he's wrong. We're all strong, both individually and as a group. One jerk can't stop us with his lame revenge scheme."

One of the kitchen windows shattered. "His lame revenge scheme is going rather well," Tessa pointed out.

"Let me think." I thrust my hands into my pockets, and was immediately pricked by the thornapple seed pod. That pod had been with me as I traveled back and forth through time, which was nothing compared to the twenty years it sat lodged in my gut. Even though it had been through more than any lone seed pod should have to weather, it still looked newly picked, what with the bright green fruit and its many spikes radiating in all directions. I rolled the seed pod around in my hand, and realized where I'd recently seen a similar image.

The blue blobs with the radiating spikes in the nexus looked exactly like thornapple seed pods.

And thornapple seeds are very, very poisonous.

I looked at the seed pod in one hand, and the glassine bone in the other.

"Tess," I said. "I know how to stop Amir and save the house." I opened my mouth to continue, but she shook her head.

"Just do it," she said. "Tell me afterward."

I hugged her, then I ran up the main stairs, to the opposite side of the house and through the library, and up the spiral staircase that led to the cupola. All the while, I heard booming shots from my father and Dan as they tried to help the guardians defend the house. I hiked up my skirts and ran up the stairs, and stopped dead when I reached the cupola.

"How do I get to the nexus?" I demanded. "Where are the steps?"

"There are no steps," my father said, not looking away as he took aim and fired. "There never have been."

"Guardian has to take you, remember?" Dan added.

I looked out the front window, pressing my hands against the glass as I watched the guardians fight off wave after wave of skeletons. Since calling one of them away from the battle was out of the question, I faced the opposite window, and said, "Stairs!"

I didn't get stairs, or a ladder, but a vine dropped down from the ceiling. I grabbed the vine and pulled myself up through the ceiling; it was quicksand again, just like when Dan and I had fallen into the library. Then I was inside the nexus, and a bright blue orb hovered above my head. I saw the spikes radiating out toward oblivion, grabbed my seed pod and the glassine bone, and threw them into the center of the orb.

Everything went blue, then white.

When I woke, I was lying on the library floor. Apparently, that was where the nexus sent all of its visitors once it was done with them. I sat up, and realized it was quiet. No gunshots rang out from above, no screams or other noises filtered in from the streets. Something warm and soft brushed my arm; the guardians were house cats again, and they rubbed their heads against me as they purred.

"I guess this means we won," I said, as I petted them all in turn.

"We sure did," Dan said, as he descended the spiral stairs. He extended a hand to help me up, then he pulled me against him and kissed me hard. "I knew you would outsmart that asshole."

"What did you do?" my father asked, as he came down the stairs. The moment he set foot on the library floor, Tess burst into the room. She looked at me and Dan, then she rushed into Dad's arms. He held her tightly, much like how Montgomery used to hold Katherine.

"This turned out to be a good day," Dan said.

I leaned my head against his shoulder. "It's not over yet."

CHAPTER 40

PARTNERS

We went outside, and were confronted by the river of bones that now occupied Essex Street.

"I haven't seen this many bones since I was in the Catacombs under Paris," I said. "These can't all be from the local clan cemeteries. Can they?"

"Doubtful, since they're not all human." Dan picked up a moose antler to prove his point. "This is a job for Jill and Angel if I ever saw one."

"Angel knows bones?" I asked.

Dan shrugged. "She's a nurse. I'm sure they covered bones in medical school."

"What we really need to do is sort them out," Tessa said, as she picked her way among the bones. She lifted her foot to step over a few, and my father was right beside her, offering his arm. After Tessa successfully navigated around the remains, she smiled at my dad, and they linked hands. "We must return every single one to its rightful clan."

"Agreed," I said. "Getting all the clans to work together will be a challenge."

"You said you wanted to create the same type of community Katherine had," Dan said, as he continued his search for antlers. "Maybe this is what will bring everyone together."

I gazed at the carnage that surrounded us. "Can we really make something good out of something so awful?"

My father wrapped his free arm around me, then he and Tessa surrounded me in the biggest, best group hug. "If anyone can do it, Bug, it's you."

"Found the asshole," Dan yelled from farther down the street, thus ending our moment of familial bliss. We approached him, all the while doing our best not to step on anyone's ancestors. Dan was standing over a severely battered Amir. Besides the slashes across his cheek and eye, courtesy of Pumpkin, he was covered in newer contusions and lay at an unnatural angle. I wondered if he'd been trampled by his skeleton army.

"Is he alive?" I asked.

"He's breathing," Dan replied. "Although, he's pretty beat. With injuries like this, he might not make it until an ambulance gets here."

"More reasons we need Jill and Angel," I murmured. "Wait, is that what we should do? Call an ambulance?"

"I don't think an ambulance can get down the street," Tessa said.

"Well, we can't just leave him to die," I said. "I know Amir would leave us to suffer, but we're not him. We're better than him."

"I can rig up a stretcher, then we can get him back to the house," Dan said. "While I move him, you call Angel. But remember, after we heal this guy, we need to figure out what to do with him, punishment-wise."

"Let's get him moved first," I said. Dan nodded, and jogged back to the house for supplies. I watched him for a moment, then I asked my father, "What should we do with Amir?"

"That's up to you," he replied. "The Mistress of Seers holds those in the wrong accountable and doles out retribution as she sees fit."

I'm finally Mistress of Seers, but Katharine never got to anoint me. I turned away, because I didn't want my father or Tessa to see the tears pricking my eyes. "Yeah. I guess it is."

While my father and Dan relocated Amir from the middle of the street to the front porch, Tessa began contacting the surviving clan elders, and I called Jill and Angel. About two hours after the skeletons collapsed, the Sanders girls arrived. Angel had brought her medical bag, while Jill carried her forensics kit. Neither one was pleased with Amir lying on the porch.

"And why isn't my patient inside?" Angel asked, as she performed an initial examination.

"The point behind all of this," I gestured toward the piles of bones, "was so Amir could get inside the house and breach the nexus. For all we know, him being unconscious is part of his plan."

"It's not." Angel stood, and snapped off her exam gloves. "Near as I can tell, this man sustained a rather severe head wound. If it's all right with you, I'd like to have your arch nemesis here transported to a hospital. He needs more help than I can give him on a porch."

"Do whatever you need to do," I said. "I trust you."

Angel whipped out her phone and began sending texts. "I've got some paramedic friends who owe me a few favors. They can quickly and quietly collect our John Doe and drop him off at the emergency room."

"His name is—"

"John Doe," Angel replied, tossing me a glare for good measure. "Remember, you trust me."

"I do," I said, then I left Angel to organize Amir's transportation and care. Tessa and Jill were walking down the street, examining the bones and taking notes. Their first task was to separate out the animal bones, then Tessa would try to determine which bones belonged to which clan. The glassine substance still coated the bones, but Jill was going to experiment on a few of the animal bones, and hopefully learn how to remove it.

As for my father and Dan, they were repairing the damage the skeletons had done to the house and surrounding property. Only two windows had been broken, but the back and side yard were in shambles, and the field of bleeding hearts I'd manifested to show my love for Dan had been destroyed.

"All the bleeding hearts were trampled," I said, more despair in my voice than I'd realized.

"Are they your favorite flower?" Angel asked.

"Not really, but this patch had sentimental value," I replied.

"Well, come spring, you can always plant more."

I smiled, because she was right. We would plant more. Come spring, we would have more flowers, and with any luck, more seers.

The sun was dipping low when Dad declared we'd done enough.

The broken windows had been boarded up, and all the bones had been moved out of the street, both so cars could get by, and to keep the ancestors' remains from suffering further damage. The animal bones had been picked out, and sat in a separate heap near the woods. With any luck, nature would reclaim them, and our offering would go toward healing all the damage Amir had wrought.

Speaking of Amir, when the paramedics arrived, they had barely questioned why we had an unconscious, bloody man on our porch. Apparently, these bone monsters had sprung up all across town, and medical personnel had been collecting casualties ever since. They assumed Amir was more collateral damage, loaded him up, and took him away.

"Think he'll end up in the same hospital as Jada?" I asked Jill.

"Doubtful," she replied. "After her stunt with Renault, she is in under lock and key. The only thing keeping her out of prison is the fact that he declined to press charges, and said she should get help instead." Jill turned toward Dan. "When are you going to call him about your job? Technically, your suspension's over."

"Good to know," Dan said. "Maybe I'll call him tomorrow. Or next week." Dan yawned. "I might still be sleeping next week. Maybe next month."

"Don't wait too long," Jill said, then she and Angel said their good-byes and went home.

"We should all get some rest," my father said. His arm was draped around Tessa's shoulders again. "There will be more of this unpleasantness to deal with tomorrow."

"It's not all unpleasant," Tessa said. "After all, those witches that have had fun shunning me for decades now get to come to me for help. I think tomorrow will be the start of a very happy time."

Dad grinned at her. "I hope you're right, Isa."

"That's our cue," I said, since those two clearly wanted to be alone. "We'll see you in the morning."

The truck given to us from the Allwoods had repaired itself during the day, which was an argument for a witchcraft-boosted vehicle if there ever was one. I spent the ride home texting Jacob, first thanking him again for the vehicle, then explaining where and when Dan and I had been for the past month. During my conversation with Jacob, we passed by more damage done by Amir's bone army.

"He was ready to destroy the entire town," I said.

"Lucky they have you to fix things," Dan, ever the cheerleader, said. "But I have to say, the policy of keeping mortals out of the supernatural community may have to be revised. Can't sweep all these bones under the rug."

"Nah. Too lumpy."

There was that side eye. "Smartass."

We pulled into the driveway, and I winced at the destroyed garage door. "I hope those aren't expensive."

"Maybe insurance covers it." We got out of the truck, and Dan headed toward the garage. "I want to check something out real quick."

"Okay," I said, even though I was dying for a hot bath. Dan activated the flashlight on his phone, and started picking through the empty cardboard boxes that had been the start of the bone army. "What are you looking for? More bones?"

"These." He handed me a three pack of purple socks. "The running socks you teased me about? I got them for you."

"Oh." I held the socks in my hands, happy and grateful and even a bit weepy, over socks, of all things. "Thank you."

"That's not all." He moved more of the cardboard aside, and withdrew something from a wide, flat box. "One of the things I love about you is your independence. You make your own way, no matter who or what has an issue with it. I also know how much it hurt you when your apartment blew up, and put a damper on your business." He paused, examining what was inside the box. "You love being a private investigator, and you're good at it. So, I got you this."

Dan turned the item toward me, and I gasped. It was a sign that read Nine Lives Investigations, and it had three cats—a gray, a tabby, and a calico—playing underneath the logo.

It was perfect.

"I was thinking that since we moved to the upstairs bedroom, we can turn the downstairs one into our office," he continued. "Or maybe we can turn the garage into an office, since we need to do some repair work out here anyway. What do you say, babe? Partners?"

I traced the outline of the letters, then I touched the calico cat. "I love it." I faced Dan. "I love you. Wait—partners? You don't want your old job back?"

"I don't know," he replied. "I was resigned to getting fired, and made peace with it. Undoing all that peace seems risky, you know? Besides, I figure it's time to move on to the next phase of our lives, whatever that turns out to be."

"The next phase." My thoughts spun with all the things we could do together, both as business partners, and life partners. Like Katherine said, all Mistresses have someone who helps them, and my someone was Dan.

"I can't wait."

CHAPTER 41

HAPPY BIRTHDAY! WAIT, WHAT?

"**I** can't believe we're doing this."

Dan squeezed my hand. "Got cold feet?"

"Never."

In fact, my feet were kind of hot. It was unseasonably warm, and I was wearing Katherine's repaired dress, along with all the associated undergarments that came with it. As for Dan, he was wearing his knee breeches again, and Tessa had sourced a matching seventeenth century shirt and waistcoat. When you called in favors from a witch, they delivered.

Speaking of favors… "Are you sure it's okay for us to take all of this?" I asked Tessa. In addition to the shirt and waistcoat, her contact had produced several bolts of wool, linen, and silk that, for some reason known only to ancient witches, they'd kept packed away for the last three hundred years. "These aren't family heirlooms?"

"They were freely given when I asked," Tessa replied. "Many clans keep supplies such as these on hand. Times past quality fabric wasn't as easy to come by, and I'm sure Katherine can make good use of them."

"I'm sure she will." We were bringing the fabric to Katherine partly as a thank you for the gift of clothing she'd given me and Dan, and partly because I wanted to bring her a present. Which was ironic, since it was my birthday, but I didn't need or want any presents. More than anything, I needed to know that she and Montgomery and little Elizabeth were okay.

Even though Katherine's letter had proclaimed that her family survived the bone attacks, and that it was an established event long before I was born, I couldn't help feeling responsible for what had happened at her equinox celebration. Yes, Amir had set things into motion that practically drove me to Katherine's doorstep, but I still felt guilty. Which, honestly, was probably part of Amir's plan. He really was a jerk.

As for the bolts of fabric, when I mentioned I wanted to bring Katherine a gift, talk turned to what sort of gift would be appropriate for an eighteenth century household. I couldn't really bring them a dozen cannolis, or any modern toys for Elizabeth; that would cause confusion, and who knows how many stressors on the timeline. But the fabric would be useful, and appropriate to the time period, which meant that Tessa's fabric hoarder friends had saved the day.

"Are you sure you don't want to come with us?" I asked Tessa and my father. What with how much my dad admired Montgomery Fletcher, I figured he'd want to meet him. Besides, after dealing with the fallout from the bone attacks over the past few days, both magical and otherwise, we could all use a break.

"Being that I'm alive in that time period, I don't think it's a good idea for me to be in two places at once," Tessa replied. "What if modern me reverts to the eighteenth century version? Or what if I begin searching for my cell phone while I'm at the market in Apulia?" She shook her head. "No, no, it's just too risky."

I nodded, because this was risky. There was a chance Dan and I would be stuck in the past, and I was trying very hard to not think about that. "I'm not even going to ask you, Dad," I said to my father. "I know you aren't going anywhere without Tessa."

"Someone needs to guard the house," he began, then Pumpkin sat in front of his feet and began cleaning her paw. "And I will help the guardians in any way I can," he finished.

"Nice save." I faced Dan. "Ready?"

"Sure am." He hefted the canvas sack that held the fabric, then he shook my father's hand. "I'll make sure nothing happens to Eli."

"I know you will," Dad said, then he pulled me into a hug. "Be safe, Bug."

"We'll be back before you know it."

With that, Dan and I ascended to the cupola, then we followed Pumpkin up to the nexus. The theory was that since we were wearing the clothes from Katherine's time, we should be able to return to the September twentieth that occurred six days after Amir's attack. For a bit of extra luck, I had the candle from my birthday cake in my pocket. Would that help? Who knew.

We climbed the stairs to the nexus's platform—apparently stairs only appeared for the guardians, and the rest of us got vines dangling from the ceiling—and took a moment to admire the brilliant blue rays cutting through the darkness. "We're ready," I said to Pumpkin, and the floor immediately became quicksand. Dan and I linked hands, and we sank down in time.

I blinked my eyes open, and wondered why I was laying out on the front lawn in this heat... and my heart fell, because I thought our time traveling hadn't worked. Then I looked at the house, and saw not the sprawling blue mansion I'd grown up in, but the stately salt box home Katherine presided over.

"Dan." I shook his shoulder. "It worked. We're here."

He got to his feet, then he extended a hand and helped me up. "Let's go say hello."

I knocked on the front door, excited and terrified and really hoping we arrived on the right day. Then Katherine opened the door, and gasped when she saw us.

I pulled the faded parchment out of my pocket.

"I got your letter."

After we'd hugged and cried and said all of our hellos, Hettie and her staff set about putting together an impromptu celebration, while the rest of us went out back to where the bonfires were held. My lower lip trembled as I took in the charred patches of lawn, and the piles of debris left over from Amir's attack. Katherine looped her arm with mine, and took me aside.

"Now, Eliza, I know what you're feeling, and none of this is your fault," she began. "The fault lays with Amir Hassan, and no one else."

"But, he followed me here," I said. "You all could have been killed."

"We could have been, but we weren't." Katherine placed her hands on my shoulders. "The best piece of advice I can give you is this: bad things can and do happen. They happen often, and as Mistress of Seers you will see more awful things than you could ever imagine. However, after the awful things are dealt with we get the good, and there is always so much more good to be had. It's our duty to handle the awful things, and remain a beacon of hope for the rest."

"A beacon of hope. I like that." I nodded toward her belly. "How are you feeling?"

She blushed as she patted her belly. "Very well, thank you. Let's get you anointed before this boy decides to join us."

"It's a boy? And you're that far along?"

"Montgomery would like a son, and honestly, it feels like I've been carrying this child half a lifetime already." We stood next to the bonfire, and Elizabeth handed her mother a vial of oil.

"Eliza Jayne Moore, do you swear to hold the line between life and death, and treat each spirit and shade you encounter with the same care you would show to your own ancestor?" she asked, as she dabbed oil onto my brow.

"I do. I swear it."

"Then I do proclaim you as my successor." Katherine stepped back, and smiled. "What will be your first act as Mistress of Seers?"

My stomach audibly rumbled, and we laughed. "Let's see how Hettie's coming along with that cake."

After we stuffed ourselves with Hettie's delicious cakes, Montgomery excused himself and left the room. He returned a few minutes later and set some red and gold silk cords on the table.

"When you were last here, Daniel inquired about handfasting," Montgomery began. "If that is still something you wish to do, I would be honored to be your witness."

"As would I," Katherine added.

I stared at the cords, then at Dan... And for once in my life I wasn't flustered or afraid. I knew exactly what I wanted. "Well, we already agreed to do it."

Dan reached across the table and took my hand. "Is that a yes?"

I grasped his fingers. "It's a yes."

Later still, Elizabeth was snuggled on my lap while we sat in the parlor around the remains of the fire. "You know, I'm named after you," I said.

"But, you're older than me."

I shrugged. "Sometimes, in our family, strange things happen, but everything always works out in the end."

Dan and I returned to our time the next morning. I wanted to stay longer, but Tessa and Jacob had warned us that the longer we stayed in the past, the greater the chance of creating unintended consequences that would affect the future. Besides, I got what I came for. We knew Katherine and her family were well, and she'd anointed me as the Mistress of Seers. I needed to get back to my own time, and begin rebuilding our community.

And I couldn't wait to start my life with Dan.

Along with my newfound sense of purpose, I had a very special gift for my father. Montgomery had written him a letter sharing all of his knowledge as a marksman in the hopes it would help my dad with his work. Dad had been the seers' marksman for over five decades, but he was the only one, and many tasks fell onto his shoulders. Montgomery hoped that by reaching across time, he could offer my dad a helping hand.

"Families help each other," Montgomery had said. "And remember, Eliza, we are always here for you. If you need us, come back."

"I will," I promised. "Be well, all of you."

Dan and I climbed up to the tower, and the now familiar blue spiky orbs were there to greet us. The nexus deposited us on the library floor, which was preferable, if harder, than the front lawn. "If we time travel again, we need to put down a rug."

"Be a shame to cover the hardwood," Dan began, then he went still. "Hear that?"

I strained my ears, at first unsure of what had spooked Dan. Then laughter wafted up the stairs.

Children's laughter.

"Why are there kids here?" I hiked up my skirts and went down to the first floor. There were children all over the place, running through the parlor, having snacks in the kitchen, and poking at the poisons in the solarium. When I was a second away from losing my mind, I saw my father.

"Dad," I called, and he smiled when he saw me. "Where did all these kids come from?"

"They're your cousins, here for your birthday," he replied. "Don't you remember?"

"Um, no." Dad felt my forehead, as if I was one of these rug rats and he was checking me for a fever.

"Perhaps the time travel confused you," he said. "Was everything well with Katherine?"

"Yeah." I withdrew the letter. "Montgomery wanted me to give you this."

Dad accepted the letter, then he rushed to shoo a child away from the oleanders. I turned to Dan, and said, "We changed things."

"Looks like Katherine didn't lose her baby," he said. "That's a good thing, right?"

"Yeah." I took in the crowds of children, and wondered why my father was the only adult present amid the chaos. "Dad, where's Tessa?"

He glanced at me, his brow pinched. "Who?"

I hope you enjoyed reading about Eli and Dan's latest adventures! If so, please consider leaving a review at the retailer where you purchased this book. Thank you!

The story continues in Wolfsbane, available here: https://www.amazon.com/gp/product/B0BTCH2313 Keep scrolling for a sneak peek!

WOLFSBANE

I stared at my father, my heart in my throat. "What do you mean, who? Tessa!"

He smiled and shook his head. "Sorry, Bug, I don't know who you're talking about."

One of the kids asked for more juice, and my father ushered her into the kitchen so he could refill her cup. I turned to Dan. "We screwed up the timeline."

He gave me a look. "Ya think?"

I narrowed my eyes at him. "Not helpful."

"Let's go upstairs and change, then we can try to sort this out," he said. "There. Was that helpful enough?"

I gave him a look, because for all of his snark, that idea was helpful. I also wanted to get out of the eighteenth century dress I was wearing, and I'm sure Dan wanted to ditch the knee breeches and hose he had on. "Hopefully Dad hasn't given my room away to one of the rug rats," I muttered, and we went back up to the second floor. On the way, evidence of my cousins was everywhere: toys, spilled snacks, and the kids themselves.

"My entire life, I've always been the youngest person in this house," I said as we sidestepped around a tricycle. "Now this place is practically a daycare."

"Where are the parents?" Dan asked. "Alex can't be the only adult here."

"Believe me, I have no answers."

We entered my old room at Gran's, and I breathed a sigh of relief when it was not only empty, but also had our modern clothes right where we'd left them. I reached for my jeans, and spied something next to the bed. It was my old backpack, and sticking out of it was my laptop.

"How is this here?" I grabbed my backpack and withdrew my laptop. It was definitely my computer, with the same scratch over the back left corner and faded stickers I'd gotten from the card shop. I opened it, and waited for it to power up.

"How much do you think has changed?" Dan asked as he pulled off his shirt.

"Hopefully, not a lot." I began unfastening the front of my dress. We'd just dealt with Amir and his bone army, and the last thing I needed was another crisis. "With any luck, we can contain the fallout and come up with a plan."

"As you say, Mistress of Seers."

I glanced over my shoulder and tried not to laugh. Dan always changed by methodically removing his clothes from top to bottom, and then putting new clothes on in the same order. Right now he was only wearing his knee high hose, and it was hilarious. "That's right, use my title."

He stood behind me and slid his arms around my waist. "What about Mrs. Lyons?"

"Big talk from a naked guy," I said, then my laptop beeped. I had a ton of desktop notifications from my social media accounts.

"I guess a lot happened while we were gone." I closed the notifications, and went to the website.

"Probably birthday wishes," Dan said, then he kissed my neck and released me so he could get dressed.

"Probably," I muttered, then I started scrolling through my notifications. He was right, they were mostly people wishing me a happy birthday. I noticed the photo icon, and clicked on it. There were hundreds of pictures of Dan and me, eating out, on vacation, and doing all sorts of couple things. However, none of those things had ever happened.

"Dan, check these out." I turned my laptop toward him, and watched his brow crease as he saw the pictures. "Apparently, we go on vacation a lot."

He tapped the screen. "This one says it was taken in Aruba two years ago." He faced me. "I don't know if we can contain this fallout."

"We need backup. Tessa sized backup." As I said her name, I realized what was missing from the pictures. Not only did I not remember any of those events, I didn't see a single picture of Tessa.

"Where is Tessa?" I withdrew my phone and opened my camera roll. I was confronted with more pictures of me and Dan, and not a single image of Tessa.

"It's like Tessa and I aren't even friends." I faced Dan. "How can that be?"

"I know how we can find out. Let's go to Tessa's and figure out what's happening. If anyone can make sense of this magical mumbo jumbo, it's Tess."

"Yeah." I scrolled through the pictures again, confirming I hadn't missed an image of her. There was nothing resembling my black-haired best friend. "I just hope she's okay."

"Tessa's tough," Dan said as he pulled his shirt over his head. "If anyone can handle this, it's her."

I closed my laptop and slid it into my backpack. "I hope you're right."

Continue the story here: https://www.amazon.com/gp/product/B0BTCH2313

About The Author

Jennifer Allis Provost is a native New Englander who lives in a sprawling colonial along with her beautiful and precocious twins, a dog that thinks she's a kangaroo, a parrot, a junkyard cat, and a wonderful husband who never forgets to buy ice cream. As a child, she read anything and everything she could get her hands on, including a set of encyclopedias, but fantasy was always her favorite. She spends her days drinking vast amounts of coffee, arguing with her computer, and avoiding any and all domestic behavior.

Find Jenn on the web here: http://authorjenniferallisprovost.com/

For up to the minute sale notifications, follow her on Bookbub here: https://www.bookbub.com/profile/jennifer-allis-provost

For exclusive content, follow her on Patreon: https://www.patreon.com/jenniferallisprovost/

Friend her on Facebook: http://www.facebook.com/jennallis

Follow her on Instagram: @jenniferaprovost

Happy reading!

Also By Jennifer Allis Provost

The Chronicles of Parthalan, a six volume epic fantasy (and one short story collection)
Heir to the Sun
The Virgin Queen
Rise of the Deva'shi
Pieces of Parthalan: Six All-New Stories From The Land Of Parthalan
Golem
Elfsong
Sunfall

The Copper Legacy, a four book urban fantasy:
Copper Girl
Copper Ravens
Copper Veins
Copper Princess
A duology based in the Copper world:
Redemption
Salvation
Poison Garden, an urban fantasy filled with seers, witches, and one seriously hot detective:
Belladonna

Oleander

Bleeding Hearts

Thornapple

Wolfsbane

Gallowglass, an urban fantasy set in Scotland and New York:

Gallowglass

Walker

Homecoming

Winter's Queen, an urban fantasy set in Scotland and Elphame:

Touch of Frost

Giant's Daughter

Elphame's Queen

Changes, a contemporary romance:

Changing Teams

Changing Scenes

Changing Fate

Changing Dates